VILLAINY AND VIRTUE

BRUCE BERGER

Cover designs
by
Pluperfyth Graphics
Saint Augustine, Florida

Printed by CreateSpace, An Amazon.com Company
Available from Amazon.com and other retail outlets
Available on Kindle and other devices

This novel is a work of fiction. The characters (with the exception of public or historical figures), incidents, settings, dialogues, and situations depicted are products of the author's imagination. Any resemblance to actual events or persons, living or deceased, is entirely coincidental.

Villainy and Virtue
Bruce Berger

ISBN-13: 978-1974372614
ISBN-10: 1974372618

For the purposes of writing this novel in as realistic a sense as possible, the use of trademarks has occurred. Use of the Brand or Trademark is minimized and used only to make the point or connection necessary. All use of trademarks is intended to be non-derivative. They are used without permission of the brand owner(s), and therefore unendorsed by the various rights holding individuals, companies, parties, or corporations.

Dedication

In memory of

Edith G. Skinner
David W. Berger
Serafina Bellu
Antonio pala

Acknowledgements

Special thanks to author and friend Bill Yancey for suggestions and editing assistance on many fronts. Any remaining deficiencies and mistakes are mine.

Many friends and family members read the first draft of this novel and offered insightful criticism and encouragement. I would like to thank Mariann Campos, Patricia Dimuzio, Marjorie Berger, Anna Berger, and Christina Berger for suggestions and devoting time out of their busy lives to improve the manuscript. Any remaining typographical errors, punctuation mistakes, or other flaws, however, are mine.

TABLE OF CONTENTS

CHAPTER 1

This is the last one—for now, anyway," the combat medic said. He set his end of the stretcher on a triage table of the 33rd Field Hospital, Anzio, Italy.

An army nurse removed the olive colored blanket from the unconscious soldier. A bandage encircled his head. Blood soaked through it over his left forehead. He wore drawers and what remained of his uniform shirt. The rest of his clothing had been cut off. Bulky bloodstained bandages wrapped both feet. A plasma IV dripped into his right arm.

The nurse took the patient's vital signs. An army major, the triage doctor, examined the soldier.

"Vital signs are normal," the nurse said. She verbalized the specifics while recording them on the medical chart.

"Cut the drawers off and roll him on his side so I can inspect his back and backsides," the major said. Two minutes later, the examination complete, he peered at the wounded soldier's dog tags and noted the religious preference imprinted on it.

A young first lieutenant, a chaplain's scarf draped over his uniform, had settled in the triage tent when casualties first arrived. His intense blue eyes appeared heavy as silent prayers crossed lips that barely moved. The major made a *C* with his thumb and index finger and nodded at the chaplain. The padre acknowledged the signal and began last rites for the fallen soldier.

The nurse draped a blanket over the patient. The doctor scanned the handwritten notes on the emergency medical tag affixed to the remaining button on the soldier's shirt.

The major eyed the combat medic. "This your man?"

"Yes, sir," the medic said. "We're short supplies at the front, so I came back with the casualties."

"What happened to him?" the major asked.

"Mortar barrage," the medic said. "A blast concussion—been unconscious since. The head bandage is only a scrape. Boots were cut off at the battalion aid station. Both feet are a mess. More holes than Swiss cheese. Lots of shrapnel. Some went all the way through. Fractures too, both feet. They cleaned his feet and took out the visible shrapnel. No serious bleeding. Doused the feet with sulfa powder and bandaged them. Gave him a tetanus booster and a dose of penicillin. The plasma IV, too."

"I don't see morphine noted on his tag," the major said.

"He didn't get any," the medic said. "The head injury worried them at the aid station. He hardly flinched while the doc worked on his feet. Do you think they'll both be okay?"

"They?" The major's eyes narrowed. "What are you talking about?"

"Him and his brother," the medic said. "The first casualty we brought in was his younger brother. Bad chest wound. Concussion too. Quinton was the name. The one on the table is his older brother. He tried to save his younger brother."

"What were they doing in the same sector?" the major asked. "That shouldn't happen."

The medic shrugged. "Snafu I guess."

The major rubbed his forehead. "His brother went to surgery right away. Wasn't stable. Collapsed lung and bleeding bad. Odds aren't good. His brother here, hard to know. Concussions are unpredictable. We'll have a medical man assess him since he's still unconscious. As to his feet, they won't kill him. Were his heels hit?"

"Heels looked okay," the medic said.

"That's a plus. I'll send him to the orthopedic tent," the major said. "They'll remove the bandages and decide whether to amputate or not. If they don't amputate now, they may need to later if infection sets in. Even if he keeps his feet, it'll be a long recovery. He'll have trouble for the rest of his life. Of course, that's assuming he survives the head injury."

The major glanced at the chaplain, who had donned his helmet and clutched his field mass kit. "Thank you, Padre. Say a prayer for these brothers. For us all. Awful situation."

The padre nodded. "I have and I will." He turned toward the medic. "Can I hitch a ride to the front?"

"Sure thing, Padre," the medic said.

"Take a look at the southeast horizon when it's dark," the major said. "You'll notice a bright area. Mount Vesuvius erupting. The spring of 1944 arrives. We're surrounded by war, and Vesuvius is erupting. Somehow, it seems fitting."

CHAPTER 2

"Get down!" Wes rammed his brother toward the foxhole. *Too late*—shrapnel ripped through his brother and Wes's boots. Pain screamed from the shattered bones of his feet. *Too late—I was too late.*

"Are you okay, mister?" a child's voice asked.

All six feet, one hundred seventy pounds of Wes Quinton lay crumpled on the floor. A hand over his forehead ruffled graying-brown hair and half hid his taut face. Sweat mixed with tears dripped from the tip of his nose. Eyes clenched; he struggled to breathe. *Quicker—I should've been quicker.* Thirty-six years ago. For both, the war ended that awful day in 1944—his brother dead and Wes never the same—the limp and pain constant reminders. The guilt, too.

The little voice echoed, "Are you all right, mister? Are you hurt?"

Wes's eyelids opened. Heavy with a lifetime of sadness, his blue-gray eyes also hinted of a resolve as sharp as a bayonet. A polished parquet floor stared back at him. He shook his head and looked up. A sandy-haired eight-year-old boy, with plump cheeks, a rounded nose, and blue-green trusting eyes, peered at him from an arm's length away. A knee-high, black-haired dog with a few white splotches, his head quizzically tilted, sat next to the boy.

The frayed edge of Wes's coat sleeve absorbed the sweat on his brow. He dislodged the leg beneath him. "What happened?"

"You yelled 'get down,' and then you jumped off the seat. All your stuff fell on the floor. Did you have a bad dream? You were asleep a long time."

"How long?"

"I don't know. For a long time. You need help standing up? Maybe I can help you."

"I'd better try myself. Maybe you can pick up my things?"

"Sure. I'm good at picking up."

"What's your name, son?"

"Timmy. Blackie is my dog." Timmy extended his hand. "My dad said to always shake when you meet someone new."

Wes took the small hand in his. "Wes Quinton. Good to meet you, Timmy. Blackie too." He turned toward the seat and pushed up with his arms, wincing as his feet twisted on the floor under his weight. *Rats.*

"You made a face, Mr. Quinton. You all right?"

"It's my feet. I'm okay now."

"What should I pick up first?" Timmy asked.

"Wait." Wes closed his eyes and shook his head to dispel the residual fog of the nightmare. A whiff of smoke teased his nose. He sniffed. It was real, not constant, but not his imagination, either. And that drone. Persistent and so tranquil that his mind filtered out what his ears heard. That also wasn't his imagination. *Clickety-clack*. It could mean only one thing.

Can't be. Wes opened an eye. A train. He sat in the back of a passenger car. An aisle ran along one side, and the rest was filled with U-shaped mahogany benches with curved backs and maroon cushions. A parade of trees, splashed with the reds, yellows, and oranges of autumn foliage, sped by the windows with rolling hills in the distance. *Rats. What am I doing on a train? Seems too soon.*

"Are you okay?" Timmy stared at him. "You look confused."

"I wasn't expecting to be on a train. Not today, anyway. Did you see me climb on?"

Timmy's face scrunched up. "No. I don't remember. It's kind of busy when it stops. You been sleeping for a long time though."

Wes frowned and rubbed his forehead. "Guess we better pick up my things. Would you hand me that leather satchel first? That's what I keep everything in."

Timmy handed the satchel to Wes. "That's nice and soft. It looks old."

"It was a gift from my parents. Now that picture, please."

Timmy peered at the aging black-and-white photograph. "Is this your family?"

Wes laid the photo on his lap as Timmy stood next to him.

"Sure is."

"Is that you?" Timmy's finger pointed as his face cocked to one side and his eyes angled up at Wes.

Wes felt a lump in his throat and held back a tear as he glanced at Timmy. The boy's expression reminded him of his little brother when they were young. His brother had always been serious like that when he asked a question. Wes was only three years older, but that was enough; an older brother knew everything and would always watch out for you. He could almost hear his little brother say, "I want to be just like you."

The portrait was of Wes and his brother in uniform with their parents behind them. His brother had just signed up for the war at the age of eighteen in 1942.

"That's me," Wes said.

"You have wrinkles now, and your nose is crooked."

"I'm sixty, so I earned those wrinkles. My nose was broken in the war."

"You're pretty old."

Wes smiled. "Sometimes I feel old, but sixty isn't that old."

"Is this your brother?"

"That's my little brother. He was killed in the war."

"I'm sorry. You must miss him."

Wes dabbed a tear before Timmy could see it. "It was a long time ago, but I still miss him, every day."

"Your mom looks like my grandma. My grandma is real nice. Is your mom okay?"

Wes swallowed and took a breath. "She became sick and died five years ago."

"How about your dad?"

"I don't know, Timmy. He disappeared four years ago. I don't know if he's alive or not."

"So you're alone?"

"Yes. Guess I am. What about you? You're not by yourself on the train?"

"Not with Blackie."

"I meant your family. Are they on the train?"

"I think it's just me and Blackie. I guess we're alone too. I know, since we're both alone, we can look out for each other."

"We'll do that, Timmy. A very good idea. You're a thinking man."

Timmy's face sparkled as a smile stretched across his face.

"Now, maybe you can hand me that catalog next to Blackie."

"This is heavy. What kind of catalog is it?"

"Sit down and I'll show you some of the pictures. Do you know what hardware is?"

"Like in a hardware store?"

"That's right. I own a hardware store. Every year there's a convention where you can order the latest hardware. The pictures are in the catalog."

Timmy flipped through a dozen pages. "What are these red and blue circles around some of the pictures?"

"Red is for things I may want to order, and blue is for what I definitely will order."

"So that's why you're on the train? You're going to buy hardware?"

Wes rubbed his neck. "Suppose so. Before we forget, can you pick up the rest of those things on the floor?"

"Sure." Timmy gathered pens and pencils, three-by-five cards, rubber bands, a yellow pad, and a checkbook. "You sure had lots of stuff in your bag. You wrote a bunch on your pad and these cards."

"Those are notes and reminders. Too much to remember in my head."

"I have that problem too. I sometimes forget to wash my hands before dinner and to brush my teeth."

"Let me give you some of these cards, a rubber band, and a pencil. You can write notes on the cards, keep them together with the rubber band, and put them in your shirt pocket. It's like having an extra brain."

"Holy cows. For me? Gee, thanks. I should've thought of something like that myself."

Wes smiled. "Well, thank you for helping me."

Timmy pointed, "Hey, look at that neat picture behind you."

A painting of a bright red caboose had a plaque above it engraved with G.F. Line in gold lettering. Wes glanced toward the front of the car, where a painting of a steam locomotive with smoke and red sparks billowing from the smokestack had an identical plaque above it.

"That's clever," Wes said. "Look up front, Timmy. A locomotive picture at the front of the car and a caboose at the back."

"What does *G.F. Line* mean?"

"That's probably the initials of whoever owns the train."

"Mr. Quinton, I better go back to my seat now—that's where I left my knapsack. I'm supposed to wait there for the conductor. I don't want to get in trouble. Sometimes I do get in trouble."

WES WATCHED TIMMY meander up the aisle walking his fingers over dark spots in the wainscoting beneath the windows. Wes leaned toward the aisle. *I'll be darned. Bird's-eye maple.* The innumerable darker bird's-eyes appeared like polka dots in the otherwise light-colored maple. Wes glanced at the ceiling. The bird's-eyes resembled dark stars, and crystal chandeliers hung every six feet. The rest of the interior was cherry and white oak. Someone who knows wood and how to work with it did this—not cheap either, he thought.

Timmy had reached his seat and busily wrote on a three-by-five card as Blackie lay beside him. A seat beyond, a young mother gazed out the window as she cuddled a baby. The rest of the car was empty.

Wes stood, shuffled his feet to ease the aching, and limped the short distance to the aisle window. A midday sun dropped tree shadows straight to the ground. The aisle exit featured a sliding door made of walnut, a brass handle and kick plate, and an etched glass panel in the upper half. A glance up the aisle revealed a matching door. Really first rate, Wes thought. The middle third of the car was special. The wider U-shaped seating included higher bench backs sporting navy-blue cushions with maroon trim. A table and lamp occupied the middle of each.

His mind wandered. Uneasy, Wes shambled to the opposite window. An unobtrusive sign caught his eye. Do Not Open Windows After Dark. An identical sign was posted at each window on both sides of the car. Odd. Wonder what that's about. He sighed. Better put my things back in the satchel.

The catalog cover read *34th Hardware Convention.* Below that, Lafayette Springs, the hosting city. Wes scanned his notes on the yellow pad and the three-by-five cards. They all dealt with the convention, items needed for the store, and hotel and train information. One card listed last-minute reminders for his store manager in red ink. *Why didn't I give him this card? Forgetful, I guess.* Wes placed the items in his satchel except for a handful of blank cards, which he bound with a rubber band and slipped into his shirt pocket.

The photograph remained on the seat. Wes wanted one more look. His eyes moved from one family member to another. All gone, he thought. Alone like Timmy said. Not much justice in this world—a little now and then but not much. Timmy reminds me of my brother. *I'll keep an eye on him. The least I can do—for Timmy and my brother.* He slipped the picture into the satchel. He always kept the photograph with him.

Wes pulled up his coat sleeve to check the time. The cracked face and motionless hands of his watch stared back. *Rats. When did I do that?* Can't have been that long ago. Would've noticed it. Must have hit it on something. He shook his head. He couldn't remember. For weeks he had worked late preparing for the convention. Too little time. Never seemed to be enough. He scanned the train car. Not a clock on the wall.

His eyes shut, Wes tapped a finger on the satchel as thoughts crowded his mind. On a train. Don't remember boarding. For the convention? Asleep a long time. That's what Timmy said. He's only a boy. Ten minutes to him can seem forever. Been overdoing it. Am I really that tired? I just don't remember getting on. Rats. Where's that conductor Timmy's waiting for? He'll know. Maybe I'll go look for him. Darn feet. Worse than usual. Better wait. *Rats. No, double rats.*

CHAPTER 3

The muted rattle of the front aisle door woke Wes who had nodded off. A towering, heavy-set man adorned in a black uniform with a gold-buttoned, double-breasted coat stepped through the door. A conductor's hat barely cleared the top of the door frame. It sported a gold braid above the visor, and gold letters, which spelled Conductor. A white shirt, black tie and vest, and black patent leather shoes completed the ensemble. His impeccable appearance harmonized with the splendor of the train's interior decor.

With a gait surprisingly light for a man his size, the conductor proceeded down the aisle. The coat buttons and lettering on his hat sparkled; light danced across their buffed surfaces. He tipped his hat and then sat across from the young mother and her baby. After a brief conversation, he moved down the aisle toward the boy and his dog.

The dog saw the conductor first. It froze with his front paws draped over the boy's leg, his head angled up. Tail wagging, it's only moving part thumped the seat. The boy's gaze followed that of his dog.

The conductor tipped his hat. "Hello, Timmy. I'm Mr. Fred Ables, the conductor. Mind if I sit and talk to you for a few minutes?"

"No. You're so tall, I can hardly see you up there."

Fred smiled. So did Wes, who couldn't help but overhear.

The conductor sat.

"How did you know my name?" Timmy asked.

"Well, Timmy, that's part of a conductor's job, to know his passengers."

"Then you know my dog's name too?"

"You have me there. What's his name?"

"Blackie. He's my best friend. We go everywhere together. He's a 'Pomian' kind of dog."

Fred chuckled. "I think you mean *Pomeranian*."

"That's it. I always had trouble with that word."

"Let me write it down, so you can practice writing and saying it." Fred pulled a pen from his coat pocket and fumbled with his other pockets. "Let's see, I have a pad somewhere."

"Use this." Timmy handed him a three-by-five card.

Fred printed *Pomeranian* in block letters. "You keep the pen so you can practice."

"Holy cows. Look at the cool train picture on the pen. Thanks. I will."

The conductor reached into his right coat pocket and withdrew a handful of dog biscuits. "And here's something for Blackie too."

Blackie inched closer, tail wagging.

"No, these are the big ones." Fred returned them and checked his left coat pocket. He pulled out a handful of smaller biscuits. "Here they are. These are a better size for Blackie. May I give him one?"

Blackie took the treat and walked further down the seat.

"Blackie loves biscuits," Timmy said. "And I think he likes you. He hasn't barked at you once."

Fred still clutched a fistful of biscuits. "Do you have something to keep these extras in? I'll give them to you, but don't give Blackie too many at once, or it may upset his stomach."

Timmy plucked a knapsack from beneath the bench and opened the snap on a side pocket. "Thank you, Mr. Ables."

"You're very welcome. Is your ticket in the knapsack? That's something else the conductor does. He checks tickets."

"I think I put it in here." Timmy rummaged the knapsack. He removed a rectangular wooden tablet. It was nearly half an inch thick, two and a half inches wide, and five inches long. "Is this it? It has my name on it in gold letters."

Fred inspected the polished piece of wood with a serious demeanor.

Timmy stared at the back of the ticket. "Look, there's a train on the back and some writing."

The conductor turned the wood over and pointed to the picture. "This is the train's steam locomotive. Underneath it says G.F. Line. Below that is Grant Fischer's signature. That's what the *G.F.* stands for. He owns the train line." Fred handed the ticket to Timmy. "Your ticket is in order. It's first-class."

Timmy looked at him quizzically. "A wood ticket? I thought tickets were made of paper. Is first class like first grade? I was in first grade when I was little."

Fred suppressed a laugh, respecting what were good questions from the young passenger. "You're right. Most tickets are paper. Mr. Fischer does things differently than other railroads. That's why you have a wooden ticket. First class is like A-OK or the best. Understand?"

"I get it. Can I keep the ticket? It's neat."

"It's yours to keep."

"Does Blackie need a ticket?" Timmy asked.

"No, but I can make him one if you want."

"That would be swell. Blackie would like that."

"There are a few things to tell you about the train." Fred pointed toward the front of the car. "If you go through that sliding door, there's another passenger car. After that, you'll find a dining car where you can order food and snacks. A few cars further on are sleeping cars. Oh, and see those signs by the windows?"

"I see them."

"Once it's dark, don't open the windows."

"How come?"

"At night, birds and bats can be attracted to the lights in the car. We'd rather not have them in here."

"I won't open them. Blackie chases birds."

"Good boy, Timmy. And if you need anything, just ask me or anyone else who works on the train. Our stewards have white jackets. Have you met our chief steward Jay Cedrick?"

"I think he carried Blackie when I got on the train. He has blue eyes and long brown hair?"

"That's him."

"Blackie liked him and licked his face. He was nice. What's a steward?"

"Stewards help the passengers in any way they can. If you need help, just ask. Any other questions?"

"Not right now. I might have some later."

"You're probably hungry?" Fred said.

"I'm kind of hungry."

"Why don't you and Blackie get something to eat? Then you can go exploring. Later I'll show you the engine and caboose, if you want."

"Wow, this is the best trip ever."

"Do you remember the way to the dining car?"

Timmy turned and pointed toward the front of the car. "It's that way."

"Good boy. Have you met Mr. Quinton?" Fred asked as he looked toward Wes's seat.

Wes lifted his head from the catalog.

Fred asked Wes, "Would you mind keeping Timmy's knapsack while he eats and explores the train? That is, if it's okay with Timmy and, of course, Blackie."

"I'll guard it with my life," Wes said. "Timmy and I have met."

"That's good with me if it's okay with Blackie," Timmy said.

"Blackie," Wes called.

"Go say *hi*," Timmy commanded the dog. Blackie turned in a circle and barked. "Go say *hi*," Timmy repeated.

Blackie ran back to Wes, who extended his hand. Blackie's cold, wet nose sniffed Wes's fingers. Its tail wagged. Its happy dark eyes peered at Wes, who scratched behind the dog's ears.

Timmy had positioned himself on the seat so he could watch. "Blackie likes you, Mr. Quinton."

"He's a fine dog," Wes said.

"Thank you, Mr. Quinton," the conductor said. "I'll bring the knapsack in a minute."

Wes nodded and returned to the catalog.

"Well, off with you, Timmy, and no running," the conductor admonished.

Fred Ables watched Timmy walk as quickly as he could up the aisle with Blackie in pursuit. Once they disappeared through the car door, he picked up the knapsack and walked back to introduce himself to Wes Quinton.

AS THE CONDUCTOR approached, Wes stood to greet him. The firmness of their handshake felt like old friends reuniting.

"Wes Quinton. Please call me Wes."

"Fred Ables. Just call me Fred. Train's conductor at your service."

It was one of those infrequent occurrences when two people, meeting for the first time, established a bond, friendship, and trust, which seemed to have permanently existed long before. There was no logic in it and no earthly way to account for it—one of those extraordinary joys of life that emerged in a moment's encounter and then lasted forever. Both Wes and Fred knew it by instinct because there was no other way to comprehend it.

Their ages were similar as were the grins on their faces. They sat across from each other on the U-shaped settee.

"I feel as though we've met before," Fred said, "but I can't remember it. You didn't cheat me in a poker game, did you?"

Wes laughed. "That's funny because I feel the same, and I can't recall it either. I think I would have. We would've stayed in touch."

"You're right; we would have. May I offer you a biscuit?" Fred reached toward his coat pocket.

Wes chuckled. "I've never been on a train where dogs are allowed, and, furthermore, where the conductor encourages such behavior by having his pockets stuffed with dog biscuits."

Fred laughed. "This is a special train in many ways. Children love their pets. The owner, Mr. Fischer, loves them both, so we welcome pets. I like animals too."

"So do I. Timmy's a nice boy. Will he be safe wandering the train? I wouldn't want anything to happen to him."

"He'll be fine," Fred said. "When children travel alone, the staff knows. They'll treat him like family. Your concern is appreciated."

"Things have changed since we were boys. I'll keep an eye on him too. And I'll keep his knapsack safe. Maybe I'll take some of those dog biscuits. After all, I'll be watching my new friend Blackie as well."

Fred passed Timmy's knapsack to Wes, who placed it under the seat.

"Thanks for watching it. Now some biscuits." Fred removed a handful from his pocket and handed them to Wes, who filled his own pocket.

"May I ask you something?" Wes cleared his throat and looked down. "I'm embarrassed to ask."

"Why sure."

"Do you remember me boarding the train because, honestly, I don't? I know it sounds silly, but I don't remember it at all."

"I'm not surprised. One of our porters had to wake you at the station. Our chief steward helped you to this very seat. You could barely keep your eyes open. You slept all morning. We put your suitcase in the baggage car. It's not that unusual. Don't worry about it."

"It bothers me, not remembering. I've been putting in long hours preparing for a convention. Too many hours and too little sleep, I guess."

"You own a hardware store with a lumberyard don't you?"

Wes's eyes widened. "How do you know?"

"We've had some passengers in the past where your name came up. Your customers think highly of you. Do you feel better now that you've slept?"

"Much better. My feet are sore from all the standing I've been doing. Otherwise, that sleep helped a bunch."

"We'll fix your feet. I'll send Jay Cedrick by in a little while. He's our chief steward. You'll like him."

"That's not necessary. They're only achy. They're not falling off."

"Now, now. You must let a conductor do his job. And I think you have a first-class ticket, like Timmy."

Wes frowned. Wonder what I did with my ticket—it wasn't in my satchel. He searched his coat and found it in an inside pocket. The polished wood bore his name etched in gold-colored letters with L.S. below it. Must be for *Lafayette Springs*, he thought. On the reverse was an etching of a locomotive. Below the picture, he saw G.F. Line and Grant Fischer's signature.

"This is a work of art." Wes passed the ticket to Fred. "I've never seen this kind of wood. It's a bit like cypress or cedar, but it's not either of them. Do you know the type of wood?"

"It's called gopherwood. It's rare. That's all I know, except it is a first-class ticket."

Wes printed *gopherwood* on the front of the convention catalog in red letters. "I'll ask around at the convention. Might learn something new."

"You mean like teaching an old dog new tricks? Sure you don't want a biscuit to chew on? You can have a big one." Fred handed the ticket back to Wes.

Wes laughed and returned the wooden pass to his pocket. "You're sure my ticket is first-class? I've never bought a first-class ticket. Can't afford it."

"It's first-class but it doesn't cost more. One of Mr. Fischer's amenities."

"Thank goodness. One thing that surprises me is how few passengers are on the train. At least this car. Did Mr. Fischer just start this line?"

"It's one of the oldest around," Fred said. "There will be more passengers without a doubt. You heard me tell Timmy about the dining car and the sleeping cars. The dining car has good food as well as snacks. It's always open. Any steward will be happy to retrieve your suitcase at any time. You'll meet Mr. Fischer at some point. He likes to chat with his passengers. And don't—"

"I know, don't open the windows at night. Birds and bats."

Fred hesitated. His eyes darkened. He glanced around, leaned toward Wes, and beckoned him to do the same. "Please keep this to yourself, but birds and bats aren't the real reason. It's enough to satisfy the passengers without frightening them. We travel through some dangerous areas at night, and we don't want to risk an incident."

"What kind of incident?"

Fred's face grew grim. "I've never seen one, but I've heard of them. Gives me the heebie-jeebies just thinking about it. Believe me, we don't want an incident. I can't tell you more, but an open window at night is dangerous. There are signs by all the windows. Plus, the windows are latched. They're deliberately difficult to open. All it takes is one pigheaded passenger . . ." Able's voice trailed off; his eyes glanced nervously around the car.

Wes nodded as the two again sat upright. Fred was a huge man, but talking about an incident had erased the color from his face. Must be bad, whatever it is, Wes thought. I'd better keep a close eye on Timmy.

The color returned to Fred's face. "I almost forgot," he said. "Tomorrow, we'll have a several hour stopover in Penceville about mid morning. It's a nice town. Maybe you'd like to stretch your legs.

Some of our passengers depart there; others come aboard. If I recall, there's someone there I think you would like to see."

"Who?"

"You'll find out tomorrow, that is, if I remember correctly. In the meantime, we'll fix your feet. I have to check on other passengers. Perhaps we can eat together later if I catch up on my duties?"

Wes watched Fred leave and wondered whom he might know in Penceville. Never heard of the place. He glanced toward the windows. The warning signs looked larger than before. *An incident.* A prickly chill climbed his spine.

CHAPTER 4

The aisle door near Wes opened. A man in his early thirties carried an oversized bucket and a canvas tote bag full of towels. He stopped in front of Wes. Shoulder-length chestnut hair framed a fervent face with sparkling blue eyes. He wore dark slacks, a white jacket, and a white shirt with a black bow tie. Embroidery on the jacket read Chief Steward and beneath that, Jay Cedrick. Broad shoulders made the weight of the bucket seem of no consequence. He smiled. "Mr. Quinton?"

"Yes, that's me."

"Jay Cedrick at your service, sir." The steward bowed slightly. "Mr. Ables asked me to see you about your feet. I'm sure I can help."

"It's very kind of you, Mr. Cedrick."

"Please call me Jay."

"I will. That bucket looks heavy. Why don't you set it down?"

"Thank you, Mr. Quinton. This water is hot, but your feet will feel like new when we're done. Do you need help removing your shoes and socks?"

"I can manage."

Jay laid a towel on the floor and placed the bucket on it. Wisps of vapor drifted from the water's surface. He knelt next to Wes. "Roll your pant legs up. I'll slide the bucket under your feet. Put them in slowly. The water is quite hot but not so much as to scald you."

Wes cautiously submerged his feet and ankles in the water.

Jay pulled a jar of multicolored crystals from his pocket. "These are Epsom salts and other secret ingredients that will take the soreness away."

"Secret?"

"My secret, but they work like a miracle given the proper soaking time."

"How long would that be?"

"About an hour. I'll know when your feet are better. So will you." Jay poured a small portion of the mixture into the water. Sparkles of vibrant light flickered as the crystals fizzed in the water.

"I've never seen salts do that."

"That's the secret ingredients." Jay rose and sat opposite Wes.

Wes wiggled his feet to insure the salts dissolved. "I don't know how to thank you. This is more than I expected."

"Pleased to be of service, Mr. Quinton. I'm glad you mentioned your feet to Mr. Ables. You've had trouble with them for a long time. It's impossible not to notice the scars. They'll be much better when we're done. Sorry they've been such a problem."

"A war injury—my brother was killed by the same mortar round. I'd swap both feet for my brother. I tried to save him, but I was too late. That's the worst scar. A lot worse than my feet."

"I'm sure you did all you could. I'm very sorry about your brother. He's in a better place now."

"I hope so."

"Mr. Ables was quite taken with you, sir. He said you own a hardware store and a lumberyard?"

"I do. After I returned home from the war, I realized our town needed a hardware store, so I started one. Later I added lumber. It's plenty of work, but the reward has been many loyal customers. Some still have tools they bought from me when I first opened."

"Has it provided a good living?"

Wes shrugged. "Up and down. There've been spells where I've carried people on credit until they were back on their feet, but those times were tough on everyone. I've also had some business difficulties, not of my making, that were trying. Almost worse than being shot at in the war in some ways. It's not always been easy, but life's about more than just making a living. I think it's the people I've met and gotten to know that's been the best part."

"You're a wise man, Mr. Quinton. The world could use more people like you."

Jay glanced out the window. "We're near our next stop; the train is slowing. I have to check if any passengers need my help. Keep your feet where they are. I'll be back shortly." Jay stood, bowed slightly, and left the car.

Wes hadn't noticed the train slowing until Jay mentioned it. The whistle sounded intermittently. Homes, roads with cars stopped at crossing gates, and telephone poles streamed by the window. Brownstones, businesses, and bustling streets crowded together as the tracks advanced into the heart of the city. Bright flashing lights from rescue vehicles illuminated a distant and otherwise ordinary city street. A bad accident, no doubt, Wes thought.

The train slowed and came to a gentle stop in a covered railway station with other parallel tracks and trains. Passenger walkways and platforms separated the numbered tracks. Travelers, porters, and luggage carts moved about in apparent randomness, masking the purposeful activity of the participants.

A sleek newer diesel train occupied the adjacent track. Wes had ridden behind similar locomotives to other conventions. Not as pretty as this train, thought Wes, and definitely not with this level of service.

Jay returned. "Mind if I sit, Mr. Quinton?"

"Please do. You don't need to ask."

Jay bowed slightly and sat opposite Wes. "It's habit, Mr. Quinton."

"You don't need to bow either. I'm not royalty, just an ordinary hardware store owner."

"That's habit too."

"You weren't gone long."

"Sometimes this is a busy stop, but there were fewer passengers than usual. My help wasn't needed for long."

"I forgot to ask you the name of this city."

"It's the state capital," Jay said.

"I visited here long ago. Looked in almost every hardware store for ideas. I'm sure it's grown since. I don't remember stopping here on my other convention trips, though."

"Our route is always changing; we stop where we need to. That's part of our service. We're more flexible than most train lines."

The train began to move and accelerated as it left the station. Wes surveyed the far side of the city through the window; it looked like the mirror image of the near side.

THE REAR DOOR slid open and Fred Ables entered the car. Wes was about to greet him but held back. Fred wore a look of exasperation that masked his usually friendly features. Loud footsteps followed him. A shrill nasal pitch penetrated the air—a voice so unmistakable that once heard, could not be forgotten.

This can't be, Wes thought. *Hope I'm wrong. I have to be wrong.*

He wasn't.

Lamar Colby, legendary for his alleged banker's expertise, was also equally notorious for his heartlessness and dishonesty. His obnoxious voice and lack of virtue dovetailed with his rodent-like face. Beady dark eyes and a diminutive-pointed nose decorated a round fleshy face. He dressed expensively and, he thought, impressively. The banker wore an elongated top hat to disguise his paltry stature. A rotund belt size and the tall hat made him appear unbalanced as though he could topple over at any moment.

A step behind Colby trailed State Senator F. W. Bryce, whom Wes also knew. Unlike Colby, he was a tall man with a stately appearance, marred on occasion by a devilish look of political ambition in his eyes. Bryce dressed as affluently as the banker; the only difference, it looked good on Bryce. He would be perfect on the front of a cereal box if you were advertising crooked, unbeatable politicians.

Colby and Bryce were friends born of a synergistic chicanery in which money and power reinforced itself. Their collusion benefited each and both simultaneously. The public both admired and feared the duo. Admiration from those with similar aspirations and a comparable deficiency of integrity; fear from those who detested corruption and the destructive carnage of their wake.

The scene grew uglier. Wes's hands tightened into fists.

Two other men Wes knew, Mack and Gus, followed Colby and Bryce. Colby publically referred to them as assistants or associates, depending on the occasion. In reality, they were errand boys, bodyguards, enforcers, intimidators, or whatever Colby required them to be. Wes used one word to describe them—thugs.

Both wore tailored suits at Colby's insistence. Mack was lean and wiry; he wore a tweed flat cap cocked over one eye. He possessed a mean streak that demanded no reason. Gus appeared overweight; a closer inspection revealed the muscularity of an ex–heavyweight boxer. Gus was the more intelligent of the two and the more vigilant, having dodged countless punches in his prior occupation. He was the one who glanced over and recognized Wes Quinton.

"Mr. Colby. Look who's here," Gus said.

The group stopped and turned toward Wes, whose, heretofore pleasant journey was now in jeopardy.

"Why if it isn't Quinton the younger," Lamar Colby snarled. "You let this kind of riffraff on your train, Mr. Conductor? And he's taking a bath in public. What kind of a train is this?"

Senator Bryce, Mack, and Gus snickered.

"We have unfinished business, Quinton. I still owe you. I haven't forgotten," Colby said.

Fred Ables glanced at Wes apologetically. "Mr. Colby, I would ask you to please respect our passengers and restrain your speech."

Colby stiffened. "Restrain myself with miscreants like this on your train. I find your remarks insulting. You'll be sorry you spoke to me like that. You don't know who you're dealing with. And you, boy," Colby continued, pointing at the head steward, Jay. "You carry my travel bag and don't drop it. What lousy service on this train."

"Yes, sir," Jay said as he stood. He leaned toward Wes and whispered, "Excuse me, Mr. Quinton, I'll be back shortly. I apologize for their rudeness."

Colby handed Jay the leather travel bag. The group resumed its trek down the aisle.

"There," Colby said. "Those seats in the middle. The others are peasants' seats."

Fred Ables stepped aside as Senator Bryce slipped into the near side of the U-shaped seating. Lamar Colby slid into the opposite side.

"Give me my bag," Colby said.

Jay didn't see Mack extend his leg to trip him. Jay staggered forward. He caught himself with one hand sliding on the table. The other gripped the travel bag, which hit Colby in the chest. The banker tumbled facedown onto the seat. His top hat fell to the floor. So did another object that landed with a *chink* and a *thud*.

"I'm so sorry," Jay said. He righted himself, set the bag on the seat, and helped Colby regain a seated position. "Are you all right, Mr. Colby? I must have stumbled over something. I'm truly sorry."

Colby's face flushed with anger. "You nitwit. You clumsy oaf. Where's my hat?"

"It fell under the seat, Mr. Colby. I'll get it." Jay retrieved the hat; he also found the source of the other sounds.

"Here's your hat, Mr. Colby. It seems to be okay," Jay said, brushing it with his forearm. "Unfortunately, your ticket must have fallen from your pocket. A chip broke off the corner." He showed Colby the ticket. "I'll have a new one made."

Colby fumed. "You're darn straight you will. I thought I paid for first class, but what we have here isn't even third-rate. How do clumsy nitwits like you ever find a job? I've never seen such incompetence."

Jay turned to Fred, and showed him Colby's ticket. The size and design matched the wooden tickets, but it was made of sterling silver. Colby's name was inlaid with gold with L.S. below it. Jay placed the damaged ticket in his jacket's breast pocket and the chipped piece in his trouser pocket.

Mack and Gus nudged past Jay and slipped into the seats opposite one another.

Fred tried his best to remain composed and professional. "Gentlemen, may I check your tickets please? That is, except for Mr. Colby whose ticket I've seen." The conductor glanced at Colby fearing another tirade, which didn't come. The horrid look on the banker's face made words redundant.

The conductor found the tickets in order. He returned them with as cordial a thank you as he could muster. Pointing, he said, "Gentlemen, there is a dining car and sleeping cars forward. The dining car is open—"

Colby interrupted. "If we want anything, we'll have it brought here."

"Yes, sir," Fred said. "And let me draw your attention to the sign at each window."

Mack, Gus, and Senator Bryce looked toward the adjacent windows. Colby simply stared at Fred.

"It is requested that you not open the windows after dark," the conductor said.

Colby again reached the shallow limits of his tolerance. "Who do you think you are? Do you not understand who I am, and who Senator Bryce is? You don't tell us what to do and what not to do. If we want the window open at night, we'll open it. In fact, we'll do whatever we please. And neither of you and no one else will stop us." Colby's face glowed crimson.

"Yes, sir," Ables said. "The windows—it's only for your own safety."

"Do we look like children?" Colby asked. "We'll decide what's safe and what isn't."

"Yes, sir," Fred mumbled, attempting to hide his frustration. "Mr. Fischer, the train owner, will stop by later to introduce himself."

"That's the first good news to come out of your mouth," Colby said. "You tell him it better be sooner than later. We have a bunch of complaints about his operation and you two clowns."

"Yes, sir," the conductor said.

"Bring us drinks," Colby demanded.

"Yes, sir," Fred said. "Jay can do that. What would you like?"

"Bourbon on ice. Four of them."

"I'm sorry. We don't carry liquor on the train."

Colby seemed ready to erupt. Instead, he opened his travel bag, withdrew a bottle, and set it on the table. He turned the bottle's label toward Fred and Jay. It was the most expensive bourbon available on the market. "Bring us glasses and an ice bucket. And make sure the glasses are clean."

"Yes, sir." Fred nodded to Jay.

"I'll be back in fifteen minutes with your ice and glasses," Jay told Colby.

Colby slammed his palm on the table. "Fifteen minutes. That's unacceptable."

"I think the glasses are all dirty," Jay said. "After all, we are nitwits. Should I bring the dirty glasses?"

Colby's fist rocked the table and nearly knocked over the bottle of bourbon. Jay headed toward the rear of the car. Fred scurried up the forward aisle suppressing a chuckle. The staff kept the glasses immaculate. Always.

JAY STOPPED AT Wes Quinton's seat and knelt in front of the bucket. "I'm sorry about the commotion," Jay said. "I wanted to check the water before I get their glasses and ice." Jay dipped his fingers in the water. "It's warm but it needs to be warmer."

"Don't bother with me," Wes said. "You'd better take care of Mr. Colby."

"This won't take long. Tell me when it's hot."

Jay placed his hands on opposite sides of the bucket and moved them back and forth so rapidly their appearance blurred.

Wes was about to tell Jay it couldn't work when he felt the temperature in the bucket rise. A few seconds later he blurted, "It's hot—it's hot."

Jay held up his hands and grinned at Wes. "I know what you were thinking. That can't work. But it did."

"How did you do that?"

"It's a trick I learned from my father. Comes in handy now and then. I have to run that errand for Mr. Colby. Keep your feet in the bucket. I'll be back."

Even seated at the rear of the car, Wes could hear snippets of Colby's conversation. I need to tell Fred about them, he thought. They could be a danger to the other passengers. That mother and her baby are too close to them—she looks worried. And Timmy and Blackie—they shouldn't be in this car. I need to tell Fred what I know. *Rats.*

CHAPTER 5

Jay passed through the rear aisle door carrying a tray with glasses, an ice bucket, napkins, and silver bowls full of peanuts and pretzels. He delivered the items to Colby's table without incident. On his way back to Wes, he checked on the mother and her baby.

"The train sure keeps you busy," Wes said.

Jay laid the empty tray on the seat. "There's always something to do. I just remembered. I need to remake this ticket." Jay pulled Colby's damaged ticket from his jacket pocket. "It chipped when it hit the floor."

"That's beautiful, striking."

"It's like yours except it's made of sterling silver with gold inlays."

"May I examine it?"

"Sure." Jay passed the ticket to Wes.

"This is exquisite workmanship, especially the locomotive on the back." Wes saw L.S. below Colby's name and hoped their paths wouldn't somehow cross at the convention. He's probably there for other business, Wes thought. And he'll stay in the best hotel, not what I can afford.

Wes returned the ticket to Jay who slid it into his breast pocket.

"I'm surprised at the craftsmanship of your tickets."

"We actually have three kinds," Jay said. "The ones like yours and Timmy's are the best. People like Mr. Colby would be insulted by a wooden ticket, even if they were told it was made of a very rare wood, so we accommodate them with a silver ticket."

"And the third kind?"

"It's made of wood, too, a reddish cedar. It's not rare, like gopherwood, but it's less common than many other woods. Otherwise, they're similar to the other tickets. They're for people who disembark at some of the towns along the way."

"You can fix that chipped ticket?"

"We could, but we'll just make a new one. We try to do things special. For some of our passengers, it's their first train ride."

The train began to slow; the whistle sounded.

"Another stop?" Wes asked.

"It'll be a short one. It's a small town. Our last stop today. I'd better return this tray and have our machinist start a new ticket for Mr. Colby. I'll be back. Your feet are almost done."

FARMS, WITH MOST of the fields harvested, passed by the window. Country roads, orchards, barns, and homes punctuated a landscape with trees decorated in the early colors of fall. A parallel track with several freight cars flanked empty cattle pens and silos.

A single traffic signal, worn brick buildings, and faded homes filled the windows as the train slowed to a crawl. Wes saw little activity: a few pedestrians, a slow-moving beat-up pickup truck, and a stray mutt.

The forward door of Wes's car opened, and a couple walked briskly down the aisle. The lady wore a maroon-colored dress, a navy blue waist-length cloak, and a scarf with a cream hue. Locks of black hair extended from beneath the scarf and framed a timeless, appealing face with luminous green eyes. A powerfully built man accompanied the woman. He dressed simply in dark brown slacks, white shirt, and a tweed coat. A trimmed dark beard with touches of gray matched his hair. His rugged face suggested a demanding life, yet his dark eyes exuded a gentleness one might not have expected. As they passed, both glanced at Wes and smiled, despite their hurry.

The train stopped at a sad weathered station badly in need of fresh paint. The faded lettering on a plank jutting over the walkway made it difficult to guess the town's name.

A young boy sat at the near end of an old bench. He clutched a small suitcase in his arms. His legs swung nonchalantly. Nearby, a sheriff stood. Farther down the bench, a nurse fussed over two baskets, each with a pastel blanket. At the far end of the bench sat two soldiers in service uniforms with duffle bags, their backs ramrod straight.

Jay, one other steward, and the couple who had walked through Wes's car appeared on the station platform. The woman peered into each basket. Jay knelt before the boy. The man spoke with the sheriff, who handed him a piece of paper and patted him on the back. The second steward walked to the soldiers. They promptly stood as if a general had arrived. The soldiers followed the steward onto the train, bags in hand.

Jay gently picked up one of the baskets; the woman carried the other. The man hoisted the young boy, carrying him and the small suitcase in one arm with ease. The nurse and the sheriff waved and turned toward town.

Soon in motion, the train left the worn station behind. Farms became sparser and then disappeared as wilderness prevailed.

JAY AND THE lady, each with a basket, entered the car followed by the man holding the boy. They stopped near Wes.

The man spoke. "Our apologies, sir. We did not have time to introduce ourselves before. I am Jonathan Holyfield. This is my wife Marielle."

"My apology for not standing." Wes pointed at the bucket. "I'm Wes Quinton and it's my pleasure. Please have a seat."

"We would like to, but we need to situate these little ones," Marielle said.

"This young fellow is Matthew," Jonathan said, "and Marielle has Lindy. Jay has Peter."

"Hello, Matthew," Wes said.

Marielle and Jay brought the baskets closer to Wes. They pulled the blankets back a bit. Lindy, a tiny baby, slept soundly. Peter, the larger infant, gazed intently at Wes.

"Sadly, they are orphans for now," Jonathan said. "We have a children's nursery car just past the sleeping cars. There we care for them while they travel to their new homes. You can visit with us if you'd like. Timmy and Blackie have been in and out of our car a few times already."

"Thank you." Wes pointed several seats forward. "Perhaps that mother and her baby would like to join you. Those other men in this car were rowdy a while ago, and she seemed apprehensive."

"That's thoughtful of you, Mr. Quinton," Marielle replied. "We'll invite her to join us."

Baby Peter began to cry, which woke tiny Lindy. She joined in.

"We've overstayed our little visit," Marielle said.

"Very nice to meet you, Mr. Quinton," Jonathan said.

"My pleasure, Mr. and Mrs. Holyfield," Wes said. "Please let me know if I can help."

Wes watched them walk up the aisle with the two babies still carrying on. Mrs. Holyfield spoke with the young mother whose baby promptly joined the chorus of criers, changing a duo into a trio.

Colby and his cohorts turned in their seats and glared at the wailing babies. Colby slapped his hand on the table. "Get those stinking crying babies out of here."

The young mother stood in the aisle clutching her baby. Jonathan Holyfield grabbed her travel bag. They navigated the remaining aisle and exited through the forward door.

THE TWO SOLDIERS Wes had seen at the last stop entered the car. They nodded, said, "Hello, sir," and sat forward of him near the windows. Both were young. The larger, a corporal, wore a green marine corps service uniform with a garrison cap. The other, an army private first class, sported a green jacket, blue pants, and a black beret. Their presence brought a flood of memories to Wes, both good and bad. The bad ones were of those comrades who didn't return from the battlefield.

Jay returned and spoke to the soldiers. "Gentlemen, I'm Jay Cedrick, the chief steward."

The soldiers promptly stood. The tall marine said, "Nick Hart, sir," and the other, "Daniel Wilson, sir."

Jay grinned. "I'm a civilian, fellows. No need to stand. The conductor will see you later. In the meantime, there's a diner, two cars forward. I've yet to meet a soldier that didn't like good chow. Are you hungry?"

"Yes, sir. Thank you, sir," they replied in unison.

"Should we wait for the conductor, sir?" Nick Hart asked.

"No, he'll catch up with you. They just pulled fresh pies from the oven."

The soldiers grinned. "We'll go now, sir. Thank you, sir," the marine said.

Nick and Daniel darted up the aisle in quick time. Colby and his thugs kept a suspicious eye on them as they passed. Anyone in uniform, police or otherwise, made them uneasy.

JAY RETURNED TO Wes and sat opposite him. "A few more minutes, and your feet are done. How do they feel?"

Wes had nearly forgotten. He wiggled his toes and rocked his feet in the warm water. "I don't feel any soreness. In fact, they feel better than they have in years."

Jay knelt and placed a towel next to the bucket. "Slowly take your feet out and put them on the towel. I'll dry them so water doesn't drip on the floor."

Wes did as told. Jay carefully wiped the water from his feet.

"Do you need help with your shoes and socks?"

"You've done too much already. I can do it," Wes said.

"I'll be back. I need to empty the bucket."

When Jay reappeared, Wes was standing, his shoes and socks on, with the towels folded next to the tote bag. "I don't believe it. My feet were awful. Worse than usual. And now they feel new. Like I could walk for miles, maybe even run. I don't know what to say, except thank you."

Jay grinned. "I knew you were hurting, Mr. Quinton. I could see it in your face. Not that it showed much, but I have a knack for reading people. Your feet won't bother you again."

"Jay, do you have a minute? I'm worried about something. Can you get a message to Fred?"

"Why sure," Jay said as they sat.

Wes leaned toward Jay and lowered his voice. "Colby and his group are treacherous men. I know from personal experience. That's how they know me. I'm not worried about myself. What concerns me are other passengers and the train staff. They could be in danger. I'm glad that mother and her baby went with the Holyfields. She was frightened. When you see Fred, please tell him what I said. I can provide more details. I don't want anyone hurt, and they are capable of it, very capable."

Jay's fingers ran over his brow. "They sure haven't given a good first impression. I'll tell Fred right away. Glad you told me. We don't need trouble."

Chapter 6

The two soldiers returned from the dining car. Conductor Fred Ables followed just behind them. Colby and his thugs eyed them surreptitiously as they passed.

"Have a seat, fellows," Fred said. He glanced at Wes with a raised finger to indicate he'd see him shortly. Sitting across from the soldiers, Fred lifted his hat and scratched his head. He continued, "Let's see, you've seen the dining car, the sleeping cars, and chatted with Mr. Fischer. You met Jay earlier. Jay and any of the stewards will be happy to assist you. Don't hesitate to ask. You've served your country, and we're here to serve you. The only thing we ask is that you don't open the windows after dark." Fred pointed to one of the signs.

"We won't, sir."

"If you don't have questions, I'll check your tickets."

"Yes, sir."

Fred examined the tickets, which were of the same wood as Wes's and Timmy's. "They're in order." He returned them.

"Thank you, sir."

Fred stood. "It's an honor to have you on the train. Please let me know if there's anything you need."

"Thank you, sir."

Fred joined Wes. He leaned in and spoke quietly. "Jay told me about your concerns. I'm worried, too, given the earlier problems. Can you meet me in the dining car in twenty minutes? We can talk there."

Wes nodded.

"Twenty minutes then." Fred strode up the aisle and exited the car.

WES SLID INTO the soldiers' booth.

They both stood. "Hello, sir."

"Sit down. Mind if I join you for a few minutes?" Wes asked.

"No, sir."

Wes extended his hand. "I'm Wes Quinton."

The men gripped Wes's hand firmly.

"Nick Hart, sir."

"Daniel Wilson, sir."

"You fellows look grand in your uniforms. You could be on recruiting posters. Have you been serving stateside or overseas?"

"Overseas, in combat. Both of us, sir," Nick said.

"There always seems to be war somewhere," Wes said. "In my day, it was the big one. We lost a lot of fine soldiers."

"Did you serve, sir?" Nick asked.

"Yes. It was a long time ago."

"What branch, sir?" Daniel asked.

"Army, like you Daniel."

"What rank were you?" Nick asked.

"Staff sergeant—promotions came pretty fast because we lost so many men. It's still hard to talk about."

"Yes, sir," Daniel said. "We know the feeling."

"I saw Jay send you to the dining car. How's the chow?" Wes asked.

"First-class. Like home cooking," Nick said.

"I think I'll try some," Wes said. He pointed to his seat. "Would you fellows mind keeping an eye on my satchel and also the knapsack under the seat? I'm watching that for a boy on the train?"

"Timmy?" Daniel asked.

"You know Timmy?"

"We met him and Blackie in the dining car. Timmy sure loves chocolate shakes," Nick said. "We'll watch them for you, Mr. Quinton. We're good at guarding things."

Wes laughed. "I know you are. See you in a while. At ease. Don't stand when I get up."

"Yes, sir."

Wes strolled up the aisle. He avoided eye contact with Colby and his cronies. His gait was smooth and easy. No limp. No pain. Amazing, Wes thought. Will it last, though?

THE NEXT PASSENGER car had few empty seats. Wes proceeded to the dining car. The teasing aroma of coffee and freshly baked pies and cakes hung in the air. Diners chatted. The clinking of cups, plates, and utensils reminded Wes of wind chimes. The aisle ran along one side of the car with dining booths on the other. In the middle of the car, the aisle curved around a half-moon shaped counter, which displayed pies and cakes on covered glass plates. A broad shelf against the wall held coffeemakers, a drink dispenser, mugs, glasses, napkins, and utensils.

White lace curtains and checkered tablecloths of country blue and white conveyed a homey welcome. Booths, upholstered in a cream color, complemented walls finished in a light colored wood with dark accents. Soft music floated in the background. An elderly lady, with short silvery hair, wore an ankle-length floral dress with an apron and sliced a fresh cherry pie. She turned at the sound of steps.

"Can I help you, sir? Why, Wes, Wes Quinton? Is that really you?"

"Mabel Hawthorne. I haven't seen you in years. What are you doing here?"

Mabel came around the counter and gave Wes a hug. "Fred, he's the conductor, told me they were short on help, so I volunteered to fill in. I could ask you the same. Would you like a menu? You must have come to eat."

"Actually, I'm supposed to meet Fred here. Have you seen him?"

Mabel pointed. "He's in the last booth at the front of the car. He's on a second piece of pie. Shall I bring you some?"

"Please. Any kind is fine and a cup of coffee would be nice too. I don't mean to run, but it's important."

Mabel smiled. "We can catch up later."

FRED WAVED TO Wes. "I got here early."

"No doubt to corner the pie market." Wes sat across from him.

Fred laughed. "You'll see why when you have a piece."

"It's on the way," Wes said. "I'm glad Jay spoke with you. I'm worried about Colby and his bunch. I've had personal run-ins with them. They can cause heaps of trouble."

"I knew they might be a problem when they boarded the train. I spoke to Mr. Fischer about them. We've kept most of the passengers in other cars to be on the safe side."

"That was smart."

Mabel delivered pie and coffee for Wes. "More for you, Fred?"

"I'm fine for now. Thank you." Fred turned to Wes. "Tell me about the problems with Colby, so I have an idea what to expect."

Wes took a bite of pie and a sip of coffee. "Let me think—where do I start?"

Fred's brow furrowed. "That complicated?"

"Lots of pieces and players. It's not just Colby. Bryce and Colby's goons are part of it too." Wes rubbed his fingers over his forehead. "Let's start here. Lamar Colby came to town a few years after I started my hardware business. He landed a job as junior bank assistant. It was the only bank in town and was well run. Everyone trusted it. The president of the bank was highly respected, too, and knew everyone. About a year later, rumors circulated that there might be a problem with the bank. Most of us didn't believe it. A month later, bank examiners showed up. They spent a week at the bank. A short while later, the sheriff arrested the bank president, and the bank closed for a few days. The newspaper ran sketchy stories of wrongdoing but also a notice that the bank would soon reopen and that all deposits were safe and insured. Furthermore, Colby had risen to bank president. Eventually, he became the sole owner by buying out other shareholders. The former bank president went to trial. The jury acquitted him, but his banking days were over. He and his family left town. The episode destroyed his reputation. It was sad; most of us knew he was a good, honest man."

"That's strange," Fred said. "There must be more to it."

"There is. A teller who was a friend quit six months after Colby took over. I have no proof of what he told me, but he's a trustworthy man. He found out Colby had falsified bank records in a way that incriminated the bank president. Colby tipped off the bank inspectors, apparently anonymously. My friend tried to assemble the proof, but the crooked records disappeared after Colby became president. My friend resigned from the bank; there was nothing else he could do. He told me to do my banking elsewhere if I could. That's what I did with my accounts. A friend from my army days was president of the bank in the next town. The only thing I left at Colby's bank was the mortgage on my hardware store.

"Colby ran things honestly for a few years to gain people's trust. Everything settled down, at least as far as appearances. About every six months, I'd see a story buried in the back pages of the paper about Colby taking ownership of this or that bank in various towns. I always wondered how he did it. Although he spent time at his other banks, our bank remained his base of operations. Maybe it had something to do with his first conquest.

"Somewhere in this time frame, Colby hooked up with F. W. Bryce. You've seen him. He's tall and stately, and looks more intelligent than he really is. Unfortunately, what he has in looks, he lacks in integrity. He's one of those smooth talkers who bamboozles people. Bryce won his first election handily when he ran for state representative because he looked the part. By the end of his first term, many stories of corruption involved him. Bryce lost reelection in a landslide. I don't know how Bryce and Colby met, but once they did, Bryce never lost an election again. Colby became as adept at rigging elections as he was at acquiring banks. He took care of the funding, bribing, and arm-twisting when needed, courtesy of Mack and Gus. Bryce did the rest. Rumor had it they could engineer Bryce's elections so well that they made money betting the spreads. Colby decided the senate would give Bryce more influence, and Bryce handily won his first senate race. And every reelection since. Bryce now has seniority. He sits on many powerful committees, some of which he chairs."

"That reinforces my dislike of politics in a big way," Fred said.

Wes shrugged. "That's what's funny about Colby. He doesn't care about politics or party. He just wants one politician, with power and influence, in his pocket for when he needs it. For him, that's Bryce. That's all he needs. And Bryce knows that without Colby behind the scenes, he'd be out of the senate. They're like symbiotic parasites. A banker and a politician. Money and power. It's a match made in heaven."

"Hell," Fred said.

"Excuse me."

"You mean a match made in hell."

"You're right, of course. And there's hell to pay for those who get in their way." Wes took a bite of pie followed by a sip of coffee.

Wes continued. "Once Colby and Bryce started working together, Colby's acquisition of other banks sped up. About four years ago, he bought one of the large banks in the state capital. The newspapers suggested it was at a bargain-basement price although the amount didn't appear in the paper. The bottom line is that Colby put Bryce in the political big leagues. Now Colby is in the banking big leagues."

Fred frowned. "How do Mack and Gus figure in the picture?"

"I remember Mack first. I'd see him hanging around Colby's bank and running errands for him. Then some stories cropped up about Mack hurting a few people around town. Later, I learned he was collecting and strong-arming for Colby. Not long after, Gus joined Colby. Gus is an ex-boxer and strong as an ox. He has a better temperament and much better judgment than Mack. I think Colby saw them as complementary and important assets for his future plans. He put them in tailor-made suits to make them presentable, but he used them as bodyguards, errand boys, and enforcers. They've been with him a long time."

"What did they do to you?"

"It was actually my parents who first had trouble with Colby."

"Dear Lord," Fred said. "What happened?"

Wes's shoulders drooped as he sighed. "Mother had been real sick and was in and out of the hospital. Between Mother and work, my father ran himself ragged. One day he received a notice from the bank that it was foreclosing on their house. He couldn't believe it because he remembered writing the mortgage check. Unfortunately, mail and bills had piled up. He found the unmailed check under the pile. He looked at the mortgage papers. The payment was overdue beyond the grace period and the penalty period. The bank had the right to foreclose. Dad rushed to the bank with the check and talked with Colby. Dad explained what happened and asked him not to foreclose. He said he would pay whatever penalty was required. Colby wouldn't relent.

"When Dad told me the next day, I took him to my lawyer, Sam Knight. Sam reviewed the mortgage papers. He told Dad the bank had the legal option and right to foreclose. The bank had foreclosed on several of his clients over the previous year under similar circumstances. In each case, Colby refused to budge. Sam told us there was no legal remedy. The only possible solution was to convince Colby not to foreclose, and those odds were about nil.

"That afternoon, Dad and I went to the bank. Colby was annoyed at seeing my father again. We begged him to reconsider. I'll never forget what he said. 'I run a bank, not a soup kitchen.' My dad saw my hands squeeze into fists. Dad put his hand on my arm and patted it. He stood without a word, and we left.

"That night, I asked Dad why he didn't respond to Colby. He told me there are times when nothing further can be done and that includes reacting to words. Colby intended for his insult to anger Dad. Dad refused to give him that satisfaction. Dad said he wanted to read me something from his Bible. He read the verses that described how Jesus drove the moneychangers from the temple courts, overturned their tables, and scattered their coins. Dad believed that even though he couldn't do anything about Colby, the day would come when justice would prevail. My dad had plenty of faith. At times, he amazed me."

"He was quite a man," Fred said.

"He was a very good man. I learned a lot from him. My parents lost the house; they rented an apartment. Mom never recovered; she died that winter. The doctor said it was the illness, but losing the house was heartbreaking. It surely didn't help."

"I'm sorry, Wes. What a tragedy."

"It gets worse. I stopped by to check on Dad every night. The loss of my mother and the house devastated him. One night, he wasn't there. I drove around town but couldn't find him or anyone who had seen him. The sheriff's office said they'd be on the lookout for him. Next day, the sheriff called and said Dad had been seen the previous night at a dingy bar near the bridge over the river. They were still gathering information and following leads. I was surprised because he hadn't had a drink since before I was born."

"Did he have a drinking problem?"

"Before Dad married Mom, he would binge drink once in a while. After they married, that stopped. I think the stress of losing the house and Mom so close together must have been too much to bear. He probably went to that out-of-the-way bar so no one he knew would see him."

"Did the sheriff find out what happened?"

"He was able to piece together most of the story. Apparently, my dad sat alone at the bar and had one drink after another. At some point, Colby's thug Mack came into the bar. My dad knew who Mack was. Dad started saying things about Colby and the bank. He was so drunk, his words slurred. Most people didn't hear him because of the music or didn't care. Mack came closer and said something. Dad swung at him, missed, and fell off the bar stool. Mack started to walk away and then turned and helped him stand up. That seemed odd to me. Anyway, Mack left. About half an hour later, Dad staggered out of the bar. That was the last time anyone saw him. For what it's worth, Mack had an alibi from his girlfriend at the time my dad left the bar. Mack also carried a gun, but the sheriff said it hadn't been fired recently. The sheriff thought my dad probably fell into the river and drowned. They dragged the river near the bar and for a mile downstream. The sheriff notified the authorities of towns downriver and the State Police. They never found his body."

"Do you think he drowned?" Fred asked.

"I don't know. About six months later, Mack saw me in town and came over. At first, he seemed serious. He told me he was sorry about my dad. Then he said, 'Drunks don't swim too well; they don't walk straight either.' He laughed and started to walk off. I grabbed his arm and asked what he meant. He laughed again and walked away. That, plus the fact that he was in the bar and had helped my dad get up from the floor, left me wondering. Did Mack help him back on the stool to avoid later suspicion? Did Mack ambush him and push him into the river? Or did my dad fall in by himself? Or, maybe, was he ashamed and hitched a ride somewhere far away from all the bad memories? I guess I'll never know, Fred."

"Do you think your dad would leave town without saying good-bye?"

Wes shook his head. "Under most circumstances, no. But he wasn't himself. He would've been ashamed of visiting that bar and drinking. Very ashamed."

Fred patted Wes's arm. "The truth has a way of coming out. I'm sure you'll find out one day. And like you said, maybe your dad is okay."

"I hope so."

"What you've told me is dreadful. I'm sorry for you and your family. Mack gives me the heebie-jeebies. They went after you too, Wes?"

"They did. You want to hear about it?"

"The more I know, the better. Let me catch Mabel for a coffee refill." Fred waved at Mabel and pointed to his coffee cup.

Mabel refilled their cups and picked up the empty plates. "More pie, fellows?"

Wes and Fred looked meekly at each other.

"One more piece for each of us," Fred said.

Mabel smiled. "I thought so. Back in a minute."

Wes stared out the window. The shadows were longer and the sun lower. Silhouettes of mountains encroached on the pale distant sky. The train labored as the grade steepened. The same warning signs he saw in the passenger car labeled the dining car windows. He couldn't help but wonder about them with nightfall only a few hours away. Strange. He felt an impending sense of war. *Rats.*

Chapter 7

Mabel returned with generous pie slices topped with whipped cream. "Enjoy it, boys."

"Thanks, Mabel. You're the best," Wes said.

"You know Mabel from before?" Fred asked.

"For a long time. She's my godmother. Used to live in our town. She's one of Colby's victims too. It upsets me; she's a sweet lady."

"What a cruel man. How'd he get like that?"

Wes shrugged. "Someone who knew him as a boy told me he was always picked on in school. He was also chosen last for teams in sports. That must be tough on a kid. Maybe he's trying to get even with the world. Who knows? Doesn't make it right, though. I guess I'm part of that world. He tried his best on me, too, both he and Bryce."

"What did they do?"

"It happened three years ago, a year after my father disappeared. I received a letter from the bank. They tried to call my mortgage for the hardware store under the force majeure clause. The letter claimed the bank had to increase reserves because of new banking legislation. They gave me ten business days to pay the loan."

Fred's eyes narrowed. "That sounds fishy."

"It sounded crazy to me too. I went to see Sam Knight, my lawyer. He looked at the loan documents and the letter. He had never seen force majeure invoked on such a flimsy basis, but he wasn't surprised that Colby would try it. He asked why I still did business with Colby's bank. I told him I took the loan before Colby worked at the bank. And I'd moved my other accounts to my friend's bank in the next town after Colby took over the bank. Sam laughed because he had done the same.

"He said I had a few options. One was to legally challenge the bank. I had a good case, but it would take time and be expensive. The second option was to pay off the loan. My loan balance was small, so that's what I decided to do.

"We called my banker friend. Sam read him the letter from Colby's bank. My friend said there was recent bank legislation, but it was minor, and Colby's letter was absurd. He also told us that Colby had twice tried to finagle his bank. He suggested the three of us meet at Colby's office and present him with a certified check for the loan balance. That way Colby couldn't claim he never received it. Sam loved the idea. He volunteered his secretary as an additional witness.

"The next morning, the four of us arrived at Colby's office minutes after it opened. Sam had prepared an affidavit, which the four of us signed when I presented Colby with the check. The affidavit had every conceivable detail, including a place for Colby's signature. Colby fumed. Sam told Colby his signature wasn't required, but his refusal to sign would be so noted. Colby signed but he wasn't happy about it. For once, he had a bad day of his own making. We went to brunch afterwards, and I heard stories about Colby worse than my family's nightmares. Sam warned me to watch out for him; he was spiteful. I asked what to watch for. He said anything that seemed peculiar."

"Hopefully that ended it?"

"Hardly. Things were quiet for a few months. Then one day, town workers showed up in a municipal truck at the corner of my hardware store. They painted over the white parking areas marked on the streets by my store. They put up No Parking signs. I asked what was going on. They told me they had a work order; that's all they knew. That left me four parking places in front of the store where it's set back from the street. There's an alley behind the store with a loading dock but no room for parking. Next to my store was a paved lot with a small warehouse that had been empty for years, but it was fenced off private property. Four parking spots weren't enough."

"I guess this is the kind of thing your lawyer warned about?"

Wes sipped his coffee. "Sure was. It qualified as *peculiar*. I drove to the town office. The person who signed the work order left town the day before on a two-week vacation. I talked with everyone in the office. They couldn't find copies of the work order or anyone who knew a thing about it. They said I'd have to wait until the fellow returned. If it was a mistake, they'd have the parking places back a few weeks after that. It put me in a bind. For all I knew, I might never get that parking back."

"Geez," Fred said. "Wasn't there anything you could do?"

"I called Sam and explained the situation. We met at the store. He looked at what the town workers had done, at the alley, and at the fenced property next to my store. Sam said he'd make some calls and get back to me later that day.

"He came back to the store after lunch. He hadn't learned any more than I did from the town office. He did find out who owned the property next to my store and had contacted them. They had tried to sell it years before with no luck. Since they no longer lived in the area, they were willing to sell it to me at a good price. Sam said the property would solve my parking problem no matter what the town did. He also suggested I use the warehouse to add lumber to my business."

"So that's how you added the lumberyard," Fred said.

"That's it. All I was thinking about was the parking. Sam thought of the lumber. He's a sharp guy. Anyway, we both wriggled through a broken part of the fence. The lot would provide plenty of parking. The warehouse was bigger than it looked. It needed minor repairs and painting but was structurally sound. Sam had checked the zoning and had done a quick title search. He didn't find any problems. He also had his secretary check for similar properties that had sold. We each wrote what we thought was a fair offer and compared our numbers. They were within a few hundred dollars.

"Sam suggested I first call my banker friend about financing and then call the owners with my offer. If they accepted, he wanted me to give him a deposit right away and sign the papers, so he could overnight them. He told me we might be able to close on the property by the end of the week, if everything was expedited."

"Is that what happened?" Fred asked.

"Sure did. My bank friend said a loan was no problem. The owners accepted my offer. By Friday morning, I was the new owner. My employees and I took down the front fence in less than an hour and put up a sign that said Hardware Store Parking. It took a month to fix the warehouse and to stock it with lumber. The lumber part of the business did great. After two years, the property had paid for itself."

"Incredible. Did you ever find out why the town ended the street parking?"

"Sam did. He could've been a detective. It turned out Bryce was in town a week before the parking spots were painted over. Someone saw him slip an envelope to a town employee at the truck stop diner up the highway. Sam raised a stink at the town office when that worker returned from vacation. The employee finally admitted he had taken money from Bryce, and that he had made up the work order. He denied accepting a bribe; he claimed it was a gift from Bryce. He knew better than to get Bryce in trouble. Of course, the town fired the employee. The town didn't press charges because they were already embarrassed and didn't want the publicity. By the time the town reinstated the street parking, several months had passed. At that point, it didn't really matter.

"Sam and I both knew that Bryce acted on behalf of Colby. The only reason Bryce ever came to town was to meet with Colby. Of course, *knowing* and *proving* are two different critters. Sam was sure right about watching out for peculiar things."

"I guess that ended the problems?"

"Not quite. Colby tried one more thing, and it ended up kind of humorous."

Fred's face lit up. "I have to hear this."

"Colby must have been desperate because he started sending Gus or Mack to my store almost every day. After one of them left, I'd find a glue container or a paint can with a hole in it and a mess to clean up. Sometimes it would be nails dumped from a box or a bag of cement cut open. It was childish but it was vandalism. They were very sneaky."

"What did you do?"

Wes grinned. "I hired a wrestler—a big one."

"A wrestler?"

"It was summer, so I hired an all-star wrestler from the high school team. This young man was enormous, in the unlimited weight class, taller than you, and incredibly strong. He worked mostly in the lumber area, but I told him to shadow Mack or Gus whenever they came to the store. He caught Gus tampering with merchandise. Gus threw a punch. The wrestler put him in a headlock and dragged him over to me. Gus's feet barely touched the floor. He looked scared. I told Gus that if he or Mack ever came to my store again or caused me problems, my big friend would practice wrestling holds on them. Gus nodded that he understood. I told him he could go after he paid for the damages he and Mack had caused. He paid, said he was sorry, and that it wouldn't happen again. It didn't. That wrestler worked for me full time after he graduated. I'm sure Colby thinks he's my bodyguard. He's not. He's just a fine young man, who happens to be huge."

"Finally some justice," Fred said.

"At least a little. Colby doesn't like me, my lawyer, or my banker friend because he couldn't beat us. What makes me sad is all the people Colby and his bunch have hurt over the years, like my parents and Mabel. Where's their justice?"

"What happened with Mabel?"

"Colby cheated her when she lived in our town," Wes said.

"Do you think she would share her story?"

"We can ask. If it might help someone else, she probably would."

"I'll ask her," Fred said.

"Mr. Ables. Mr. Ables." The elderly steward stopped at the booth, hands on knees, catching his breath.

"Good God, man. Are you all right?" Fred asked.

"Fight—there's going to be a fight."

"Who? Where?"

"Passenger car. The one with those four dandies."

Fred stood, a grimace on his face. "That's Colby and the others."

"I'll go with you," Wes said.

"You better stay here, Wes. You might give them more reason to fight. I'll send for you if I need help."

CHAPTER 8

First the bourbon, next the cigar, then the poker game. Colby cheated, as always. He thought he was adept and no one was aware. He was wrong. Bryce knew and so did Mack and Gus. It didn't matter. He was the boss. Colby was smart enough never to win more than four hands in a row. More would raise suspicions. Worse, if caught, no one would play with him. If any of the others won two in a row, questions arose. Three, well, that just wouldn't happen.

Mack had been called. He held three jacks. That beat Colby's two pair and Bryce's one pair. A smug grin traversed Mack's face.

Gus laid down his cards one by one: three of hearts, five of clubs, seven of hearts, and six of spades.

"You ain't got nothing," Mack said.

"Here's the last." Gus set a four of diamonds on the table and arranged the cards in sequence. "A straight beats you all."

Mack's grin evaporated. "This stinks. That's the last two hands you won. I should've won."

Gus crossed his arms and raised his voice. "I had the better cards."

"And how did that happen?" Mack's jaw jutted.

"Go ahead and say it, Mack," Bryce said. "Say what we're all thinking."

Colby saw Gus's hands tighten. Colby liked fights but this wasn't the time. "Gus was lucky. Nothing wrong with that. Whose deal?"

FRED SCURRIED FROM the dining car to the passenger car and peered between the glass etchings of the aisle door. Colby and his comrades sat immersed in a poker game. They looked as though they could've been playing tiddlywinks. No fight. No raised voices. The two soldiers at the back of the car stared out the window. I should've questioned the steward more, Fred thought. A false alarm. Might as well head back.

But his feet wouldn't move. Beads of worry became sweat on his brow. The steward *must* have seen or heard something, Fred thought. Enough to run to tell me. *Better stay.* Fred stared through the glass and slid the door back several inches so he could listen.

MACK RAMPED UP the bidding and was called. Three queens and two eights, a full house. Disgusted, Colby threw a flush on the table. A dejected Bryce had three nines. Mack began to gloat but didn't like what he saw in Gus's face. He had a feeling he wouldn't like Gus's cards either.

The cards dropped from Gus's hand onto the table. A full house: three kings over two tens. His third winning hand in a row. Gus reached for the pot; his fingers curved around the pile of chips.

Mack's eyes bulged. He grabbed Gus's forearm. "Cheater!"

Gus stared into Mack's eyes. "I don't cheat."

Bryce scowled. "You gonna let him get away with it, Mack?"

Gus pulled away from Mack's grasp. "I don't cheat; I don't cheat."

Colby snorted. "Sure you don't. You wouldn't be working for me if you weren't a cheat."

Gus drew in a deep breath and slowly exhaled. "I don't cheat. I don't."

Mack stood, his eyes fixed on Gus. Speckles of light reflected from the brass knuckles woven among the fingers of his right fist. The words came like spittle. "You lousy cheater."

Gus slid from the booth and stepped back.

Mack knew he wasn't big, but he had advantages. Weapons. He'd forget his wallet but never his weapons. And his biggest was always there: he was as mean as a mad mongrel.

"Teach him a lesson, Mack," Bryce said as he glanced at Colby, who nodded approval.

Colby rubbed his hands together and ran his tongue over his lips.

FRED FROZE, HIS hand poised to fling the door open, but fragments of doubt plagued his thoughts. My duty to stop this. Or is it? If someone gets hurt, then I go? Maybe better if Colby loses some manpower? Should've brought Wes. Nick and Daniel, maybe they'll help? Fred rubbed the tightening muscles in his neck. *Darn these heebie-jeebies.*

MACK LUNGED WITH a wild roundhouse that tagged Gus's chin.

Gus retreated and rubbed his jaw. He glanced at his fingers. No blood, he thought. The brass knuckles had only grazed him. *Need to be more careful. Mack's unpredictable.*

A jab from Mack swiped Gus's cheek. Mack followed with a kick that hammered Gus's groin. Gus dropped to one knee gasping. Another kick targeted his head. Gus parried and struggled to his feet. Mack charged and laid a brass knuckles uppercut into Gus's solar plexus. He doubled over as air whooshed from his mouth.

"Come on, Mack. Finish him," Bryce yelled.

A glint from the knuckles caught Gus's eye. He slipped his head as a punch whizzed by his ear. *Enough. I don't want to hurt Mack, but I gotta stop this.*

Gus feinted to keep Mack off him and regained his stance. A combination of a jab, hook, and an uppercut staggered Mack. His eyes became glazed donuts. Mack threw a haymaker. Gus caught the fist in his open hand and closed his fingers like a vise. The pressure ground the brass knuckles into Mack's fingers. Gus twisted counterclockwise locking Mack's elbow and shoulder. Mack couldn't move. Gus saw Mack's free hand sneak toward his pocket and increased the pressure on the hand he held. He torqued the arm until Mack flinched.

"Move your hand away from that pocket. I don't want to see a gun or blade," Gus told Mack.

Mack grimaced. His hand edged away from his pocket. "Okay, okay. I give. Let go."

"You say it first."

"Uncle. Now let go."

"You know what I'm talking about." Gus ratcheted the pressure on Mack's arm.

"Okay, okay. You're not a cheat," Mack muttered.

"Didn't hear you."

"You're not a cheat. You don't cheat."

Gus glanced at Colby and Bryce. "Everyone hear that? You'd better remember it. You ever call me a cheat again, Mack, and you'll need a new arm. Pick a fight with me again, and it'll be your last." Gus released Mack's arm.

Clink. The brass knuckles fell to the table. They left red notches pressed into Mack's fingers. He massaged his hand and arm.

Gus kept an eye on Mack and glanced at Bryce and Colby. Bryce seemed disgusted as he handed a wad of bills to Colby.

"Nice fight, Gus," Colby said. "Knew you'd win." Colby slipped the chunk of cash into his coat pocket.

Gus stared at the two. *They bet on this? Colby made money off me?*

"Have a seat, boys," Colby said. "My deal."

THE BRUTALITY OF the fight put a shiver in Fred's spine. Mack and Gus were time bombs with hair-trigger fuses. If they could do this to each other, no one on the train was safe. Mack was a vicious street fighter, and Gus could drop an ox with his power. Who could stop them? Maybe I should've done something? And maybe I'd be out cold on the floor right now.

It had been quite a fight. He thought Mack would win until he realized Gus had held back. Why did he do that? Gus's quick combination took but seconds. And what's the big deal with cheating? They're not exactly a quartet of meditating monks. Maybe Wes would know.

Fred peered through the glass. The poker game began anew. No squabbling. Quiet as tiddlywinks. Fred inched the aisle door closed and left for the dining car.

CHAPTER 9

Fred returned to the dining car table with a slice of cherry pie, a coffee mug, and a fresh pot of coffee. "Don't touch that pie, Wes," he said. "It's for Mabel. Just spoke with her." He refilled their cups and filled the mug for Mabel. "She'll be here in a few minutes." Fred sauntered to the counter with the pot, refilling passengers' cups along the way, and then rejoined Wes.

Wes stared as Fred slid into the booth. "You ought to put an ice pack on that," Wes said.

"On what?" Fred shrugged.

"That shiner and the mouse under it. You really took a beating."

"Huh." Fred felt his face.

Wes laughed. "I'm joking. Was there a fight or not? I don't see a scratch on you."

"I watched from behind the door. Mack and Gus. One heck of a fight." Fred recounted the events and gave a blow-by-blow description.

"You were smart not to get involved," Wes said. "Those two are dangerous."

"Yeah. Like you've been saying. The four of them worry me."

"Me too," Wes said.

"Two things I don't understand." Fred stroked his chin. "Why did Gus hold back? He could've taken Mack out right from the start."

Wes shook his head. "Don't know. Sounds like he took some shots too. Makes no sense."

"And why would Gus get so riled about being called a cheat? From what you've said, they're all scoundrels. With theft, fraud, and beating on people, what's the big deal about cheating?"

"Darned if I know," Wes said. "Maybe he didn't cheat. If someone called me a cheat and I didn't, I'd be mad about it. Maybe Gus has lines."

"What do you mean?" Fred asked.

"Lines. You know—lines he won't cross. Maybe he doesn't cheat. And maybe there's other stuff he won't do. More lines. Everyone has lines."

"Maybe that's it." Fred glanced up. "Here comes Mabel."

FRED AND WES stood when Mabel approached the table. She sat next to Wes and took a sip of coffee.

"I've smelled that coffee all afternoon; it tastes even better. Nice to sit for a change."

She looked at Wes. "Fred told me Lamar Colby is on the train. That scares me with the troubles he's caused and what he did to me."

"I don't like it either," Wes said. "His henchmen and Senator Bryce are with him too."

Fred patted her arm. "Don't worry, Mabel. We'll watch them. They're two cars back. It's unlikely they'll come to the dining car. They'll expect the staff to bring things to them. Jay and the other stewards will do that. We'd rather keep them where they are."

"That's a relief," Mabel said. "I don't want to be anywhere near them."

"Wes told me a lot about them," Fred said. "I don't like hearing bad stories, but I need to look out for the passengers. The more I know, the better. Wes mentioned you had trouble with Colby. Can you share it? That is, if you feel up to it."

"It brings back awful memories," Mabel said. "But I'll tell you. I don't want anyone else hurt."

Mabel took a deep breath. "It happened a few years after my husband died. I lived off my husband's pension and our savings, and kept our home because of the memories. My husband never made a lot of money in his line of work. But he was very thrifty. Over forty years, our savings had grown. The pension and savings would have been enough for the rest of my life.

"The savings were in Mr. Colby's bank. We started the account thirty years before he came to town, so we never thought about moving it. It was the only bank in town. After Colby foreclosed on Wes's parents' home, Wes stopped by one night and spoke with us. We'd known Wes since he was a baby. He told us what happened. He planned to move his accounts to a friend's bank. He didn't trust Mr. Colby one bit. We told Wes we had paid off our mortgage. We thought a savings account had to be safe. As it turns out, we should've listened to Wes."

"Don't blame yourself, Mabel," Wes said. "It should've been perfectly safe."

"Well, one day I went to the bank with my passbook to withdraw some savings. The teller pulled my account record and kept looking back and forth between it and my passbook. He said they didn't match. The bank record had a balance of less than half of what my passbook showed. He was sure the bank record was wrong. He wanted to show the passbook to Mr. Colby. After a few minutes, he returned and said Mr. Colby was certain there was an error in the bank record. Mr. Colby would need the passbook for a few days to find the mistake. It seemed reasonable, so I left the passbook with the bank. I was sure the problem would be resolved. Leaving that passbook with Mr. Colby was a big mistake."

"That was your only bank record?" Fred asked.

Mabel looked at Fred with a tear in her eye. "Yes. I was so stupid."

"A lot of people would have done that, Mabel," Fred said. "You don't expect a bank to be crooked. Don't be hard on yourself. Colby is the villain here."

Mabel dabbed the tear with her napkin and took a small bite of pie. She continued, "When I returned to the bank, the teller gave me the passbook without saying a word. I knew something was wrong. I opened it and looked at the balance. It was what the bank records had shown two days before. I looked through the passbook and never saw a balance like I'd had before. I checked the name and address. It looked just like the other passbook, except it wasn't as worn, and, of course, all the balances were wrong. I knew it wasn't my original passbook. The teller knew it too. I was horribly upset and asked to see Mr. Colby.

"Mr. Colby was polite at first and told me they had checked the records. He said everything was okay, including my savings passbook. I told him it wasn't my passbook. He took it, pretended to look carefully, and said it was. I told him my account had more than twice what the passbook showed. He said that couldn't be true because the passbook and the bank record balances matched. He became angry when I said someone must have switched the passbook and changed my account record. He said the bank would take me to court if I spread stories I couldn't prove."

"How awful," Fred said. "Cheated, lied to, and threatened."

"It was horrible," Mabel said. "I had this terrible feeling I'd probably never see that money again. It was over half of the life savings my husband had been so careful about. I started to cry and begged Mr. Colby to straighten everything out. He said there was nothing to be done and left the bank for lunch."

"I'm so sorry," Fred said. "What did you do?"

"I went to see Wes at his store. He had warned us about Mr. Colby, so I thought he might be able to help. I told him what happened. Wes was upset too."

"Upset," Wes exclaimed. "I was angrier than you know what."

"I remember," Mabel said. "Wes thought Mr. Colby had targeted my account after my husband died. He thought Colby kept double books on the bank and my account record. Once he had my passbook, Wes thinks he forged one with numbers that matched the double account record and the double bank book. Then Mr. Colby probably destroyed the original records and the original passbook. Wes didn't think there was much chance of recovering my money because any proof of what I had was gone. Wes wasn't sure though. He called his lawyer, who asked us to come over right away. Wasn't his name Sam?"

"Sam Knight. You have a good memory, Mabel," Wes said.

"He was nice, smart, and honest," Mabel said. "You remember people like that."

"That's Sam," Wes said. "You finish your pie, Mabel. I'll tell Fred this part since I was there. You can fill in anything I miss."

Mabel glanced at her slice of pie. "That's fine with me."

Wes sipped his coffee and then leaned forward. "Sam wanted to know every detail. He spent a few minutes reviewing an older case file on his desk. Sam asked what I thought. I repeated what I'd told

Mabel at the store. Sam looked frustrated. He thought what I'd said was spot-on and agreed there was no way to prove it. He also thought the odds of retrieving the money were slim. Sam pointed to the older case file. Three years before, the same thing happened to another widow at Colby's bank. Sam said if you put Mabel's name in that file, you wouldn't need to change anything except the dates and the dollar amounts. He had talked with the teller on that case and had obtained a sworn affidavit but knew it wouldn't help because the phony records would appear to be legitimate.

"Sam wrote to the state's Bank Regulatory Board about the previous case and requested a review by a bank examiner. They replied that the lack of evidence didn't warrant it. Sam wrote and called them several more times. He felt the examiner had stonewalled him. Political pressure and bribery may have played a roll."

"That could be Bryce?" Fred asked.

"That's what Sam thought," Wes said. "Sam called a friend from law school who practices near the state capital. His friend told him corruption was so widespread that the case was a lost cause.

"Sam told Mabel to withdraw her money from Colby's bank without delay. He'd also obtain an affidavit from the bank teller while the teller's memory was fresh and before he either quit or was fired. He'd also write Colby requesting information related to Mabel's situation. Lastly, he would file a formal complaint with the state's Bank Regulatory Board about Mabel's case and request a review by a bank examiner. He didn't expect anything positive from it, but at least, it would become part of the complaint file on Colby's bank. Perhaps Colby would be snared one day. Sam told Mabel there wasn't much else to do. He'd hope for some kind of break, but it was a long shot."

"Did I forget anything, Mabel?" Wes asked.

"The accountant," she said.

"That's right," Wes said. "Sam asked Mabel about her finances. Mabel said she still received her husband's pension, but she had to dip into her savings now and then to make ends meet. She knew she had enough in savings before the theft, but she wasn't sure if that was true after the theft. Sam referred her to a good accountant."

"Were you okay, Mabel?" Fred asked.

"The accountant said I had been fine before, but now he thought I'd probably outlive my savings because of the loss. If I sold the house and rented an apartment, I'd be better off, financially, that is. He said I didn't need to do anything right away, but I probably should within a year or two."

"What did you do?" Fred asked.

"A year later, I sold the house and moved in with my daughter and her family in another town. I had to sell most of the belongings we had accumulated over the years. It was hard to do." Mabel wiped a tear from her eye.

"There was one curious thing, though. A few months after Mr. Colby stole my savings, I'd find an envelope stuffed with money stuck in my back screen door. It happened almost every month. When I moved in with my daughter, it came in the mail. There was no return address. I never found out who was doing it. At first, I thought it might be Mr. Colby. Perhaps he felt guilty. The more I thought about it, the less likely it seemed because he's such a coldhearted man. It's still a mystery."

Fred scratched his cheek. "That's odd. Wherever it came from, it doesn't make up for what Colby did. I'm sorry, Mabel. Someone who cheats widows is someone capable of almost anything. Thank you for telling me what happened. I will do my best to keep other passengers away from them."

"I don't want anyone else hurt," Mabel said.

"You look tired," Wes said. "Why don't you take a nap? A little rest would do you good."

"I think I will," she said.

Wes kissed Mabel on the forehead. Fred helped her up. She headed toward the sleeping car.

FRED REFILLED THEIR coffees. He stared at his cup and rubbed his forehead. "Wes, this is a bad situation. I can keep that passenger car with Colby empty. But I need to keep an eye on them too. They'd become suspicious if I kept a steward in the car. I hate to ask, but—"

"No problem," Wes said. "I'll watch them. I know more about them than anyone on the train. I'll see if I can move closer, in case they say anything worrisome."

"You think they have guns?" Fred asked.

"I know Mack and Gus carried pieces around town. We should probably assume they do. As for Colby and Bryce, I doubt it."

"I should've checked when they came on board."

"You had no reason to. Asking now would create trouble," Wes said.

"What about Nick and Daniel?"

"I'll brief them and ask if they want to stay in that passenger car. My hunch is they will. That works a little to our advantage. Their uniforms make Colby and the others nervous. Maybe they'll think twice before doing something."

Fred sighed. "I hope we don't have problems."

"It's unlikely. Colby usually plans in advance, plus his connections aren't at his fingertips. We'll probably be okay; just need to be vigilant."

"Colby has that bad temper. He gives me the heebie-jeebies," Fred said.

"Where's Timmy?" Wes asked. "I worry about him. It'd be better if he stays out of that car. I still have his knapsack."

"He and Blackie have traipsed all over. He finally ran out of gas. Right now, they're with the Holyfields. I'll come for the knapsack. Don't worry about Timmy. He'll be fine."

Wes nodded. His brow furrowed. Despite Fred's reassurance, nuts and bolts of worry tumbled in his stomach. *Rats.*

The two stared through the glass in silence. The train had reached the foothills of the mountains. Snowcaps on the highest peaks glittered. The sun brushed the horizon, painting distant clouds in pastels of lavender, pink, and orange. It would soon be dark.

CHAPTER 10

"Gentlemen." A deep resonant voice interrupted their reverie. Preoccupied with the sunset, Wes and Fred had not heard the dining car door open.

"Mr. Fischer, please join us," Fred said. "Let me introduce one of our passengers, Mr. Wes Quinton." Wes and Fred stood and shook hands with Fischer.

"Grant Fischer," said the train's owner when he shook Wes's hand with a sturdy grip. "I've heard good things about you. I hope your trip has been pleasant thus far." The three men sat.

Solidly built, Fischer's features included radiant dark eyes, silvery-gray hair, and an impeccably groomed beard of the same shade. His seasoned face bore a timeless quality and an innate dignity, which emanated a gregarious nature and the distinct impression of wisdom. He was dressed in white with a well-cut suit and tie. The tie color matched his hair.

"Your train is remarkable, Mr. Fischer," Wes said. "The interior wood design and craftsmanship are beautiful. I've never seen anything like it."

Fischer replied, "You would appreciate it more than most because of your business. Have you met the Holyfields and Jay?"

"I briefly met the Holyfields," Wes said. "Jay fixed my sore feet with his secret soak."

"Jay does many things well," Fischer said. "Did he tell you he and Mr. Holyfield designed the train's interior? They did some of the carpentry, too, although they mostly supervised."

"Jay didn't mention that," Wes said. "I've also never ridden a train where dogs are allowed. I like that. I met Timmy and his dog earlier. The two are inseparable."

"I must confess a soft spot for animals as well," Fischer said. "People become attached to their pets. For a child, it makes a trip less intimidating. We don't mind the bit of extra work it entails. We enjoy the little travelers too. Fred has become famous for his pocketfuls of dog biscuits. And in different sizes, may I note."

"Just between you and me, Mr. Fischer, Fred may be losing it. Earlier, he offered me a dog biscuit." Wes's eyes darted toward Fred.

Fischer erupted in laughter. Fred feigned indignation, then chuckled. A few *woofs* from Wes and the three exploded hysterically like school-aged boys.

"I can't remember when I last laughed like that," Fischer said. "Laughter is good for the soul."

"I wish we could laugh the entire trip," Fred said. "Unfortunately, we have a few passengers who are problematic."

"Would that be Mr. Colby, his two associates, and Senator Bryce?" Fischer asked.

"Yes, sir," Fred said. "You've heard already?"

"Their reputations precede them," Fischer said. "Jay informed me of their earlier antics. I also heard about their recent little fracas."

"How'd you know about the fight?" Fred asked. "I was the only one who—my apologies. Of course, you would know."

"What do you suggest we do, Fred?" Fischer asked.

"They're in the rear passenger car," Fred said. "I'd like to keep them there. It'd be best to keep other passengers away from them. Wes knows them well. He has agreed to be our eyes and ears in case trouble is brewing."

"Thank you, Wes, but please be careful," Fischer said. "Is anyone else in that car?"

"There are two young soldiers," Fred said. "Wes will talk to them. He's pretty sure they'll choose to stay in that car."

"That must be Nick and Daniel," Fischer said. "I met them earlier. Fine young men."

"The best," Fred said.

Fischer tugged on his beard. "Take menus to Mr. Colby and his group next time you're back that way. Better to feed them where they are."

"Good idea," Fred said. "Wes is returning shortly. I'll follow later to retrieve Timmy's knapsack. I'll take them menus then. I'll ask Jay to send a steward through the car periodically in case they want to order anything."

"Splendid," Fischer said. "I'll visit Mr. Colby and his party this evening. Anything else I should know? Any suggestions, Fred? Wes?"

Fred's brow furrowed. "We don't know if they have guns. Wes thinks Mack and Gus probably do."

Fischer grimaced. "Just be extra careful. I need to go; have some things to take care of. Good to meet you, Wes. Keep me informed, Fred."

"Yes, sir. I will."

As the multicolored sunset faded to shades of gray, a three-quarter moon reflected pale light onto the mountains through which the train wound. Wes flinched when sudden darkness and a *whoosh* surrounded the train. They had entered a tunnel. There would be more.

WES MAY AS well have been invisible when he walked through the passenger car. The four miscreants engaged in a game of serious poker. Haphazard stacks of money laid about the table. A half-empty bottle of bourbon stood in the center. Colby and Bryce puffed on cigars; a cigarette dangled from the corner of Mack's mouth.

Nick and Daniel nodded as Wes approached. He grabbed Timmy's knapsack and his satchel from his seat and continued walking toward the soldiers.

"Don't stand," Wes said. He took a seat beside them.

"What's up?" Nick asked.

Wes leaned toward them. "Boys, there's a potential problem. You'll need to decide whether to stay in this car or leave. Your choice, of course. Let me fill you in so you can decide."

Wes spoke for ten minutes with an occasional interruption for a question. Nick and Daniel alternated between widened eyes and clenched fists.

"So that's the story," Wes said. "I hope there won't be trouble, but there could be. You saw the fight between Mack and Gus first hand."

"Doesn't worry us," Daniel said. "If you care to take a walk, we'll make sure they won't cause trouble."

"I know you could," Wes said, "but for now, it's just recon. They haven't done anything, yet, except for being obnoxious and fighting each other. Do you want to stay or go? Your call."

"We're in, for sure," Nick said. Daniel nodded in agreement.

"Good," Wes said. "Thought you would be. Keep an eye on them but don't be obvious. They're suspicious by nature. Don't stand when Fred or anyone else approaches; it draws attention to you. Fred will be back soon. I'll move up a seat or two, so I can pick up any chatter. Keep an eye on me, too, so I can signal you if needed. We'll alternate chow times, so we always have eyes on them. Any questions?"

"No, Sarge." Nick grinned. "Sorry, I couldn't help it."

Wes smiled. "I would have been proud to have both of you under me when I served. Now, use your heads and be careful. Fred should be here soon."

They waited in silence. Moonlight replaced darkness, followed by a long stretch of pitch black. Another tunnel we've passed through, Wes thought. He gazed out the window. The reflection of the two soldiers reminded him of his own youth. Strange how life seems to circle around over time. He was glad Nick and Daniel had stayed, despite the nagging premonitions of an old soldier. Maybe it was just an overreaction, but the wisdom and experience of his intuition gnawed at him. *Something's about to happen. I can just feel it. Rats.*

AT COLBY'S TABLE, the poker game continued amid the pungent odor and haze of cigar smoke. Fred handed menus to Gus, who was the only one to notice him.

Fred headed back to Wes, Nick, and Daniel and sat. "I brought extra menus," he said. "We have folding tables if you want to eat here. You fellows in with Wes?"

"Wouldn't miss it," Nick said.

"Please be careful. All of you," Fred said. "And thank you."

"Glad to do it," Wes said. He handed Fred Timmy's knapsack. "I'll move forward when you stand, Fred. They won't notice with their game and the smoke."

Wes grabbed his satchel and followed Fred into the aisle. He slid into the next seat. The convention catalog would provide good cover, and he could jot notes if needed. The time to hurry up and wait had officially arrived.

THE SMOKE BEGAN to bother Colby's eyes. "Open the window, Gus," Colby said. He slid over to give Gus access.

"We're not supposed to at night," Gus said. "The conductor—"

"I don't care what he said. Open it," Colby ordered.

Gus unlocked the latches and tugged at the window's lower section.

Fred saw Gus's silhouette through the cloud of smoke and yelled, "Don't open the—"

CHAPTER 11

Too late! Gus opened the window.

Whoosh! The air speeding by pulled drifts of smoke from the car. The wind chill from the moving train aggravated the frosty mountain air. Colby wrapped a black scarf around his neck.

The tumultuous air roared as the train entered a tunnel creating a vacuum at the open window.

Rats. Wes sprung to the aisle and signaled Nick and Daniel. The three men sped toward the erupting turmoil.

Fred leaned over the table trying to draw Colby's attention.

Then it happened.

The blowing ends of Colby's scarf jerked through the open window, and the scarf tightened around his neck. The ferocious vortex of screaming air tugged on the scarf ends and pulled Colby toward the window. The back of his head slammed into the glass and against the opening, despite his efforts to oppose it.

Mack and Gus, unaware of Colby's plight, pushed Fred away. Senator Bryce, oblivious as well, snarled at Fred's intrusion. Fred pointed to Colby who clutched at the scarf as his face reddened. The howling turbulence made conversation hopeless. Whirlwinds scattered cards and money wildly about.

Fred didn't hear Wes and the soldiers as they drew near.

Bryce and Mack gawked at Colby.

Wes stepped in and leaned toward Bryce and Mack so they could hear him over the blast of air. "Out of the way! Now!" They could barely hear but saw his somber face and slid from the seat.

Nudging Gus's shoulder, Wes put his mouth close to the man's ear and said, "Hold Colby's arm. Don't let go!"

Gus, his face contorted by confusion, gripped Colby's arm.

Wes tapped Fred's arm. He pointed and yelled, "Move the table!"

Fred slid the glasses, the bottle, and the ice bucket to the middle. With a man at each corner of the table, it was quickly out of the way. They returned their attention to Colby.

Wes cupped his hands over Daniel's ear. "Keep Bryce and Mack out of our hair."

Daniel gave a thumbs-up and marched over to the pair, who seemed satisfied to stay back on their own accord.

Nick saw Wes gesture and turned his ear toward him.

"Hold Colby's other arm," Wes said. "Don't let go or we'll lose him."

Nick nodded, slid next to Colby, and gripped his upper arm.

Fred leaned toward Wes and shouted, "Loosen the scarf. I'll keep his hands out of the way." Fred yelled in Colby's direction as he secured his hands, but it was impossible to tell if Colby understood. Colby's eyes bulged with fear as he struggled to breathe.

Wes reached behind Colby's neck and felt the tangled mess of the scarf ends. The frigid air streaming by numbed Wes's fingers. He loosened the matted jumble of scarf knot in an attempt to relieve the pressure on Colby's throat.

A blotch of black smoke and soot resembling dark ghostly fingers wafted eerily in front of the scarf before drifting away. The scarf tightened. Wes shook his head. *What was that?* He glanced at Fred, who gestured toward the window. Dark fleeting wisps at the edge of the window seemed to push it farther open, almost by stealth. Wes shook his head and refocused his eyes. The vague specter had disappeared, but there was no doubt the window had opened a few inches more.

Gusts of icy air roared from the tunnel through the open window deafening the passengers. More of Colby's head exited the train through the window, arching his neck, despite the firm grip on him by Gus and Nick. The scarf constricted his airway. Spittle drooled down Colby's jaw. His eyes protruded, terror evident. Slowly, the scarf choked him.

Wes shouted to Fred, "This isn't working. We have to pull his head completely inside the car. Put your arm around his neck and grab my arm on the other side. Your hand will go numb out there. Need to do this quick."

Fred nodded.

Wes put his arm in place, and Fred reached around with his. They pulled inward. Colby's head didn't budge. They looked at each other in disbelief. A nod signaled another try. They strained again. No movement. None.

Wes glimpsed a fleeting strand of dark vapor snaking around their arms and over Colby's scarf. That has to be engine smoke, Wes thought. Must be. But it's almost like something's fighting us. *That can't be; it's not possible.*

Colby's face turned a ghastly purplish hue. He gasped for breath as the scarf closed his airway.

Wes's fingers felt dead in the freezing air. They had one last try. This is no way for any man to die, Wes thought. *Not even Colby.*

Fred and Wes signaled each other with another nod. Wes raised a clenched fist to indicate maximal effort. Colby had to be freed *now*. They leaned into it with all the force they could muster. Their arms throbbed. Their muscles burned. Their fingers froze like icicles.

Wes neared exhaustion. He looked at Colby. Please, don't die, he thought.

Flakes of white ash blew onto Colby's scarf and then disappeared as white wisps out the window. Ashes to ashes, dust to dust, Wes thought.

Fred and Wes groaned; they expended the last of their strength. Their frozen fingers, unable to grasp any longer, lost their grip. Both men toppled to the floor, acutely aware of their failure to save Colby.

But their last effort *had* freed Colby and the scarf from the suction of the outside air. Hands on throat, Colby wobbled in his seat before sprawling forward onto Fred and Wes. Nick disentangled and removed the scarf from Colby's neck. Gus forcefully closed and locked the window, keeping as much distance from it as he could.

The howling ceased. The chill dissipated as quickly as it had arrived. Gus and Nick lifted Colby to the seat. His gasping had ebbed into deep breaths. Fred and Wes glanced at each other, the closed window, and Colby.

Colby sat stunned, his face blanched a ghastly white from the exposure and devoid of expression. Wes had seen it before in war:

the vacant blank look of men who had narrowly escaped death and knew it.

Wes turned to Daniel. "Bring him a stiff drink, no ice."

Daniel handed a glass containing two fingers of bourbon to Gus. Colby's hands shook so badly that Gus had to direct the glass to his lips.

"Just a small sip at first, Mr. Colby," Wes said.

Gus tilted the glass as Colby took a small swallow. The banker coughed as the warmth of the liquor spread within him.

Wes massaged his own icy hand trying to restore the circulation and feeling in it. He saw Fred shake his hand and clench his fingers with the same goal.

Colby took another sip of bourbon, his hands steadier. Color returned to his face as crimson blotches overcame the hideous pale features. He stared at the glass, his mental faculties impaired by the horrific ordeal.

MOONLIGHT FLOODED THE mountainous landscape as the car emerged from the tunnel. Fred surveyed the others. "Everyone else all right?"

All nodded except for Senator Bryce. "What was that?"

Fred grappled for an answer. It was an incident, just like the stories from the old-timers. He hadn't expected to experience an occurrence firsthand. Now that he had, he knew nothing more except that is was terrifying. Terrifying and inexplicable. "That's why you don't open the windows at night. Don't do it again!" Fred used his most commanding voice. He hoped Bryce would not question further.

Colby's face was almost back to normal and the glass of bourbon near empty.

Fred motioned to Mack and Daniel. "Why don't you pick up the cards and money, so we can move the table back."

Mack sneered at Daniel. "You get the cards. I'll pick up the money. Wouldn't want any of it to disappear."

With the table returned to its original position, Colby's cronies slipped into their seats. All of them sat farther from the windows than before.

Fred looked at Colby. "Are you okay, Mr. Colby? I'm sorry about what occurred. It's never happened while I've been conductor. The window is closed. There's no danger. Can I bring you anything?"

Colby erupted. What he said was not what Fred expected from someone they had saved from death moments earlier. "What you can do is get me the owner of this train. Mr. Flimflam. Mr. Flapjack. Whatever his name is."

"It's Mr. Fischer," Fred said.

"Whatever. And I want to see him now. What kind of a train is this? Don't you care about your passengers' safety? You have danger outside the windows, and nobody says anything?"

Fred turned pale. "I clearly remember asking you to not open—"

Colby's face reddened. His fist pounded the table. "A stinking liar for a conductor, a clumsy oaf steward, and you and Quinton trying to pull my head off and throwing me on the floor."

"You tell him, Lamar," Bryce piped.

Colby continued, "I'm going to have you fired. I'll have that clumsy steward fired. I'll ruin Fischer. You'll pay for what you've done. You'll regret the day you met me. I'll destroy you. I'll destroy Fischer. I'll destroy this railroad company. You bring me Fischer. Now! And get out of my sight."

"Yes, sir," Fred said. Anything more would have continued the harangue and probably made it worse.

Fred nodded at Wes, Nick, and Daniel, who headed toward the back of the car. He wanted to thank them, but it would have to wait. Fred went the other way, preoccupied with the incident and Colby's reaction. Mr. Fischer wouldn't be pleased. Colby would be more dangerous than ever.

WES STARED BLANKLY at the upside-down convention catalog. How could something like that happen? he wondered. And the strange smoke and ashes. That was odd. No, more than that. It was creepy. My imagination? But Fred saw it too. Hope I'm not going crazy. He righted the catalog. Maybe I already am.

The sound of shuffling cards brought his attention back to the foursome. Colby and Bryce leaned toward each other. Wes shut his eyes and strained to hear their conversation. He discerned but a half-dozen words. He heard *shut* and *out of b—* from Colby. Bryce said *board* and *knots*. Colby added *bank* and *pennies*. He heard no more. The poker game resumed.

Wes wrote the words on the back of the catalog. He tried to conjure a discussion containing the list but soon gave up. They were up to something. Something no good, for sure. His stomach growled. Better eat, he thought. This could be a long night. Wes scanned the menu and wrote on a blank three-by-five card: 2 BLTs on toast, chips, pie, coffee.

He motioned to Nick and Daniel. The soldiers joined him. "Thanks for your help, guys. Without it, Colby would've been in bigger trouble."

"Glad to help," Nick said. "That was one of the strangest things I've ever seen."

"I can't make sense of it either," Wes said. "Anyway, while it's quiet, why don't you two go eat. Take this card if you would. Takeout for me."

Nick looked at the card. "No problem."

"And if you see Timmy, tell him to stay away from this car. It's not safe," Wes said.

Nick and Daniel strolled up the aisle toward the chow car.

Wes rubbed the tight muscles of his neck. He thought of his own brother and Timmy. Have to keep Timmy safe. At least it's not war. Starting to feel like it though. How did I get into this? Started with a bad dream. Now it's becoming a nightmare. *Rats*.

CHAPTER 12

Fred entered the dining car; his feet dragged and his shoulders slumped. An incident occurred on his watch. It nearly killed Colby. Maybe he should resign as conductor. He had to tell Mr. Fischer. Hopefully, Colby would behave in a civilized manner when Mr. Fischer went back to see him. If he resigned, perhaps that would satisfy Colby.

Fred cherished his time on the train: the familiar sounds, the constant motion, and the ever-changing landscape. Mostly, he loved the people he worked with and the many passengers they served. There were the few who were difficult, like Colby and his group, but that only contrasted with many wonderful passengers, like Wes, Timmy, and hundreds of others he remembered. Shaking his head, he navigated the car. He would miss it all. He doubted he was fit to be the conductor anymore. Trudging along the aisle, eyes on the floor, he passed Fischer, who sat talking to diners.

"Fred. Fred," Fischer said.

"I'm sorry, Mr. Fischer. Didn't see you. I need to speak with you. It's important."

"Of course, Fred. Grab an empty booth. I'll be with you in a minute."

Fred lifted a mug of coffee from the counter. He picked a booth away from the passengers. Mind blank, he added sugar and stirred mechanically. Stars near the horizon disappeared and reappeared as the mountains gave way to craggy hills. He recognized the terrain. They were on the down slope from the highest peaks.

Fischer slid into the booth. "We're picking up speed. The engine's getting a rest. You look like you could use some too, Fred. Haven't seen you like this before. What's wrong?"

Fred's shoulders sagged. His eyes remained fixed on his coffee. "It happened. I tried to stop it. It was too late. He almost died. I'm really sorry, Mr. Fischer. I let you down."

"Somebody opened a window?"

Fred nodded. "In the tunnel. It was Gus. Mr. Colby ordered him to do it. I told him to stop. It was too late. I told them not to when they came aboard. Colby wouldn't listen. Now he says I didn't warn him."

"Was it Mr. Colby who almost died?" Fischer asked.

Fred's face appeared ashen. His eyes remained lowered. "Yes," he said. "The wind caught his scarf, almost pulled him through the window. Wes and I tugged him back in, but barely."

"How is Mr. Colby now?"

"At first he looked terrible," Fred said. "We gave him a drink. He came around; seems okay now. He chewed me out; said lots of awful things. He said he would ruin you, Mr. Fischer. He demanded to see you immediately."

"Tell me about the incident. Every detail."

His eyes slowly meeting Fischer's, Fred continued. "I think Wes and I saw the same things, but we haven't had a chance to talk. Nick and Daniel helped. They didn't see everything we saw. Gus helped too." Grant Fischer listened attentively while Fred related the entire episode. "I'll have to resign as conductor. Maybe it would be better if you fire me. I don't want you to have trouble with Mr. Colby."

Fischer smiled and patted Fred's arm. "You're as good a conductor as I've ever had, and I've had many. What happened was in no way your fault. These incidents happen rarely. When they do, it has never been because of a blunder by the conductor or staff. They occur when people, like Mr. Colby, refuse to adhere to simple rules, to simple authority you might say. Disobedience brings consequences although not always immediate or obvious. In this case, it was immediate. We've had instances where someone opened a window at night, not out of willful disobedience, but simply because they forgot. Those have never resulted in a problem, and they close the window as soon as they are reminded.

"What happened was entirely due to Mr. Colby's actions. You, Wes, and the others saved him. Your reaction was virtuous and your efforts commendable. And, considering Mr. Colby has not given a kind word to you or anyone else since setting foot on this train, your actions on his behalf are that much more remarkable and worthy of acclaim. Mr. Colby blames you. He should blame himself. Instead, he accuses, curses, and threatens you, when he should express his gratitude to all of you. Fred, you are a fine man and an outstanding conductor. What happened is done. Don't fret about it further."

"But Mr. Colby still wants to see you," Fred said. "He's angry. He said terrible things."

"Let me worry about that," Fischer said. "You know I care about all of my passengers, even those lacking good behavior. I'll go see him in a while."

"He wanted to see you right away."

"The wait will do him good. Patience is a virtue, eh Fred?" Fischer smiled and winked.

Fred sighed and sat straighter. "Do you want me to tag along when you talk to him?"

"No," Fischer said. "You've been subject to enough venom for one day. It's my turn. I've dealt with it for longer than you can imagine."

"Please be careful, Mr. Fischer," Fred said.

"I will. Shall we eat? Better to see Mr. Colby on a full stomach, I think."

"Sounds good to me." Fred waved at a waitress.

Nick and Daniel sauntered by the counter looking for a booth. Fred motioned to them.

"Please sit with us," Fischer said. "Is Mr. Quinton joining us?"

"He sent us to eat while he stays on reconnaissance. That is, he's watching Mr. Colby," Daniel said. "We'll bring him takeout when we go back."

"Bless him," Fischer said. "He's a considerate man. Fred and I thank you both for your help with Mr. Colby."

"Happy to," Nick said. "We didn't do that much."

"You fellows are too modest," Fischer said.

Nick's eyes narrowed. "I saw something crazy while I was holding Mr. Colby's arm. It looked for a second like crooked dark fingers opened the window more. Not real fingers, but I don't know how else to describe it. It was the weirdest thing I've ever seen. Did anyone else see that? Maybe I need to have my eyes checked."

"I didn't see it," Daniel said, "but I was watching Mack and Senator Bryce in the aisle."

Fred glanced at Fischer before speaking. "I saw it too. So did Wes. I can't describe it any better—gave me third-degree heebie-jeebies."

"What do you think it was, Mr. Fischer?" Nick asked.

Fischer stroked his beard. "Fred informed me of the affair. The human mind understands ordinary events reasonably well. However, certain phenomena challenge the mind. Consider evil. It assumes various forms; it deceives in many ways. Evil may portray itself as pleasant and desirable. Then again, it may appear as a vicious, unyielding force. Generally, evil prefers trickery and misdirection; a sneaky and sly approach. That strategy succeeds repeatedly. What you witnessed at the window could have been an encounter with evil. An evil force is conceivable, but perhaps it was too blatant. The other possibility—it was simply smoke. Maybe distorted by the turbulence of the tunnel but only smoke, nonetheless. Those are the two choices. I leave it for you to decide."

Nick's mouth hung open, his eyes wide. "I hope it was just smoke," he said.

"In any case, let's return to our menus," Fischer said. "I'm sure you're hungry."

The waitress took their orders. Half an hour later they had finished dessert and were sipping coffee, having discussed the state of the world.

"We'd better head back," Daniel said. "Mr. Quinton's probably starving. Thanks Mr. Fischer, Mr. Ables."

"Thank you, fellows," Fischer said. "I'll be back soon to see Mr. Colby."

They ambled down the aisle toward the passenger car, pausing at the counter for Wes's takeout.

Fred eased out of the booth. "If you'll excuse me, Mr. Fischer, I'll start my evening rounds."

NICK AND DANIEL passed Colby and his partners unnoticed, thanks to a poker game. The two soldiers sat across from Wes and handed him a brown paper bag and a cup of coffee.

"Thanks, fellows. Smells good." Wes started on the takeout, making an *okay* sign with the thumb and forefinger of his free hand. "How was dinner?"

"We ate with Mr. Fischer and Mr. Ables," Nick said. "The food was first-class. That Mr. Fischer knows more people and stories than anyone I've ever met. He mentioned he was coming back to see Mr. Colby."

Wes glanced toward Colby. "Why don't you two return to your seats while they're busy with the game. I'll try to finish eating before Mr. Fischer arrives. If it stays quiet, maybe you can get some shut-eye later."

"You think they'll have a quiet conversation?" Daniel asked.

"Probably wishful thinking," Wes said, "but there's always hope."

CHAPTER 13

Grant Fischer entered the passenger car and nonchalantly approached Colby and his party, who were immersed in their poker game. He stood motionless with one hand resting on the back of the seat. Gus glanced up and nudged Colby, who raised his head.

"Gentlemen, permit me to introduce myself. I am Grant Fischer, the owner of this train and rail line."

Colby sized him up. Fischer presented an impressive appearance. His demeanor conveyed gentlemanly tendencies. Colby suspected Fischer was also intelligent given his position. Colby read people as well as he could decipher a bank ledger. That skill advantaged him when he set up his marks. He would need to be careful with this Fischer. His mind made up, Colby decided he would break Fischer. The question was how? He needed to probe the train owner's character and find a weakness he could exploit. Colby would begin with a restrained approach and then attempt to make Fischer flustered and angry. He found that a reliable way to expose flaws.

"We wondered when you would show up, Mr. Fischer. Don't you know who we are?" Colby asked.

"My apologies, sir," Fischer said. "Of course, I know who all of you are." Fischer nodded to each as he continued. "You are Mr. Lamar Colby, renowned banker. Next to you is legendary State Senator F. W. Bryce. Your associates are Mack and Gus. I can assure you, gentlemen, your reputations precede you. I am quite aware of who you are."

Colby's eyes narrowed. He forced a smile. Fischer's answer unnerved and irritated him. And he did know them; even so, he did not defer to them. The notoriety normally would please Colby, but this time it didn't. It wasn't what Fischer said, but how he said it, as though his words were loaded with secret knowledge. It seemed as if Fischer had a dossier on each of them. Fischer's response seemed like a warning. Colby felt a tingle on the back of his neck. Fischer would be a challenge, maybe a difficult one. Colby knew he would win any confrontation. Nevertheless, he remained wary of Fischer.

"I almost forgot." Fischer reached into his jacket pocket. "Here's your new ticket, Mr. Colby."

Colby examined the silver ticket. "It's a fancy ticket for a mediocre train."

Unfazed, Fischer said, "We do special things on this train, including the tickets. I regret your impression is of mediocrity. That is not our intent at all. Of course, a man of your stature has probably ridden the very best railcars. And I do apologize for the incident with the window. Conductor Ables related it to me. I trust you are experiencing no adverse effects?"

"Adverse effects? I was nearly killed," Colby fumed. "What kind of a train is this? Do you not care about the safety of your passengers? You have dangerous windows and nobody says anything?"

"Mr. Colby, Conductor Ables requested that you not open the windows at night. In addition, there are signs at each window that serve as reminders. Furthermore, Mr. Ables tried to stop your associate from opening the window. I sincerely regret the incident, but it *was* avoidable."

Colby's face reddened. "Well, your staff is a most unimpressive and bungling bunch. If someone had told me of the danger, I would have told Gus *not* to open the window."

"I can assure you, Mr. Colby, my staff is handpicked," Fischer said. "They are people of the utmost integrity and competence. However, given your opinion of my staff, you may very well have disbelieved Mr. Ables, no matter what he said, and opened the window anyway. An open window at night will usually not cause a problem, so warning people of possible danger is an unnecessary overstatement. We have found the conductor's request and the signs sufficient for almost everyone."

Colby felt his hands clenching and a growing warmth in his face. Fischer was getting the upper hand. He was unflappable. That unsettled Colby, who was accustomed to being in the driver's seat. Fischer threw Colby's own words back at him and used them to mock and insult him. Colby was sure of it because that was his own game plan even though it wasn't working. "I am not *everyone,* Mr. Fischer. I am Lamar Colby. I am not your ordinary *everyone.* Not by a long shot. I expect to be treated in a respectful manner. My employees carry out my orders. I expect things to be done exactly as I specify. If not, there are consequences. I assume your employees do your bidding also. Any mistake they make reflects on you."

"Indeed, you are not ordinary, Mr. Colby," Fischer replied. You are as unique as Gus, Mack, Senator Bryce, Mr. Ables, or anyone else. Furthermore, I am pleased that you so well grasp the significance of commands, details, and consequences. I have very few rules for my staff and only one for the passengers. That, of course, relates to the windows. It's quite simple: don't open the windows after dark. Call it a rule, a command, or an order. If you violate that command, there can be consequences as there are in your organization. If disobedience has no penalty, then of what use is a rule? I am gratified that you understand such principles. It is a distinct pleasure, I might add, to converse with a man of your intelligence."

Colby suppressed his exasperation, attempting to match Fischer's relaxed composure. Colby rarely met his intellectual equal or was bested, for that matter. It wasn't over though. Colby intended to continue probing and prodding in order to gain the upper hand. The time had come to raise the stakes. "Mr. Fischer, I find you a quarrelsome and unpleasant man, despite your seemingly tranquil performance. Many of your remarks and innuendos are insulting and patronizing. I will tolerate it no further."

Fischer shrugged and smiled. "My good man, I assure you this is no performance. I am sincere where we're in agreement. The same is true where our thoughts differ. By choice, you can believe what you wish. The truth binds me. It is simple, straightforward, and not subject to manipulation or revision. I care for you, Mr. Colby, as I do for all of my passengers. Your opinion of me will not alter that. Thinking you have been slighted is a product of your own sensitivity, certainly not my intent or design. I make every effort to live by integrity in all aspects of my being, and I shall continue to do so. I do not act or speak frivolously."

Colby's irritation vanished as soon as he heard *integrity*. He would exploit Fischer's weakness, the man's desire to be honest. That's what had been annoying Colby. Yes, Fischer's parries to his verbal thrusts had been aggravating, but that wasn't all of it. Indeed, Fischer *was* a man of integrity. Colby had sensed it but not fully realized it until Fischer mentioned the word himself. He and Bryce were masters of corruption, deceit, and whatever means were necessary to accomplish an objective. They were virtuosos of villainy. Fischer wouldn't be able to thwart their underhanded tactics because it was not in his nature. Fischer would not possess the devious connections to counter the financial and political machinations that he and Bryce would unleash. Colby was certain he would prevail. He would repay Fischer for the physical terror he had experienced at the window. The suffering he would inflict on Fischer would result from financial ruin and the loss of his train and line. Colby would render it even more atrocious by telling Fischer what he would do. That would provide Fischer with two unwelcome companions: anguish and distress. Integrity—indeed! That would be Fischer's downfall. Colby relished the thought with great anticipation.

Colby raised his eyebrows. "Mr. Fischer, I have had enough of you. I do not like you and find you distasteful and repugnant. I do not like your staff or your passengers. I have decided I will put you out of business and ruin you. Furthermore, I will tell you how I will do it. Senator Bryce, who has great influence, sits on the Transportation Committee. He will have little difficulty in arranging your indictment for regulatory and safety violations that will shut you down. We will bankrupt your operation, and then I will buy this train and your rail line for pennies on the dollar. I may even expand my empire from banking to transportation. I may rename this train *The Colby Connection*. You will rue the day you crossed Lamar Colby."

Colby watched Fischer's face for evidence of trepidation and dread. There was none, whatsoever. His demeanor changed not at all. And neither had the calmness of his voice throughout their conversation. Fischer's lack of fear disquieted Colby. *Who is this Fischer?* Colby searched his memory for some recollection of the man in any situation. Nothing came to mind.

"Mr. Colby, I regret you have found your circumstances so unpleasant," Fischer said. "I also am disappointed that my staff and I are repugnant to you. I would ask that you reconsider your intentions. Perhaps you could redirect your considerable skills to virtuous objectives that would prove beneficial."

Colby scoffed. "My decision is irrevocable. We will leave your train at the next stop and board a returning train, so we can put our plans into action immediately. You will be surprised at how quickly a train inspector knocks upon your door."

"Mr. Colby, I regret to inform you that there are no returning trains on this line."

Colby's jaw dropped and his eyes widened. "Why certainly you are joking. That cannot possibly be true. Why it's preposterous."

"Quite true, I assure you," Fischer said. "The rail grade on this side of the mountains is far too steep for a train to climb. Traveling down is no problem, but returning is not possible."

"Well, then how does your train return to where it started?" Colby asked.

"There are various routes. With the flexibility of our schedule, we eventually arrive there."

"Frankly, I don't believe you, Mr. Fischer. We *will* catch a returning train. If not, we will go by other transportation. A bus, if necessary."

"Mr. Colby, the towns along this route are small communities having no need for buses or automobiles. You can walk almost anywhere in town in twenty or thirty minutes. There are some bicycles, carts, and wagons, but that is the extent of the transportation. Except for this train. The train is one of the special things we do to serve these remote locations."

Colby's brow furrowed in thought. *I don't believe him.* No returning trains. No buses. No automobiles. It's ludicrous and inconceivable. And there was something else Fischer said: remote locations, remote locations. That was it. Fischer had a monopoly and didn't even know it. Monopolies were for exploitation. He would make more money from this train in a week than he would pay for it. Fischer had a potential fortune with this line but was probably too foolish and sanctimonious to profit from it. Colby would. That episode with the window may have been my good luck. I don't need Fischer's back talk anymore. *Time to be rid of him.*

Colby settled back and crossed his arms. "Mr. Fischer, my party and I will leave your train at the next stop and make our own arrangements. Please have our luggage removed from the train at that time. I bid you a good evening."

"Certainly, Mr. Colby. I will see to it. We will arrive in Penceville in mid morning. A good night to you, gentlemen."

IT WOULD HAVE been impossible for Wes not to have heard the conversation. Wes turned to the back of his catalog. The words and phrases he had heard and written earlier were now in context: *shut down, out of business, bankrupt, pennies on the dollar*. The discussion over the open window was no longer business as usual. Colby had made it personal, very personal. Wes shuddered. He was in the middle of it. He'd been worried about Timmy. Now he worried about the whole train. The only blessing in the sordid affair was that Colby would be off the train tomorrow.

From what Fischer had said, there was no returning transportation. That would be a problem for Colby. At least it would slow his efforts against Fischer. It would also greatly aggravate Colby. *That*, Wes would like to see firsthand.

Wes wondered if Fischer would tell Fred about the threats. He would certainly tell Fred that Colby was leaving. As to the threats, he wasn't sure. There was nothing Fred could do about them. Perhaps there was little Mr. Fischer could do. Wes's jaw tightened. Colby and Bryce were formidable adversaries, even for Mr. Fischer.

It had been a long day. Wes gazed out the window. Moonlight illuminated jagged hills and gorges that mimicked the ups and downs of the day's events. Nick and Daniel slumped in their seats. Fatigue overwhelmed Wes. His chin soon rested on his chest; a gentle snore escaped from his throat.

CHAPTER 14

The sun peeked above the horizon; its rays dissolved the darkness above. Bridge girders flashed by the window as the train traversed a deep gorge bound by jagged hills. A glint of light nudged Wes from his slumber. The savory aroma of coffee revived his senses. A covered cup and a handwritten note rested on the seat beside him: *Thought you'd want coffee. Come back to the caboose and freshen up. Your luggage is there. Jay.*

The coffee was fresh and hot. Wes glanced around the car. He didn't see Nick or Daniel. Colby and his party slumped in their seats. The only reason to watch them now was to make sure they woke in time to depart the train in Penceville.

Wes grabbed the coffee and his satchel and headed toward the caboose. He traipsed through a utility car, a baggage car, and two cars loaded with boxes, barrels, and crates before entering the last car on the train.

"Hi, Fred," Wes said as he slid back the heavy door and entered the caboose.

"Morning, Wes. Rise and shine." Fred wore an apron over his T-shirt. He mixed batter in a bowl. "Your suitcase is on the bunk if you want to clean up while I fix breakfast."

Ten minutes later, Wes emerged to the scent of bacon, pancakes, and steaming coffee. The two men said grace and then added butter and syrup to the pancake towers.

"Delicious," Wes said. "Have you seen Nick and Daniel? They were gone when I woke up."

"They came back earlier to tidy up. Thought I wouldn't have enough food, so they went to the dining car. I'm sure they can pack in the chow."

"No doubt. I walked through the supply cars. Looks like you could feed an army."

"Maybe a small one," Fred said. "Most of the supplies are for the towns where we stop. Sometimes we add more freight cars if needed. This train is the only good way to get out here."

"I guess you know Colby plans to get off the train in Penceville?"

"That's what Mr. Fischer said. He gave me the gist of his conversation with Colby. If they do leave, that's the good news. Those threats he made against Mr. Fischer have me worried though. Mr. Fischer didn't seem bothered, but he never seems to be. You probably heard it all?"

"Every bit," Wes said. "Colby didn't believe what Mr. Fischer said about no returning trains, no cars, and no buses. That ought to slow Colby down."

"He'll find out for himself that Mr. Fischer doesn't lie. Then he'll have to find a way out. I don't know how he can, but he seems determined. I say good riddance."

"Me too," Wes said. "He was lucky last night with that window. He could've been gone already."

Fred frowned. "Don't remind me. I never thought I'd be part of an incident. You hear stories, but it's not like being there. It's even scarier because it's so strange. How can an open window pull someone with such a strong force? We couldn't budge Colby. And what were those black smudgy things? I'm still not sure if it was real. And those white flakes. Did you see all of that, too, or have I gone nuts?"

"I saw it. Can't explain it either. And I swear that window opened further by itself—or maybe with some help. Did the stories mention that?"

"The stories had everything we've talked about in one way or another."

"If I didn't know better, I'd think the train was haunted," Wes said.

Fred's eyes widened. "Don't say that. It gives me the heebie-jeebies. Don't say stuff like that."

Wes snickered. "I'm sorry, Fred. Didn't mean to laugh."

"What's so funny? You're making fun of me."

"No. It's just that you're such a big guy, and you get the heebie-jeebies. It's like oil and water; they don't mix. I said, 'If I didn't know better.' Geez, Fred, I don't believe in spooks. There's either some logical explanation, or it was just weird coincidence. Anyway, now you have your own story to tell."

"I wish I didn't. I'd rather forget about it. Let's talk about something else."

"Tell me about Penceville," Wes said.

"It's a nice place. Lived there myself until I became conductor. I still have friends there."

"What did you do there?"

"I worked in one of the factories that makes goods for the shops. Eventually, I became foreman. Later, I ran all the factories. When the last train conductor retired, Mr. Fischer asked me to take his place.

"Penceville is the size of a big town or maybe even a small city. It has a first-rate train station with an area to off-load supplies. It's a short walk to town down a promenade. The town is full of different kinds of streets: straight, winding, narrow, and wide. Most are paved in cobblestone or setts, except for the dirt roads that go to the farms or sawmill. There's every kind of shop and store you could imagine and different styles of buildings. Many people live above their shop. Others live in apartments or in small homes. There's a big square in the middle of town and small parks all around town. There's even a carnival area with a roller coaster, a Ferris wheel, other rides, and games. There are plenty of cafés and restaurants. You would never know the factory area because it blends with the rest of the town. It probably sounds like a hodgepodge, but it's quaint and charming. You'll see when we stop there. More coffee? Have enough to eat?"

"Coffee please. Who lives in Penceville?" Wes asked.

"Just about anyone you can imagine. Everyone's friendly. There are always people coming and some leaving. There's a welcoming committee, to help those arriving settle in. The pleasant surroundings make you feel at home."

"What about those leaving? Where do they go?"

"Some travel to other towns, some work on the train, and some continue as far as your stop. It depends."

"You said there's someone in Penceville I should see. I've never heard of this place. I can't imagine who I would know."

"I'm not completely sure, so I don't want to say," Fred said. "If I'm wrong, you'd be disappointed. We'll know soon. We'll be in Penceville in an hour. Are your feet up to walking?"

"My gosh. Forgot all about them." Wes rocked his feet. "They feel fine. I think Jay performed a miracle. Hope it lasts. Need help with the dishes?"

Fred removed the apron and donned his uniform and cap. "Let them soak. I'd better shake a leg. Leave your luggage here, satchel too, if you want."

"Thanks. Guess I won't need to watch Colby anymore," Wes said.

Fred rolled his eyes. "If he leaves; I'm sure he will. The rest of the train ride will be enjoyable once they're gone."

"Amen to that. I'll head back and see if Colby needs help packing."

Fred laughed.

WES FOLLOWED FRED to the passenger car and joined Nick and Daniel. "Morning, fellows. Did you have enough to eat, or did they run out of food?" Wes asked.

Nick rubbed his belly. "We had plenty. There's more if you haven't eaten."

"I ate with Mr. Ables," Wes said. "Did he tell you about Penceville?"

"Sure did," Daniel said. "Nick and I plan to visit."

"You know that Colby and his friends are departing there too?"

"We heard," Nick said.

"Watch out for them in town." Wes stood. "I'm moving closer to their seats. We don't need any last-minute surprises."

Colby and his cohorts chatted and ate. Wes heard nothing to suggest a change in plans. Relieved, Wes turned his eyes toward the changing landscape.

Rugged precipices and gorges transformed into rolling hills tinseled by rivers and streams. Sunlight glittered off cascading water. The hills gave way to a flat terrain spotted with scattered knolls. Tree leaves, spiteful of autumn's onset, preserved their greenish hues.

The train slowed. Clusters of cattle dotted an open range. Orchards, fields, scattered barns, and farmhouses followed, connected by a web of dusty roads. A rutted dirt road paralleled the track. It linked the farm community to whatever lay ahead.

The train's whistle pierced the air. The monotonous *clickety-clack* became a deeper drumbeat. The whistle sounded twice more as the train came to a crawl and then stopped in Penceville.

CHAPTER 15

Wes ambled to a passenger car window. The train station nestled on a knoll. Beyond and below it spread the kaleidoscope of architecture and colors known as Penceville. The hues varied from pastel to primary and every combination thereof. A centrally located town square bore lofty trees, which projected above the taller buildings. A single church steeple bested the height of even the tallest trees. Streets radiated from the town square like the spokes of a wheel. The top third of a Ferris wheel poked above a line of trees on the far side of town. Near it, a collection of curved peaks gleamed in the sun, the fearful summits of a roller coaster. Penceville reminded Wes of a cozy patchwork quilt: comfortable, homey, and appealing.

A wide covered platform of cut stone, with ornate benches of wrought iron, stretched beside the train. Leading to town, a broad granite arch opened to a gently sloping walkway. The brass lettering on the arch read Welcome to Penceville. Beneath it, another sign read Visitors. Arrivals labeled a smaller archway on the right and served as a foyer entrance to the station. Constructed of granite with expansive windows and a red tiled roof, the station appeared solid yet inviting.

A shoulder high stone wall with a gate separated the freight portion of the platform from the passenger and luggage side. Workers loaded freight into horse drawn wagons for deliveries about town. Porters filled luggage carts. A steward checked baggage tags against a clipboard.

Jay and Mr. Fischer strolled toward the arrivals' entrance of the station. Nick and Daniel weren't far behind but zagged under the visitors' arch and down the promenade toward town. Stewards and station workers positioned themselves on the platform. Moments later, a crowd of passengers exited the train. A handful departed through the visitors' arch, but most were directed to the arrivals' entrance. The platform emptied as quickly as it had filled. A few people carrying travel bags exited a station door and walked toward the train.

"Time to go," Colby exclaimed.

Colby's shrill voice startled Wes, who was engrossed with the view of the town and station. Gus carried Colby's travel bag. The men advanced up the aisle and disappeared through the door. On the platform a moment later, they marched toward the porters to retrieve their luggage, which sat on a four-wheel handcart. The foursome left through the visitors' arch with Gus hauling the cart.

The forward aisle door opened. Fred peeked in. He strolled down the aisle; his eyes darted back and forth in obvious exaggeration, scrutinizing where Colby and his group had been seated. "They're gone; they're gone. Hallelujah, hallelujah."

Wes chuckled. "Don't jinx us. Hope we don't run into them in town."

"We won't. You ready to go? I need to check in at the station. I'll show you around, and then we'll hit the big town."

Minutes later, they entered the station. Fred led them to an office separated by glass from other areas, which were also mostly constructed of glass walls.

"Have a seat," Fred told Wes. "Let me log a few things, and then I'll show you around."

Wes scanned the station's interior. The transparent walls inspired a sense of openness. Two separate waiting areas connected to a receptionist in a small office. From there, a glass door led to a larger office occupied by a mahogany desk, two chairs, and a cluster of leather armchairs around a floral oval rug. Lilies decorated side tables. Etched pictures of trains decorated the glass walls. Wes saw two exit doors. A paneled wall behind the desk had its own door. Wes recognized some of the train's passengers in one of the waiting areas. He could not identify the inhabitants of the other waiting room.

As Wes watched, Fischer and Jay entered the paneled door of the office and sat in the chairs next to the desk. Jay stacked tickets while Fischer checked a list. By intercom, Fischer communicated with the receptionist, who would call someone from a waiting area and direct him or her to the larger office. A conversation followed between that person, Jay, and Fischer, in the comfort of the armchairs. Expressions of shock, surprise, and joy overcame a few. Each person either surrendered a ticket or received a ticket and then left through one of the exit doors.

"I'm done," Fred said. "Sorry. Took longer than I thought."

"That's okay," Wes replied. "I've been watching people meet with Mr. Fischer and Jay. I don't understand it. Some of the folks seemed kind of emotional too."

"It's not that complicated. The people who just arrived by train are in one waiting area. When called, they meet with Jay and Mr. Fischer, who explain about Penceville. They also turn in their ticket. They leave through the exit door that leads to the front of the station. That's where a welcoming committee greets them; they receive their luggage; and they meet their sponsor who helps them get settled.

"The other waiting area is for those leaving Penceville. Those people also talk with Jay and Mr. Fischer and receive a departure ticket. They leave through the other exit, which leads to the platform where they board the train. The porters make sure their luggage is put on board. It all works well."

"Jay and Mr. Fischer seem to take a personal interest in everyone," Wes said.

"They do." Fred moved closer to the glass. "Looks like they're almost done. There's one more person waiting. I'll be. That's Joe Croft. I was his sponsor when he came to Penceville."

Fischer signaled Fred to come to the office. He motioned to Wes as well.

"Hope I'm not in trouble," Fred said.

Fred and Wes walked into the hallway, around the corner, and entered the office.

"Hello, Fred. Wes," Fischer said. Jay smiled.

"There's one more person in the waiting area," Fred said. "Looks like Joe Croft."

"He's last for a reason," Fischer said.

Jay left the office and returned with Joe, who greeted everyone.

Fred patted Joe on the back. "Joe, meet Wes Quinton, one of our passengers visiting Penceville. Wes, this is Joe Croft."

"You're probably wondering why Jay and I arranged this meeting," Fischer said. "This is your last trip as conductor, Fred. You're retiring at the end of the line. We're pleased to give you this ticket. Congratulations."

Jay handed Fred a gopherwood ticket. "Congratulations, Fred."

Fred sighed. A tear slipped from his eye. "I don't know what to say. I'm happy to be retiring, but I'll be sad to leave the train too."

"I also wanted you to know that Joe will be the new conductor," Fischer said. "You can fill him in on the duties during the rest of the trip. This will be your on-the-job training, Joe."

Fred smiled. "Joe, they couldn't have picked anyone better. Have a porter take your luggage to the caboose. There's plenty of empty drawers and storage space. Need help with anything?"

"No," Joe said. "Have to pick up my uniform in town. It needed a few alterations. And I want to say good-bye to some friends. My luggage is already on the train."

"The conductor's manual is in the top drawer of the desk in the caboose if you want to thumb through it," Fred said.

"I'll make that a priority," Joe said.

"Jay and I have some errands of our own," Fischer said, heading for the door. "We'll see you later on the train."

"I'd better get that uniform," Joe said. "Don't want to miss my first train ride as *conductor-in-waiting*."

Fred turned to Wes. "Let's finish up the station tour and head to town."

Wes would have gotten lost in the station complex if left to explore it himself. The luggage corridors ran below the station thanks to the sloping knoll. Storage areas overflowed with supplies. Near Fischer's office, he saw a utility room with equipment for tooling tickets and stacks of wooden blanks, both gopherwood and cypress. Wes looked twice but didn't see any silver ticket blanks. He figured they needed to restock. The assistance counter at the front of the building marked the end of the tour.

Wes pointed out the window. Two figures walked toward the promenade. "Isn't that Colby and Bryce?"

Fred shielded the window's reflection with his hand and turned to the man working the counter. "Jim, were those two men just in here?"

Jim took a quick look. "Sure were. Couldn't get rid of them. And before them, there were two others. I hope they're not staying here."

Fred shook his head. "They're visitors. Jim, this is my friend Wes Quinton."

"Nice to meet you, Mr. Quinton."

"Tell me what happened," Fred said.

Jim scratched his cheek and then spoke. "First a pair of fellows came to the counter. One was big and well built, almost your size. The other was wiry and plain mean looking. He had a flat cap cocked over one eye."

"Gus and Mack," Fred said, nodding at Wes.

Jim continued. "The big one did most of the talking. He asked me a hundred different ways about getting a return train ticket. The mean one interrupted now and then. 'You better not lie to us. You better not lie to us,' he said repeatedly. Of course, there is no returning train, but they wouldn't believe me. After about ten minutes, they finally gave up and left. About five minutes after that, two other fellows came in. One was short with a tall top hat, and the other was a handsome man. They were both well dressed."

"That was Mr. Colby and Senator Bryce," Fred said.

"That's right, they said that near the end," Jim said. "They were as bad as the first two. The short one kept asking about returning trains and tickets. He kept trying to trick me into saying there was one when there isn't. The other one acted like he was on my side at first, but when I kept saying there wasn't any train back, he stopped acting friendly. The short one got mad and slammed his hand on the counter. That's when they asked me if I knew who they were. I told them I had never seen them in my life before. How would I know who they were? Besides, it didn't matter anyway because there's no train back. The little one hit the counter again but with his fist. He told me who they were, how important they were, and that I'd better give them return tickets or they'd cause me problems. I told them if I had any, I'd give them the tickets just to be rid of them. But there weren't any because there are no return trains. They pestered me for a good twenty minutes before they left. They weren't happy when they did."

"Mr. Fischer told them the same thing on the train. They didn't believe him either so don't feel bad," Fred said.

Jim's eyebrows rose. "They didn't believe Mr. Fischer? They really are stupid aren't they. Besides being mean."

Fred glanced out the window. He saw Colby and his troupe pulling the luggage handcart down the promenade near the edge of town.

"Jim, I don't think they'll be back to bother you. You did well putting up with them."

WES AND FRED left the station, strolling the short distance to town. A stuccoed arch read Welcome to Penceville where the promenade merged into the adjacent streets. An azure sky and overhead sun offset the touch of autumnal chill. Fred led the way. They zigzagged through lanes and streets full of shops, stores, and cafés with colorful awnings. Quaint shops lined cul-de-sacs that sprouted at odd angles from many streets. Antique stores, florists, bakeries, delicatessens, grocery stores, a watch repair, clothing goods, furniture stores, shoe stores, book stores, music stores, and restaurants of all cuisines stretched in every direction.

"How about coffee?" Fred asked. "That café serves all kinds."

They sat under the café's awning around a wrought iron table. Wes scanned the menu. "I'll have a cappuccino and a pastry."

"I'll have the same," Fred said.

A waiter took their order. A few minutes later it arrived.

"This is quite a town," Wes said. "Quaint, like you said. I bet there's a hardware store."

"Several."

Wes's eyes widened. "Several? Really? I'd like to see them if we have time. I'm always searching for ideas to improve mine."

"We should have time. About a half hour before the train leaves, its whistle will blow twice. Even if we miss the train, it's only traveling five miles up the track. It'll stop at the sawmill for a few hours to restock wood for the locomotive. We burned plenty climbing the mountains. A wagon can haul us there if we miss the train at the station."

"I'm surprised Timmy didn't want to come with us," Wes said.

"I asked, but Mr. Holyfield was teaching him how to play checkers. He told Timmy if he became good at it, he'd teach him chess. Timmy said he wasn't leaving. He'd learn checkers first and then chess. He's a smart boy. Determined too. I bet he'll be playing chess by the time we return."

Wes sipped the cappuccino. "That gives me an idea. Is there a toy store?"

"Just past the pet store. What are you thinking?" Fred asked.

"I'd like to buy Timmy a chess set that'll fit in his knapsack. He'd like that. Who knows? Maybe one day he'll be a chess master."

"I'll go in on it with you. We'll buy him a nice one."

"I want to get you something, too, since you're retiring," Wes said.

"I really don't need anything. Your friendship is a gift in itself."

"Thanks, Fred. But would a bottle of champagne be out of order? We can have a toast in the caboose and invite Jay, Mr. Fischer, and anyone else you want. That is, if it's sold here."

"It most certainly is, and I know just the store."

"I'd like to stop in some other stores, too, if you don't mind," Wes said.

"Which ones?" Fred asked.

"I'll let you know if I see them."

WES WENT IN and out of several antique stores before acquiring a small package.

"Find something?" Fred asked.

"My secret. Are there any arts and crafts stores?"

"Next street over."

Wes entered and exited that store in a few minutes.

"Find what you needed?"

"In the bag," Wes said.

Fred pointed up the street. "The toy store is over there."

The *boy* in them had to stop for a gander at the pet store windows. In one, three puppies jumped on each other and rolled off, only to right themselves and repeat the process. At another window, four puppies had worn themselves out. They curled together sleeping. In the last window, three energetic kittens performed. One played with another's tail; one played hockey with a piece of dry cat food; and another had its paws on the window, mewing at the people on the other side of the glass.

"Ready for the toy store, Fred?"

Fred stared spellbound at the pet store windows. "Just a minute more."

"We need to watch the time," Wes said five minutes later.

"Sorry. When I lived here, this was my favorite store. You can play with the kittens and puppies if you go inside. You're right. We'd better go."

The toy store brimmed with every imaginable plaything that might delight a child. Wes and Fred perused everything from baseball gloves to tin soldiers to model trains. In the game section, a selection of chess sets captured their attention.

Wes pointed to a set with black and white alabaster playing pieces. It also had a folding box made of cherrywood with an alabaster playing surface. "How about this one? The pieces store in the box."

"I was thinking the same thing," Fred said. "It's a nice one, something Timmy could keep for a long time."

Wes carried the chess set to the checkout counter.

"Come and look at this, Fred." Wes walked to a corner of the store. He turned the windup key under the belly of a small toy dog and returned it to the shelf. The dog moved to and fro as its mouth opened and shut, accompanied by barking sounds. "I think this one looks like Blackie."

Fred rummaged through the others on the shelf. "That's the one. Timmy would like that as much as the chess set."

"I'll buy it for him," Wes said.

The clerk wrapped both gifts. Wes added them to his bag.

"I almost forgot," Wes said. "There's someone I should see?"

"Patience. Let's get the champagne. It's on the way. We'll pass through the town square to get there."

CHAPTER 16

Colby and Bryce ambled in front followed by Mack and Gus, who took turns pulling the cart with the luggage. They had entered Penceville under the welcoming arch, not feeling particularly welcome. Colby fumed about the lack of a returning train.

"I tell you, F.W., this Fischer is smarter than we thought. I smell a rat. I bet he has a monopoly on this town, just like the train," Colby said.

"That would take a lot, Lamar. This is a big town," Bryce said. "It'd take a lot of muscle to keep it in line."

"There are other ways. Let's find a phone or a telegraph office. We can have our connections do some checking on Fischer. I never heard of him before. I want to know everything about him—and his train line. Maybe we can start tightening the screws on him now, before we return."

"Yeah, I don't know anything about him either," Bryce said. "But I can sure start the worm turning with the transportation committee. We have to find a phone."

Colby turned to Mack and Gus. "Keep your eyes peeled for a phone or a telegraph office."

"Watch out, boss!" Gus yelled.

A mammoth pumpkin had toppled off a farmer's wagon and bounced erratically across the street. Colby couldn't tell which way the orange monster would travel because each time the stem hit the pavement, its direction wobbled. Colby moved this way and that, fitfully dancing, trying to escape. At the last moment, Gus yanked

Colby's arm, and the pumpkin bounded by. It came to a rest near a streetlight fronting a small park.

Mack grinned. "That was close. You could've been squashed."

Colby glared at Mack. The grin disappeared.

Two farmers ran over from the farmers' market where the orange heavy roller had originated.

"Are you okay, sir?" one asked Colby. "I'm really sorry. That's my prize pumpkin for the competition. I should've tied it on my wagon."

Colby glowered at him.

The two farmers struggled to lift the pumpkin. Gus walked over. The three men managed to carry the awkward orange sphere to the market and place it on a large table with other pumpkins waiting to be judged.

"Thank you, sir, for your help," the farmer said. "Again, my apology. Wait here. I'll bring a bag of apples for you and your friends."

Gus watched the farmer return to his wagon. The farmers' market filled a wide expanse between buildings. A striped red and white tent cover shaded it. Fruits, vegetables, eggs, chickens, and even piglets filled the stalls. Behind the stands, Gus saw a half-dozen wagons, a few with horses hitched. Other horses grazed on hay in an adjacent corral.

"Here's the apples." The farmer showed them to Gus from the open bag. "Just picked them this morning. Hope you'll like them. Thanks for helping us. Please tell your friend I'm sorry."

"Thanks." Gus extracted one of the apples and bit into it. He strolled back to his colleagues. "Have an apple. Courtesy of the pumpkin farmer," he said. Bryce and Mack each took one.

Preoccupied, Colby growled, "Keep looking for a phone or a telegraph office."

They walked several more blocks, stopping at corners to peer down intersecting streets. Colby periodically sent Gus into stores or shops to ask about a phone or a telegraph office. The answer never varied. No one had a phone or knew where one might be, and no one remembered a telegraph office in town.

At a small park, they rested on benches beneath a maple tree. Colby and Bryce gazed up and down the street, hoping to see anything they might have missed.

"This is insufferable," Colby said. "These stores and shops all seem to be well run. The streets are full of shoppers carrying bags, which means they have money to spend. The town is clean and well kept. Yet there's not a phone to be found. How can that be? How can a town appear so prosperous and not have phones? There must be phones."

Bryce shrugged. "Maybe just certain businesses have phones. What business couldn't function without a phone? Maybe that's the question."

Colby pointed down the street. "There."

"Where? What do you see?" Bryce asked.

"There—on the corner."

Bryce squinted and strained. "You mean that bank?"

"Exactly," Colby said. "Not only should we get some straight answers, but they must have a phone. You can't do banking today without one. It's not possible. And I'm sure they'll let us use it. One banker to another. Let's go."

Colby rose first. He strode toward the bank followed by the others. The bank occupied a prime corner location with elm trees and benches on each side. Impressive columns stretched to the second floor. A marble slab engraved with 1st Savers Bank hung between the columns. The revolving-door entrance of tinted glass enhanced the prestigious appearance.

"F.W., come with me," Colby said. "You two wait here with the cart. We may be on the phone for a while."

"Sure thing, Mr. Colby." Gus reached for the bag of apples.

Colby and Bryce scooted through the revolving door.

A receptionist at a desk with several high-backed chairs in front of it greeted the men. The desk sat in a spacious lobby with offices along one wall and a row of tellers straight ahead. "Gentlemen, may I help you?" she asked as she eyed their attire.

Colby pulled a business card from his pocket and nodded at Bryce to do the same. They handed her the cards.

"We're visiting Penceville and would like to speak with your bank president or manager," Colby said.

The receptionist's eyebrows lifted as she examined the cards. "Our manager is in, Mr. Colby. Please have a seat while I give him your cards." She left through a heavy door past the desk and returned a minute later. "Mr. Evan will be delighted to see you. Just go through that door."

Colby didn't like what he saw. Lanky and bespectacled, Donald Evan wore a quality suit that looked a size too big. He parted his black hair in the middle until it reached a bald spot where the part became irrelevant.

The bank manager stumbled over his own feet as he lurched to greet them. "Donald Evan, bank manager. Please have a seat. It's a delight to have visitors. Especially, men of your esteem."

"You have heard of us then?" Colby asked.

"Why no, neither of you," Evan said. "But I must say, your business cards are most impressive. Indeed."

Colby's jaw tightened. *Don't say it. How could he not recognize my name? And especially at a bank—what kind of nitwit is this?*

"Have you been the bank manager long?" Colby asked.

"Oh yes," Evan said. "For quite some time. It's a rather pleasant job."

"You must know Penceville well then?" Bryce asked.

"Indubitably. Quite well," Evan said.

"We've been told there are no returning trains. Is that true?" Bryce asked.

"I've never asked," Evan said. "I've heard the track's too steep for a train to return, but I can't verify it."

"Mr. Evan, it's very important that I communicate with my largest bank," Colby said. "Senator Bryce also needs to contact a committee chairman on a matter of some urgency. If you would be kind enough to let us use your phone, we will gladly pay for any long distance charges."

"Phone?" A quizzical look crossed Evan's face. "We have no phone. If we had one, I would certainly let you use it—and with no charge as a matter of courtesy."

Colby's eyes widened and his mouth dropped. "That's not possible, Mr. Evan. How do you conduct your banking without one? How do you do bank wires? It must be by phone or maybe telegraph. And how do you contact your other branches for customer information and balances?"

"We are an independent bank like all the others in Penceville. We have no need for bank wires. Our banking is simple and straightforward. I can't think of any reason why we would need a phone. I don't know of any telegram services in town either."

Colby glanced up as he thought for a moment. "Mr. Evan, what if you had a bank robbery? How would you call the police?"

Donald Evan cackled and slapped his hand on the desk. "Oh really, Mr. Colby. You have such a sense of humor. A bank robbery, a bank robbery. Those kinds of things just don't happen here. Wait. I take that back. Some time ago, I attended a play at the theater by the town square. It was a comedy. In one scene, they acted out a bank robbery. It was simply ludicrous. People were falling out of their seats because they laughed so hard. Did you see that play too, Mr. Colby?"

"I must have missed that one." Colby rolled his eyes and shook his head. "Is there someplace in town that rents automobiles? Is there a taxi stand?"

"Pardon my saying, Mr. Colby, but you ask the strangest questions," Evan said. "Oh, my apologies. I forgot you are just visiting. No, I'm sorry. There are no automobiles or taxis that I'm aware of. You have given me an idea though: a horse-drawn trolley. Now that would fit well with our town. Yes, I like that idea. Would your bank be interested in partnering with us on the financing? Why we could—"

Colby angled his eyes toward Bryce and tilted his head toward the door. It was time to go. Bryce caught the motion and none too soon. Both had had enough and stood.

"Mr. Evan, thank you for your time. We have other business to attend to," Colby said.

"My pleasure," Evan said. "Let me know about that financing, Mr. Colby."

"I'll think about it," Colby said as they rushed out of the office.

GUS AND MACK stood when Colby and Bryce returned.

"You were in there a long time," Gus said. "Did you make the calls?"

"He was a buffoon," Colby said.

"Pardon?" Gus said.

"That banker. A buffoon. A clown. A dunce. A dolt. A nitwit. A simpleton. Take your pick. Why, Mack could do a better job," Colby sneered.

"Hey," Mack said.

"Sorry, Mack," Colby said. "I didn't mean it like that. No phone, no telegraph, no autos, and no taxis. And he was intolerable to boot."

"Do you think he was lying?" Gus asked.

"He was too stupid to lie," Colby scoffed.

"A first-class imbecile," Bryce said. "This business of no phones and no telegraph office makes me think you may be right about one thing, Lamar."

"What's that?" Colby asked.

"Maybe Fischer does have a monopoly on this town," Bryce said.

"What do we do now?" Mack asked.

"Let's stop at that café down the street," Colby said. "These aren't good shoes for walking. My feet need a rest. There has to be some way out of here."

Chapter 17

"Four coffees," Colby said to the café waitress.

"Yes, sir. Would you be interested in today's pie special? They're fresh out of the oven."

"What kind of pie?" Senator Bryce asked.

"Pumpkin."

"No pie," Colby grumbled.

Bryce glanced at Colby who was morose, an unusual condition for him. Colby hadn't walked this much in years, and his expensive shoes weren't designed for it. Aching feet and fatigue seemed the least of it although they surely didn't help. Bryce knew he experienced the same thing that Colby must have felt: the uneasy sensation of a problem with rapidly disappearing options. Perhaps none. Were they trapped? Bryce wondered. That couldn't be; options always existed. One had to think of them. That was the hard part. What haven't we considered? What have we overlooked that, perhaps, is right in front of us? Bryce stared into the street with blank eyes as he contemplated their predicament.

The *clink* of coffee cups ended the visual torpor. Something across the street caught Bryce's eye. An option existed but his mind couldn't fathom it. *What am I seeing?* An empty shop with a vacancy sign. Below that, another sign: Outstanding Location on the first line and Business Opportunity on the second. The clue was right there, but Bryce couldn't quite grasp it. Something in the signs. There is something there. He scrutinized each sign, letter by letter. The second sign, the first three letters of the second line: B, U, S. That was it. BUS. They hadn't asked the moron banker about buses. They were in too much of a hurry to leave his office. Fischer said there were no buses. But who trusted him? It was an option they hadn't looked into. At least there's a chance, Bryce thought.

"Your coffee, gentlemen." The waitress placed the cups on the table.

"Miss, is there a bus station in Penceville?" Bryce asked, hoping for but not expecting a positive response. Bryce saw a glimmer in Colby's eyes.

"Why yes, sir," she said. "And it's always busy with people coming and going."

"You understood me? A *bus station*?" Bryce repeated.

"Certainly, sir. The bus station is on the other side of town past the town square. It's not far from the Ferris wheel." She pointed. "You can see the top of the wheel from here."

"Do you know when it's open?" Bryce asked.

"All day and in the evening," the waitress said. "Like I said, it's a very busy place. I've been there myself."

"And you said people come and go?" Bryce asked.

"Why yes. From all over," she said.

"We'll take that pie now." Colby's cloud of gloom dissipated.

"Which kind?" the waitress asked.

Colby smiled. "Why pumpkin, of course."

"Right away, sir. I'll be back shortly."

"You're a genius F.W.! How did you think of that? I was drawing blanks and kicking myself because of it. Maybe it's time to promote you from senator to governor," Colby said.

"It just came to me somehow," Bryce said. "We forgot to ask that banker about it. Maybe because Fischer said there were no buses."

"Well, Fischer's a liar for sure. I just knew he was lying," Colby said. "We'll head for that station as soon as we're done here. Leave that waitress a big tip." It wasn't generosity but Colby's habit of paying for useful information when he otherwise couldn't return a favor. To the waitress, unaware of the motivation, it would simply be a big tip.

IN SHORT ORDER, Colby and his party arrived at the town square with Gus tending the luggage cart. The stone-paved square featured a central park with decorative benches and stout elm and maple trees.

A majestic church, flanked by grassy courtyards, dominated one side of the square. Its steeple rose seemingly to heaven, and sunlight sparkled from its bronze shingles. A theater and numerous other shops and stores bordered the remainder of the square.

Colby gauged the best course through the square. He eyed the top of the Ferris wheel poking above the trees. On the square's far side, the bordering streets merged at odd angles. He lost sight of the wheel.

"Excuse me, sir," Colby said to a passerby. "Is this the way to the bus station?"

"It is." The pedestrian pointed. "Take this street about three or four blocks to the carnival area. Continue across the park. The bus station is on the other side."

"Thank you." Colby gestured the others to follow and started down the street.

"You know, this is a nice place," Gus said.

The others turned toward him with odd looks.

Colby wondered if Gus needed a rest. Maybe too much sun? "You pull the cart for a while, Mack."

"I'm okay, Mr. Colby," Gus said. "This town reminds me of where I grew up. Everything's pretty simple. Kind people. That's all I meant. It's nice in that sort of way."

"You wouldn't fit in," Colby said. "Everyone acts pleasant enough, but they all seem to be overdoing it. Why do you suppose that is?" Colby glanced about. "Anybody see the top of that Ferris wheel?"

As they emerged from a sharp turn in the street, the Ferris wheel towered above them in its magnificent entirety. Glimmering steel composed the spokes and rims. Each passenger car carried up to six people. It looked to be over one hundred feet to the peak, surpassing most of the tallest trees. *Oohs* and *aahs* drifted down from the occupants when the cars reached the zenith.

A broad promenade wound between the Ferris wheel on the left and a roller coaster further ahead on the right. Smaller walkways sprouted from the promenade to less daunting rides and a variety of carnival games. Past the Ferris wheel, an open grassy expanse contained sports fields and areas for general activities. Trees bordered the entire area. People animated the landscape. They enjoyed the rides, games, and sports activities. Others relaxed on benches, watching or reading under the radiant warmth of the sun.

The eyes of Bryce, Gus, and Mack darted about in an attempt to absorb all the activity. Colby alone remained focused. He searched for any sign of the bus station as they proceeded along the promenade. The encircling trees proved an effective shield, hiding whatever lay beyond them.

Colby heard the subtle *whizz* but didn't recognize it. Bryce saw the source a split second later.

"Duck, Lamar!" Bryce yelled.

"Where?" Colby asked.

It was too late. A spinning plastic disk angled off Colby's top hat tumbling it from his head. Bryce nimbly caught the hat before it hit the ground. A collie bounded by, determined to retrieve the disk.

Colby scratched his head and glanced around. "Where's the duck? I don't see any—" His face flushed. "Now aren't I stupid?" He realized what had happened. *Duck* was intended as a verbal command and not a noun.

"Sorry, mister," a teenager told Colby. "A breeze caught it. I wasn't aiming for you. Honest."

Colby glared at him. "You juvenile delinquent. You—"

The teenager's eyes widened. "How did you know? Did someone tell you? I'm not like that now. Honest, I'm not."

Colby, taken aback, stood with an mouth open, speechless.

"Why don't you go farther down the field, son, so you don't hit anyone else," Gus said. "You have a stronger arm than you thought."

The young man smiled at Gus and blushed at the compliment. "I will, sir. It's a good idea. I should have thought of it."

"You were too busy having fun. Next time use your head a little better," Gus said. "Say, do you know where the bus station is?"

The teenager pointed. "Sure. It's near the street on the other side of those trees. Stay on this path until you reach the street and then turn right."

"Thanks," Gus said.

COLBY AND BRYCE led Mack and Gus, who struggled with the burdensome luggage cart, along the pathway. Even Bryce found it difficult to stay abreast of Colby, who scurried on his short legs, almost jogging at intervals. By the time Mack and Gus reached the street, Colby and Bryce had a fifty-foot advantage. The street ended in a sweeping cul-de-sac where Colby and Bryce stopped. They stood in the middle of it, motionless and staring straight ahead, when Mack and Gus caught up to them.

It was there as the waitress said, but it wasn't what they expected. The street ended with an extension of the carnival atmosphere that spilled over into a sports store, an indoor arcade, a toy shop, a candy store, and a cluster of themed restaurants. *The Leaning Tower of Pizza* looked off-kilter, a shorter, stubbier and less ornate version of its Italian counterpart in Pisa. *The Great Wall of China* bore a sign along its fortresslike wall, which read Best Chinese Food in Penceville. And there were the competitors: *The Chicken Coop* and *The Fish Wharf*. The latter had a smaller sign beneath the name stating We Don't Bait and Switch.

The Bus Station nestled between *The Coop* and *The Wharf*. Architecturally clever, it resembled an oversized double-decker bus. Red bricks composed the bulk of the building with bricks of other colors affording the trim. Protruding black and white bricks simulated tires on white rims. A sign beneath the establishment's name read Home of the famous Double-Decker referring to a specialty menu item. Customers filled windows on both levels. Outside, a waiting line evidenced the popularity of the eatery.

Colby's face blanched. Bryce's slumped with his mouth gaping. Mack's jaw clenched. Gus gawked and dropped the cart handle, which hit the pavement with a *thud*. The sound stirred Colby and Bryce from their trance.

Bryce stuttered, "S-s-she said it's always busy with people coming and going. She said it's open all day and in the evening. She said people come and go from all over. All over where? Penceville?"

Colby stared at his feet. His shoulders sagged. "Let's go."

The four wandered glumly down the street. No destination. No plan. The promenade they had left shortly before with much promise now seemed a pathway infested with evil trolls. They turned onto it with vacant minds and struggled for any morsel of thought or revelation that might be forthcoming.

"Those benches," Colby said. "Let's sit. My feet—"

A long silence ensued. Penceville had never seen a more sullen quartet.

Bryce broke the silence. "I'm sorry, Lamar. It never crossed my mind that the waitress was talking about something other than a real bus station. I feel like an idiot."

"We all do," Colby said. "She wasn't lying. It was miscommunication pure and simple. She was talking about a restaurant and we were talking about, well, a bus station. With real buses that go somewhere. I hope you didn't tip her too much. She gave us bad dope. Not on purpose but it didn't help. We wasted time; and my feet hurt again. It's all this blasted walking."

"Maybe we should stop at a shoe store and find you some better shoes, Mr. Colby," Mack said. "You been complaining a lot about your feet."

Colby glared at Mack but then considered it. Actually, that was not a bad idea. Colby looked at Mack more pleasantly. "Good thought, Mack."

Mack grinned.

"Does anyone have any ideas?" Bryce asked. "My last one didn't pan out so well."

Gus hadn't said a word. He stared across the park. His eyes revolved in slow circles. "Let's take a ride on the Ferris wheel."

"What!" Colby exclaimed. "Have you given your brains to Mack?"

"Look at it," Gus said. "Look at the top of it. What do you see?"

"It's a Ferris wheel, a big one," Colby said. "It goes way up there—"

"That's the point," Gus said. "It's taller than most anything around here. When you're on top, you can see the whole town and probably for miles around. What if there are things we don't know about, like a highway with cars, or another railroad track, or roads with a bus, or another town? Maybe it's unlikely, but we won't know if we don't look. It's the only idea I have right now."

"Let's ride the Ferris wheel," Colby said, a bit of hope in his voice.

"YOU'D BETTER REMOVE your hat, sir. Sometimes it's windy on top," the Ferris wheel operator said. Colby put his hat in the cart, and the four men climbed into the passenger car.

"Can you stop at the top for a little while each time we go around?" Colby asked. "We're visitors. We'd like to have a good look at the town."

"We're not too busy right now. Sure. Be glad to oblige," the operator said. "You can see everything from up there." The wheel turned raising the car ever higher. Penceville shrank as buildings and streets took on the semblance of a model. At the apex, the wheel stopped.

The spectacular view silenced the car's occupants. A continuous dirt road, providing wagon access, surrounded Penceville, which was pentagonal in shape. Beyond the town, countryside stretched in every direction. The glistening railroad tracks extended in both directions from the red-roofed station. The promenade from the station to town resembled ribbon candy. On a cluster of distant lakes, V-shaped wakes doggedly trailed boats. Dirt roads wove between the lakes and connected the town to the lake region.

With a slight jerk, the wheel resumed its rotation. The car began its descent. Halfway down, the wheel stopped as riders disembarked. Moments later, their car reached bottom.

The operator leaned toward them. "I'll get you back up. No one else is on the wheel, so I can give you five minutes, maybe more, at the top."

"Do those lakes connect to any rivers?" Gus asked.

"No rivers. There are a few streams but that's about it," the operator said.

"Thanks." Gus tipped two fingers to his forehead, giving the man a casual salute.

Within a minute, they reached the zenith. Following the railroad tracks backward led to a vast expanse of farms with interconnecting dirt roads and a longer road extending to the one encircling Penceville. Orchards, whose trees aligned with the precision of a marching band, alternated with growing fields. Moving dots, likely cattle or horses, populated patches of open range. Tracing the tracks forward, a lengthy dirt road ended at a structure with adjacent piles of logs. At that distance, the logs resembled toothpicks. A network of smaller roads wound into the nearby forest. Another road angled away from the forest and terminated in a deep pit. The rock quarry possessed its own collection of paths and scattered buildings.

No roads appeared to extend farther than what they saw from the Ferris wheel although the dense countryside made it impossible to be certain. There were no visible highways, autos, buses, other towns, or additional railroad tracks.

"I'm not seeing anything helpful," Colby said. "Ready to go down?"

"Give me a minute," Gus replied.

"You see something?" Colby asked.

Gus pointed. "That big red-and-white tent cover is the farmers' market where the pumpkin almost hit you. You can see three other places like it, except smaller, around the edge of town. They're probably smaller farmers' markets. Most of the wagons and horses are at the bigger one. It's close to that dirt road that goes to the farms.

"I was looking for an airport. I didn't hear any planes today, so I didn't expect to see one. But you never know. I suppose we could ask. There was one strange thing I noticed." Gus pointed again. "See those black clouds and lightning on the horizon back from where the train came? That's a big storm, but the rest of the sky is as clear as it can be. It's just odd. I don't see much else. Wish I did. It's a pretty view though."

Colby glanced at Gus. Somehow over the years, he had overlooked an intelligence that could have been useful. On the other hand, he also saw glimpses of a sentimental nature that weren't befitting an enforcer. There was more to Gus than he had previously appreciated. He left the thought at that for the time being.

Colby signaled the operator with a thumbs-down. In short order, they stood on terra firma. Colby took a few deep breaths; he felt better simply from the Ferris wheel excursion. *We still have no course of action, but something will come up,* he thought.

"Thank you for indulging us." Colby slipped the operator a tip. "Would you point us to the nearest airport or private air service?"

"I'm sorry, sir, but there's no airport in Penceville. I've never seen a plane here at all," the operator said.

"What about a helicopter or a blimp?" Bryce asked.

"No, sir. None of them either," the operator said. "There was a hot air balloon once, before I came here. Heard the story."

"Tell us," Colby said.

"Well, sir, a visitor decided to stowaway in Penceville. Supposedly a nasty fellow, he refused to return to the train. Over a few months, he built himself one of those hot air balloons. He brought it to the field in this park and took off. Wish I could've seen that."

Bryce's eyes widened. "Did he get away?"

"Not for long. The balloon went up and up. A freak thunderstorm popped up out of nowhere. Lightning hit the top of the balloon. It started coming down and drifted toward the town square. The balloon snagged on the church steeple. It took half a day to bring him down. They said he wasn't right after that."

"He was hurt?" Colby asked.

"No. Just his mind. He kept saying, 'I learnt my lesson—I learnt my lesson,' over and over again. He ran all the way to the train station and stared down the tracks waiting for the next train. As soon as it came, he jumped aboard. No one's heard about him since."

Colby frowned and donned his hat. "Let's find a restaurant. I'm starved."

THEY PASSED SEVERAL fancy restaurants, but Colby wasn't interested. At a shop with outdoor tables, Colby said, "This one's good. We'll eat outside." The deli sat on one of the four corners where two streets intersected. The foot traffic was hectic if not frenetic. Pedestrians dodged and weaved to avoid collisions. A checkered tablecloth of red and white covered the square table. Colby turned his seat to view the streets.

"This isn't your style, Lamar," Bryce said. "Let's go inside. It's too darn busy and noisy out here."

"There's a reason," Colby said. "Keep your eyes peeled for anyone we know. We're running short on luck and ideas. I don't want to return to that blasted train. Fischer would have me over a barrel. I won't stand for it. There has to be somebody or something that can get us out of here."

A waiter arrived with menus and glasses of water. "I'll be back in a few minutes to take your order," he said.

They all picked up a menu except for Gus, who sipped the water.

"Mr. Colby, remember the farmers' markets I showed you from the Ferris wheel?" Gus asked.

"Sure," Colby said. "What's the point?"

"Well, the big one had plenty of wagons and horses by it," Gus said. "We saw roads leading to the farms. Past them, it's hard to say with all the trees and vegetation. I'm wondering if there's a road we couldn't see that leaves this place. If so, maybe it connects to some other town too far away to see from the Ferris wheel."

"Gus could be right," Bryce said. "It's a possibility."

"What are you suggesting, Gus?" Colby asked.

"Why don't I go back to that big farmers' market before it closes and see what I can find out," Gus said. "When you're done eating, you can follow. If there's a way out, I'll line up a ride."

"On a horse wagon?" Mack asked.

"It's better than walking," Colby said.

Gus shaded his eyes and looked for the sun's position. "It's about noon, I'd guess. I'll go now. I'm sure the market's open for most of the afternoon so take your time. Sorry to leave you with the cart, Mack. You remember where that market is, Mr. Colby?"

"We'll find it," Colby said.

Mack looked down at the cart and kicked it.

Chapter 18

Wes flashed a childish smile with his eyes aglow. "One more stop?" It was half wish and half question.

Fred glanced at the store window that had brought Wes to a standstill and then at the store's sign, Square Hardware Store. The shop sat at the intersection of a street with the town square.

"You have no choice," Fred said. "It's calling your name."

About the size of Wes's store, the layout of aisles and goods also appeared similar. Wes walked each aisle inspecting the merchandise as both a consumer and a business owner.

"What do you think?" Fred asked.

"A lot like mine. There's one thing I want to buy."

"What's that?"

Wes led Fred down an aisle. "This dowel jig. I carry one at my store, but this is much better. It accommodates different dowel sizes too."

"What's it for?" Fred asked.

"It helps you line up and drill holes for dowels when you're gluing boards together. Without a jig, it's a very difficult task. Maybe I'll find this at the convention, too, but I don't remember it in the catalogue."

"You've chosen a fine product, sir," the checkout clerk said.

"I've never seen one this clever, but it looks easy to use," Wes said. "It's a woodworker's delight."

"Funny you say that. Another customer said the same thing a few months back. Small world. Enjoy it, sir."

"I hope you're happy now," Fred said as they exited the door.

Fred faced Wes and didn't see the heavyset man who strode toward him. The man looked elsewhere and didn't see Fred either. The collision produced a resounding *thump* that would have knocked Fred off his feet had he not been clutched by the man and braced by Wes.

"I'm so sorry," said a voice behind Fred. "I wasn't watching where I was going."

"I wasn't either," Fred said, turning to see into whom he had crashed.

"Why, Mr. Ables, Mr. Quinton," Gus said. "Are you okay, Mr. Ables?"

"Gus! I knew something big hit me," Fred said. "You caught me quickly too."

"I used to be a boxer, Mr. Ables. My reflexes are still pretty good. I didn't expect to run into you, Mr. Ables, or you, Mr. Quinton."

"I'm glad you didn't run into me," Wes said. "I wouldn't be standing if you did."

"I didn't mean it like that, but I'm glad to see you both," Gus said. "I'd like to talk to you. Some things have been bothering me."

"Sure, Gus," Fred said. "There's a sandwich shop over there. Let's have a bite to eat."

"Mind if we sit outside?" Gus asked. "If I see Mr. Colby coming, I'll have to scoot."

"No problem," Wes said. "Lunch will be on me."

THE FOOD ARRIVED quickly, and the three were hungrier than they'd realized. "I'm not sure where to start," Gus said. "I guess I should first apologize for opening that window on the train. If I hadn't done that, Mack would have or even Mr. Colby. He doesn't like to be told what to do or not to do."

"We know that," Fred said. "You didn't have much choice. At least Mr. Colby seems to be all right."

"Well, thanks to you and Mr. Quinton," Gus said. "He never thanked you, but I didn't expect him to. So I'm saying thank you. I'm sorry, too, for the way the others behave. It's not right to treat people the way they do. Mr. Colby and Senator Bryce aren't very good men. They've both done a lot of bad things. Mack is the meanest person I've ever known. He tripped that steward on the train so fast I couldn't warn him."

"That was Jay," Fred said.

"Yeah, Mack did it to be mean, pure and simple. No reason for it."

"It seems you don't belong with them, Gus," Wes said.

"I don't. I really don't," Gus said. "Not to say I'm perfect. Far from it. I've done plenty of things I'm not proud of and for which I'm sorry. But I'm not like them. I hope you understand that."

"How did you become involved with Colby?" Fred asked.

"Like I told you, I used to be a boxer, and I was pretty good," Gus said. "I lost a few of my early fights, but then I had a long winning streak. A crooked promoter wanted me to throw my next fight. I wouldn't do it. He saw to it that my career was over. My name was mud, and I couldn't find any kind of job anywhere. Somehow Mr. Colby heard about me and gave me a job." Gus rubbed his forehead. "That's an odd thing about Mr. Colby. He can be as cunning and crooked as the worst of them. But, sometimes, he has a soft spot for a person down on their luck, or someone who helped him without being asked.

"At first, the job seemed like normal business, but then it became shady, then crooked, and then finally immoral. I found out he was stealing from widows. What kind of person does that? It happened gradually, not all at once. It's easier to see looking back on it."

"Why didn't you just quit?" Wes asked.

Gus shrugged. "That's complicated. And it wasn't because of money. Mr. Colby paid me and Mack real good, but I didn't stay because of that. I would have been happier digging ditches. You see, I figured if I quit, Mr. Colby would replace me with someone as mean as Mack. They'd do more damage than if I stayed. Especially when I started working against Mr. Colby."

"Against him? What do you mean?" Wes asked.

"Not completely against him. No one could do that because he does a lot of things I wouldn't even know about. When I could, I worked against him. Or if I found out something he did that maybe I could undo a little. That's what I meant. And I had to be careful too. If he ever found out, I probably wouldn't be around for long."

"Can you tell us some of the things you did to thwart Colby?" Fred asked.

Gus leaned toward them and lowered his voice. "Please don't tell anyone else. If any of this leaks out—"

"We won't," Wes said.

"I believe you. I can tell you're both honest," Gus said.

Gus glanced at the street and continued. "Mr. Colby had Mack and me be his enforcers. We'd intimidate people and rough them up a little if we needed to. Sometimes we'd go alone. If it was just me, and Mr. Colby was shaking down a good person, I'd tell them to leave town for a few weeks, so I could tell Mr. Colby they were gone. Or I'd have them pay only part of what Mr. Colby wanted and make up the difference with my own money. Some of these people had families and kids. It just wasn't right."

"How did you keep them quiet?" Fred asked.

"Quiet? What do you mean?" Gus asked.

"I think Fred means, how did you keep Colby from finding out what you were doing?" Wes said.

"That was a worry," Gus said. "Mostly, I tried to help good people. I didn't care about helping crooks or shysters. If I helped someone, I'd have him swear on a Bible that he wouldn't tell anyone. Not even his wife if he was married. And I'd tell him it would get me in big trouble, and Mr. Colby would come after him even harder. Good people won't swear on a Bible unless they really mean it. You can tell it in their eyes. No one ever talked that I know of. If Mr. Colby ever found out, I would know real fast."

"Where did you get a Bible?" Fred asked.

Gus pulled a worn Bible from his jacket pocket. "I'd use this one."

"That looks well used," Fred said.

"I read it when I can," Gus said, "and I've been carrying it for a long time."

Wes tapped Fred's arm. "Why don't you ask Gus about the fight?"

Gus looked perplexed. "What fight?"

"The one between you and Mack in the passenger car," Wes said.

Gus's eyes widened. "You were there?"

"I was," Fred said. "Behind the car door. A steward warned me about it. Saw it all."

Gus squirmed. His cheeks flushed. "What about it?"

"Seemed like you were holding back," Fred said. "Mack hit you with some good shots. That is, before you dazed him with that combo."

"Yeah, Mack's tough," Gus said. "I was holding back. I could've knocked him out from the start. I even held back on that combination. And I could've dislocated his arm but I didn't."

"Why not?" Fred asked.

"I didn't want to hurt him. You know, permanently," Gus said. "I don't like to hurt anybody. Even when I boxed as a pro, I never tried to take someone out for good. I had some tough fights where I gave it everything I had against someone as good as me. But, if I was fighting a journeyman, I'd hold back. Wouldn't want to take away his living."

Fred nodded. "I wondered, too, why you became so upset when Mack called you a cheat. You don't keep the greatest company. I'd think you'd be used to it."

"He called me a cheater, and that's one thing I'm not. I don't cheat. I don't," Gus said. "Just like I wouldn't take a dive when I boxed. That cost me my career. There's a bunch of things I won't do. You gotta keep your dignity. No one else will keep it for you. A man who starts whittling away at his dignity won't have spit left."

"May I ask you something, Gus?" Wes said. "You don't have to answer if you don't want to."

"Go ahead."

"Do you know a Mabel Hawthorne?" Wes asked.

Gus's face turned grim. He clenched his fists. "I sure do. That was one I found out about afterwards, by chance. Mr. Colby did that by himself. I heard he did another one before, but I could never find her name. I know they were both widows. It made me sick."

"Mrs. Hawthorne used to find money in an envelope stuck in her screen door. Later it came by mail after she moved. Was that you, Gus?" Wes asked.

"It was me," Gus said. "It was my own money. I couldn't undo what Mr. Colby did, but I hoped it would help Mrs. Hawthorne."

"You're a good man," Wes said. "That was a kind thing to do."

"That means a lot coming from you, Mr. Quinton," Gus said. "I might as well tell you about your hardware store. Remember when Mack and I were vandalizing your store?"

"Sure. That was after I got Colby mad at me," Wes said.

"Oh, you made him real mad," Gus said. "Do you remember what we did at your store?"

"Sure," Wes said. "Glue containers with holes, paint cans with holes, cement bags sliced open, and spilled nails."

"You have a good memory," Gus said.

"Well, that glue and paint made a mess," Wes said. "It took a long time to clean up. You remember that kind of thing."

"I only did one kind of vandalism. Can you guess which one?" Gus asked.

Wes thought for a moment. "I'd say the nails."

"Why the nails?" Gus asked.

"Well, from what I know about you now, the spilled nails were in a neat pile on the shelf. In a way so they wouldn't fall on the floor."

"You're right," Gus said. "I had to do something in case Mack showed up. I knew the nails would be easy to put back in the box. I didn't want them on the floor where somebody could step on them, or a youngster might get hurt."

"Mack did the others?" Wes asked.

"He did and I'm sorry," Gus said. "You can see that mean streak in what he did."

"Remember that big young man, the wrestler?" Wes asked.

Gus's eyebrows lifted. "How could I forget? I've never seen anyone that big and strong. I'm glad you hired him, though. It helped me convince Mr. Colby to call off the vandalism."

"You threw a punch at him if I remember," Wes said.

"Yeah," Gus said, 'I could've knocked him out with one punch, but I just faked one. He was only a kid and there to help you. Even so, I sure didn't like that headlock. I couldn't move at all; it was scary. He's one strong boy."

"Gus, I'm astonished at what you've told us," Fred said.

"Same for me," Wes said. "You have a lot of good in you. And you're working against tough odds."

"I just wanted you to know I'm not what you probably thought I was," Gus said. "At least, not for a long time. It's hard trying to spoil Colby's plans. Especially since he was the only one who offered me a job. And I have to worry about him finding out. It's awful to be in this position. It wears on you. Maybe it is time for me to quit. Somewhere like Penceville would be nice. The people here seem decent."

"Can I see your train ticket again?" Fred asked.

"Sure," Gus said.

Fred examined the ticket, which was made of cypress. Beneath Gus's name was an F. "That's what I thought I remembered."

Gus frowned. "Is something wrong?"

"No," Fred said. "You might be pleased with what I have to say."

Gus's face relaxed.

"Your ticket takes you to the next stop," Fred said. "The *F* stands for Fontville. It's a lot like Penceville and full of friendly people. I think you'll like it there."

"What about Mr. Colby and the others?" Gus asked.

"They don't leave the train until much later," Fred explained. "They have different tickets. Maybe you noticed when I checked them on the train."

"Yeah, I did and sort of wondered about it," Gus said. "Why do I get off before them?"

"I don't know the answer, but I suspect it's a good thing for you," Fred said.

Gus looked down and slumped in his seat.

"What's wrong?" Wes asked.

"I won't be on the train. I wish I was, but I'm helping Mr. Colby find a way out of Penceville."

"You can return to the train right now," Fred said.

"I can't do that, Mr. Ables," Gus said. "Like I said, Mr. Colby gave me a job when I was down and out. I have to finish helping him now. Maybe when that's done, I can catch the next train by myself."

"You can do that," Fred said. "The ticket doesn't have an expiration date. Just hang onto it."

"I didn't know that," Gus said. "I'd like to leave now but I can't. Hope you understand."

"Don't worry about it, Gus," Fred said. "Things have a way of working out."

"I'm glad we could talk," Gus said. "I feel better now. I should run before Mr. Colby shows up. I'm behind schedule. Thanks for the lunch."

FRED AND WES watched Gus disappear up the street.

"What a surprise," Wes said. "You think you have someone pegged, and you're dead wrong. Count me guilty. Gus is a good man in a difficult spot."

"And he's been in that spot for a long time. That's tough," Fred said. "I shouldn't be surprised. I kind of sensed it from his ticket when I first saw it on the train."

"What does his ticket have to do with it?"

Fred looked away. "Uh—we better buy the champagne before we run out of time. Let's go." He jumped to his feet.

Wes's eyes narrowed and his brow furrowed. "What about the ticket?"

"Later, Wes. Let's get moving."

Wes shrugged. "Okay. You lead and I'll follow."

Chapter 19

Fred led the way. For Wes, the trek seemed like an expedition through uncharted wilderness. Crossing the town square required no particular navigational skill. But afterward, Fred darted down multiple streets. The first winding street departed the square at an odd angle. After several blocks and a series of right and left turns, Fred stopped and pointed. "The store is at the end of that cul-de-sac."

"I should've brought a compass," Wes said. "I hope you remember the way back because I didn't leave any bread crumbs."

Two story specialty shops with contrasting colors lined the street, creating a charming appearance. A minute later, they stood in front of a canary-yellow shop. Windowpanes in a diagonal pattern and interior lace curtains adorned its facade. A decorative sign above the entrance read Fine Spirits, and below it a smaller sign stated: Liquors - Fine Wines - Imported Beers - Specialty Spirits.

Fred gestured. "After you."

A bell jingled when Wes opened the door.

"Be with you in a minute." The muffled voice came from a backroom.

The owner had appointed the cozy shop with displays by category. The shelves brimmed with bottles of all sizes, shapes, and colors. Humidors lined one side of a checkout counter. The dull *ticktock* of a wall clock above the counter echoed in the silence. A corridor extended into a wider hallway that led to the back of the building.

Fred and Wes located the champagne section. The diverse collection befuddled them.

"May I help you? Why Fred, how are you?" Even with their backs turned, the man recognized Fred from his conductor's uniform and stature.

Wes knew the voice and turned. "Dad!"

Father and son stared in mutual disbelief and then embraced with tears in their eyes.

"I thought I'd never see you again," Wes said.

"Same here, Son."

"How did you know Wes is my son, Fred?" Walt Quinton asked.

"I remembered you told me you had a son," Fred said. "When I saw Wes, I thought it might be him because of the resemblance and last name. The only way to be sure was to bring him here."

Walt dried his eyes with a handkerchief. "Let me see if Eric will watch the shop for a bit, so we can go upstairs and talk." He turned his head and spoke loudly to an unseen colleague. "Eric, can you come here please?"

A young man in overalls came through the hallway. Walt introduced him. "You know Mr. Ables, Eric. This is my son, Wes. Eric helps me now and then. Especially when supplies come from the train. Eric, would you watch the store while we go upstairs for a while?"

"Glad to."

"Holler if you need any help," Walt said.

Walter Quinton led them down the hallway and up a set of stairs to a sitting area. Sunlight splashed through the bay window onto a braided rug surrounded by a floral sofa and oversized chairs. A framed family picture, a copy of the print that Wes kept in his satchel, sat on an end table next to the sofa. Between the chairs, his father's Bible rested on a table with a brass floor lamp behind it.

"Follow me and I'll show you the rest." Walt started down the hallway.

A doorway on the right opened to a cheery kitchen with a table and two chairs. A modest bedroom occupied the other side of the hall. The end of the hallway spilled into a sizeable utility room. A card table and folding chairs sat at one end of the room, and a workbench and shelves, jammed with woodworking supplies, filled the other end. Pegboard loaded with tools covered the nearby wall. A stack of lumber perched on a pair of sawhorses. A partially finished project rested on the floor next to the workbench. A broom, dustpan, and trash can sat in a corner.

"What are you building, Dad?" Wes asked.

"A bookcase for one of my friends."

"You have nice tools. How do you like that dowel jig?" Wes asked.

"It works great. Clever and easy to use. A real delight," Walt said. "I'm using it on the bookcase. Purchased it at the hardware store by the town square."

"I bought one there today," Wes said.

"I'm not surprised. You always had a good eye for gadgets. Anyway, this is my gadget room. Sometimes my friends visit and we play cards. I like living here. It's quiet, and the commute to work is just one flight of stairs. Let's head back to the sitting room. Can I bring you anything?"

"We're fine," Fred said.

Fred and Wes parked on the sofa. Walt sat in the chair next to his Bible.

Wes took the family picture from the table and laid it across his lap. "You told Fred you had two sons, Dad? You told him about Tommy, didn't you? We can't forget Tommy." Wes stared at the picture. "Tommy should be here. I promised to bring him home safe." Wes's head sagged. He buried his face in his hands.

"Fred knows," Walt said. "War is hell. Even a just war. Any war. Bad things happen. That's what happened to Tommy. You did your best, Wes. No one has ever faulted you. Tommy wouldn't have either. You need to let it go, Wes. Tommy's in a better place and so is your mother. That's where the justice is."

Wes raised his head and returned the picture to the table. He spoke softly. "I'm sorry. Seeing you and the picture . . . missing Mom and Tommy. It's too much at once. Too much."

Fred patted Wes on the back. "Tell your dad about our friend Timmy."

Wes's eyes brightened. "There's a boy on the train—Timmy. He's eight. He has a cute little dog, Blackie. Timmy has sort of adopted Fred and me. He's a smart little fellow. Reminds me of Tommy at times. I've been keeping an eye on him. I want to make sure he stays safe on the trip."

"You should have brought him," Walt said. "Where is he now?"

"He wanted to stay on the train. A Mr. Holyfield is teaching him how to play chess," Wes said.

"I know the Holyfields; wonderful people," Walt said. "Timmy should be safe on the train or even here in town. Watch him, though. He's a boy. You and Tommy were magnets for trouble, now and then, when you were boys."

"What happened to you, Dad? The sheriff's office put all the pieces together except for your disappearance. They even dragged the river thinking maybe you fell in and drowned."

Walt frowned. "Then you know I went on a binge. I hadn't done that since before I married your mother."

"I know, Dad."

Walt sighed. "I guess I was overwhelmed with your mother dying and losing the house. And like you, I miss Tommy. It's not a good excuse, none of it. The stress got the better of me. I went to that bar by the river because it was out-of-the-way. I didn't want to see anyone I knew. One drink led to another. Soon, I was pretty well gone. It was then I started thinking of what an embarrassment I would be to you and my friends. A drunk in a public place. That made me even more miserable. All of it kept circling in my head. I finally decided I'd leave; leave everything behind and start someplace else. I kept thinking of you, Wes, because you were all I had left. But then I'd think how disappointed and embarrassed you would be of me. Anyway, somehow I must have staggered to the train station and gotten on a train. That's where I was when I came around. The people on the train were very nice. I got off in Penceville and have been here ever since."

"It would have been all right," Wes said. "Everyone knew you were having a tough time. It weighed on me, too, Mom and the house. And I was worried about you too. Everyone would have understood."

"I know that now, but I didn't at that bar," Walt said. "Everything was twisted around; I wasn't thinking straight. That's in the past now."

"The sheriff's office questioned Mack because he was seen in the same bar that night," Wes said. "Apparently you took a swing at him. Do you remember Mack?"

"Oh, sure. I know who Mack is," Walt said. "I remember him at the bar, but it's a bit fuzzy. I don't remember him afterwards, but who knows?"

"Colby, Bryce, Mack, and Gus are in town right now," Fred said.

"In Penceville?" Walt asked.

"Sorry, but they are," Fred said.

"I hate to say it, but I hope they don't stay, that is, unless they've changed their ways," Walt said.

"They're trying to leave Penceville and find a way back," Wes said.

"They're not going on the train?" Walt asked.

"They're supposed to, but they had a spat with Mr. Fischer. Colby vowed to ruin him and take his train," Fred said.

"Fat chance of that happening," Walt said.

"That's their plan," Wes said. "That's why they're trying to leave. To use their crooked contacts."

"It's unlikely you'll run into them," Fred said. "They'll either find a way out or reboard the train. Their tickets aren't for here."

"Thank goodness for that," Walt said. "You watch out for them, Wes. Keep Timmy away from them too. And you be careful, Fred. Colby's a heartless man and a viper."

"We know," Wes said. "I've had my problems with them, too, but I came out on top. Fred has had run-ins with them on the train."

"Your son nailed them good," Fred said.

"I'd like to hear about that," Walt said.

Wes related how Colby called in his hardware store mortgage, the parking problems that Bryce had a role in, and the vandalism by Mack and Gus. His father listened intently at Wes's counterattacks and chuckled at the episode with the young wrestler.

"So Colby actually helped you expand into the lumber business," Walt said.

"That's how it worked out, Dad."

"Maybe you should've thanked him," Walt said. "On second thought, probably not a good idea. He would've thought you spiteful. In any case, someone was looking out for you. I've told you justice eventually prevails. You have to have faith."

"Perhaps that time," Wes said. "Wish it happened more."

"I noticed you're walking better, Son. You've always had that limp since the war."

"It was a steward on the train, Jay. He fixed it," Wes said.

"Why, of course. I should've known. Jay's the master of all things," Walt said. "How's your business?"

"Busy. I have good people working for me and plenty of loyal customers. I'm traveling to the hardware convention to see what's new. Hope someone has that dowel jig. I'd like to carry them in the store. Say, why don't you come with me, Dad? It's in Lafayette Springs."

"Is that where your ticket takes you?" his dad asked.

"Sure does." Wes pulled the ticket from his pocket.

His father recognized the gopherwood and saw L.S. below his son's name. "I'd like to, but I'm busy here. There are only two of these stores and on opposite sides of town. If I closed, it would inconvenience a lot of people. One day I'll come stay with you, promise, if that's okay?"

"Of course it is, Dad," Wes said. 'You know, it's sort of ironic that you run a store like this. You don't—"

"No, I don't' drink except for a beer now and then when my friends come over for cards," Walt said. "I'm surprised to be here, too, but this is where my sponsor brought me. I asked if it was a mistake, but it wasn't. Maybe it's like avoiding temptation or something like that. Anyway, I like running the store and living here. Penceville is nice too. No Colby types that I've ever heard of."

"It's odd that we were coming to this store anyway," Wes said.

"You were coming to buy something?" Walt asked.

"A bottle of champagne. Fred's retiring," Wes said. "We're planning a little party for him on the train."

Walt shook Fred's hand. "Congratulations. Who's taking your place?"

"Joe Croft," Fred said. "He's a good man."

"That he is," Walt said. "Are you traveling to Wes's destination?"

"Same ticket," Fred said.

"Watch after my boy," Walt said.

Fred nodded. "You don't have to ask. We should be leaving. I expected to hear the train whistle by now, but I haven't. I need to get back and find out what's happening. I'm still the conductor."

Walt rose from the chair. "I'll walk you downstairs. We'll pick a special champagne."

Wes gazed around the sitting room and at the picture on the table before following his father and Fred downstairs. He had more questions, but the time had been too short. His dad was okay; that was the important thing.

"Thanks for watching the shop, Eric," Walt said. "See you at cards tomorrow night?"

"I'll be here."

Walt took Fred and Wes to the champagne section. "Let's see. This is a good one. Suitable for a retiring conductor." At the checkout counter, Walt wrapped the bottle. "And let's add a handful of these." He opened the humidors and removed a half-dozen cigars. "This is all my treat, Fred."

"Thank you, Walt," Fred said.

Wes and his father embraced.

"I'll come as soon as I can, Wes," Walt said. "Keep an eye on your little friend, Timmy."

"I will, Dad."

WES GLANCED BACK at the shop as he and Fred strode up the street. His father watched from the window. It was too short a visit. He thought about staying and catching the train the next time it passed through town. Who knew when that would be? Besides, he had an obligation to Timmy. And there was the convention too. *Rats.* Things were too complicated. Always that way, it seemed.

"Thank you, Fred," Wes said. "That was the nicest gift I've ever received."

"I'm glad it worked out that way," Fred said.

"You think there's something wrong at the train?" Wes asked.

Fred glanced toward the sun. "We should've heard two whistles by now. We would've heard them, even in your dad's shop. There's some kind of problem. Could be the train, or the tracks, or something else. We'll be back in less than half an hour. Then we'll find out. Hope it's not serious. I'm worried though."

Wes's mouth went dry; his throat tightened. What if something happened to Timmy and not to the train? he thought. *I'm being irrational. Timmy's on the train, and Colby and his crew are off it. The train's the safest place to be.* "Fred, let's go a little faster." *Rats.*

CHAPTER 20

Gus stopped to catch his breath. He had scurried from the restaurant near the town square to where they first entered Penceville. He scanned the street but didn't see the farmers' market or any landmark that jarred his memory. Speaking with Mr. Ables and Mr. Quinton was an opportunity he had to take. But he also needed to arrive at the market before Mr. Colby or face tough questions. He asked directions from a passerby, who pointed down the road. A few blocks later, the street jogged to the right. He was back at the market with its red and white tent cover. He glanced around; Mr. Colby hadn't yet arrived.

The market bustled. Farmers unloaded bushel baskets and boxes of produce. Shoppers wove their way through haphazard aisles. A makeshift table in front buckled under the weight of hefty pumpkins. The most ponderous, in the center, boasted a blue ribbon.

"Hey, weren't you here this morning?" asked a lanky farmer in bib overalls.

"You have a good memory," Gus said.

"Yeah, you helped carry that big pumpkin across the street after it darn near knocked down that little man with the big fancy hat. I tell ya, that was the funniest thing I seen in a long time. That little guy was dancing back and forth like he was at a Saturday night hoedown. And that pumpkin seemed darned out to get him the way it kept bouncing around. We're still all laughing about it. Why that pumpkin took first place. It's right there on that table with that blue ribbon. Ain't that something? You don't think it's funny?"

"That man is my boss," Gus said.

"Oh. Well, didn't mean no harm. He's okay, I hope?"

"He's fine. He'll be back here in a little while. Maybe you can back off some. It kind of embarrassed him."

"Will do," the farmer said.

"Also, maybe you can help me," Gus said.

"Why sure, if I can."

"We're looking for a wagon ride and a road out of Penceville if there is one."

"I ain't been here too long. Let's go back by the wagons. Some of these fellows been farming here for a while and would know a lot more than me."

They worked their way through the crowded market, squeezing between people and tables. Behind the market, farm wagons clustered near the dirt road that encircled Penceville. A corral of grazing horses ignored the commotion of farmers unloading goods.

"Say, Jack this fellow is—"

"I'll be darned. How are you Gus?"

"You two know each other?" the farmer asked.

"Old friends," Gus said.

"Well, I'll leave so you can catch up."

Jack Bart featured broad shoulders, a chiseled face with black eyes, and black hair that he combed back. His initial impression was menacing, but a closer look revealed mellowness in his eyes.

"Jack. What in the world are you doing here?" Gus asked. "I was here this morning and didn't see you."

"I'm glad you came back," Jack said. "I was at the smaller markets this morning. Just got here."

"I'm trying to recall the last time I saw you. Wasn't it when you told me you we're leaving the business?" Gus asked.

"You're right," Jack said. "And I *did* leave the business."

"I remember what you said back then, 'It grates on my conscience.' Those were your exact words. I never forgot that," Gus said. "Didn't you work for some hotshot that Mr. Colby knows?"

"That I did. Both cut from the same cloth. And that's what happened. My conscience finally got the better of me. That's when I quit."

"What did you do after that?" Gus asked.

"Same thing I'm doing now. Found a job on a farm. I didn't know anything about it at first. Over time, I worked my way up to foreman. Went to the library whenever we went to town; read everything I could about farming. It was nice to be growing things instead of destroying things. Eventually, I bought my own spread. Never regretted quitting the business. Best thing I ever did; should've done it sooner."

"You look good, Jack. Tanned. Relaxed. You look a little thinner too."

"That's the hard work. It takes the fat right off. I'm in better shape now than ever. What are you doing here, Gus? Did you come to stay?"

Gus frowned and lowered his head. "No. Just passing through with Mr. Colby, Senator Bryce, and Mack."

"You still work for Colby?" Jack asked.

"Sort of," Gus said.

"What does that mean?"

"Well, it's like you and your conscience. Mine bothered me, too, and I've been working against Mr. Colby at the same time I'm working for him. He'll be here shortly. Please don't say anything."

"I won't. Why didn't you just quit?" Jack asked.

"By staying with him, I stopped some bad stuff and tried to fix some of the damage he did. If I quit, I couldn't have done that. He would have replaced me with someone worse."

"You put yourself in a risky spot," Jack said. "I admire what you did. I think I took the easy way out."

"I look at you and wonder if I made the right choice," Gus said. "Sure is nice around here."

"Amen to that. First-class farmland too. You must have gotten a train ticket, Gus?"

"I did. I'm supposed to get off in a place called Fontville. I think it's the next stop."

"From what I've heard, it's a lot like here," Jack said. "I'm sure you'll like it. Good for you."

"Except we're not returning to the train," Gus said. "Mr. Colby wants to leave here. You can't go back by train or any other way we've found. In fact, that's why I'm here."

"I'm confused," Jack said.

"From the Ferris wheel we saw all the dirt roads. We wondered if any of them leave here, so Mr. Colby can return."

"That I don't know. I've never heard of anyone leaving Penceville except by train. Heck, I've never heard of anyone wanting to get out some other way. Running the farm keeps me busy, so I don't know all the roads. That doesn't mean there's not a road out. I just don't know. I'm trying to think who might know."

"Is this your wagon, Jack?"

"Sure is."

"Can you take us to your farm?" Gus asked. "Maybe we'll find out something about the roads. We don't know what else to do."

"Fine with me," Jack said. "You sure Mr. Colby and the Senator won't mind riding on a farm wagon? Mack too, for that matter."

"At this point, they'd probably be happy to be off their feet. Especially, Mr. Colby. He's been moaning about his feet all day."

"He still wears those high-class shoes?" Jack asked.

"The finest. But they're not made for walking. And we've been doing some hiking today."

"I just thought of something," Jack said. "One of my farmhands has explored all over this area. He owns a good horse, and sometimes he's gone for days. If anyone would know about roads or trails, it's him. His name is Pete. He'd be the one to talk to."

"Is he at the farm now?" Gus asked.

"Should be. We're harvesting today. You said Colby and the others will be here soon?"

"Any minute now," Gus said.

"Give me a hand unloading the rest of the wagon, so we'll be ready to go."

JACK AND GUS relaxed under the tent cover and sipped cider while they watched for Colby.

Gus had removed his jacket and tie, loosened his shirt, and rolled up the sleeves. He stared at his powerful forearms and flexed his fingers. Gnarled hands, from old fractures and injuries, reminded him of his boxing years. A light breeze slipped through the tent, carrying the scent of fresh-baked bread from a nearby bakery. Gus closed his eyes and smiled. Serenity. That was what he felt. He couldn't remember when he had last felt this much at ease.

Fred Ables, Wes Quinton, and Jack. Gus had talked with all three today. Right here in Penceville. They were good people. He thought about Fontville and wondered if he would know anyone there. What would he do there? Where would he live? It didn't matter for now. He needed to fulfill a last obligation to Mr. Colby, who had given him something when no one else would: a job. It turned out to be a lousy job that became worse over time. Fontville seemed a dream. It would have to wait; maybe he'd never get there. That's what worried him because he really wanted to.

THE LANKY FARMER who recounted the pumpkin tale to Gus giggled when a cart arrived bearing the very same short man with his top hat. Stacked luggage filled the bulk of the cart. The man with the tall hat sat in the back, his legs dangling. Two other men pulled the cart, struggling with the weight of its contents. Colby appeared mortified and in no mood to talk. Gus yanked the laughing farmer's overalls. The farmer turned toward Gus, noticed the solid forearms and clenched fists, and decided Gus's expression meant he should stop. The laughing ceased.

"The legendary Mr. Colby," Jack said.

Gus rose to greet his colleagues. "I was expecting you sooner."

"We were delayed," Bryce said. "Can we move this cart off the street? Lamar's not too happy right now."

Gus grabbed the handle and pulled the cart toward Jack. "We'll move you out of the sun, Mr. Colby," Gus said.

Jack brought chairs. Colby remained in the cart and stared straight ahead. Bryce and Mack each sank unsteadily into a chair.

"Where were you?" Gus asked.

"All this walking has been tough on us, especially Lamar," Bryce said. "His feet mostly. His shoes aren't meant for it. We stopped at a shoe store to buy something better."

"Find anything?" Gus asked.

Bryce explained, "They had all kinds, but the only thing that fit was a pair of fleece-lined workman's boots. He tried them on. They felt good, so he bought them. But he won't wear them because they look funny with his suit. The pant legs don't fit over the top of the boots and stay bunched up on top of them."

"That's why you pulled him in the cart?" Gus asked.

"That's it," Bryce said.

"Where are the boots?" Gus asked.

"On the cart," Bryce said. "Hey Mack, pass me the box with the boots."

"These are nice," Gus said. "Good leather, steel tipped toe, soft lining."

"Very chic," Jack said.

"Fellows, you remember Jack Bart," Gus said. "He used to work for one of Mr. Colby's friends."

"Sure, I remember you," Mack said.

Bryce and Colby glanced toward Jack and nodded.

"Jack runs one the farms. He has a wagon and horses," Gus said. "He's willing to take us back with him. Jack doesn't know if there are any roads out of here, but one of his farmhands goes exploring all over on his horse."

"If anyone knows a way out, it's Pete," Jack added.

Colby stirred from his near catatonic state. "How soon can we go?"

"Right now if you want," Jack said.

"The sooner, the better," Colby said from the back of the cart. Gingerly, he stood on his aching feet. He grasped the nearby table to help maintain his balance. Lamar Colby had picked the wrong structure to lean on. The improvised table of sawhorses and a sheet of plywood already bowed under the weight of pumpkins on display from the day's earlier contest. A *crack* split the air. The middle edge of the plywood fractured from the added weight. Colby jerked backward and fell on his derriere. His top hat tumbled between his open legs. The pumpkins wobbled and then rolled into the break of the sagging plywood. Colby's hat crumpled when the prize pumpkin, its blue ribbon proudly attached, landed upright between his legs with a *thud.* The prize pumpkin mercifully deflected the remaining pumpkins to the right and left.

"Egads!" Colby exclaimed.

Gus moved the pumpkins and helped Colby to his feet. "You okay, boss?"

Mack held the damaged hat, which resembled an accordion. "Here's your hat, Mr. Colby."

Gus heard cackles originating from behind the market. It was the laughing farmer, who, no doubt, had witnessed what transpired.

"Maybe we can stuff newspaper in your hat to fix the shape," Mack said.

Colby looked at his hat, glanced at the pumpkins, and stared at Bryce. "Fischer will pay for this."

"Let's go to the wagon," Gus said. "You ready, Jack?"

"All set."

Gus and Jack helped Colby through the farmers' market and onto Jack's wagon. Mack brought the cart. He transferred the luggage and the box of boots onto the wagon bed where Colby sat.

"Go ahead and climb on," Gus told Bryce and Mack. "I'll return the cart to the tent."

Gus walked to the tent. The laughing farmer slapped his knees, hooted, and cackled about Colby's misfortunes. Others joined in. With his back to Gus, he didn't see Gus's glare. One by one, the other men noticed Gus and ceased laughing. The farmer finally sensed a presence and peeked over his shoulder. One look at Gus and his face turned ashen. He ran from the market and rushed down the street. He glanced over his shoulder to make sure that Gus was not in pursuit.

Gus returned to the wagon and joined Jack in the seat.

"Where we're you?" Mack asked.

"It was a laughing matter," Gus said.

"Huh?"

"I was getting rid of some trash," Gus said.

"Okay," Jack said, shrugging his shoulders. "Let's get moving. Giddyup."

CHAPTER 21

Fred and Wes made good time through the crisscrossing streets of Penceville as they proceeded toward the train. Even at his father's shop, Wes sensed Fred's unease. It wasn't until Fred mentioned the absence of the train whistle that he understood why. Most people react to something that's happened, but few react to something that hasn't happened that should have. The dog that didn't bark that should have. In this case, the train whistle that should've sounded but didn't. Of course, Fred would be attuned to the train's schedule. Still, the intuitive deed impressed Wes.

They reached the entrance arch and promenade that ended at the train station. The back of the arch held a sign so clichéd as to be almost meaningless: "We hope you enjoyed your stay in Penceville." Wes glanced at the words. He *had* enjoyed his stay. In fact, those words understated his joy. The anguish of his father's disappearance had departed. He and Fred reveled in the pleasant surprise of Gus's revelations. Gus had placed himself in harm's way for the sake of goodness. That was it, in a nutshell. Many would not have done that. Wes felt a newfound respect and admiration for Gus. Was there something mystical about Penceville? The visit had indeed been like a cozy quilt. It was a different place without a doubt.

Timmy. Wes felt certain he was okay. The absence of the whistle probably resulted from a train problem like Fred said. Wes had become attached to the boy. His presence reminded Wes of having a little brother again. Maybe his father was right. Perhaps he should've brought him to town. *I'm sure he's all right.*

"Do you hear that?" Fred asked.

The sound of spirited children's voices drifted to the promenade. They played on a grassy field adjoining the train station. Scattered adults kept a watchful eye and occasionally intervened.

"Children from the train," Fred said. He left the promenade and angled toward the field. "Looks like Jay, Mr. Holyfield, and some of the stewards are supervising them. There's a definite train delay."

The older children played kick ball. So did Blackie. The dog darted back and forth across the field each time the ball changed directions. Smaller children played tag, turned somersaults, spun like tops, and attempted cartwheels. The cacophony of voices grew louder as Fred and Wes approached.

"Hi," Jay said. "I didn't hear you coming with all this wonderful noise. We're delayed. Thought we'd give the children some fresh air and tire them out a bit."

"Is there a problem with the train?" Fred asked.

"No. The train's fine," Jay said. "It's Gaash Pass. They've had rains up that way. A mud slide covered the tracks. Mr. Fischer knows the details. We won't be leaving until sometime tomorrow. That's all I know. We brought the children out for a while before it cools down. Oh, and Joe Croft boarded a half hour ago; said he'd help in any way he can."

"Good," Fred said. "I'll go talk to Mr. Fischer right away. No need for you to go with me, Wes. I'll fill you in when I know more."

Wes watched Timmy chase the ball. He exhaled as his body relaxed from a tension of which he hadn't been conscious.

"YOU MUST BE tired after all the walking, Mr. Quinton," Jay said. "Let's sit on the bench. How have your feet held up?"

"My feet are wonderful, thanks to you. And please call me Wes."

"Okay, Mr. Quin—I mean, Wes."

Wes set the shopping bags on the bench. "May I ask a favor of you, Jay?"

"Sure, anything."

"I bought a gift for Fred for his retirement. I need to paint part of it. Could I use the utility room on the train? Won't take long."

"Sure. You need help?" Jay asked.

"No, thanks though. Was it your idea to bring the children outside?"

"Actually, Mrs. Holyfield thought of it. The children can become rambunctious on the train. The fresh air does them good. I like being out with them too."

The kick ball rolled to the bench with Blackie and Timmy not far behind. Jay picked up the ball and threw it halfway across the field. That delighted the children who watched it arc high into the afternoon sky.

"Hi, Mr. Quinton," Timmy said. "Where have you been? I haven't seen you all day."

"In town shopping. What've you been doing?" Wes asked.

Blackie looked at Wes and drew closer, smelling his shoes. "Go say *hi*," Timmy said.

Blackie put his front paws on Wes' knee as Wes scratched behind the dog's ears. Blackie seemed to have a smile on his face. Wes reached into his jacket pocket. "If I remember correctly." He drew out a dog biscuit.

Blackie turned in a circle and barked. Wes handed the treasure to Blackie. The dog carried it a few feet away and started chewing on it. "Blackie sure likes you, Mr. Quinton," Timmy said.

"Maybe it's the biscuits. He's a fine fellow," Wes said. "Now, you didn't tell us what you've been doing."

"I forgot you asked," Timmy said. "Mr. Holyfield taught me how to play checkers. He said he'd teach me chess if I got good at checkers. Well, I did. Now I'm learning chess. It's a whole lot harder. Mr. Holyfield said it's a *what-ifs* game. You have to think ahead a whole lot of what-ifs for all the different pieces. I know how all the pieces move, but the what-ifs make it hard. I've only won one game. I think Mr. Holyfield let me win. He made some dumb moves that even I probably wouldn't do. I'm going to keep practicing. Mr. Holyfield is a good teacher. He said being able to play chess will help your mind get sharper, whatever that means. That's the only thing that worries me. I don't want my head to grow pointy."

"Mr. Holyfield means it will help make you smarter," Jay said.

"Your head won't get pointy," Wes said.

"Whew, that's good," Timmy said. "I was kind of worried. I looked in the mirror before I came outside. Time to play some more. Come on, Blackie."

"Fred and I bought Timmy a nice chess set in town," Wes said after the boy was out of hearing range. "Sounds like he plans to stick with it. I'd better take these bags on the train. I should paint now while the train's still. You'll watch Timmy for me?"

"Will do," Jay said.

FRED FOUND MR. Fischer and Joe Croft in the dining car. He slipped into the booth next to Joe.

"Hello, Fred," Fischer said. "Joe's getting a head start on the conductor's job with the problem we have."

"I feel like I'm looking in the mirror, Joe. You look great in that uniform," Fred said. "Jay told me there was a mud slide at Gaash Pass because of rains up that way."

"That's right," Fischer said. "We've had problems there before. For you, Joe, it's one of those things a conductor needs to be aware of. We perform routine track inspections and sometimes extra ones in areas prone to trouble. About an hour ago, a horseback rider informed me of the landslide. Crews are clearing it. They don't expect to finish until tomorrow morning. After they finish, it'll take another hour to inspect the track the avalanche buried. The bottom line, we won't be leaving until tomorrow. About mid morning, we'll head for the sawmill to restock firewood for the locomotive. Then we'll leave from there."

"Does the sawmill know?" Fred asked. "And what about the passengers?"

"The rider stopped at the sawmill, so they know about the mud slide, but they don't know we'll be there tomorrow. Perhaps you would send someone to tell them. Joe informed the passengers about the delay. No one was upset; so we're covered there."

"Good," Fred said. "I'll send someone to the sawmill."

"You said this Gaash Pass has been a problem before, Mr. Fischer," Joe said.

"It's roughly fifty miles ahead," Fischer said. "Fred will point it out when we go by. There will probably still be crews working on the right side of the pass. The Gaash Pass cuts through an area of low rolling hills. The hills are mostly clay. They absorb water and are prone to landslides with prolonged rain. The left side of the pass is cut well back, and a retaining wall diverts mud slides. The right side is higher. Construction crews need to cut it back further and extend the retaining wall, which we've been working on. Sometimes a mud slide on the right will overrun the retaining wall. The clay is miserable when it turns to mud and hard as a rock when it's dry. It's a challenge no matter what. It's a great place to work only for those needing to improve on the virtue of patience. Other than that, it's miserable."

"Anything else I need to know, Mr. Fischer?" Fred asked.

"That's all I know at this point."

Fred rose. "I'd better send someone to the sawmill before it gets too late."

"I have plenty to learn," Joe said. "I'll tag along, Fred."

"After you've done that, Fred, I need to ask you about something," Fischer said. "If you see Wes, bring him too."

"You'll be here?" Fred asked.

"Will be, unless something else comes up."

WES BOARDED THE train and hurried back to the utility room with the shopping bags. He removed a slender brush and an undersized bottle of beige enamel from one of the bags. Carefully, he unwrapped the package from the antique shop. The modifications would take just a few moments but required a steady hand and good lighting. The small workbench near the ticket blanks was a perfect place to do the work. Wes dipped the tip of the brush into the paint. Meticulously, he changed what had been a maroon color into beige. Satisfied, he placed the gift for Fred in a nook where the paint could dry. Wes grabbed the shopping bags and headed toward the caboose.

FRED ENTERED THE caboose with Joe behind him. "Hey, Wes. Thought you might be here."

"Did you find out more about what's happening?" Wes asked.

"A little," Fred said. "I'll fill you in on the way to the dining car. Mr. Fischer wants to talk to us."

"Me too?" Wes asked.

"You too."

"Do I have time to empty these shopping bags?"

"Be quick," Fred said.

Wes handed the champagne and cigars to Fred. He placed the dowel jig on a shelf. The small package with the mechanical toy dog slid into his pocket. "Should we take the chess set?" Wes asked Fred. "We might be able to catch Timmy when he boards the train. It's from both of us."

"Timmy *is* hard to track down. Good idea," Fred said. "Joe, we're meeting with Mr. Fischer. Can we bring you anything from the dining car?"

"I'm fine," Joe said. "I'll continue studying this conductor's manual."

FRED AND WES joined Fischer in the dining car booth.

"Thanks for coming, Wes," Fischer said. "I wanted to hear your thoughts about something."

"Happy to oblige," Wes said.

"Did either of you see Mr. Colby and his group in town today?" Fischer asked.

"We saw Gus and actually had a pleasant conversation with him," Fred said. "We were surprised by what he told us. Didn't see the others, but they were somewhere in town."

"Gus is a better man than most people appreciate," Fischer said. "From that perspective, he doesn't trouble me. The other three do. I thought they might have returned to the train by now. I assume they're still searching for a way to leave Penceville."

"That's the impression Gus gave us," Wes said. "If I know Colby, he'll look at the remotest possibility before he'd set foot on this train again."

"Therein resides my concern," Fischer said. "It is rather unlikely they will find a way out. Should that prove true, it is probable they will return to the train as a last resort. Under that circumstance, Mr. Colby is likely to feel like a caged animal. He might become more vengeful, more dangerous, and more treacherous. I am worried about what he may be capable of doing. Do you know how he might react, Wes?"

Wes shrugged. "That's difficult to predict, especially if he feels trapped. His temper is also an issue because it could aggravate anything else he does. Colby and Bryce are high stakes con artists. Mack and Gus have been the muscle, but now we know that Gus is okay. That leaves Mack as a worry. Could Colby or Bryce become violent? I think it's unlikely, but I wouldn't swear to it. People do strange things when they snap. I saw plenty of that in the war. Do you really think they'll be back?"

"I think it likely," Fischer said. "My concern is for the others on the train."

"Not to argue, Mr. Fischer," Wes said, "but I know Colby pretty well. If there's a way out, he'll find it. It seems like there should be some way to leave. If you're troubled about Colby boarding the train, couldn't you go to the sawmill now? Then take the train partway to the pass where the mud slide is. That way, Colby can't reboard the train. You'll have no worries about the other passengers."

Fred straightened his back and flinched as he glanced at Wes. "Wes, Mr. Fischer knows what he's—"

Fischer placed his hand on Fred's arm. "Wes, that's a good thought, but I also wouldn't want the fine people of Penceville left at Colby's mercy. On the train, we at least have some control of the situation. There are fewer people on the train than in Penceville. I know Penceville and the surrounding area better than anyone. For Mr. Colby to find a way out would require a miracle. I don't think he believes in them. We should be prepared for their return to the train."

"I understand," Wes said. "Probably the best we can do is watch them like before. I'll try to sit close enough to eavesdrop. If we know what they're planning, we may be able to stop them. The other factor is Gus. What he knows could certainly help us."

"Gus is due to depart in Fontville," Fred said. "Hopefully he will. I'll talk to him then. If Colby and the others return, I'll direct them to the same seats and keep other passengers away from that car. Other than what we've discussed, I can't think of anything else."

"Fred, we should keep tabs on Timmy if Colby reboards the train," Wes said. "Timmy likes to roam around."

"I'll keep Timmy away from them," Fred said. "Don't worry about him. Do you have any other ideas, Mr. Fischer?"

"Unfortunately, no. We'll do the best we can. Thanks for your input. If you'll excuse me, I need to speak with the engineer," Fischer said, standing to leave.

THE JINGLE OF children's voices cascaded through the dining car when the rear car door opened. Jay marched up the aisle, kick ball in hand, followed by tired youngsters in tandem.

"Mind if we borrow Timmy?" Fred asked as Jay passed their booth.

"All yours," Jay said.

Wes moved the gift from the seat to the tabletop when Timmy approached. The store clerk had wrapped it in blue paper and added a red ribbon. "We have a gift for you, Timmy," Wes said. "Have a seat next to Mr. Ables."

"For me! Really?" Timmy sat. Blackie jumped onto his lap and sniffed the package.

Fred rumpled Timmy's hair. "Just for you."

"What is it?" Timmy tried to loosen the ribbon.

"Let me do that for you." Wes unfolded a pocketknife and sliced through the ribbon.

Timmy removed the paper, his face beaming with surprise. "A chess board!"

"Unlock the clasp on the side," Wes said. "Open it slowly. Maybe there's something inside."

Timmy cautiously unfolded the board. An insert held glistening alabaster chess pieces. Timmy removed a black rook and a white knight, examining their detail. He returned the pieces to their spots and hugged Fred and then Wes. "Holy cows. It's the nicest thing I ever saw. Thank you, Mr. Ables. Thank you, Mr. Quinton. Now I'll really get good at chess."

"Now, close the board and lock it," Wes said to Timmy. "Always double check the clasp so the chess pieces don't fall out."

Timmy closed the board, secured the lock, and checked it again. "Like that, Mr. Quinton?"

"Perfect, Timmy," Wes said.

"Can I show it to Mr. Holyfield?" Timmy asked.

"It's yours, Timmy," Fred said.

"Gee thanks." Timmy grasped the set in both hands, as if it was an egg balanced on a spoon, and walked up the aisle as Blackie followed.

"We made a good choice," Fred said.

"Couldn't have done better," Wes said. "The hug was worth a thousand chess sets."

"I just thought of something," Fred said. "I should brief Joe on Colby and his group in case they reboard the train. Joe doesn't know anything about them."

"Hadn't thought about that," Wes said. "You're right; he needs to know."

"Better do it now," Fred said. "Who knows when they might show up?"

WES THOUGHT ABOUT Mr. Fischer's pointed question about how dangerous Colby could be. The return of Colby to the train would be bad news. That he was sure of, but the nature of the looming disaster wasn't so predictable. Wes stared out the window of the dining car, his brow furrowed equally in contemplation and concern.

"Mind if I join you, Mr. Quinton? That is, if you're not busy," a pleasant female voice asked.

Wes looked up and quickly stood. "Please do, Mrs. Holyfield. I'm sorry. I didn't see you. I was thinking about something. Please call me Wes."

She gracefully slid into the booth across from him. "And you must call me Marielle. You did look rather pensive."

"It's been a busy day," Wes said. "The children and babies must keep you busy too."

"They do. The children are napping after their outing. That is, all except for Timmy. He's playing chess with Mr. Holyfield on that beautiful set you and Fred gave him. That was thoughtful. The babies are sleeping too. I thought I'd take a short coffee break."

Wes signaled for two cups of coffee, which the waitress promptly delivered. "How many children and babies are you caring for?" Wes asked.

Marielle took a sip of coffee while calculating. "Counting the young mother's baby, there are four babies and seven children."

"That's a lot of responsibility," Wes said. "I admire you and your husband for doing it."

"Jonathan, that's Mr. Holyfield, loves children. I couldn't do it without him. Of course, Jay loves them, too, and is always helping. If you can't find Jay, that's where he is. He's been that way ever since he was a boy."

"Jay is remarkable," Wes said. "I've never met anyone kinder."

"I'm glad to hear you say that about my son," Marielle said.

"I didn't know he was your son," Wes said. "It's obvious that kindness runs in your family."

"That's very nice of you to say."

"Are all of the babies and children going to homes?" Wes asked.

"Every one of them has relatives waiting for them," Marielle said.

"That's a relief," Wes said. "There's nothing more important than family."

"That's so very true. I'd best head back and check on everyone. It was nice to talk to you, Wes."

Wes stood as Marielle rose to leave.

WES SIGNALED THE waitress for a coffee refill. Through the window, he saw Nick and Daniel stroll onto the station platform, each with a shopping bag. Minutes later, they sat in the dining car booth with Wes.

"We've been dreaming about this pie all the way back to the train." Daniel took a bigger bite than he should have. "We came back double time. Thought we missed the train. Never heard the two whistles Mr. Ables told us to listen for."

"Actually, the train won't leave until tomorrow morning," Wes said. "There was a mud slide on the tracks that's being cleared."

"Must have been a big one," Nick said. "Anything else happen while we were in town?"

Wes thought for a moment. "Mr. Ables will retire at the end of this run. Joe Croft will be the new conductor. Nice fellow; you'll probably meet him. Also, Mr. Fischer believes Mr. Colby and the others will reboard the train. He's concerned about it."

"They're not the friendliest bunch," Nick said. "I guess I'd be worried too."

"The only decent one is Gus," Wes said. "Mr. Ables and I ate lunch with him in town. In fact, he's a nice guy."

"That's something. Go figure," Nick said.

"If Colby returns to the train, we'll have to watch them again," Wes said. "Colby's likely to be peeved to the limit." Wes turned his attention to the men's packages. "Didn't know you were shoppers."

"I bought clothes and books," Nick said. "I like to read. Daniel dragged me through every antique shop he found. Adding to his collection, as usual."

"What do you save, Daniel?" Wes asked.

"Old police stuff. Badges, hats, medals, handcuffs, nightsticks, and things like that. I've been collecting since I was a boy. Found a bunch in town today. In good shape too."

"Can you show me?" Wes asked.

Daniel's eyes lit up. "Sure. I'll include the history too."

An hour later, Wes sipped a third cup of coffee while Daniel continued his show and tell. The contents of his shopping bag covered the table.

CHAPTER 22

Joggled now and then by ruts and potholes, Colby, Bryce, and Mack watched Penceville grow smaller from the back of the farm wagon as it rolled along the dirt road. The luggage bumped against and annoyed Mack, who elbowed it back into place. The ride still beat hauling the darn stuff around Penceville. A glum Colby sat silently. Content, Bryce watched farms and orchards dawdle by.

"You okay back there?" Jack asked.

"Bumpy," Bryce replied. "How much farther to your farm?"

"About three miles; at the end of the road," Jack said.

Gus perched on the driver's bench next to Jack. He examined their surroundings. "Nice country. I see why you like farming."

"Surely do," Jack said. "It's harder than most people think. You can't cheat or coerce crops and critters. If anything, it's the other way around."

"Hadn't thought about it like that," Gus said. "Do these roads that branch off go to other farms?"

"Every one of them goes to a neighbor. See the farmhouse straight ahead? That's home. Five more minutes."

Jack stopped the wagon halfway around the circular drive. A cobblestone walkway led to a house where steps rose to a covered porch. The house, a boxy wooden structure, stood two stories tall. Red storm shutters contrasted with the off-white house color. A porch swing, three rockers, and two plain chairs testified to the porch's popularity. Worn floor paint under the seats confirmed it.

Gus and Mack helped Colby dismount from the wagon, climb the steps, and drop into a chair.

"Bring those boots from the wagon," Colby said to no one in particular.

Gus retrieved the box. Colby removed the boots and stared into the distance as he caressed the fleece lining. He had made up his mind. The patent leather shoes came off. A disgusted grimace crossed his face as he tossed them into the box. He rubbed his feet, inserted them inchmeal into the boots, and laced the boots to the top. All eyes watched as he rocked his feet back and forth. The pant legs bunched up at the top of the boots. It didn't matter. Colby looked at the others. "That's better. I don't care if it looks ridiculous."

"Doesn't look bad at all," Jack said. "Pass me your hat. I'll see what I can do with it, Mr. Colby."

A few minutes later, Jack returned with a hat less deformed than before. "I put a roll of cardboard inside and stuffed paper in to hold it." He placed it on Colby's head. "Looks better than it did. Sit tight, I'll go find Pete. He's our explorer. Get something to drink if you're thirsty."

GARBED WITH A vest, a ten-gallon hat, and boots, he looked more like a cowboy than a farmhand. A droopy moustache framed a nonchalant grin. Years in the saddle had resulted in a touch of a bowlegged gait.

"This is Pete," Jack said when they reached the porch. "Pete's been all over these parts, Mr. Colby. If anyone can help you, it's Pete."

"We're searching for a way to leave Penceville," Colby said. "And not by train. Specifically, we want to return to where we came from. Is there a way to do that?"

Pete tugged at his moustache. "I reckon there should be. Now it won't be by road. I've travelled every road there is. Actually, me and Dollar, my horse. Some of the roads turn into paths; they peter out pretty quick. You have to make your own way after that. It'd be easy to get lost. I always carry a compass to be on the safe side. Unless you're used to camping, it's not the way I would try."

"What else is there," Bryce asked.

Pete removed his hat and thought for a moment. "Well, sir. You could walk along the train tracks. I been up and down those tracks both ways. The way the train goes, I've been all the way to Gaash Pass. That's about fifty miles. The other way, I been about the same. It's easy riding next to the tracks, and there's a line shack about every twenty miles."

"What's a line shack?" Colby asked.

"It's a cabin where work crews or inspection crews can stay overnight. They have bunks, a stove, cooking gear, and a table and chairs. Some of them have a well with a hand pump. I've stayed in some myself. They're pretty nice. Beats camping, for sure. Most of them have wood already cut for the stove and extra cans of food. The crews are good about that."

"So we could follow the tracks back and stay in the line shacks?" Colby asked.

"I don't see why it couldn't be done," Pete said. "It'd be hard to walk it. If you traveled light, you could probably get by with six horses."

"Six horses?" Bryce stammered.

"Yeah. Six would probably do you. You'll need the extra two for carrying supplies. Y'all know how to ride don't you?"

Pete watched Colby and the others shake their heads. "That's a problem," Pete said. "You can learn but if none of you knows horses, you can run into trouble. The horses need care too."

"We can't do horses," Colby said. "That is, unless you come with us. I'll make it worth your while. I'm a banker."

"It would sure be an interesting trip, Mr. Colby, and I do appreciate the offer," Pete said. "We're just too busy here. What you're talking about may take a few weeks or more."

"There must be a way," Colby said. "Following the tracks back is the obvious solution but how? Too bad there's not some kind of car you drive down the tracks."

"That's it, Mr. Colby!" Pete exclaimed. "I just remembered. There is a car. And it's faster than walking and a whole lot less trouble than horses."

"Really? A car?" Colby said.

"It's called a handcar," Pete said. "It has four wheels, a platform, and a seesaw pump that you push and pull to keep moving. If all four of you pumped hard, you could go close to fifteen miles an hour.

With normal pumping, you could probably average eighty miles a day where the track's flat."

"Where do we find such a car?" Colby asked.

"That's what I remembered," Pete said. "There's one in a shed next to the track not a half mile from here. I saw another handcar shed near Gaash Pass the other way. There's probably more of them up and down the line. The crews use the handcars to travel along the line for inspections and repairs."

"Jack, can you take us in the wagon to see this handcar?" Colby asked.

"Sure," Jack said. "Everybody hop in. Sit with me, Pete, so I don't miss it."

THE HANDCAR SHED, a drab wooden structure, connected to the track by a plank runway. Pete opened the shed doors and rolled out the handcar. A steel frame with a wooden platform sat above four pressed-steel wheels. An A-shaped support in the middle of the platform held an I-shaped structure that pivoted at its apex, allowing as many as four men to propel the vehicle. One side of the car had a foot operated braking mechanism. A makeshift bench ran the length of the car on each side. The benches sat over the wheels so as not to impinge on the platform. The benches seated extra riders or a pumper taking a break.

"This is it," Pete said. "I worked on a train crew for a while, so I know how it works."

The others observed as Pete rolled one set of wheels onto one rail and maneuvered the back set close to the other. Pete signaled Gus for a hand. With a quick lift, all four wheels of the handcar rested on the track.

"It'll be easy with four of you," Pete said. "The line shacks all have a set-off platform so you can park the handcar off the track. There are plenty of set-off platforms along the tracks too. You want it off if you're not using it or if you hear a train coming. Most of those who die on handcars are killed by the train they didn't see coming. To go, just turn a wheel with your foot to begin moving or push from the ground. Then start pumping. The handcar will coast to a stop, or you can use the foot break."

Pete pumped the car thirty feet down the track and back while the others watched. "You can stack luggage and supplies in the middle of the car next to the support and rest on the bench if you're not pumping. There's a bench on each side, so you can keep the handcar balanced if two of you take a break. Now you try it. Two at a time. Go about a hundred feet, stop, and then come back."

Colby bounded onto the handcar. "Come on, F.W. Let's get this thing moving."

Bryce stepped onto the car and grabbed the pumping handle. Colby pressed his boot to a wheel and initiated a forward movement, which accelerated as the two men pumped. They were back where they started in a matter of minutes.

"Let's see you beat that," Colby exclaimed.

Gus and Mack repeated the exercise.

"Now all four of you," Pete said. "Be careful because it's more crowded. See what kind of speed you can reach with all of you pumping. On the way back, take turns so you can try the benches."

Pete watched the handcar accelerate as it moved a hundred yards up the track. Returning, the four men switched about on the platform and benches.

"I think you have it down," Pete said. "Now, take the handcar off the track. It's the reverse of how we put it on. Lift one end off the tracks, then twist it and drag the other side off." Pete observed their efforts with an approving nod.

"Just one more thing to show you," Pete said. He walked into the handcar shed and returned with an oiler that had a long tapered nozzle. "Watch me oil these wheel bearings. You ought to do it each day you run the handcar. And do these mechanical, moving parts too. There's an oiler in every line shack and handcar shed, so you don't need one with you. It keeps the parts from wearing out too quickly. Go ahead and put the car on the track while I return the oil can."

The handcar sat on the rails when Pete returned. "You fellows are quick learners," Pete said. "You can make good time with that car. As you reach the hills and mountains, you'll slow down a lot. In fact, there'll be stretches where it'll be easier to push the car. You could even leave it behind and walk. Just remember to take the car off the track. On the other side of the mountain, there's sure to be more handcar sheds. You won't need to pump going downhill. More than likely, you'll probably have to do some breaking so you don't lose control. Too fast around a corner is dangerous."

"So you think there's a good chance of returning using handcars and staying in the line shacks?" Colby asked.

"Like I said before," Pete said, "the tracks are probably the only way. I can't think of a reason why it wouldn't work. You should take food and canteens with you. Those mountains get cold even though it's not winter, yet. You'll need extra blankets. Take gloves, too, not just for the cold. You'll likely have blisters from pumping—you might want to bring some salve and bandages."

"Can you help us with those things, Jack?" Colby asked.

"Sure," Jack said. "Got plenty. Have an extra can opener I'll throw in too."

Pete looked up with a hand shading his eyes. "There's about five hours of sunlight left. You could make forty or fifty miles by sundown. You could be at the mountains in a few days."

"How long to collect those supplies?" Colby asked.

"I can be back in thirty minutes," Jack said. "You want your luggage off the wagon?"

"We'll take it with us," Colby said. "Mack, Gus. Stack that luggage on the handcar. Leave space for what Jack's bringing. Put my shoes in my travel bag. We don't need that box."

"One other thing I remembered," Pete said. "Watch out for Delusion Gorge."

"For what?" Colby asked.

"It's about forty miles down the track where the land changes from valley to rocky hills. A bridge crosses that gorge. Sometimes there's nasty weather there. And I mean *nasty*. Other weird stuff too."

"I saw black clouds and lightning in that direction from the top of the Ferris wheel," Gus said. "The rest of the sky was clear. Really odd. Is that what you mean by weird?"

"That's part of it," Pete said. "You be careful there. I could tell you stories about that place."

JACK RETURNED IN twenty minutes with three bulging burlap bags in the farm wagon.

"Give me a hand with these, Pete," Jack said.

The bags filled the remaining free space on the handcar platform. Jack pointed at each bag and explained, "This bag has blankets and medical supplies. Here are gloves. This bag is full of canned goods.

This one has bread, fruit preserves, coffee, towels, and canteens. I threw in playing cards too."

"Thanks, Jack, Pete," Colby said. "I owe both of you. Next time we're back this way, this will be my railroad."

Jack and Pete watched the handcar accelerate as the occupants pumped at a smart pace. It disappeared around a curve minutes later.

"What did he mean—it'll be *his* railroad?" Pete asked.

"I have no idea," Jack said. "Maybe he just likes trains?"

Pete hopped onto the farm wagon next to Jack. "Hope them fellows have a good trip on that handcar. Not sorry to see them go, though."

"Something happen when I went for supplies?" Jack asked.

"Nothing important," Pete said. "I tried to tell them the stories about Delusion Gorge, but nobody would listen."

"I'm surprised," Jack said. "They're heading that way. You'd think they'd want to know about it."

"Actually, Gus wanted to hear, but Mr. Colby and Senator Bryce kept interrupting. Those two kept yammering about Mr. Fischer this and Mr. Fischer that and their big plans. You know, bigwig talk. Too busy to hear stories about the gorge. I could've told them my own too. It's pretty much like the others."

"I didn't know it happened to you too," Jack said. "You never told me."

"Haven't had a chance," Pete said. "It was only a few weeks ago."

"I'll be darned. Tell me what happened."

Pete twirled his moustache. "I'd been as far as the gorge before but never past it. I figured I'd walk Dollar across the bridge, and we'd do some exploring on the other side. That was the plan, but it got shelved for a while. Overnight, to be exact."

"A storm?" Jack asked.

Pete nodded. "A big one, right at the gorge. Fierce and nasty as it could be. I left Dollar a ways back from the gorge. Didn't want him spooked. Followed the tracks on foot right to the edge of the gorge. You couldn't see a thing; it was as black as an outhouse hole. Low dark clouds and thick fog. A chain saw wouldn't have cut it. The tracks seemed to end with no bridge. Even with the lightning, no bridge, not a sign of it. I could've sworn on a stack of Bibles that it wasn't there."

"My gosh," Jack said. "How could that be?"

Pete rubbed his forehead. "I surely don't know. I'd seen that bridge before. It's solid construction: cut stone and thick steel. Built to last. Can't explain it."

"You're right about that bridge being well built. I saw it close-up once too. What'd you do?" Jack asked.

"Walked back to Dollar and rode to the nearest line shack. Stayed overnight. The next morning was beautiful, sunny, and warm. Rode back to the gorge. There was the bridge as nice as it could be. I walked Dollar across, and we went exploring for a few miles. Awful rocky on that other side. Dollar didn't like it none, so we came back."

"Your story's like the others I've heard," Jack said. "Whoever named it Delusion Gorge got it right. Wonder why it happens?"

"Must be the work of the devil," Pete said. "I wasn't drinking. I don't do that when I'm working or exploring. You ask me; the work of the devil."

"Those boys should've listened to your story. Suppose they find themselves in a storm and don't see the bridge. They'd probably turn around and come back."

"Probably would," Pete said. "Those bigwigs don't seem to have much patience; too busy scheming. Hope they don't have trouble; we don't need them back here in Penceville."

CHAPTER 23

The *whir* of steel wheels and the continuous *clickety-clack* mimicked the train, except it was louder and sharper. Countryside streamed by. Combined with the wind of the handcar slicing through air, the noises created an impression of great speed. It was more a product of the mind than reality. The car was, nevertheless, at maximum speed. The four men ardently pumped as if enamored with a newfound toy.

Colby glanced behind them. He saw the farm wagon disappear when the handcar followed a curve in the tracks. He pumped as energetically as the others. His spirits improved in proportion to the growing distance between them and Fischer's train. The two rails converged in the distance. Colby focused on that far spot vowing to toil until they reached it. Once there, he would measure his effort. That would be more sustainable in the days to come.

Colby's chin jutted as he widened his stance. They had been on the verge of failure. Now, they had turned that prospect around. Fischer almost had the last word. Now, he and Bryce would have the final say. Fischer would pay dearly for his insolence. He should have feared me, knowing my reputation, Colby thought. For now, the difficulty was reaching the top of the mountain. Then it would be an easy downhill journey to a town where they could catch a bus or taxi to the state capital. There they would unleash a fierce barrage against Fischer, which would become the new standard for vendettas. Colby felt a prickly warmth radiate within him. It reinvigorated his pumping, despite the fatigued muscles of his arms.

The vanishing point of the distant rails failed to move closer. The tracks continued straight to the horizon. Colby realized he could not keep his vow. His arms throbbed from muscles unaccustomed to even minor physical labor.

"I need to rest," Colby said. "I'm not used to this."

"Me either," Bryce said.

They sat on opposite benches. Mack and Gus centered themselves over the pumping handles. The handcar continued, its speed barely diminished.

"How far have we gone?" Colby asked.

"I'd guess maybe six or seven miles," Gus said.

"Seems like it should be more," Bryce said.

"That's because your muscles are sore, and it feels like we're moving faster than we really are," Gus said. "This'll be a long trip. We have to pace ourselves. Even Mack and I will need a break now and then so rest up."

A rhythm developed based on endurance and strength. Gus and Mack powered the handcar for fifty minutes, then Colby and Bryce for ten. Ten minutes wasn't long, but they made a determined effort to maintain the car's speed.

Colby pointed. "There's a set-off platform. I think we passed another one a few miles back."

"We should reach a line shack in a few more miles," Gus said. "Keep your eyes peeled. I'd like to stop and take a peek. There should be a set-off platform too."

Mack and Gus passed a canteen between them as they pumped. Clouds gathered in the distance but did not infringe on the mid afternoon sun.

"There it is," Colby said. A quarter mile ahead, a line shack merged with the tree line thirty feet from the track.

"Let it coast to a stop," Gus said once they were closer.

They strolled to the shack, curious about their living quarters for the next few weeks. A rust smudged tin roof capped the weather-beaten, wooden cabin. Amenities included bunks for six, plenty of blankets, and a potbelly stove for heating and cooking. A beat-up table and cluster of chairs occupied what remained of the floor space. Against a wall, two cabinets flanked a utility sink. One held plates, cooking and eating utensils, and towels. The other stored canned goods, supplies, and a can opener. Pots and pans hung from nails on the wall. Two oil lanterns rested on the table. A wall shelf yielded boxes of safety matches, lamp oil, and an oiler for the handcar. Two buckets sat in a corner next to a broom. An overhead shelf contained bars of soap and boxes of powdered soap. A stack of cut and split logs leaned against another wall where an axe, hatchet, and bow saw hung from nails.

"Not bad," Gus said. "It's a little tight but has all the basics. I saw a well pump outside and a lean-to. What do you think, Mr. Colby?"

"It's worse than the lousiest hotel I ever stayed in. Not much else to do though," Colby said.

"It's not that bad," Mack said.

"I don't think Lincoln ever had it like this," Bryce said. "Say. That gives me an idea for my next campaign."

"We better move on," Gus said. "We have a long way to go."

The scenery became as monotonous as the clamor of the handcar. The initial excitement of new transportation and adventure wore off. The reality of the difficulties ahead loomed larger. Colby pointed out nearly every set-off platform for the first twenty miles. Presently, he paid them no heed.

"Another line shack ahead, about a half mile on the right." Gus said as he peered at the sun, which rested above the treetops. "Probably two hours until sunset, maybe more. You want to push on to the next shack or stop here, Mr. Colby?"

"How long to the next one?" Colby asked.

"If we speed up, we can probably reach it by sunset or a little before," Gus said.

Colby looked down and stroked his forehead. Of course we should keep going, he thought. It puts us further from Fischer and closer to home. That's the whole idea. *There's time.* He shivered and his stomach tightened. A tiny voice escaped the depths of his mind: *Dark's coming.* He shook his head. *I'm not scared of the dark. What is this? The train window signs. Remember? You need to be safe when it gets dark. Ridiculous. This is ridiculous. Who's being a nitwit now? We keep moving. As long as it's light, as long as—*

"We're at the line shack, Mr. Colby," Gus said. "Stop or go?"

"Let's go, but I want to be inside by dark," Colby said. "Understand? Inside by dark."

"I got it," Gus said. "Let's crank it up, Mack."

THE HANDCAR MOVED faster thanks to Gus's brawny arms, strong back, and iron legs. Distant clouds thickened and darkened. A cross breeze of cool air stirred leaves. The sun sank below the treetops. Sunset drew nearer: an hour or less, probably less.

Gus saw it first because he was the only one looking forward. The vague object, indistinguishable from the track, lay a few miles away. The clouds had curdled into a black mass overlying the horizon. A lightning bolt flashed through the thunderhead. A deep rumble of thunder reached the handcar a half minute later. Gus had counted the seconds.

"We're heading toward a storm, Mr. Colby," Gus said. "About five or six miles. And I think there's something on the track. I can't make it out, yet."

The others turned. Ominous black clouds formed an angry wall. Something blocked the track.

"What is it?" Colby strained to discern the dark shadow.

"I can't tell," Gus said. "We're almost there. Ease up, Mack. I don't want to hit it."

The steel wheels shrieked as Gus braked the handcar to a stop. A haphazard pile of railroad ties covered the track. The side facing the handcar was splashed with red paint. "I'll see what's past here," Gus said, jumping from the handcar. "Back in a minute."

"Somebody's messing with us," Colby said. "I bet it's Fischer."

"You're probably right," Bryce said. "Fischer knew we were leaving. He's trying to slow us down."

Gus returned. "You need to see this. A hundred feet ahead. Don't get too close to the edge."

The track continued on the other side of the roadblock until the ground dropped precipitously into a deep gorge. Scrubby bushes protruded from cracks and jagged outcroppings along the canyon's rocky walls. White caps danced in the raging river rapids at the winding depths of the chasm. The turbulent water spawned a murky fog that clashed with heavy black clouds pressing down from above. On the far side, drenched by torrents of rain, craggy hills emerged when bolts of lightning illuminated their glistening features. Howling gusts interrupted a stiff breeze.

Colby gripped his hat and peered over the ledge. "The bridge must have fallen in."

"That's what I thought at first," Gus said.

"What do you mean?" Colby asked. "It's gone."

"Maybe the bridge was never there." Gus pointed into the gorge. "Look. No debris. It's hard to be sure; visibility is awful. That's a deep hole, too, almost straight down. No way to know. All I know is, we can't cross."

"We'd better start back right now," Colby said, panic evident in his voice. "We have to reach that shack before sunset. It's becoming dark already. Where's the sun? That storm looks like it's coming across the gorge. Anyone see the sun?"

The threat of the storm eclipsed all thoughts of the bridge. The handcar zoomed over the rails. So far, they outran the tempest except for intermittent squalls that nipped at their nerves. Stretched shadows clawed toward the tracks from a sun banished behind the tree line. A gloomy chill filled the air.

"Keep pumping," Gus said.

"How much further to the shack?" Colby asked.

"Ten minutes at this speed," Gus said.

Colby looked straight into Gus's eyes. "We have to be there before dark."

Gus hadn't seen Colby like this. His eyes seemed vacant and terrified at the same time. Sure, a bad storm chased them, Gus thought. Maybe they'd get wet and cold. No big deal. They'd dry out and warm up in the line shack. No, something else was wrong. Was it that episode on the train with the window? Is it the dark? Colby really doesn't want to be out in the dark? He's worried that something might happen when it gets dark?

"Pump harder," Gus bellowed.

WITH HALF THE sun below the horizon, Gus stopped the handcar by the set-off platform. Colby jumped off and dashed into the shack. Between the waning sun and a looming storm, darkness swiftly descended. The luggage and burlap bags sat in the shack, now illuminated by an oil lamp. Gus glanced at the generous stack of split wood against an inside wall and a hand-operated well pump over a utility sink.

Mack and Gus hauled the handcar onto the set-off platform and secured a tarp over it. After filling a bucket with twigs for kindling, they retreated to the security of the shack.

The split wood atop the kindling ignited readily. The glow from the potbelly stove added warmth and illumination to the shack's interior. Gus and Mack sorted through the burlap bag of foodstuffs and the shack's cabinets to set the evening's menu. They prepared a meal of canned meat, beans, peaches, and bread. Colby contributed bourbon, which mixed agreeably with the well water. No culinary complaints arose since all were famished from the physical exertion of the day.

Gus set a bucket of water on the stove. "Everyone have enough?"

"More than adequate, Gus." Colby added a finger of bourbon to each cup. "That gorge must have been the place Pete mentioned. What did he call it?"

"Delusion Gorge," Gus said. "It's an odd name. He warned us about the weather there. Said something about other strange things too. We should've let him tell us the stories."

"Too late now," Colby said. "Makes no difference at this point."

Gus flexed and extended his fingers. "I'll do the dishes as soon as the water's hot. It'll feel good on these old hands. Maybe we can play cards when I'm done. Listen to that wind picking up. Sounds like a few raindrops on the roof too. Glad we're in here. That storm's coming."

Colby always carried poker chips in his travel bag. Strewn around the table, the chips added a bit of color to the functional but otherwise drab shack. The cards looked small in Gus's beefy hands, reddened from dishwashing and a day of powering the handcar.

"I'm still thinking about that missing bridge, Mr. Colby," Gus said. "Maybe it was knocked out by a storm. Someone piled those ties on the track and painted them red. Had to be a railroad crew, I suppose. It's strange. How can a bridge be gone with no debris left? That's why I wonder if it was ever there. Maybe we should look again tomorrow morning?"

"It'd be a waste of time," Colby said. "With no way across, it doesn't matter. If it fell apart, then Fischer's not maintaining his line. If there was no bridge, then I don't know what's happening because the train had to have come this way. It's not possible that the train came some other way."

"It's a monopoly," Bryce said. "He controls the train, the line, the town, and who knows what else. Maybe he demolished the bridge to prevent you from taking his railroad. Who knows? No phones. No telegrams. No autos. No buses. Think about it, Lamar. You'd probably do the same if you were in his shoes. He has us over a barrel; he's putting the screws to us."

"You're right. It's darn suspicious," Colby said. "We have no choice but to head back to that tr . . ." Colby's mouth dropped and his eyes widened. "The train won't be there; it left this afternoon. We're stuck in Penceville until the train comes again. And the bridge is out so how does a train return? Oh, Fischer got us good, really good. If I ever see him again, he's had it. He'll pay for this."

"No way out? I can't stay around a place like this," Mack said. "There's no action. I can't stay here."

"We can go the other way," Gus said.

Bryce frowned. "What other way?"

"The same way the train goes," Gus said. "It might be longer, but eventually we'll return to where we started. There'll be other towns for supplies and hopefully no mountains to cross. Since the train travels that way, the tracks should be okay too."

Colby took a deep breath. He leaned toward the others. "Good thinking, Gus. That'll work. Fischer probably thinks he has us trapped, but we'll follow his train. He won't expect that. It's as if we're hunting him down. I like it. And we'll get him. It'll take time but we'll get him. Or I'm not Lamar Colby."

WITH A FRESH plan in place, the poker game became a serious matter. Gus threw more wood into the stove to combat a dropping temperature. A gloomy darkness surrounded the windows except when shafts of moonlight pierced the clouds. Menacing shadows appeared and faded as trees swayed from angry gusts of wind. The rain began as a drizzle and then pelted the tin roof in a frenzied torrent. Flashes of lighting split the darkness, followed by a deep roar. The *crack* and *rumble* of thunder joined the whistling and howling squalls. A ghastly evening assailed the shack.

A deafening *crash* rattled the tin roof. The chairs scattered as the four men jumped to their feet. Screeches, scratching, and clawing skulked to and fro above them. The windows clattered and the door shuddered as violent gusts battered the humble refuge.

Mack pulled a snub-nosed revolver. "What's on the roof?"

"Don't open those windows! Are they locked?" Colby frantically glanced from window to window.

Gus checked the windows and then ran to the door, which relentlessly banged against its frame. Rivulets of water snuck beneath the door, escorted by sinister wispy shadows that accompanied the lightning strikes.

Colby stared wide-eyed at the door's threshold. "Block it! Stuff something under it! Don't let it open; don't let anything in!"

Gus jammed a towel into the crack beneath the door. "Mack, help me slide this cabinet in front of the door."

With the door secure, the rattling windows and unnerving noises above them persisted and intensified. Blasts of wind buffeted the shack.

Mack pointed the revolver toward the roof. "What is *that*?"

Gus walked to a bunk and stepped up. His head neared the spot of the ghastly sounds. A bloodcurdling *screech* clawed the roof as a squall pounded the shack. Gus flinched but kept his place. He closed his eyes and tilted an ear toward the cacophony. Gus jumped to the floor. "Put the piece away, Mack, before you shoot somebody."

"I'm not putting anything away. Something's attacking us."

"It's a branch."

"Huh?"

"A broken branch that's probably hanging from a tree," Gus said. "The end of the branch is sitting on the roof. The wind is blowing it back and forth. That's what's making the sounds. I saw the tip from the window."

"Leave it there." Colby had backed into a corner. "Don't open that door. We'll put up with it."

"When the wind dies down, the branch will stop moving," Gus said. "The worst might be over. I think the rain is letting up."

Colby nervously glanced around the shack. "Let's play cards. That'll keep our minds off this blasted storm. Throw more wood in that stove. It's nippy in here."

"I'll do it," Mack said.

Colby added bourbon to their cups as a calming elixir more than anything else. A harrowing evening warranted it; demanded it, in fact. The rains intensified once again. The windows clattered. Forceful winds swirled. The clawing on the roof annoyed but was no longer a cause for apprehension. Poker chips shifted around the table by virtue of the best card hand or best bluff. The elixir and distraction of the game had done their work: anxiety alleviated.

A piercing *pop* exploded in the shack. Cards flew through the air. Chips clinked to the floor. The men sprang to their feet. White plumes shot from the stove and the joints of the stovepipe. Mack vaulted across the room, his back to the wall, gun in hand. The others stepped back from the stove. Particles of white soot hung in the air and then settled, speckling everything that wasn't white.

"What now? We're being attacked from inside!" Mack yelled.

"It was just green wood," Gus said. "Green wood in the stove."

"I didn't put any green wood in the stove," Mack said. "It's all the same color. Look at the pile. None of it's green."

"Green means it hasn't dried," Gus said. "It's wood that was recently cut. It has a lot of moisture in it. The sap hasn't dried out. That's why it's heavier than dried wood. That noise was sap exploding. What shot out of the stove was steam and white soot."

"That's the last time I add wood to a stove." Mack returned the revolver to his pocket.

The card game resumed after the men dusted the soot from their clothing and moved the table farther from the stove. A few additional minor eruptions belched from the potbellied contraption but nothing of consequence. The outside winds diminished. The rain slackened to a drizzle pecking at the tin roof. The lightning flashes ceased.

"The storm's about over," Gus said.

"Good. I want to be out of here at sunlight," Colby said. "We have a big trip ahead."

"But you don't get up that early," Mack said.

Colby glared.

"We'd better call it a night," Gus said. "Tomorrow will be a long day."

Chapter 24

Darkness shrouded the shack. Still, the lowered wick of the lamp cast sufficient light for Gus to reignite the stove's fire and brew coffee. Arising early was an old habit from his boxing days when he jogged before the cock crowed. The shack warmed quickly. The aroma of fresh coffee aroused the others while the first hints of daybreak crept into the sky.

Oatmeal, bread, preserves, and coffee provided a decent breakfast, at least filling as far as Colby and Bryce were concerned. It seemed odd for the shack to bask in the morning sunlight after such a miserable night, but the change was welcome.

Colby gulped what remained of his coffee. "Let's load the car. Time to go."

"We're not ready yet," Gus said.

"We're all packed," Bryce replied. "What's the problem?"

"I'm not leaving here with dirty dishes, cluttered bunks, and a fire in the stove," Gus said. "Besides, I need to remove the tarp from the handcar, oil it, and put it back on the track."

"It's a peasants' shack. Let them clean it," Bryce said.

Mack nodded. "Yeah, it's their problem."

Gus placed his hands on his hips and glared at them. "We had the privilege of staying in one of their sorely needed shelters last night. It protected us from a vicious storm. Their stove and the wood they cut kept us warm. We ate their food. We slept in their bunks and snuggled in their blankets. Peasants! These are hard working and thoughtful people with tough jobs. They look out for one another.

I'd rather be a peasant than any one of you ungrateful weasels. Go by yourselves. I'm not leaving until this place is in proper order, and I'll decide when that is."

The others stood speechless, unable to meet his gaze. Colby broke the silence. "Mack, you wash those dishes. Bryce and I will straighten up in here. That is, unless you need help with the handcar, Gus?"

Gus grabbed the oilcan and a rag and headed for the door. "I'll do it myself."

The tarp had protected the handcar and kept it dry. Gus oiled it and placed it on the tracks by the time Colby and Bryce emerged with luggage. "There's the branch that clawed the roof last night." Gus pointed to a hefty branch on the ground near the tree line. "You can see where it hung from that tree. Lucky it didn't put a hole in the roof. I'll clean out the stove, and then we can leave."

Mack finished the dishes and dried his hands, unhappy for the assigned task. Gus scraped the stove's embers into a bucket and doused them in the sink.

Gus surveyed the interior of the shack before closing the door. He wanted to add to the woodpile. They hadn't burned much wood. Everything outside was wet from the storm. He would make up for it at the next shack in which they stayed.

With everyone aboard, Gus set the handcar in motion. The sense of urgency and novelty that prevailed the day before had dissipated. They backtracked toward Penceville. From there, the journey would take a new direction.

"JOE, YOUR BREAKFAST is as good as Fred's," Wes said. "Must have something to do with conductors or maybe this caboose."

"It's obviously the conductors," Fred said, sipping his coffee.

"Heard anything more about the mud slide?" Wes asked.

"There was another rider from Gaash Pass about an hour ago," Fred said. "They expect the tracks to be cleared by noon. Mr. Fischer said we'll leave in a few hours for the sawmill. Once the wood is loaded, we'll be on our way. We'll arrive in Fontville by late afternoon."

"Any sign of Colby?" Wes asked.

"No, thank goodness," Fred said. "Maybe we'll be lucky, and Mr. Fischer will be wrong. I do feel sorry for Gus, though. He doesn't belong with them. The idea of staying in Fontville appealed to him."

"I feel bad for him too," Wes said.

"I'm planning a buckboard ride to the sawmill and to reboard the train there," Fred said. "I can use a little fresh air. Joe will watch the shop. You want to come, Wes? Timmy and Blackie are going. Timmy's excited about it."

"Wouldn't miss it," Wes said. "Did Fred tell you about Colby and his crew in case they show up, Joe?"

"Fred filled me in," Joe said. "I'll do my best to return them to the same car."

"That could be humorous in one way," Fred said. "If Colby sees Joe in his uniform, he'll probably figure Mr. Fischer fired me. That would make Colby happy. Then when he spots me in my uniform, he'll think Mr. Fischer is doubling down on him, and he'll have a fit."

"Do you have an extra uniform that would fit me?" Wes asked. "How about tripling down?"

Fred laughed. "Meet me in front of the train station in about two hours. I'll be there with the buckboard, and Timmy and Blackie. Meanwhile, I have errands to run."

"THERE'S THAT HANDCAR shed," Gus said. "Jack's farmhouse isn't far from here. The Penceville train station is probably only twenty minutes away. We've made decent time. It's only mid morning."

Colby and Bryce sat on the benches, content to let Mack and Gus propel the car at a modest pace. It still beat walking; Colby's fleece-lined boots testified to that. Colby had considered wearing his shoes today but threw them back into his travel bag after trying on one of them. For comfort, the ridiculous looking boots couldn't be beat.

"I can make out the roof of the train station," Gus said. "There's something red on the track. Can't tell what it is. Can you?"

Colby and Bryce strained to see. Mack glanced over his shoulder as he pumped.

"I think it's a caboo—" A loud whistle pierced the air and repeated twice more, drowning Colby's words. "It is a caboose!" he yelled. "The train's still here. Everyone pump. Maybe we can catch it before it leaves."

The handcar's speed doubled. Now within a hundred yards of the caboose, the train began to move. They narrowed the distance to less than fifty yards. Colby waved wildly at the unoccupied caboose. No one knew they were nearby. Less than twenty yards. The sounds from the engine obliterated their shouts. The handcar came closer. Only five yards. Now within an arm's length. Mack turned toward the caboose. He stretched, attempting to grasp any part of it. Inches. Just inches. The train gathered speed. The inches turned to feet. The handcar couldn't keep up. The feet lengthened to yards, then tens of yards. Their manpower was no match for the locomotive. The four men sat on the car's benches gasping for air, sweating profusely, muscles aching from the exertion. The handcar coasted, slowed, and stopped.

"W-w-we almost caught it," Colby stammered between quick breaths. "That blasted Fischer. He did this on purpose. Probably had someone watching for us. I'll ruin that man."

"That was so close," Gus said. "Pass the canteen. I need a few minutes. I'll get us moving again but not like that."

AS HE WALKED across the grassy field by the train station, Wes saw Blackie and Timmy playing fetch. Fred checked the horses hitched to the buckboard. The dog noticed Wes first and ran over, his tail wagging cheerfully in recognition. Wes reached into his jacket pocket and retrieved a biscuit, which Blackie appreciatively accepted.

"Hi, Mr. Quinton." Timmy ran over to him. "Look what Mr. Ables gave me for Blackie. He told me he would make one for him." Timmy handed Wes a train ticket identical to theirs except it bore Blackie's name. "Isn't it swell, Mr. Quinton."

"That's a fine ticket, Timmy," Wes said. "Mr. Ables is a good man; he keeps his word. That reminds me. I have a little gift for you too. Come back to the passenger car after dinner tonight. That'll give me time to find it."

"For me! Holy cows. What is it?" Timmy asked.

"You'll see later. Mr. Ables is calling us. Have you ever been on a ride like this?"

"No. I've never seen horses close-up before. They sure are big. A lot bigger than Blackie."

Fred lifted Timmy and Blackie onto the wagon bed and then climbed onto the plank seat next to Wes. The train whistle sounded several times. The horses trotted onto the dirt road leading to the sawmill.

"Who will get there first? Us or the train?" Timmy asked.

"It's only five miles," Fred said. "The train won't be traveling very fast, but it'll still beat us there. We could keep up with it for a while. That would tucker out the horses, though. We'll take our time and enjoy the ride."

"WHAT'S THAT BEHIND the train, Mr. Ables?" Timmy asked. "It looks like it's chasing the caboose, and it's almost caught it."

The train had moved ahead of them. A handcar with four men trailed close behind. One of the men waved his arms frantically. The car momentarily seemed to touch the caboose. That proved short-lived as the distance between the caboose and handcar grew. The car slowed and coasted to a stop.

"That's a handcar," Fred said. "You push up and down on handles like a seesaw to make it go. I can't imagine a crew chasing the train like that. Makes no sense."

"One of those men has a top hat," Wes said. "The one who waved his arms. That's not Colby, is it? Oh, rats. Has he gone nuts? What are they doing on a handcar?"

Fred flicked the reins. The horses increased their pace, and the buckboard drew even with the handcar.

"It *is* Colby and the others," Wes said. "They're sitting still, probably tired from chasing the train. If they take off again, they'll catch the train at the sawmill. How long would it take them, Fred?"

"If two pump, probably a half hour or more. If they all pump, maybe twenty minutes or less."

"They don't know the train is stopping at the sawmill," Wes said. "Maybe they'll take their time. Will we get there ahead of them?"

"Not at this rate," Fred said. "If they start moving again, we'll speed up. Mr. Fischer needs a heads-up. If needed, we'll run the horses the last mile."

"Timmy, we may need to go fast," Wes said. "If we do, you hold Blackie and hang onto the wagon."

"Are we going to race that handcar?" Timmy asked.

"Not a planned race," Wes said. "But we do need to reach the train first. I hope it doesn't become a race."

THE HANDCAR SAT motionless while the occupants recovered from the race with the caboose. The train vanished in the distance. Colby bore a look of dismay and anger, mixed with perplexity. Why didn't the train leave yesterday? he wondered. Was something wrong, or was this part of Fischer's scheme? If it was Fischer, what else was he plotting?

"Must be farms up this way," Mack said. "There's a farm wagon on the road over there. It's kicking up dust."

Gus stared at the wagon a hundred yards away. "That's strange. There are no farms here. I looked this way when we were on the Ferris wheel. That road ends at a sawmill. And that big guy is dressed in black. That's no farmer, not a sawmill worker either. Could be that train conductor. The hat is black too."

"I think you're right," Bryce said. "My eyes are pretty good. I'm certain it's that moron conductor."

"I wonder why he's not on the train," Colby said. "Maybe Fischer canned him. He's a nitwit; they're both nitwits. But why is he heading toward the sawmill? And why the uniform? It makes no sense."

"Maybe he's boarding the train at the sawmill," Gus said.

"Why would the train stop there?" Bryce asked.

"For wood," Gus said. "That train has a steam locomotive. They're probably loading more wood. If we hop to it, we can probably arrive before it leaves. I'd guess that sawmill is only four or five miles from here."

"Everyone start pumping," Colby yelled. "We have a train to catch."

WES LOOKED TOWARD the tracks. "They're pumping that handcar now. Moving at a good clip too. Wonder if they recognized us and figured out the train will stop ahead?"

Fred flicked the reins. "Keep an eye on them. They may gain on us for a while, but they can't keep up that pace. When we reach the train, put Timmy and Blackie on board. Then find Mr. Fischer and tell him what's happening. Joe too, if you see him. I'll set the steps so Colby returns to the same passenger car, and I'll open the side of the baggage car for their luggage."

"Ready to hold on, Timmy?" Wes asked.

Excitement filled Timmy's eyes. "Are we going to race?"

"Sort of," Wes said. "When we reach the train, you and Blackie climb on board quickly. Go to the Holyfields. Understand?"

"Got it." Timmy gripped the side of the wagon and held Blackie with his other arm. "Is this what you call a 'venture'?"

"*Adventure*, Timmy. *Adventure.* It is, indeed," Wes said.

THE HANDCAR LAGGED the buckboard by a quarter mile. Colby and Bryce pumped too. Their faces drooped from a growing fatigue.

"Those horses started running," Gus said. "That wagon's pulling away."

Colby gasped for breath. "I can't pump any faster. That conductor will tell Fischer to leave right away. I just know it."

"Pick it up, Mack," Gus said. "Five minutes. We can be there in five minutes."

THE WAGON ARRIVED first. Timmy and Blackie safely boarded the train. Wes found Mr. Fischer and Joe Croft in the dining car. They listened while Wes related what had happened.

"A handcar, oh my." Fischer chuckled. "Mr. Colby is persistent and clever, too. I will give him that. How remarkable. How remarkable, indeed."

"They'll probably be angry at you, Mr. Fischer," Wes said. "They'll blame you for not being able to leave. I'm sure Colby will demand to see you again. Be careful with him."

"I'd rather him focus on me than on the passengers," Fischer said. "I know his type quite well. Sadly, I see it far too often. You'll keep an eye on them, Wes?"

Wes nodded. "If anything comes up, I'll let you know."

"Things should be quiet for a while," Fischer said. "They'll be tired and hungry. I'll stop by after lunch and hear what they have to say. Why don't you take something back for lunch, Wes?"

"Thanks, I will. I'd better take my seat before they reboard the train. I imagine they'll be worn around the edges."

FRED STOOD BEHIND the caboose and watched the handcar roll to a stop. The car's occupants stared at him. They slouched on the plank benches, breathing hard, attempting to regain enough energy to speak.

"So nice to see you gentlemen again," Fred said. "I could've taken you for a handcar ride if you wanted. Where have you been?" Fred glanced at Colby's boots, the bunched up pant legs, and his rumpled hat.

"What are you gawking at?" Colby sneered, well aware of his fashion deficits.

"Nothing worthwhile, I mean nothing in particular," Fred said. "I placed the steps by your train car. Your seats are waiting."

"Why is the train still here?" Colby asked.

"There was a mud slide at one of the passes. We're restocking wood for the engine. The train will depart in about an hour."

"Let's get on," Colby said. "And you, Mr. Conductor, bring us food. And tell Fischer I want to see him. I don't know what the heck is going on, but I know he's behind it. Mack, bring my travel bag."

"Anything special for lunch, Mr. Colby?" Fred asked.

"No. But it better be good. And no pumpkin pie."

"Certainly," Fred said. "I'll take care of it as soon as your luggage is on board."

"You stay with him, Gus, so he doesn't steal anything," Colby said.

Bryce and Mack trudged toward the passenger car with Colby in tow.

"I'M GLAD YOU'RE back, Gus," Fred said. You look tired. Where've you been?"

Gus narrated their movements since leaving the train, including the episode at the gorge with the missing bridge.

"I've heard about that gorge," Fred said. "Gives me the heebie-jeebies. Delusion Gorge. Strange weather and odd things happen there. Maintenance crews are always working out that way. Mr. Fischer knows more about it than I do. I'll tell him what you said about the bridge, just in case."

Gus scratched his head. "Maybe we didn't see it because of the bad weather. I wanted to go back the next morning, but Mr. Colby was in too much of a hurry."

"What are those burlap bags on the handcar?" Fred asked.

"That's food and blankets Jack Bart gave us for the trip," Gus said. "Do you know Jack?"

"Why sure. Jack's a good man."

"Can you have someone return the bags to him?" Gus asked. "It was nice, what he did for us."

"Be happy to," Fred said. "Someone has to return the handcar to its shed anyway. They can take the bags to Jack."

Gus squinted one eye. "Was that you on that wagon on the dirt road?"

"How'd you know?" Fred asked.

"The black uniform," Gus said. "Seemed like you were racing us."

"We were, mostly to let Mr. Fischer know you had returned. Didn't want Colby to surprise him," Fred said. "How's Mr. Colby after your escapade?"

Gus shrugged. "He held up better than I thought. Tired, though. He's mad at Mr. Fischer. Mr. Colby is dangerous when he's like this, unpredictable too. This isn't over, not by a long shot. Colby doesn't give up. You need to be careful."

"Did he say what he might do?" Fred asked.

"Nothing specific but he didn't know we'd reboard the train. Colby's probably thinking about it already. He's obsessed about getting even with Mr. Fischer."

"Will you let me know if he plans something?" Fred asked.

Gus nodded. "I will, somehow."

"We'll arrive in Fontville late this afternoon," Fred said. "That's your stop. You should get off while you have the chance. You deserve it, Gus."

Gus paused in thought before speaking. "Maybe I should. I tried my best to get Mr. Colby home, but it couldn't be done. That wasn't my fault. Fontville would be a nice change. I'm tired of worrying about what Mr. Colby might do next. I will get off in Fontville."

Fred patted Gus on the back. "Wonderful. When the train stops there, I'll drop by to verify your ticket in case Mr. Colby objects. You'll like Fontville. The people too. Let's load this luggage. I'll have the stewards bring lunch right away."

"A big lunch please, Fred."

Chapter 25

Wes sat in the passenger car eating his take-out lunch more quickly than he should have. His neck felt tight. He sat stiffly, glancing back and forth between the front and rear aisle doors. Colby would soon be several seats away. *Rats. I'm on edge.* His emotions weren't based on fear; they arose from instinct. He had learned not to ignore his intuitions during the war, and he wouldn't now. Big trouble brewed. When and what it might be was unknowable, but it was coming. Nick and Daniel had returned from the dining car and lounged a few seats back. They know the situation, Wes thought. That gave him some comfort. Otherwise, the passenger car remained empty but not for long.

Colby entered first, followed by Bryce and Mack. Wes stifled a snicker when he noticed Colby's boots and the deformed top hat. Colby made a beeline for the fancier seats in the middle of the car, the same they had claimed previously. All three appeared dusty and weary. Wes wondered about the extent of their travels, certain the tale would intrigue him. The boots, the misshapen top hat, and the handcar practically guaranteed it. Gus looked as fatigued as the others when he entered the car. Making his way toward Colby, he massaged his hands, sliding into the seat beside the group. Jay and another steward approached, carrying trays loaded with sandwiches, chips, pitchers of lemonade and iced tea, glasses, and a pile of napkins.

Colby, surprised at how quickly the food had arrived, could not contain himself. "What took so long?"

"Sorry, Mr. Colby." Jay said, unloading the trays. "We came as quick as we could put things together. I'll be back with cake and coffee. They're brewing fresh coffee now."

Colby grunted. Mack tried to trip Jay again, but his tired feet refused to cooperate.

Jay returned with coffee and cake within ten minutes and cleared the empty plates. "Anything else I can bring you?"

"Do you have any liniment?" Gus asked. "My hands are sore. Old injuries acting up."

"We have some in our first aid kit," Jay said. "Shall I bring it?"

"I'll get it later," Gus said. "Where do I find it?"

"Stop by the dining car. I'll leave a tube of it at the counter."

"Thanks. And for the lunch also," Gus said.

"You're most welcome," Jay said. "My pleasure."

Despite the coffee, exhaustion and the meal took their toll. The four men fell asleep where they sat. The train whistle sounded, and the train jerked as it departed the sawmill.

"HOW NICE TO see you again, Mr. Colby, Senator Bryce, Mack, Gus. I stopped by earlier, but you were snoozing. Must be the fresh autumn air," Fischer said. "What happened to your hat, Mr. Colby? I like your boots. Were they a purchase in Penceville?"

"No thanks to you," Colby grumbled. "A pumpkin smashed my hat in Penceville. The pavement pounded my feet. I had to buy these absurd boots. Nothing else would fit. I don't ever want to hear about that stupid town again."

"I'm sorry it was problematic," Fischer said. "Most people find the town rather charming. I understand you took a lengthy handcar ride. That is excellent exercise, and I commend you for choosing it."

Colby's eyes narrowed. "You know very well, Mr. Fischer, that it's the only possible way to leave here except for this train. It was not a choice. It was the only option, since there are no automobiles or buses, and no roads that go anywhere."

"I told you there were no automobiles and buses," Fischer said. "There is no need for them. As such, there is also no need for roads except those essential to the community. I trust you were not surprised by what I truthfully stated?"

"You didn't tell us there were no telephones or telegraphs," Bryce said.

Fischer smiled and shrugged. "My dear man, had you asked, I surely would have told you. It's certainly no secret. Everyone in town is aware of it and thinks nothing of it."

Bryce crossed his arms and shot Fischer an icy look. "Well, I think you have a monopoly and control everything. Everywhere we turned, there were problems. There's no way to leave except this train. That's part of the monopoly. You must be making a fortune off it."

Fischer laughed. "Senator, I generate no revenue from this train, the town, or the community. The people appreciate where they are and what they do. As to leaving, there is the train. It travels only one way because of the track grade. The handcar could take you back although the grade would make it challenging. Why didn't you just continue with the handcar? It would require some stamina, of course, but men of your determination usually stay the course."

Colby's face tightened, and his eyes became slits. "I think you know what stopped us. The bridge at the gorge was missing. The weather was bad. We saw no bridge or any sign of it. There was a pile of ties blocking the tracks. The tracks stopped at the edge of the gorge. I think you had the bridge destroyed to keep us from leaving, to force us back onto your train. You pretend to act nice, but you're no better than us. At least we don't try to act like somebody we're not. What about that bridge, Mr. Fischer? Explain that."

"The bridge concerns me," Fischer said. "Gus related the same information to Mr. Ables earlier. I've already sent a crew to check on it. Having said that, it is quite unlikely that the bridge is gone and ludicrous to suggest that I would demolish it. That is a deep gorge. The construction of a bridge to cross it is a difficult and dangerous task. The gorge itself is unusual because it separates these flatlands from the rocky hills on the other side. It is prone to sudden violent storms producing poor visibility, powerful winds, intense rains, and lightning. Add fog from the tumultuous river that courses through the gorge, and it becomes a peculiar place at such times. The maintenance crews call it Delusion Gorge because of the adverse weather and strange things that occur. This isn't the first time someone has reported the bridge missing. When the weather is vicious, the bridge is difficult to see. Crews often work out that way. The rails corrode more quickly; workmen replace them more often than elsewhere on the rail line. That's could be why track was missing. The ties were piled up as a warning. It doesn't take them long to replace them if the weather cooperates."

"So you're claiming the bridge was there?" Colby asked.

"It most likely is," Fischer said. "I won't know for sure until a messenger catches up to us in Fontville.

"Fontville?" Bryce said.

"It's our next stop," Fischer said. "It's about the same size as Penceville. We'll be there in a few hours."

Colby glared at Fischer. "Nobody told us the train would stay in Penceville overnight. I think you were waiting to force us back onto the train. Your gorge story sounds like a fairy tale. I think you're scheming against us."

"Why, Mr. Colby," Fischer said. "You are one of the most suspicious individuals I have met in some time. Most people aren't schemers. You left the train before we found out about the mud slide on the tracks. Crews have cleared it, but that's the cause of the delay."

"I don't believe you," Colby sneered. "Too many excuses and weird things are happening."

"Can you believe your eyes? We're traveling through Gaash Pass now." Fischer pointed out the window. "See the workers clearing mud near that retention wall."

"You could have set that up too," Bryce said. "Ever since Mr. Colby said he would take your train, we've had nothing but trouble and flimsy excuses. And now you've forced us back on the train. You think you can manipulate us. It won't work. Not against us."

"Gentlemen, please," Fischer said. "I'm not out to control anyone or plotting to do anything. I wish you would dispense with your false notions and simply enjoy the ride. There is no conspiracy against you by anyone on this train. You have concocted straw men in your imagination and act as though they are vanquishing you. Please desist in this folly before it consumes you."

"I'm warning you again, Mr. Fischer," Colby said. "All your subterfuge, delays, and lies haven't changed a thing. It only increases my determination to bring you down and take your railroad. I will do that. You may have slowed us, but that's all. I'll make you a pauper and take your monopoly empire. By the time I'm done, you'll wish we had never set foot on your stinking train."

Fischer sighed. "Mr. Colby, I'm sorry I can't dissuade you from such adverse thoughts. I would ask that you please be considerate of the other passengers, with whom you have no grievance. There is nothing more I can say at this point. If I can be of further service, please call on me. In the meantime, I bid you good afternoon."

WES COULDN'T HELP but overhear the conversation between Fischer, Colby, and the others. He winced at Colby's harsh words and accusations. In the face of such glaring insults, Fischer exercised admirable restraint and patience. It seemed as if the world had turned inside out and upside down. Another subversion of justice, Wes thought. Not much seemed right anymore. Surely there was a higher justice. Where was it, and when would it come? Wes shook his head. Not soon enough. His dad had always told him to be patient. Justice would come. Wes still waited.

Colby seemed to be spinning out of control, on the edge of madness, and nearing a point of irrational desperation. The behavior reminded Wes of battle fatigue. Here, it was not army against army but Colby against Fischer. Colby was the aggressor. Fischer kept his wits about him, but Colby seemed to be losing his.

Any hint of Colby's intentions would be welcome information. Wes closed his eyes. He hoped the lack of visual distraction would enhance his auditory senses. He strained to hear Colby's conversation. He needed clues.

"MACK, GRAB MY shoes from the travel bag," Colby said. "Time to ditch these stupid boots. I'm tired of the insults."

"What will we do now, boss?" Mack asked. "We've tried a bunch of plans; nothing's worked. Something always stops us."

"It's Fischer and his monopoly," Bryce said. "He'd be a perfect politician. Tell you something with a straight face and then do whatever benefits him or his buddies. Control it all while you smile and lie. He'd go far in politics. I know the type."

Colby looked down at his feet. The shoes looked better than the boots. After two days absence, they again felt comfortable. The change had been auspicious, the change, the change. *That's it*, Colby thought. A flood of ideas invaded his mind. His eyes darted about while his brain sorted, processed, and organized the inputs. The details were sketchy, but a basic plan had solidified. *That'll work. What a simple idea.* Colby rubbed a smudge from his shoe with his handkerchief.

"Mack, the answer to your question is we'll change the shoes." Colby settled back in the seat and crossed his arms. "That's our plan."

The others looked at Colby as if he had gone mad. "But you just did that," Mack said.

Colby looked around the car. He noticed Wes several seats away. "Lean in. Keep your voices low. Let me explain what I mean."

Bryce shrugged. "I hope this is good."

Colby glanced around the table before he spoke. "It's an analogy. By changing shoes, I mean we'll change who controls the train. Right now, that's Fischer. But I shall take over. Once that's done, we won't stop the train until it reaches the state capital. The eminent Senator Bryce will then initiate the regulatory and safety violations that will terminate Fischer's operation and bankrupt him."

Mack shrugged. "But we don't know how to run the engines. And there aren't enough of us to keep everyone in line. We're outnumbered."

Colby grinned. "We don't have to run the engines, and we don't need to rule over everyone. We only have to be in charge. Most of the people on the train don't even need to be aware of it."

"I still don't get it," Mack said. "Fischer's the boss now. How do we take control from him?"

"We'll force him to do what we say," Colby said. "That's how."

"I have my gun," Mack said. "That might do it."

"It could work," Colby said, "but I don't think he scares easily. He might even walk away. And if you did shoot him, they'd probably stop the train at the next town. No, must be a better way. That part I haven't thought through yet. Try to think of something he really cares about. Something he'd be willing to surrender the train for. Any ideas?"

Bryce stared at the table. "I can't think of anything off the top of my head."

"Well, we have a plan," Colby said. "Now, it's merely adding the details. Let's drink to it."

Colby pulled a bottle of aged bourbon from his travel bag. "Where's a steward when you want one? We need glasses and ice."

"I'll take care of it." Gus stood. He stretched and flexed his fingers. "These hands need liniment anyway. That handcar did them in."

WES STRUGGLED TO hear any tidbit from the huddled conversation. The only sound that reached his ears was muffled mumbles. He'd heard Colby say something about *changing the shoes* before they hunched in their seats. Change the shoes. It meant something, but what? One solitary clue. *Rats.* It didn't help. They were hatching a new plot. Mr. Fischer was right about Colby. Persistent and clever, excellent traits for a man of virtue, undesirable for a man of Colby's temperament and inclinations. Wes knew Colby. That's what worried him.

THE CONGESTION IN the next passenger car initially perplexed Gus. My gosh, it's because of Colby, he thought. Mr. Fischer's isolating the other passengers because of Colby's rotten behavior.

Gus's mouth watered as he entered the dining car. The aroma of pot roast, fries, apple pie, and coffee filled the air. Comfy and homey, the diner reminded him of better and simpler times. A waitress at the counter smiled when he approached.

"Jay said he would leave some liniment here for me," Gus said.

"You must be Gus," the waitress said. "Jay told me you'd be coming. Here's a tube you can keep."

"Thank you. Is Mr. Ables around?"

"I think he's busy somewhere," she said. "Mr. Fischer and Jay are in the end booth. I'm sure they can help you. Is there anything else I can get you?"

"I'll be returning to my car in about five minutes," Gus said. "Could you have an ice bucket and four glasses ready to go?"

"Why, certainly. Oh, Jay's waving at you."

Gus walked to the booth. "Ma'am, Mr. Fischer, Jay."

"Gus, this is Mrs. Holyfield," Fischer said. "She and her husband care for the children and babies. Please join us."

"My pleasure, Mrs. Holyfield." Gus sat. "And thank you, Jay, for the liniment. I can't stay long. Mr. Colby will become suspicious. Mr. Ables asked me to tell him about anything Mr. Colby was planning."

"We'll pass it on," Fischer said. "We appreciate what you're doing, Gus. I worry about my passengers."

"I saw how most of them are in that crowded passenger car," Gus said. "I'm sorry, Mr. Fischer."

"It's not your fault," Fischer said. "You're trying to help."

"Do you mind if I rub liniment on my hands while I talk?" Gus asked. "It smells bad, but it would be better if I return to Mr. Colby with my hands smelly."

"I'll do it while you talk," Mrs. Holyfield said.

"Thank you," Gus said.

Gus cleared his throat. "Mr. Fischer, I'm sorry to tell you this. Mr. Colby plans to take over the train and run it nonstop until it's back at the state capital."

"How will Mr. Colby gain control of the train?" Jay asked.

Gus shrugged. "That he's still thinking about. Mr. Colby plans to force Mr. Fischer to do what he says, somehow. They talked about using a gun. Mack has a piece, but I don't think that's how Mr. Colby plans to do it. He intends to pressure Mr. Fischer in some other way. He hasn't figured it out yet, but he will. He will do something, that's for sure. If I hear anything else, I'll let you know if I can."

"Thank you, Gus," Fischer said. "Mack with a gun worries me because of the other passengers. Are Mr. Quinton, Nick, and Daniel still in your car?"

"The two soldiers?" Gus asked.

Fischer nodded. "Correct."

"All three are there but no other passengers," Gus said.

"Good. The three of them are aware of trouble brewing," Mr. Fischer said.

"I'm supposed to get off the train in Fontville," Gus said, "but I'll stay on board if it'll help."

Fischer smiled. "Gus, that's very considerate of you, but you've been a great help already. You're a good man. I know you're looking forward to Fontville and being free of Mr. Colby. We'll deal with Mr. Colby. I want you to depart at your stop. We'll be there in about an hour. Fred told me he'll come back for you in case there's any problem with Mr. Colby."

"I appreciate that," Gus said. "I'd better return before they come looking for me. They're waiting for glasses and ice. Please be careful. And thank you, Mrs. Holyfield. My hands feel much better."

MACK HAD DEALT poker hands before Gus returned. Poker chips were stacked at Gus's place. "Here's glasses and ice," Gus said.

"About time you got back. What's that awful smell?" Colby asked.

"That's the ointment," Gus said. "It's rubbed in all the way, but that's how it smells."

"Don't let any of it rub off on the cards," Colby said. "This is the only deck I have."

WES HALFWAY PAID attention as the card game continued. Colby and his men limited their conversation to poker talk or requests for more bourbon or ice. Judging from the shadows zooming by, mid afternoon approached. In an hour or so, the train would arrive in Fontville. Wes wondered how Colby would react to Gus's departure. He thought he knew, but he would find out soon enough.

CHAPTER 26

The train emerged from a thick forest, bathed in the late afternoon sun. Farms painted the landscape. The train whistle blared while the train slowed. Five minutes and two whistles later, they stopped in Fontville. Wes walked to the window for a closer view. He noticed Gus gazing as well. It would be his new home.

The layout mimicked Penceville, but the architecture featured an ornate gothic style. Medieval towers and spires jutted upward throughout the town. A smaller version of the Eiffel Tower projected above the trees on the far side of the town square. A gothic emerald-green roof topped the train station. As in Penceville, a broad promenade led to town.

Fischer and Jay entered the station before any passengers disembarked. Porters shuffled luggage; Joe Croft checked tags. Fred directed a group of passengers to the station's arrival entrance. Several new passengers boarded after he checked their tickets. The process was a repeat of Penceville, except for different passengers leaving or boarding. Fred saw Wes in the window. He pointed toward Colby's group, so Wes would know he had not forgotten Gus.

The front car door opened. Fred walked toward Colby and his cohorts, stopping in front of them.

"What in the world do you want?" Colby blurted. "We didn't call for you."

Fred ignored him. "May I see your ticket, Gus?"

Gus pulled it from his jacket and handed it to Fred.

Mack's eyes narrowed. "What is this?"

Fred glanced at the ticket and returned it to Gus. "This is your stop, Gus. The porters put your luggage on the platform. Follow me. I'll show you where to go in the station."

Gus stood. The jaws of the others dropped as if they would scream, but no sound came. Colby stiffened in his seat, his eyes staring in disbelief. Bryce's eyes glazed over. Mack's looked ready to pop from their sockets.

"This must be a mistake," Colby said. "We work together. We're traveling together. We have the same tickets."

"My ticket is different," Gus said. "I get off here."

"That can't be," Colby said.

"Gus, show him your ticket," Fred said. "It's wooden and there's an *F* for Fontville, Mr. Colby. It *is different* from your ticket."

Colby eyed the ticket. "What a cheap piece of junk. Gus is with us. Give him an expensive ticket like ours. I thought he had one. I don't care what it costs."

"Gus has the correct ticket," Fred said. "It's not a matter of cost."

"Everything has its price," Colby said. "Everyone does, too."

"Maybe in your circles, Mr. Colby, but not here," Fred said.

Gus's face was firm. "I'm leaving."

Colby, Bryce, and Mack realized he was serious. Gus was determined to depart the train. Colby's face tightened. His eyes constricted to slits. "You can't leave."

"This is Fischer's doing," Bryce said. "How much did he pay you? I know he bribed you. How much was it? We'll double it."

"No one paid me anything," Gus replied. "This is my stop. My ticket is different from yours. I'm ready to get off. I want to get off. I'm getting off."

"Stop him, Mack!" Colby screamed.

Mack didn't know what to do. He pulled his gun and halfheartedly pointed it at Gus.

"Are you aiming to shoot me, Mack?" Gus asked. "If so, it'll have to be in the back because I'm leaving."

Colby pounded his fists on the table. "You turncoat; you lousy rat. I should have never given you a job in the first place."

Bryce glared at Gus. "It's Fischer. He's behind it all."

"Fischer has had it," Colby yelled. "This is the last straw. I'm not putting up with anything else from him."

WES WATCHED FRED and Gus walk toward the station entrance. Gus turned for a last look at the train and saw Wes in the window. Wes waved. Gus clasped his hands signifying both victory and gratitude and then disappeared into the station with Fred. Wes hoped he would see Gus again. Colby had lost a fine man. Now, Wes and the train staff had only to contend with Colby, Bryce, and Mack. Gus had been the moderating factor. Mack had been quick to pull his gun on Gus. Both Colby and Bryce seemed to have shortened erratic fuses. Moderation had left the train with Gus.

AFTER GUS'S DEPARTURE, Colby, Senator Bryce, and Mack hunched over the table in animated conversation. Wes heard nothing except for a *bravo* from Senator Bryce and sporadic pounding of the table by Colby's fist. They hadn't even looked up when the train whistle sounded as they departed Fontville. The sun sank low in the sky.

Wes turned toward Nick and Daniel. "You fellows want to beat the crowd and eat now?"

"It's about that time," Nick said. "Do you want to eat first?"

"I'm not that hungry," Wes said. "Maybe you could bring me a sandwich and coffee?"

"Will do," Nick said. "See you in a while."

Wes watched them stride up the aisle.

"Hey you, soldier boy," Colby snarled. "Tell them we want dinner and coffee."

Nick looked at the three of them, thought about saying something, but changed his mind. "We'll tell them. Let's go Daniel."

Ten minutes later, Jay and another steward unloaded trays of food and coffee at Colby's table. The other steward left when they finished. Jay walked back to Wes and sat.

"Hi, Mr. Quin—I mean, Wes," Jay said. "Here's your sandwich and coffee. Nick told me. Is that all you're eating? You feel all right?"

"Thanks," Wes said. "I'm fine. Not much of an appetite. I'm worried about the three you just served. They're plotting something."

"Gus told us Mr. Colby plans to take control of the train," Jay said.

"Control? How?" Wes asked.

"Gus didn't know," Jay said. "He said Mr. Colby hadn't figured it out yet. He also told us Mack has a gun."

"That I know," Wes said. "Mack pulled it on Gus. Tried to stop him from leaving the train in Fontville. Colby was enraged. They thought Mr. Fischer bribed Gus. After Gus left, the three of them huddled over their table for the better part of an hour. I think they've hatched their plan. I couldn't hear a thing about what it might be. Those three are wound up tighter than a cuckoo clock. Something could happen at any time."

"What can they do? There are only three of them," Jay said.

Wes frowned. "The gun. That makes it more than three. They have lethal force. If they pulled it on Gus, they'd pull it on anyone. And their frame of mind is twisted. They're on edge, close to the precipice, ready to go over. No way to know when. Probably depends on their plan. I wish I knew more."

Jay's shoulders drooped. "This is bad. I'll tell Mr. Fischer and Fred. It looks like Colby's finished eating. I'd better clear their plates before they start throwing them." Wes watched as Jay emptied their table.

"Bring us ice and glasses, steward," Colby said.

Shortly after Jay left, Nick and Daniel returned to their seats near the back of the car. Wes nibbled at the sandwich and sipped coffee. The Colby trio resumed their poker game. A steward returned with an ice bucket and glasses. Colby meted out two fingers of bourbon to each glass then added ice. Wes could have used a little himself.

Perhaps he was more on edge than necessary. There seemed to be nothing imminent. As long as they played cards, what else could happen? Wes gazed out the window. A glorious palette of twilight colors welcomed nightfall as the sun slipped beneath the horizon. Such beauty and such danger, Wes thought. How can they coexist? Magnificence and malice, seems like oil and water. Some day justice, but not today, not tomorrow, not—who knows? Wes stretched. His face reflected in the window and seemed older than he'd remembered. Wear and tear. Pay attention old soldier. Honor and duty. You're on watch. Forget the philosophy; just pay attention.

THE FORWARD DOOR of the passenger car opened and Timmy scampered through. "Come on Blackie. Let's go see Mr. Quinton."

Unusual for him, Wes felt a sense of panic. He had told Timmy to stop by after dinner for the gift he promised the boy. That had happened before the buckboard ride when Colby was nowhere in sight. There didn't seem to be a chance of Colby returning to the train.

With all the activity, Wes had forgotten about the gift. *Rats.* He should've sent word to Timmy or taken the gift to him. Or had someone else do it. It hadn't crossed his mind. Stupid, how stupid. This is no time for Timmy to be here. Too dangerous. They wouldn't grab Timmy, would they?

Memories of his own brother crept into Wes's thoughts. Tommy's gone. I was too late. Timmy. Have to keep him safe; have to. His hands felt clammy. An icy shiver stiffened his spine. He's just a boy. They wouldn't stoop that low. Would they? They wouldn't hurt him. Would they? Colby couldn't; he just couldn't. Wes wiped his hands on his pants and took a deep breath. Settle down, he told himself. He'll pass by them. Then I'll take him to the caboose. He'll be safe there, out of the way.

Wes glanced at Colby. *He's the key. If he ignores Timmy, we're okay. So far, so good.* His eyes darted between Timmy and Colby.

TIMMY'S VOICE ANNOYED Colby. In general, he disliked children. More specifically, the sound had interrupted his concentration on the card game.

Colby shifted in his seat. The cards didn't matter that much. Fischer. Ruining Fischer; taking his train. That's what mattered. Obviously, the best way to capture the train was to gain control of Fischer. That was the simple part of the plan. They had also decided that taking a hostage was the best way to force Fischer to comply. It would work. Fischer wouldn't risk harm to one of his beloved passengers. That was pretty simple too. A more complex and not yet resolved question prolonged the discussion. Who would make a good hostage?

Who could they threaten that would compel Fischer to surrender command of the train? That was the crucial question. They had ruled out Jay. In fact, they eliminated any of the men, whether passenger or crew. Too much risk of a confrontational type. A lady, a child, or even one of the babies would be easier to manage. That would yank Fischer's heartstrings. There were pros and cons for each scenario. They hadn't yet decided. Actually taking a hostage would pose its own difficulties. More planning. Additional risks.

"Beat you," Bryce said. "Can't believe you bet on a pair of fours. Your deal."

Colby stared at the cards on the table. Bryce held a flush to Mack's three queens. Colby was low man. Rare for him to lose like that. He usually would fold with a crappy pair.

Colby's focus on the game had been disrupted. It was that nitwit boy who cost him a game, he thought. That annoying boy. Wait, that was it. The boy. Here was a gift on a platter. Colby sat upright and looked toward Timmy. Their hostage had just arrived.

TIMMY DREW EVEN with Colby's table. Wes saw Colby stiffen in his seat as his head swiveled toward Timmy. Wes knew what it meant.

"Go back, Timmy!" Wes yelled as he stood.

"Grab the kid, Mack!" Colby screamed.

Mack lurched. He grabbed Timmy and jerked him from the aisle despite the boy's kicking legs and flailing attempts to free himself. Blackie growled and jumped at Mack with bared teeth as the thug dragged Timmy to the seat.

"Stop moving and call your dog off, or I'll shoot him." Mack drew the revolver from his pocket. He pointed the gun at Blackie and then toward Wes, Nick, and Daniel, who had jumped from their seats. "You three," Mack snarled. "Get back in your seats or I'll hurt the boy."

Tears rolled down Timmy's cheeks. "Please don't hurt my dog."

"Call him off—now," Mack yelled.

"Go say *hi* to Mr. Quinton, Blackie. Go say *hi*," Timmy said. "Mr. Quinton, call him. He'll come for a biscuit."

Wes pulled a biscuit from his pocket and whistled. "Come here, Blackie. Here's a treat. Come on, boy."

"Go get it," Timmy said. "Go say *hi*."

Blackie walked halfway down the aisle, then turned and looked at Timmy.

"Go on Blackie. Go say *hi*," Timmy said.

"Come on, boy," Wes said, waving the biscuit.

Blackie continued to Wes, who gave him the biscuit and picked him up.

"Daniel. Take Blackie. Don't let him go," Wes said.

"We'll hurt the kid unless you get Fischer right now," Colby said.

Wes started to move toward the aisle.

"Stop right there, Quinton," Colby said. "I don't trust you one bit. I want to keep my eye on you."

Colby pointed at Nick. "You go, soldier boy. Stay on the far side of the aisle when you walk by. You better not try anything, either."

"Please let Timmy go," Wes said. "He's only a boy."

"Isn't it great," Colby said. "Now I have Fischer right where I want him. Shut up, Quinton, or the boy gets hurt."

"Timmy, stay still and do what they say," Wes said as calmly as he could.

THE AISLE DOOR opened. Fischer, Jay, Fred, and Nick entered. Marielle Holyfield had come, also, but stayed behind the door and peered through the etched glass.

"I see you brought an army with you," Colby sneered.

Colby pointed to Fred, Nick, and Jay. "You three to the back of the car and sit. Nothing funny or we hurt the kid. And you, Mr. Fischer, stand against that wall across the aisle from us. Don't make any sudden moves."

Grant Fischer cautiously moved opposite them. "Are you all right, Timmy? Have they hurt you?"

"I'm okay, Mr. Fischer. Just scared," Timmy said.

"Where's Blackie? Is he all right?" Fischer asked.

"He went back to Mr. Quinton," Timmy said.

"Stay still, Timmy," Fischer said.

Colby's eyes grew cold and narrow. "Now, Mr. Fischer. You will do exactly as I say, or Mack will hurt the boy. He has no compunction against doing that. Frankly, neither do I."

"Please let him go, Mr. Colby," Fischer said. "Surely you wouldn't hurt a child. I know you wouldn't do that."

Colby nodded to Mack who twisted Timmy's forearm behind his back and then raised it. Timmy cried out in pain. Tears welled in his eyes.

"Please stop," Fischer said. "You're hurting him."

"Hurting kids doesn't bother me at all." Mack released Timmy's arm. "Maybe I should do the other one now."

"No!" Timmy screamed. "Don't let them hurt me again, Mr. Fischer. Please don't let them hurt me."

"So you see, Mr. Fischer, we mean business," Colby said. "The boy means nothing to us. You can do what I ask or watch the boy suffer. Your choice."

"What do you want?" Fischer asked.

"It's really quite simple," Colby said. "Run this train nonstop to the state capital where we boarded it."

"What about my other passengers and their stops?" Fischer asked. "You'll inconvenience many people."

Colby shrugged. "Do I look like I care? You mean passengers like Gus? How much did you pay him to leave? I know you bribed him. Probably a good riddance; he was starting to act like you."

"Mr. Colby, I assure you, I didn't bribe or pay Gus anything," Fischer said. "There would be no reason to even consider it."

"You'd expect Fischer to lie about that," Bryce said. "He's blocked everything we tried to do and used his whole monopoly against us. He's more crooked than we are. He turned Gus against you, Lamar. One of your own. That's really low down. We don't need Fischer. If he's out of the way, who can stop us?"

"Now look, Senator Bryce, you've said many things that just aren't so," Fischer said.

"Are you calling me a liar?" Bryce snarled. "Me? Senator F. W. Bryce?"

Colby's jaw clenched and his eyes bulged. Veins protruded from his temples. "Are you calling my friend a liar? Give me the gun, Mack."

Mack's eyes widened.

"Come on, Mack. Give me the gun." Colby glared at him.

Mack reluctantly moved the gun toward Colby who snatched it and pointed it at Fischer.

"What are you doing with that gun?" Timmy stammered.

"How do you like this, Mr. Fischer, you sniveling excuse of a man. I can put you out of your misery and ours too." Sweat beaded on Colby's forehead.

"Please, Mr. Colby. Put the gun down," Fischer said.

"Liars, huh?" Colby sneered.

Colby swiped at his eyes. Sweat rolled from his brow. His hand trembled from the weight of the gun and nerves frayed beyond repair.

Wes felt his stomach tighten. His mouth was as dry as a desert. This couldn't be any worse, he thought. It will be if he shoots. Would he? Does he have it in him? Wes focused on Colby: the sweat, the quivering hand, the look in his eyes. Wes had seen it during the war. Some men lose it. Everything boils over and they just lose it. Colby seemed close.

I can't let this happen, Wes thought. His eyes drifted to Timmy, Fischer, then back to Colby. *I have to save Tommy. Rats. Timmy. I told him I'd look after him, keep him safe.* But Colby has that gun pointed at Mr. Fischer. That's who he'll shoot, if he shoots. I'd have to try to push Fischer out of the way. Could I even make it there in time? What about my feet? Are they still okay?

Wes rocked his feet. *Rats.* My left foot. Something's wrong. Did Jay's treatment wear off? He ran his hand down his leg and reached the shoe. The lace is undone; hope that's all. He glanced toward Colby. They wouldn't notice. Wes furtively bent over. He tied the lace and checked the other. He shuffled his feet. Okay, now. Thank God, they're okay. Just the lace. He glanced again at Colby who sat trancelike with the gun aimed at Fischer.

Better plan this right now, Wes thought. Three options. Go for Timmy; go for the gun; go for Mr. Fischer. What's the best move? Wes couldn't do all three. He was closest and had the best chance to do something, but it could only be one of the three. Maybe those behind him would take care of the others.

Going for the gun would risk Timmy being accidentally shot. If he went for Timmy, the same could happen. Colby might move the gun and hit Timmy. Fischer was Wes's only play. He would have to try to push him or shield him before Colby shot. That was the best Wes could do. Maybe the others could snatch the gun and Timmy during the confusion.

If Wes failed, Fischer would drop from a bullet. Maybe it would shock Colby to his senses. Then again, he might continue shooting until the gun was empty. No way to know. Timmy would probably be safe as long as Mack held him. Mack wouldn't want to be shot by his own gun.

If Wes succeeded, there was a decent chance he would be shot. Soldier's risk, Wes thought. Better him than Timmy or Mr. Fischer. He should've saved Tommy. He had to save Mr. Fischer and Timmy; he simply had too.

Turning, Wes flashed hand signals to Nick and Daniel in the seat behind him. His goal was Fischer. They should try to disarm Colby and free Timmy. Wes would time it as best he could. With a bit of luck, he could shove Fischer out of harm's way and maybe avoid a bullet himself. It would be a short sprint. The timing needed to be perfect.

Wes stared at Colby. He didn't like what he saw. Call it soldier's instinct. Colby intended to shoot Fischer. There was no doubt. And it wasn't in a matter of minutes—it was any *second.*

Wes positioned his feet for a quick start and stooped, making himself nearly invisible. The element of surprise would give him an edge. Wes peered at Colby over the top of the seat.

Colby wiped the sweat from his eyes and ran his tongue over his lips. His trigger finger twitched.

Wes said a quick prayer. He expected pandemonium no matter what he did.

CHAPTER 27

Wes darted up the aisle in a crouched position. He closed half the distance to Fischer then transitioned to a full-fledged sprint. The sound of other hurried steps followed him.

Colby glanced toward Wes, a startled expression on his face.

Fischer now stood less than five feet away. Wes sensed another runner a split second behind him. He had no time to look. The other runner closed the gap between them.

Colby's glare returned to Fischer. His gun hand shook, but the twitching of his finger ceased. He squeezed the trigger.

Wes lunged with extended arms to shove Fischer from harm's way. The runner behind Wes dove at the same time, pushing past Wes and grazing him. The revolver flashed. The blast echoed through the car. A sickening *thud* sounded as the bullet struck. The acrid smell of burnt gunpowder filled the air.

Colby's hand jerked upward as the gun fired. He reflexively pulled it down, squeezing the trigger again. A wild second shot struck low on the opposite wall.

Wes winced as his elbow slammed into the floor. His arms had knocked Fischer off balance. Fischer tumbled to the floor, sprawling on top of Wes. Jay lay facedown next to Wes. He had outrun Wes and thrown himself between Colby and Wes.

Colby's arm jolted up after the second shot. Nick vaulted from a seat into a running dive. He crashed onto Colby's table tilting it wildly. The spinning table knocked Bryce flat onto the seat. Glasses, cards, and poker chips, fluttered into the air and onto the floor. Nick crashed into Colby pinning his arm against the seat back. The gun dropped from his hand.

Mack froze, a blank look on his face and his mouth gaping. Timmy wriggled free. He slid under the table and ran to the back of the car. Nick righted himself. He located and grabbed the gun. He positioned himself across the aisle, pointing the revolver at Colby, Bryce, and Mack.

Unhurt, Fischer struggled to his feet with help from Fred. Wes knelt on the floor and tapped Jay's shoulder. No response. Jay did not move. The gun had fired at point blank range; Jay had put himself in the line of fire.

Wes's stomach churned. This can't be, Wes thought. Not Jay. He took the bullet. He has his whole life ahead of him. That should be me. Yet there lay Jay, facedown and motionless. A tear slid down Wes's face.

Marielle Holyfield rushed through the door, eyes wide and moist. A grim expression gripped her face, her lips pressed together in a thin line. She inched closer to Jay and glanced toward Wes.

Wes looked up at her and shrugged. *Was Jay dead? Or was he badly injured?* He didn't know.

Jay's limbs flopped when Wes rolled him onto his back. Wes saw a round hole, surrounded by scorch marks from powder burns, centered over the left breast pocket of Jay's white steward jacket.

Marielle gasped. She knelt on the floor. Lifting Jay's head and upper body, she cradled him in her arms. Tears rolled down her cheeks.

She glared at Colby. "You shot my son, Mr. Colby. You shot my son."

HIS FACE PALLID, Colby's eyes turned away from Mrs. Holyfield. He swallowed hard. His foot nervously tapped the floor. She probably thinks I'm remorseful, Colby thought. Scared and genuinely concerned, his nerves shook his foot, but not from remorse. He was worried about himself. He shot a man. Not the one he intended to, but a man, nevertheless. And that man looked to be dead. How will I get out of this? What will the newspapers say? Can I somehow squelch the story? Can a good lawyer get me off? How much would it cost to bribe a judge—maybe a jury too?

Colby clenched his hands in frustration. His shot missed Fischer. Why didn't I shoot as soon as I had the gun? You idiot, Lamar. If he had gotten Fischer, he wouldn't care about the other problems. But he had missed Fischer. He waited too long. He wasn't done with Fischer. Everything would take a little longer. That was all.

Quinton had meddled in his business again. What's that clown's problem? Maybe he was a war hero once. Playing hero again? I'm not done with him either. I owe him more trouble. And that stupid steward. What a moron. He jumped in front of Quinton and Fischer. Trying to save the world? Well, that stupid steward got what he deserved for acting like such a nitwit. Why couldn't that be Fischer lying on the floor?

WES PLACED HIS fingers against Jay's neck. He felt a pulse. Jay's chest rose and fell with each shallow breath. No blood stained the white coat. Wes loosened Jay's tie and unbuttoned the shirt collar and the jacket. Maybe the injury wasn't as bad as it seemed. Maybe the bullet bounced off a rib and fell to the floor. Or maybe it ended up in the soft tissues of the arm or chest wall, which wouldn't be mortal. Wes glanced around the floor, hopeful for a miracle.

A glimmer, within arm's reach, flashed from under the seat. Wes stretched toward it. His fingers curled around it. Metal. He held his breath. A bullet, the nose flattened from impact. It hit something hard. Maybe it bounded off a rib. But then again, maybe it was the second shot.

Jay remained immobile. At least he was breathing and had a pulse. Wes lifted the side of the jacket where the bullet pierced the pocket, surprised at the weight. Still no blood and no sign of injury to Jay's chest. He examined the inside of Jay's jacket and his shirt—no holes.

Wes glanced at Marielle, who gently bit her lip. Wes reached into the jacket pocket and removed a rectangular piece of metal. It was Colby's chipped silver ticket with an indented center and adjacent cracks. The flattened bullet and the dent matched perfectly. Marielle's eyes glistened with a sliver of hope.

What irony, Wes thought. Jay shot by Colby. Colby's damaged ticket stopped the bullet. Was it irony? Fate? Divine providence? A miracle? Wes shrugged. Jay was still out cold. Something else was wrong.

Wes surveyed the rest of Jay's body. No sign of damage anywhere. Wes ran his fingers over Jay's scalp. He felt a swollen area. A goose egg. Wes examined his fingers. No blood. He parted Jay's hair. Just a lump, no laceration. Wes glanced at the rounded edge of the seat back. Probably the source of the head injury.

"Jay's knocked out," Wes said. "He has a good sized bump on his head. Probably hit the seat. The bullet struck the metal ticket in his pocket. Can you bring ice, towels, and smelling salts?" Wes asked Fred.

"On the way," Fred replied.

"Jay, it's Wes. Can you hear me? You bumped your head. Open your eyes. Everything's okay. Timmy's safe. So is Mr. Fischer. Your mom's here. Jay. Jay." Only minutes had passed since the shooting although it seemed longer. Jay should come around pretty soon, Wes thought. That is, if the head injury's not worse than he suspected. "Jay, it's Wes. Time to wake up. Your mom wants to talk to you."

Jay's eyelids fluttered and opened. "What happened?"

Marielle leaned over and kissed him on the forehead.

"Stay still," Wes said. "You have a lump where you hit your head. You were knocked out. Colby's old ticket was in your pocket and stopped the bullet. How's your head feel? You feel dizzy? Do you hurt anywhere else?"

Jay felt the lump. "Ouch. That's sore. I'm okay everywhere else, I think. Don't feel dizzy. I kept forgetting to take that ticket out of my pocket. Guess it's good to be forgetful sometimes."

"You remember what you did?" Wes asked.

"Sure. Caught up to you in the aisle and jumped in front of you," Jay said.

"You saved my life, Jay. That bullet would have hit me," Wes said.

"And you were saving Mr. Fischer's life," Jay said.

"Trying to," Wes said.

"Here's the . . . Jay, you're back with us," Fred said.

Jay smiled at Fred. "Not that easy to get rid of me."

Wes wrapped ice in a towel and laid it gently on the swelling.

Marielle took the towel from Wes. "I'll hold it."

"Jay, you ought to rest for a while," Wes said. "Get up slowly in case you feel woozy. We'll finish up here. We'll keep your jacket, though. It's evidence. I'll hold onto the ticket and bullet too. Maybe I can find the other bullet that hit the wall."

Jay stood slowly with help from Fred. "I'm okay," Jay said. "I think I will rest, though."

Marielle led her son out of the car.

COLBY'S EYES GLOWED. He would've danced a jig if the soldier didn't have Mack's gun pointed their way. No one died. In fact, nobody was even scratched by a bullet, Colby thought. The worst they can charge me with is attempted murder. A good lawyer will get me off. I'll buy my way out of it if I have to. If I play my cards right, I might not be charged with anything. I don't know about guns. I wouldn't shoot anybody. I was just trying to scare Fischer. I didn't know the gun was loaded. The gun went off by itself when that soldier crashed into the table. That's what did it. It wasn't my fault. Colby smirked. Mack and Bryce will back up whatever I say. We'll plan it out. There are no police on the train. The three of us will arrange our story long before anyone questions us. I'll have to put up with that nitwit Fischer until we leave the train. Our plans to take the train are derailed for now. I'm at Fischer's mercy but don't expect any. If I were in Fischer's shoes, I wouldn't give any either. I'll still ruin Fischer. The day of reckoning is just delayed.

"FRED, FIND SOME stewards to clean up this mess," Fischer said. "There's ice, poker chips, and cards everywhere. We'll figure out what to do with our friends while you're gone."

Nick still had the gun trained in the general direction of Colby. "We'd better check for other weapons," he said.

Daniel frisked them and examined Colby's bag. They were unarmed except for Mack, who had a six-inch switchblade strapped to his leg, and brass knuckles and extra bullets in his pocket.

"Mr. Fischer, do you have a lockup on the train?" Nick asked. "We can't let them move around. Too dangerous."

"No, we don't," Fischer said.

"Daniel, didn't you show me some old handcuffs you bought in Penceville yesterday?" Wes asked.

Daniel nodded. "Yes, sir. Two pair and in working condition. Have the keys too. But there are three of them."

"With two pair, we can shackle them together at the wrists or the ankles. Either way, where one goes, they'd all have to go, and that won't be far," Wes said.

Daniel retrieved the cuffs from his bag. After a little experimentation, the three instigators sat cuffed at the ankles. Mack to one of Colby's legs and Bryce to the other. With Colby's short legs in the middle, it would be difficult for them to travel more than a few feet on foot. That arrangement also left their hands free. No one would face the unpleasant task of feeding them.

"We can take turns watching them," Nick said. "They probably won't try anything, but you never know. Better to be safe." Nick lowered the revolver, flicked the safety on, and removed the bullets. He handed it all to Fischer. "We don't need the gun with them cuffed. Better to not have it around. Maybe you can stow it for evidence, Mr. Fischer."

"Are you all right, Mr. Fischer?" Wes asked. "I knew Colby would shoot. I had to move you out of the way."

"I'm fine. Thank you. What about you?" Fischer asked. "I landed on top of you."

"My elbow's sore where it hit the floor. Otherwise, I'm okay. Here's Colby's old ticket and the bullet. Probably should keep all the evidence with the gun. We might be able to find the other bullet. I think it hit the wall."

Wes examined the interior siding for the second bullet. The cherry framing and the handrail remained intact. The bullet evidently struck the bird's-eye maple. Wes didn't see an obvious hole. That necessitated meticulously checking each of the bird's-eyes. "Here it is." With the tip of his pocketknife, Wes removed the bullet and gave it to Fischer. "It's the darnedest thing I've ever seen. The bird's-eye almost swallowed it up. If you didn't know it was there, you'd never see it. We ought to keep it with the other evidence."

Wes ran his fingers over other bird's-eyes. He felt indentations in a few others as well. Wes looked closer and scratched his head. A *woof* from the back of the car caught his ear. Better check on Timmy, he thought.

The stewards had cleaned the area. Fischer pocketed the second bullet. He turned toward the troublemakers. "Mr. Colby, Senator Bryce, Mack. Because of your actions and the danger you pose to my other passengers and the crew, you shall remain cuffed for the duration of this trip. You will stay in this car and these seats. Your meals will be brought here. You will eat with a spoon. What you have done is unconscionable. To kidnap that boy, hurt him, and threaten his dog is a most despicable act of cruelty. Firing that weapon with the intent to end an innocent life is loathsome and odious. Should you misbehave further, there are other unpleasant options at my disposal, which I shall not hesitate to utilize. You will not want to learn what they are. Do you understand me?" Fischer's eyes were clear, deep, and forceful. His demeanor bore a strength and power that commanded attention. He meant business.

Colby nodded.

WES HURRIED DOWN the aisle and sat next to Timmy and Blackie. "Are you okay, Timmy? You were very brave. They can't do anything else to you. We have their gun, and they're handcuffed together by their ankles. They won't hurt anyone else."

"I'm all right. My arm hurt when that man twisted it. It doesn't now. Are Mr. Jay and Mr. Fischer okay? That was really scary."

"Mr. Fischer's fine. Jay bumped his head. He'll be all right."

"I'm glad," Timmy said. "If they're okay, then Blackie and me will be okay."

"Timmy, I'm sorry. When I told you to come after dinner, I didn't think Mr. Colby would be on the train," Wes said.

"That's not your fault, Mr. Quinton. They're just bad people."

"Do you still want the present?"

Timmy's eyes brightened. "Do I? Sure I do."

Wes felt around his jacket. "Here it is."

Timmy removed the paper from the mechanical dog. "Holy cows. This is swell."

"Wind up that key on the belly side. Then put it on the floor," Wes said.

The spring clicked tighter with each turn of the key. Timmy placed it on the floor. The toy dog began to jump and bark. Blackie cocked his head and added his own woofs.

"It looks just like Blackie." Timmy threw his arms around Wes's neck in a hug. "Thank you, Mr. Quinton. You're my best friend ever, well, after Blackie, of course."

Wes grinned. Timmy would be okay.

Chapter 28

Surprise!"

Fred stopped in mid stride in the dining car aisle with an emerging smile. He received a standing ovation from Mr. Fischer, Jay, Wes, Nick, Joe Croft, Marielle, and Mabel, followed by hugs and handshakes. The staff had rearranged several booths, so the partyers could dine together behind a long table.

"Please be seated," said Fischer, who remained standing. "Tomorrow, our trusted companion and conductor, Fred Ables, begins his retirement. We honor you, Fred, and graciously thank you for your dedicated service. We know you missed dinner tonight because of your many duties. In light of this, we have arranged your favorite meal. Jay will say grace."

Everyone's head bowed. Jay said a prayer of thanks.

Fred's mouth watered while stewards served the table. Filet mignon, lobster tails, mashed potatoes, and brussels sprouts steamed with delectable aromas. A side salad bathed in blue cheese dressing and buttermilk rolls with butter complemented the course.

"How did you know my favorites?" Fred asked.

Fischer pointed. "Jay let me know."

"How did you know, Jay?" Fred asked.

Jay flicked his eyebrows up and down. "I know many things."

Joe Croft elbowed Fred. "Come on, Fred. You're being silly."

Fred blushed. "Well, of course, you would know. Both of you. I forget sometimes. I'm embarrassed; I wasn't thinking. Maybe I've been on the train too long."

Wes glanced at Fred. Why was he embarrassed? he wondered. What was he forgetting? Wes saw Mabel glimpse at Fred, then at him with a quizzical look. Wes scanned the others at the table. No one else seemed to notice. Wes shrugged.

Fred savored a chunk of lobster dipped in melted butter. "Where did you find lobster? It tastes like it was just caught."

"Many places in the world have excellent lobster," Fischer said. "These are from Maine since that is what you're accustomed to. And they're fresh as you presumed."

Wes looked at his plate. Fresh lobster? Maybe there's a tank. Probably in the kitchen. But what if there isn't? He peeked at Fischer. He'd ask Fred later.

"We wanted to do something special for you, Fred," Jay said. "After all, it's your last supper on the train as conductor. Of course, you are welcome to ride at any time as a guest."

"After what's happened, I'm not sure I ever want to see a train again," Fred said. "How's your head, Jay?"

"It feels fine," Jay said. "The bump's smaller. The ice helped. Almost as good as new."

"Don't let him fool you, Fred," Marielle said. "Be careful. It's his funny bone that was bumped."

Jay kissed her on the cheek. "Real funny, Mom."

Coffee and Fred's favorite dessert, chocolate-layer cake, followed the meal. Mr. Fischer made sure Fred's piece was the largest.

"AND NOW THAT our meal is finished," Fischer said, "we shall toast Fred with champagne. One bottle was provided by Wes. Given our numbers, I am providing another vintage bottle for this special occasion. There are cigars for those so inclined."

The vintage champagne filled an unusual slightly asymmetrical bottle. The glass container looked handcrafted. Wes examined it closely. He saw no label, but a date was etched into the glass: 1825. He blinked and looked again, certain he had misread. He hadn't.

"Mr. Fischer, this bottle has a date of 1825 on it unless I'm missing something," Wes said. "Is that right?"

"It most certainly is, and it's an excellent champagne," Fischer said. "The champagne house is French, founded in 1811. I'm confident you will find it delectable."

Wes raised an eyebrow and rubbed his chin. "Can someone help me? 1825. What happened then? History wasn't my best subject."

"Plenty of things," Fischer said. "Let's see, John Quincy Adams became the sixth president of the United States succeeding James Monroe. There were only twenty-four states then. Charles X became the king of France, and Nicholas I became the emperor of Russia. King George IV sat on the British throne. The Daoguang Emperor ruled China."

"Interesting events happened in 1825 too," Jay said. "The first modern railway, the Stockton and Darlington, began operating in England. The Erie Canal opened. It's a remarkable 363 miles long. Ezra Daggett and his nephew, Thomas Kensett, patented food storage in tin cans. And, Rensselaer Polytechnic opened in 1825, the first engineering college in the United States."

"They forgot to mention a few other things," Marielle said. "The first hotel in Hawaii opened in 1825. Malden Island was discovered in the central Pacific Ocean by the British warship HMS *Blonde*. Uruguay seceded from Brazil. Oh, and Johann Strauss II was born in 1825. I just love 'The Blue Danube.' Of course, he didn't compose it until 1866."

Wes, Mabel, and Nick sat motionless with dazed eyes. It wasn't just the stream of information, but how quickly it burst forth. And not only from Fischer but, also, from Jay and Marielle.

Wes shook his head. "That was more than I bargained for. How do you know so much about history?"

"Perhaps I can answer," Fischer said. "The events we related are but a sliver of what happened that year. You see, history is a record of the actions of people, whether as individuals or groups. My, perhaps I should say, our fascination is people. History reflects what they do in time. By knowing the people, the events are easy to recall. Recorded events are but a minute part of the totality of human history although it often captures the essence of an era. Novels, diaries, letters, newspapers, and other literary devices also provide reflections of history because they come from people. Our interest in people is what makes history second nature to us. I hope that answers your question."

Wes smiled. "I feel like I'm back in school. Can I ask how you obtained an 1825 champagne? It must be difficult."

"That it is," Fischer said. "Of course, I have my resources."

Wes gazed at the antique bottle. Can't be many of these that even exist, he thought. How would you know where to look? Wes rubbed his forehead.

Fischer raised the vintage bottle. "Now, let us toast our good friend and capable conductor, Fred Ables. Also, our heroes, who were courageous in the face of fire today: Wes, Nick, Daniel, and Jay. We thank you all."

Wes sipped the 1825 champagne—smooth, fresh, and still a bit bubbly. Whoever had made it and the bottle were long gone. They probably could not have imagined it being opened over a century and a half later.

"I'd better return to relieve Daniel," Wes said. "I'm sure he's tired of looking at our cuffed friends. Is there a plate for him? I know he'd appreciate it."

"A plate's in the warmer awaiting his arrival," Fischer said.

"I'll relieve him, Sarge," Nick said. "You stay. Mr. Ables is your friend."

Five minutes later, Daniel sat beside them enjoying the meal.

"What are Mr. Colby and his comrades doing?" Wes asked.

"What else? Playing poker and drinking bourbon," Daniel said. "At least, they're keeping to themselves. Say, is that cake as good as it looks?"

FISCHER LIT THE first cigar. "Haven't had one of these in a while. Does a man good every now and then. Anyone else?"

Wes, Fred, and Jay each reached for one.

"A special night for me," Fred said. "I'll indulge myself."

"A special night for you," Wes said. "I think I'll indulge myself too."

"I got bumped on the head. And shot," Jay said. "I'll indulge myself as well."

The table erupted in laughter.

"It's been an eventful trip for us all," Fischer said.

"That's an understatement," Wes said. "I think I'm done with train travel."

"It's been a bumpy ride." Jay grinned and rubbed the top of his head. "I could've done with one less bump."

"Wes, thank you for what you did," Fischer said. "Not many people would've done that."

"Jay did it too," Wes said. "If it weren't for Jay, I wouldn't be here."

"I guess I have to thank Mr. Colby for his broken ticket and myself for forgetting to take it out of my pocket," Jay said. "I was lucky."

"You can go further than that and thank Mack," Wes said. "Gus told us Mack tripped you on purpose. If he hadn't, Mr. Colby's ticket wouldn't have been damaged."

Fischer tugged at his beard. "Odd how things work out. Almost as though there's some purpose behind it. Coincidence or complex design? Either way, it's a remarkable chain of events." Fischer stood. "I'd better open the window and let this smoke out."

"Don't! It's dark!" Wes and Fred shouted.

Fischer flinched.

"Sorry," Fred said. "That's what Mr. Colby did. It's a fresh memory for us."

"My apologies," Fischer said. "I should have explained first. For the present company, there is no risk whatsoever. There is, of course, more to it, but I'll enlighten you some other time. If you wish, you can stand on the other side of the car while I open the window."

"No need for that," Wes said. "We trust you. Fred's right about it being a scary experience. And we weren't even the one being pulled out the window."

Fischer opened the window.

"Boo!" Jay yelled.

Everyone jumped except for Fischer, who flashed him an incriminating glance.

Jay shrugged and grinned sheepishly. "Sorry. Couldn't help it. Don't forget. I had a head injury. Maybe I'm not quite right up there yet."

"You know better than that, Jay," Marielle said.

"Sorry, Mom."

Wes laughed. "Thanks, Jay. We needed that, probably deserved it too."

"I'll leave the window open until the cigars are done," Fischer said as he sat.

"What will you do with Mr. Colby and the others?" Wes asked.

"We'll let them off the train tomorrow," Fischer said. "The authorities will deal with them soon enough. Justice will prevail. Their days of causing problems for others are coming to an end."

Wes sagged in his seat and rubbed his eyes. The day had taken its toll. "I'd better call it a night. Time to give Nick a break. It's monotonous watching those three. Good night."

"I'll stop on my way back," Fred said. "Can I bring you coffee?

"I'll get some to go. Thanks, Fred."

WES SLID INTO the seat next to Nick. They sat directly behind Colby and his cuff-linked friends, who played cards.

"Any problems?" Wes asked.

"None," Nick said. "I don't know how they can play for so long. Nothing else they can do except sleep, I guess."

"Hopefully, they'll do that shortly," Wes said. "Appreciate your help. Go catch some shut-eye."

Wes didn't think Colby paid attention to anything except the poker game. Colby proved him wrong. The banker peered over his cards. "Quinton, guess you think Fischer's beat us. It's just a temporary setback. This isn't over. I know good lawyers, and I have judges in my pocket. I have the services of the good Senator Bryce and Mack too. My contacts will make Fischer's head spin. It's just a matter of time. I don't have a worry in the world."

"Do you drink champagne?" Wes asked.

Colby's eyes turned toward Wes. "That's a strange question. Bourbon. That's what I drink. Good bourbon."

"What's the oldest bourbon you've had? I assume you like it aged."

"Of course," Colby said. "The older the better. Sometimes I can buy twenty-five year old bourbon through my connections. What's it to you?"

Wes shrugged. "That's the best your connections can do?"

Colby's eyes widened. "Now look here, Quinton. Twenty-five year old bourbon isn't easy to find."

"Mr. Fischer just served us champagne from 1825," Wes said.

The players all looked up from their cards.

"What did you say?" Colby asked.

"You heard me. 1825," Wes said. "The bottle was handmade. It was like no champagne I've ever tasted."

Bryce snarled. "That's another Fischer lie. He's full of them."

"You know very well he's never lied to you. Not once," Wes said. "So here's my question. What kind of connections are needed to acquire an 1825 champagne?"

Silence filled the passenger car. A troubled look crossed Colby's face.

FRED SLIPPED INTO the seat beside Wes. Colby, Bryce, and Mack slouched in their seats, a snore escaping now and then. Fred bore fresh coffee, which Wes gratefully accepted. The night was overcast and starless. The *clickety-clack* of the train rolling down the tracks seemed especially monotonous in the quiet of the passenger car.

"Looks like they won't be a problem for a while," Fred said.

"The problem for me will be staying awake," Wes said. "This has been one long day."

Fred sighed. "Hard to believe. Penceville this morning with no Colby. Now we're guarding them. I'm glad Gus is in his new home."

"Me too," Wes said. "Nice party Mr. Fischer threw for you. I'm amazed at the lobster and champagne. And impressed with how he rattled off that history. It was akin to stating your family members' names. That quick. He seems to be more than a train owner. What else do you know about him, Fred?"

Fred pinched his nose and closed his eyes. "Gosh, I'm tired."

"Did you hear me, Fred? What else do you know about Mr. Fischer?"

Fred looked away. "Not much more than you. A special man. Very kind, very sharp, good to work for."

Wes glanced at Fred and wondered. Seems like Fred knows more. Does he? Or is he just tired? "What's the schedule tomorrow?" Wes asked.

"In the morning, we'll stop in Roseville, a town like the others. We'll reach the last stop after lunch. That's where we get off. I'll pack as soon as I'm back in the caboose. Then I'll relieve you. Joe will take my spot later. That way, we can all sleep a little. I'll fix breakfast in the caboose tomorrow morning."

"I need to pack too," Wes said. "Remind me not to forget that dowel jig."

"I'll do that," Fred said. "Be back in an hour."

Wes leaned back in the seat and stretched his legs. His eyes closed; his thoughts wandered. In his mind's eye, he saw his brother Tommy. A tear rolled down Wes's cheek. Sorry Tommy. I tried. Tommy's face faded; Timmy's appeared. Timmy was safe. We kept him safe, Tommy. He's safe; he's safe; he's . . . Wes drifted into sleep.

A snore woke Wes. He shook his head. *Rats.* Dozed off, he thought. Supposed to be on watch. He took a gulp of coffee. Colby, Bryce, and Mack slumbered. He'd be free of them tomorrow. Finally. Wonder if they ever have nightmares. Probably not. Then there was Gus. Wes smiled. Had to be others like Gus trying to do some good in a world too often devoid of it.

Fischer. He'd become somewhat of a mystery, Wes thought. Had a way about him, something special. More than a train owner. What else did he do? Fred seemed to know more than he would say. Why was that? More questions than answers. Wes shrugged and shook his head. At least for now, tranquility had returned to the G.F. Line.

Chapter 29

Night surrendered to morning. Joe Croft, Wes, and Fred each worked on a third cup of coffee in the caboose, weary from the guard duties, which had precluded a full night's sleep. The men had devoured a hearty breakfast, courtesy of Joe. A joint effort cleaned and dried the dishes, pots, and pans.

"This has been a wild train ride," Joe said. "I hope nothing like this happens when I'm conductor."

"It's been unusual," Fred said. "Not likely to happen again for a long time. I'm ready for some peace and quiet. Retirement sounds better and better."

"What will you do, Fred?" Wes asked. "It starts this afternoon."

Fred stroked his chin and gazed at the coffee cup. "That's a good question. Of course, I've thought about it off and on ever since Mr. Fischer told me. I don't know what I'll be able to do."

"Wish I could help," Joe said. "I haven't heard any stories, so I don't have a clue either. Must be special though."

"No doubt about that," Fred said. "It'll be different. I'll know soon enough."

Wes glanced back and forth between them. "What are you fellows talking about? Don't you have hobbies or other things you like to do, Fred?"

"Oh, sure. I like bowling, and I'm pretty good at it. Fishing, too, even though I don't catch much. I like to tinker with old cars. Fixed up quite a few of them over the years."

"Then do those things," Wes said.

"I will if I can," Fred said. "It's not that simple. I hope it's possible but I don't know. Anyway, I'll figure it out once I'm settled."

"Do you have a place to stay?" Wes asked.

"I'm sure there will be a place," Fred said. "I haven't been told any specifics. That's something else I'll have to reckon with."

"I can help you look," Wes said. "I don't have to be at the convention all day every day."

Fred fiddled with the buttons on his jacket. His gaze wandered about the caboose. "We can talk about it later, Wes. I still have plenty to do before I'm retired. In fact, I'd better shake a leg." He quickly stood and left.

"Did I say something wrong?" Wes asked.

"No," Joe said. "It's a big day for Fred. He has a lot on his mind. Big day for you, too, for that matter."

"For me? What do you mean?" Wes asked.

"Well, uh—um—well, you'll arrive at your destination," Joe said. "That's it. That's what I mean."

Wes closed his eyes and pinched the bridge of his nose. The events of the past three days had worn him out. Both Fred and Joe seemed evasive. Some of their talk made no sense. Was it just his own fatigue? he wondered. Theirs too? Odd that Fred didn't plan better for retirement. That wasn't like Fred. Maybe I'm missing something? I'm probably just tired. Overreacting, that's probably it.

"Joe, I forgot to ask Fred something," Wes said. "You probably know the answer."

"Sure. Go ahead."

"Has Fred taken you on a tour of the train?" Wes asked.

"Of course," Joe said. "Much more than a tour. He showed me every nook and cranny. As conductor, I need to be familiar with everything."

"Is there a lobster tank anywhere? Maybe in the kitchen?" Wes asked.

"No," Joe said. "Didn't see one anywhere. Wouldn't have missed that. Fred was thorough. Why do you ask?"

"Last night, Mr. Fischer said the lobster was fresh and from Maine," Wes said. "If there's not a tank, how did Mr. Fischer get it? That's what I wanted to ask Fred."

Joe scratched his head and looked away. "Mr. Fischer did say that. Suppose it could have been frozen. You know, fresh then frozen.

You need to ask Fred or Mr. Fischer. Well, I have things to do." Joe hastily exited the caboose.

WES KEPT AN eye on the Colby trio while he reviewed his notes in the convention catalogue. He glanced up when the train's whistle announced their arrival at the Roseville station and strolled to the window for a better view. The layout of Roseville mirrored the other towns, but it was built on a series of hills in a Mediterranean style. Tiled roofs, with colors ranging from reddish brown to bright orange, crowned stuccoed buildings in a variety of hues. Balconies, patios, courtyards, gardens, and fountains decorated the panorama. Stone stairways linked streets and pathways, which traversed the town. A duplicate of the Leaning Tower of Pisa graced a grand park on the far side of town past the central piazza.

Fischer and Jay exited the train first, followed by porters, Joe, and Fred. Luggage, passengers, and freight found their way on and off the train, following the protocol he had seen at prior stops. Wes glanced at the promenade from the station to town. Seems as though the same architect planned all three towns, he thought. The overall design is the same. The difference is the style. Maybe I'll visit Fontville and Roseville some day. His gaze returned to Colby, Bryce, and Mack. Given their proclivities to the contrary, they behaved. Thankfully.

The brief stop in Roseville ended. The train jerked and the whistle blew. The final leg of their journey began.

WES ENTERED THE dining car for his last lunch on the train. He wanted to say good-bye to Mr. Fischer, Jay, and the Holyfields. Their paths were unlikely to cross again. The car should have bustled with passengers, but it didn't. Wes saw Mabel Hawthorne behind the counter making fresh coffee. "Hi, Mabel. I've never seen the dining car this empty."

"They tell me it's always like this at the end of the trip. A lot of people wait until the last minute to pack. I did mine last night, but I still have a few things to do."

"Me too," Wes said. "I know I'll forget something, but I can't remember what."

"Oh, Wes, you have a subtle sense of humor. It's been so good to see you. I hope we see each other again."

"So do I," Wes said. "I wanted to say good-bye to Mr. Fischer and Jay. Have you seen them?"

"Jay finished lunch, but he's having coffee and pie. He'll be back in a few minutes." Mabel pointed to a booth. "Jay's sitting there. What can I bring you?"

"A sandwich, coffee, and a piece of cake would be great," Wes said. "I'll sit at Jay's booth."

Wes stared out the window. Sunshine cheered him, pushing the troubles of the last few days to the back of his mind. He would arrive at the convention soon. He'd see old friends and new faces; new gadgets and gizmos; and the old trustworthy merchandise. There would be much to take in. He hadn't seen the dowel jig in the catalog but would search for it at the convention. After all, not every product made it into the catalog.

Jay had grabbed Wes's order and delivered it to the booth. Jay sat across from Wes.

"How's your head today?" Wes asked.

"Fine. The bump's almost gone. Good thing, too. This will be a busy day."

"I hoped to say good-bye to you, Mr. Fischer, and the Holyfields, but I guess everyone's busy. It'll probably be a long time before I see any of you again."

"It'll be sooner than you think," Jay said. "I'm sure we'll run into one another in next to no time."

"I'm not likely to be on a train again for a while," Wes said.

"That doesn't matter. Mr. Fischer and I travel around quite a bit."

Wes sighed and rubbed the back of his neck. "I hope so. I feel like you're part of my family after what we've been through."

Jay smiled. "You are. We have been through a lot."

"I also wanted to thank you again," Wes said. "That bullet would have hit me if not for you. It's a debt I can never repay. I'll never forget it."

"You were doing the same for Mr. Fischer," Jay said. "That was a real sacrifice. I couldn't stand by and let Colby shoot you. Consider any debt repaid many times over. You're a good man. I have to run, Wes. Lots to do."

DANIEL GUARDED THE Colby threesome. They finished lunch as Wes returned to the passenger car.

"Did you and Nick eat?" Wes asked.

Daniel held up a crumpled brown bag. "Takeout."

"I'm proud of you and Nick," Wes said. "You've been a big help. You're good soldiers and fine men."

Daniel blushed. "Thanks. It means a lot coming from you."

"I'll be at the back of the car if you need me," Wes said.

The front door opened, followed by the voices of Mr. Fischer, Fred, and Joe. The three men strode to where Colby sat.

"Mr. Colby, Senator Bryce, Mack. We'll arrive at our final destination in less than half an hour," Fischer said. "That's where you will depart. We'll remove the cuffs if you pledge to remain in this passenger car until Mr. Ables or Mr. Croft comes for you."

"What happens when we leave the train?" Colby asked.

"You will depart the train station through the exit for your particular ticket," Fischer said. "Attendants will check the tickets."

"The police will arrest us?" Bryce asked.

"No," Fischer said. "You'll be free to go about your business as long as you keep your appointment."

"Appointment? What appointment?" Colby asked.

"That information will be provided shortly after you leave the train," Fischer said. "Someone will notify you when it's time."

"I want my things back," Mack grumbled.

"What things?" Fischer asked.

"You know. My gun. My knife. My brass knuckles," Mack said.

"Mack, you are a brash one. Sorry, but no," Fischer said. "Your luggage, though, will be available after your appointment ends. Again, gentlemen, on your solemn word, will you stay in this car until one of the conductors calls for you?"

"I promise," Colby said.

"You have my word," Bryce said.

"Me too," Mack added.

"Daniel, you may remove the cuffs," Fischer said. "Thank you for their use."

"Legs, please." Daniel said, removing the keys from his pocket.

Colby's legs flew out from under him when Senator Bryce and Mack eagerly raised their cuffed legs. Colby flopped back in the seat. His hat toppled to the floor. Mack glanced at Colby and snickered. Bryce shook his head and rolled his eyes.

In moments, Daniel released the three from the handcuffs. They massaged their ankles, grateful to be free of the hindrance. Colby had two ankles to rub. As the chief instigator of their troubles, that seemed fitting.

AS SOON AS he felt the train slow, Wes returned the catalogue to his satchel. He stared out the window and tried to recall the station at Lafayette Springs and the surrounding city. His last visit had been too long ago. Once he saw it, he felt certain the town would look familiar.

The train whistle sounded. Ornamental gardens of sculpted bushes and bright flowers flanked the train. The vivid landscape flowed by uninterrupted until the train came to a halt. A platform of polished marble stretched the length of the train, with a tall decorative fence of wrought iron bordering its back edge. Centrally located at the rear of the platform sat an undersized station building with two round windows and a single door. The modest sign above its door read L.S. Station. Uniformed attendants provided assistance at arched exit gates located on each side of the station's platform.

The exit on the left glistened with silver and gold embellishments matching the ostentatious style of the structures beyond the fence. Lavish buildings surrounded a central square adorned with flamboyant fountains and benches. Magnificent spires capped the larger buildings, further enhancing the opulent atmosphere.

Polished woods of different hues decorated the arched exit to the right of the station, creating a design both simple and dignified. The buildings beyond appeared unpretentious: whitewashed wooden structures with cheerful colorful roofs and matching shutters. Winding and crisscrossing pathways connected the buildings. Grassy areas, trees, and benches filled the spaces between the walkways along with chirping birds and frolicking squirrels.

Behind the station, an imposing stone building separated the two exit areas. The round upper portion of the building featured a domed roof and supporting columns. Majestic tinted windows of vibrant colors sparkled in the sunlight.

Wes scratched his head. Nothing looked familiar. Lafayette Springs was a city, and what he saw was barely the size of a village. Maybe they had moved the station to the city outskirts and added shopping areas. When last here, he seemed to recall the local paper talking about proposed renovations, possibly relocation. Things were always changing. Perhaps the city had. He'd ask Fred.

MR. FISCHER AND Jay disembarked first. They disappeared through the station door. Joe and a few stewards gave directions and answered questions as the passenger car emptied.

Everyone exited the train; no one waited to board. Wes watched Marielle Holyfield push a double stroller across the platform. Her husband directed the children in single file. Timmy and Blackie brought up the rear. The young mother and her baby, Nick, Daniel, Mabel, and other passengers that Wes had not met filled the platform. Most of the passengers exited the archway on the right. A few departed to the left. Attendants checked each ticket. Porters filled carts with the passengers' belongings.

A frown gripped Wes's face. There hadn't been a chance to say good-bye to Timmy and Blackie. He'd grown fond of the boy and the little dog. He felt his jacket pocket. A few dog biscuits remained. Maybe he would see them later. He hoped so.

Wes rubbed his chin, peering out the window. Something troubled him about the station. Not just the unfamiliarity. Why were there two exits from the platform? he wondered. Why were attendants checking tickets? The trip was over. Examining tickets seemed pointless. The two exits lead to two very different areas. On the left, ritzy. On the right, unassuming. Where were the passengers for the return trip? Was that on a different train? Maybe a separate station? How would he travel from the station to his hotel in Lafayette Springs?

If not for the voice, Wes might not have recognized Fred, who ambled toward him. He had exchanged his uniform for civilian attire.

"Time for Colby and his buddies to leave the train. Then we can go," Fred said to Wes.

Fred strode to Colby's seat. "Mr. Colby, Senator Bryce, and Mack, please follow me. Conductor Croft will point you to the appropriate exit from the platform. You'll be reunited with your luggage later."

Wes watched as the men exited the car, glad to be free of them.

Fred returned with a grin. "Finally rid of them. Do you have everything, Wes? Your satchel?"

"Right here. The dowel jig is in my luggage. That's it I think. Oh, wait! Give me a minute. I just remembered the most important thing."

"And what's that?" Fred asked.

Wes didn't hear Fred. He scurried out the back of the passenger car and returned a few minutes later.

"Sorry, Fred," Wes said. "I'm usually not this forgetful. The last few days must have done me in."

They stepped onto the platform. An autumn sun glistened off the marble.

Joe Croft approached them, his hand extended. "I'll miss you Fred, Wes. I'll join you when I retire. You know where to go?"

Fred smiled. "Of course. And I'm grateful for it too."

AN ATTENDANT AT the exit checked Wes's and Fred's tickets and allowed them to pass. A dozen paces later, they strolled amid the whitewashed buildings, which consisted of small shops, restaurants, cafés, and a tavern. A squirrel on a bench nibbled on an acorn. It watched them nonchalantly.

Wes shook his head and looked at Fred. "This isn't how I remember the station at Lafayette Springs. Nothing seems familiar. Something's not right about this."

Fred sat on a bench. "Have a seat, Wes. We need to talk. I have to be careful about what I say, at least until after your appointment. We can talk more when it's over."

"What appointment? What's going on? I'm here for the hardware convention."

"Someone will come for you soon," Fred said. "It's nothing to worry about, I promise. I know you've been puzzled. Everything will make sense."

"How do you know, Fred?" Wes asked. "And why have you been keeping things from me? Especially after all we've been through."

Fred looked down. "I can't tell you right now. It's not that I don't want to. It's just that, well, it wouldn't be appropriate for me to be the one. You're my good friend; please trust me on this. Your father asked me to look after you. That's what I'm trying to do. Everything will be okay. You'll see. After it's over, we'll have a drink in the tavern and talk."

Wes's face relaxed a bit. "I trust you. There have been things that seemed odd. We've been so busy I haven't had a chance to sort them out."

"You have a sharp mind. You notice things most people don't," Fred said.

"Who's this meeting with and what happens?" Wes asked.

"Wes, you ask questions I can't answer. I don't know everything, either. After all, I'm waiting for mine, too, just like you."

Wes's eyes widened. "You have an appointment?"

"Everyone who arrives here does. Mr. Colby, Senator Bryce, and Mack too. Considering their exit, I'd like to be a fly on the wall for theirs."

"What do you mean by that?" Wes asked.

"See, I've said too much already," Fred said. "I'm getting myself in trouble. I can't say any more right now."

"Colby tried to shoot Mr. Fischer. Mack hurt Timmy. And Bryce is cut from the same cloth," Wes said. "They should all be heading for jail. But they have appointments? I have an appointment? You have an appointment? Everybody has an appointment? Where's the justice in all of this? I don't understand any of it."

"You'll understand. Be patient."

Wes's fingers tapped the bench. "Yeah. Hurry up and wait. Rats. I'll wait. I don't like it, but I'll wait. Rats."

COLBY GAZED AT the ornate buildings. "This is my kind of place."

The three had passed through the left exit of the platform. Now seated under an umbrella outside a bar, they sipped aged bourbon. Other taverns, fine restaurants, high-end specialty shops, and a casino surrounded the central piazza.

"I expected the police to be here to arrest us," Senator Bryce said. "I don't trust Fischer."

"I haven't seen a single cop," Mack said. "No security guards, either. I don't know about this appointment, though. Maybe that's where they bag us. Want me to scout around for a way out?"

"No, don't bother," Colby said. "I've been looking. Haven't seen any way to leave here. Seems this place is out in the boondocks too."

"Probably more of Fischer's monopoly," Bryce said. "What will we do, Lamar?"

"We'll keep the appointments, whatever they are, and carry on from there. We should know more then," Colby said.

A young woman in a black business suit approached their table. "Is one of you Mack?"

"That's me," Mack said. "What's it to you?"

"It's time for your appointment," she said. "May I check your ticket, please?"

Mack pulled his ticket from his pocket. "This is when I'm arrested?"

"Oh, no, sir. There are no police here."

"Then he's being arraigned?" Colby asked.

The lady's eyes narrowed. "Arraigned? I don't understand."

"You know, charged with a crime in front of a judge," Bryce said.

"That's a strange way of putting it," she said. "No it's an appointment."

"Why is he first and not me or Senator Bryce?" Colby asked.

The woman shrugged. "I don't make the appointments. I only notify people."

"Well, when will our appointments be?" Colby asked.

"I don't know exactly. Someone will come for you when it's time."

Colby pointed across the piazza. "Is there poker in that casino?"

"I believe there is," the lady said.

"That's where we'll be. You tell them I don't like to wait," Colby said.

"Yes, sir," the young lady said. "Now, if you'll please follow me, Mack."

Colby and Bryce watched them walk toward the stone building. It was a solid looking structure as one might expect of a courthouse or a state capital edifice. What they didn't know was that Mack would not be returning.

WES AND FRED sipped coffee at an outdoor café awaiting their appointments. A bronze door on the side of the stone building opened. The Holyfields emerged with children and strollers.

"There's Timmy," Wes said. "Blackie too. I want to say good-bye before we leave."

"I'm sure we can do that later," Fred said. "Your appointment should be soon."

"Mr. Ables? Mr. Quinton?" The voice came from behind them. It belonged to a young man in a white suit.

"That's us," Fred said.

"May I see your tickets, please?"

"He sounds like you, Fred," Wes said.

Smiling, the young man examined their tickets. "Thank you for showing me your tickets. If you would both follow me, it's time for your appointment."

Fred's eyes widened. "Both of us?"

"Yes, sir. Those are my instructions."

Fred shrugged. "Time to go. Be nice to finally see the inside of that stone building. I wondered about it every time the train stopped here."

COLBY HAD NEVER experienced such luck at poker. He even irritated Bryce. The last player finally threw his cards on the table and left muttering, "Cheater."

"I guess that's it," Bryce said. "You've cleaned out everyone willing to be fleeced."

Colby squinted at Bryce. "Fleeced? Why this casino merely has my lucky cards. And, of course, I'm the best."

"There's that gal again," Bryce said. "She's coming this way."

"Mr. Colby, Senator Bryce. It's time for your appointments," the young lady said. "If I may check your tickets, please."

"Where's Mack?" Colby asked.

"I'm sure he's left. It's likely you'll see him later."

"Where did he go?" Bryce asked.

"I'm sure you will be told. Now please follow me."

"Where?" Colby asked.

She pointed. "The stone building. It's quite lovely inside, at least what I've seen of it."

CHAPTER 30

The young man led Wes and Fred through several halls within the stone building. A receptionist in a white dress rose from her desk when they entered a waiting room. Her radiant eyes and beaming smile instantly put them at ease.

"Mr. Ables, Mr. Quinton. I am Serafina. It's so very nice to meet you. If I may see your tickets. Please have a seat. We are waiting for two others. Then you will be seen."

"Isn't that unusual?" Fred asked. "I thought appointments we're one-on-one."

"It's extremely unusual," Serafina said in a soft voice. "Occasionally we schedule two at the same time. Four is extraordinary. I cannot recall it occurring before except when children and babies are involved. For adults, it's unheard of. I'm quite sure there's a good reason."

"No question about that," Fred said. "It wouldn't happen otherwise."

Wes glanced back and forth between Fred and Serafina. "I have no idea what you're talking about."

Serafina touched Wes's arm. "I'm sorry, Mr. Quinton. Please forgive me. I only now realized that Fred would know more than you. I didn't intend to make you anxious. Your tickets are in order, perfect. Couldn't be better. You'll understand why very soon. The others should arrive momentarily. Please have a seat and relax."

Oversized armchairs surrounded an oval coffee table in the modestly sized and cozy room. Classical music floated in the background. Subdued lighting completed the soothing ambiance. Fred and Wes eased into adjacent seats. Both remained silent, their heads lowered in contemplation.

Wes rubbed the back of his neck and frowned. He had only his imagination to guide his thoughts, which proved unhelpful. He wondered about the entire trip. His presence on the train from the start still puzzled him. Sure, there was the convention. But where was he now? Waiting for an appointment. What for? With whom? There was more that was troubling. If not for Fred, he'd, he'd, who knows? Maybe he would've tried to go back himself. But he trusted Fred. It provided him some solace that otherwise wouldn't exist. Fred seemed to know what to expect. Wes didn't. It worried him.

The sound of Serafina's voice carried across the room. Fred and Wes stiffened in their chairs, heads turning quickly in her direction. The sound of her voice didn't startle. What she said did. "Mr. Colby and Senator Bryce, please come in. I am Serafina. If I may see your tickets, please. Good. You may be seated with the other gentlemen. You will all be seen shortly."

In the dim lighting, Colby and Bryce didn't realize the identity of *the other gentlemen* until they sat.

"You two," Bryce blurted. "I thought we were rid of you."

"We had hoped the same," Fred said. "Must be a reason for it, though."

Colby sneered. "And what might that be?"

"We'll know soon enough. He'll tell us," Fred said.

"Who will tell us?" Colby asked. "You seem to know so much. Who will tell us? The man in the moon?"

"I bet it's Fischer," Bryce said. "Want to bet? He's been a big pain."

"At least Fischer finally fired you, Mr. Conductor," Colby said. "No fancy uniform. You can't boss people around anymore."

"Fred's retired," Wes said. "Mr. Fischer didn't fire him."

"We're here because of our problems on that stupid train," Bryce said. "What kind of trouble are you two in? You're in the same place as us. You're not as goody-goody as you think."

Serafina walked over and flashed a stern look. "Sorry to interrupt, boys. They're ready for you, all of you. Enter through that bronze door and be seated in front of the desk."

MUTED DIRECTIONAL LIGHTING revealed four armchairs and the front of a substantial desk made from polished marble. Colby and Bryce took the farthest seats, Fred and Wes the two closest to the entrance. Otherwise, the room remained dark with indiscernible boundaries. A profound silence settled over the room. The four men waited. Time dragged. Measured only by their thoughts, perhaps time ceased to exist.

A subtle breeze of fragrances swept over them: the smell of the sea, a light rain, blooming roses, incense, and dozens of other scents. Illumination, like the dawn of a fresh day, blossomed in the room's darkness. A cloud of fog shrouded the desk and then dispersed from a blast of roaring wind. A towering man in a glistening white robe stood behind the desk. His white beard and windswept locks framed a bronzed face scored with lines that spoke of ages and wisdom. His dark piercing eyes commanded attention. A sizeable tome rested on the massive desk.

The man gazed at each of them and then sat. With deliberation, he opened the voluminous book and spoke in a powerful voice. "Do you know who I am?"

Colby, Bryce, and Wes sat wide-eyed, too astonished to answer.

"I know who you are, sir," Fred said. "It's an honor to be in your presence."

The others glanced at Fred, their brows furrowed with uncertainty.

"Perhaps it would be preferable to assume a more familiar appearance for the sake of the others, Fred. What do you think?" the man asked.

"Maybe that would be better," Fred said. "Of course, you know best."

"I think you're probably right," the man said. "Perhaps it was an excessively dramatic entrance for them."

The cloud of fog reappeared and enveloped the man. When it scattered, Grant Fischer sat behind the desk. "I know all of you recognize me now. There is much we need to discuss."

"You," Colby yelled. "What is this, some kind of magic show? You could hide an elephant behind that desk. You're not fooling us."

"Put your hands on the desk. All of you," Fischer commanded.

Once their hands were placed, the desk and book vanished along with Grant Fischer.

"Do you see an elephant, Mr. Colby?" It was Fischer's voice.

Colby's eyes darted about the room. "No."

"Then what's that?" Fischer asked.

An elephant with its trunk swaying stared at them from the side of the room.

"Would you like a closer look, Mr. Colby?

"No. That's not necessary," Colby said.

Fischer shrugged. "You were the one who mentioned it. Very well. Let's put everything back in order."

The desk, book, and Fischer reappeared. The elephant had disappeared.

"How did you do that?" Bryce stammered. "Nobody can do those things. Nobody."

"You're beginning to catch on," Fischer said. "I am not *nobody* as you put it. I am also—"

The swirl of fog reappeared and dissipated. Jay levitated, arms outstretched, above the polished surface of the desk in a luminous white tunic. "I am also—"

Jay vanished. A milky apparition wafted about the room. It transformed into a galaxy of scintillating lights, which scattered before their eyes. In another instant, Fischer again sat behind the desk. Fischer interrupted the silence that followed. "Do you know who I am now? Don't provide them with any more clues than I already have, Fred."

Colby slumped in his chair. "I have no idea. Some kind of trickster."

Bryce stared wide-eyed, his face pale. He shook his head sideways.

Wes knew. At least he was fairly sure. Nothing else made sense. Even then, the thought boggled his mind. He shifted in the seat. His mouth felt dry and he fiddled with his coat sleeve. He glanced at Fred and Fischer seeking confirmation in their eyes. The answer had implications that were too overwhelming to consider. Nevertheless, it had to be so. No other explanation fit, as strange as it seemed. He had wondered about it now and then over the years. Now it had come like a thief in the night. So soon.

Wes looked at Fischer and bowed his head. "There can be but one explanation as to who you are. Forgive my confusion. I am having trouble believing what I've seen. You cannot be other than the Father, the Son, and the Holy Spirit."

Fischer smiled. "You have spoken truthfully, Wes Quinton. I know your conclusion brings realizations that seem difficult to reconcile with your experiences of the last several days. I shall delve into it in greater detail. Perhaps you will share the critical element with Mr. Colby and Senator Bryce. Fred already knows. I suspect that you have reasoned it as well."

"I will," Wes said, "but first, I am unsure what to call you."

"As you addressed us on the train is satisfactory for now," Fischer said.

Wes rubbed his chin, struggling with his thoughts. "Mr. Colby, Senator Bryce. I am still grappling with this myself. There's no other way to say it: we are dead. And we have been ever since we boarded the train. I know it seems otherwise, but we wouldn't be in the presence of God if that weren't true. Is that correct Mr. Fischer?"

Fischer nodded. "That's correct."

Colby crossed his arms and shot Fischer a stony look. "Is this some kind of sick joke? You expect us to believe this fairy tale?"

Bryce pointed toward Wes and Fred. "I get it now. Both of them are on your payroll. They'll say whatever you want. You can't fool us."

"Perhaps a few details might convince you," Fischer said. "From the train, Wes saw the flashing lights of the rescue squad heading toward the automobile accident that killed you in the state capital. Mack drove. He was speeding and reckless. The crash killed Mack, Gus, Senator Bryce, and you, Mr. Colby. That's why you boarded the train in the state capital. I am correct that Mack was driving and in a dangerous manner because you were in a hurry, Mr. Colby? How would I know these details if I am not who I say I am?"

Colby looked at Wes. "You saw us crash?"

"No," Wes said. "I was on the train and saw the ambulance's flashing lights as we entered the city. I didn't know it was for you. You boarded the train not long after that while it was in the state capital. You don't remember?"

Colby scratched his head. "Mack was speeding; he was always reckless. I don't remember an accident, though. Odd, I don't remember boarding the train. I remember seeing you on the train but not climbing aboard. Strange, but I never thought about why we were on the train."

Bryce's eyes narrowed. "I don't buy it that we're dead. I don't feel like it, either. I can walk, talk, move my fingers, and do everything that I could before."

"Hold out your left arm, Senator Bryce. You too, Mr. Colby. Watch carefully," Fischer said.

They did as told. Starting at the tips, their fingers began to turn to dust, flake off, and dissipate into thin air. Their eyes widened in horror. As their hands vanished, they grabbed for the missing limb with their other hand. They found nothing to take hold of.

"Is that sufficient or do you require further proof, gentlemen?" Fischer asked. "Perhaps I should leave the bones and ligaments."

"That's enough." Colby said, his face ashen. "Please put it back. You've made your point."

Colby and Bryce stared as the absent parts reappeared from forearm to fingertips. They balled their hands into fists and wiggled their fingers to be certain.

Colby stared at the edge of the desk and swallowed hard. "Maybe you are God. Let's suppose you are. Why do you make it seem as though we're alive if we're not?"

"It's a fine and legitimate question, Mr. Colby," Fischer said. "You have an intellect capable of understanding truth when you choose to exercise it. Let me first explain that by death, I expressly mean the death of your body, which is the lesser part of you. The greater part, and that which is immortal, is your soul, or what some call your spirit. The body is the vessel of your soul during your earthly life. Once the body dies, the soul is freed of it. Because the human is so accustomed to their senses, the separation of the soul from the body can be a disturbing event for some. Because I love my creation, I retain a semblance of a body for those to whom the loss of a body might prove distressing. Of course, even the semblance of a body requires a means of transportation. Thus, the rational for a train. I also use buses, ships, caravans, and so forth. In essence, I provide whatever is appropriate for a given period and the individual person. It is not a ruse by any means but a gentler way for many to make the transition. Your soul is most certainly alive. Your body is not and will not be unless you participate in the resurrection. For now, that is looking much too far ahead. Do you understand thus far, Mr. Colby?"

Colby nodded. "There's some sense in it."

"Fine," Fischer said. "We are making splendid progress. You know you are in the presence of God, and you know that your bodies have died. Incidentally, the initials of my pseudonym, Grant Fischer, and thus G.F., represent God the Father. The same for Jay Cedrick: J.C. or Jesus Christ. Out of humility, he simply goes by Jay. Make no mistake though, God the Son and I are in one another as one God. The same applies to the Holy Spirit, who was also active on your recent journey, as I shall elucidate later. Now, Wes, would you mind explaining why Fred was already aware of what we just discussed? Your mind is astute. I know you have reached the proper conclusion."

Wes sighed. "I'll do my best. There were many things during the train trip that seemed odd here and there, but nothing big that would jump out at you. Looking back, those little things point to something that I could not have understood earlier. I'll give a few examples. When I saw my father in Penceville, I wondered why he hadn't called or written me. That was out of character. After I saw him, I looked for phones and mailboxes around Penceville and never saw any. I also asked him to come with me on the train. He said he couldn't. Why was that? I realize now that Penceville is part of purgatory. He can't leave until his time there is complete. Certainly anyone there would not be able to communicate with those still living. Another thing I noticed was that all three towns, Penceville, Fontville, and Roseville, had the same basic design as if planned by a single architect. I wondered why. It seems now that each is simply a different part of purgatory. Am I on the right track, Mr. Fischer?"

Fischer nodded. "You're doing fine. Please continue."

Wes took a deep breath and slowly exhaled. "Mr. Fischer and Jay were always the first off the train and into the stations. Inside the station in Penceville, I saw them meet with both arriving travelers and those leaving town. There were separate waiting areas for each group. That seemed curious. Fred told me he had been in Penceville until he became the conductor. That means that Fred had probably met with Mr. Fischer and Jay when he first arrived. It would be nerve-racking for anyone to find himself uprooted and in a new town without explanation. I can only conclude that Mr. Fischer and Jay revealed and proved who they were to each new arrival and explained why they were there. That's why Fred already knew who Mr. Fischer and Jay were and that we are dead. What Fred knew because of his time in purgatory was something he couldn't tell me or other newcomers. I think that's the reason for the separate waiting areas. It reduces the risk that someone leaving, who knows what's happening, lets something slip to a new arrival. That information has to come from Mr. Fischer and Jay first. Is that correct?"

"That is absolutely so," Fischer said. "And you are right about the separate waiting areas. Secrets are difficult to keep. Even small gaffes can raise the suspicions of a perceptive person. I am aware, Wes, that you experienced consternation as a result of comments made by Fred, which seemed nonsensical at the time. Your questions about Fred's retirement come to mind."

Fred's face flushed. "I didn't spill the beans. I tried to be as careful as I could. It wasn't easy, especially with a good friend."

Fischer laughed. "Relax, Fred. You did as well as anyone could. Indeed, even the fresh lobster and vintage champagne contributed to Wes's bewilderment. Those were my contributions to his confusion. I know it was difficult for you, Wes, but we had to watch our p's and q's too."

Wes shook his head. "It's all finally making sense."

"Wes, perhaps you would briefly explain to Mr. Colby and Senator Bryce the nature of purgatory," Fischer said. "I know you are knowledgeable on the subject, and they have not given it thought for a very long time."

"Knowledgeable is probably too strong a word for me," Wes said. "My understanding is that after death, there are ultimately two possible destinations for souls. One is heaven and the other is hell. To enter heaven, souls must be pure and free of sin. For those who still carry minor sins or, perhaps, have not made a full remittance for their sins, there is a time of cleansing or purification in purgatory. This allows souls to reach a state of holiness such that they can enter heaven. If there were no purgatory, the only place for them would be hell. That would be tragic because there are many fine people whose flaws are relatively minor. As I understand it, every soul that reaches purgatory will eventually proceed to heaven after the required time to overcome whatever deficiencies are in need of repair. Of course, it's all in accordance with your particular judgment of each individual when they die."

"Excellent, Wes," Fischer said. "You have eloquently summarized it. And as you pointed out, purgatory is of great benefit to many people. That is why it is part of my creation. Perhaps you would say a few words about Gus, so that Mr. Colby and Senator Bryce might have a more concrete and meaningful example."

Wes smiled. "Gus is a much better man than I had ever thought. That became apparent when Fred and I had lunch with him in Penceville."

"What?" Colby exclaimed. "I knew something funny was happening. Is that how you bribed him away from us? You arranged to meet him. Behind my back."

"You're wrong, Mr. Colby," Wes said. "We happened to run into Gus by accident. Actually, he ran into Fred and it was quite a collision. In any case, he wanted to talk to us. I won't go into detail, but it became clear that he was quite a good man. He was always grateful to you, Mr. Colby, for providing him a job when no one else would. He was very loyal in that regard. But he didn't belong with you two or Mack either. That's why he left the train in Fontville. His ticket was for there. He was glad to be getting off. I'm happy for him. His time in purgatory has begun, but he'll be coming to heaven in time."

"Why, that's preposterous," Colby said. "He was just like us."

"Wes has spoken fittingly about Gus," Fischer said. "He was indeed overjoyed to be in Fontville. He is a man of considerable virtue. I'm rather fond of Gus and proud of much that he has done."

"Well, what about Mack?" Colby asked. "He's had his appointment with you already. Where is he?"

"He has departed," Fischer said. "Wes, I'm sorry to tell you this, but I know you've wondered about it for some time. It was Mack that pushed your father into the river that night after he left the bar. You've seen your father, of course. Mack, on the other hand, will not be a bother to anyone again."

A tear rolled down Wes's cheek. "I knew it. I just knew it. That's how he disappeared. Does my father know?"

"No," Fischer said. "He didn't want to know how he died. He only asked for reassurance that you were okay. I was happy to provide that comfort. I should also add, to their credit, that Senator Bryce and Mr. Colby had nothing to do with your father's death. It was Mack's doing, his idea. He did it alone. His girlfriend helped him cover it up with a false alibi. Mack was a bad one, sad to say. He's gone now."

Colby's eyes were wide. "You sent him to hell? You condemned him?"

"Mr. Colby, perhaps I should point out a few things that you and many other people simply ignore during their lives," Fischer said. "Before I do though, there is a reason why the four of you are here together. I rarely do this, but your lives were intertwined extraordinarily on the train and also with Wes previously. The contrast between the two pair of you could not be more stark. You and Senator Bryce do not fully appreciate the disparity. Fred and Wes do. Therefore, I do this primarily for your edification and contemplation, Mr. Colby and Senator Bryce.

"As I was saying, many people forget the day will come when they die, and that they will be judged by me. Some choose not to believe in me, and therefore rationalize that they will not be judged. Thus, they can conduct their lives as they wish. That is a mistake. Judgment shall happen regardless of what they choose to believe. And that particular judgment is really not that difficult. Each person builds toward his or her own verdict over a lifetime. There is no shortcut to heaven or to hell. One chooses their path and builds upon it. The course may be altered through free will, reason, faith, grace, repentance, and forgiveness. A bad path can be abandoned and a good one chosen. The angel, by virtue of its superior intelligence, cannot recover if it sins. It joins Lucifer's lot. People, however, can make mistakes, fall down, and pick themselves up again in the valiant pursuit of the high road of redemption and salvation. That, I applaud and assist."

Colby's face whitened. "Are you implying that Senator Bryce and I will be sent to hell?"

Fischer frowned. "I need not even look at the book before me. I know your deeds and so do you. Must I remind you of the evil you imposed on others? Both of you made a career of iniquity. You provided the record in this book yourselves. Your have bequeathed your own condemnation with no assistance on my part. I simply ratify it. In your case, it is so apparent that a child would have no difficulty."

"But," Colby stammered. "I, we—"

"We're not murderers like that awful Mack," Bryce said. "And that gun accidentally went off in Mr. Colby's hand. He didn't kill anybody."

Colby glared at Bryce. "Shut up F.W. Just shut up."

"Perhaps we should take a break," Fischer said. "That will allow a few moments for you to reflect on your lives, Mr. Colby and Senator Bryce. It will also provide you time to digest what we have discussed so far. Unfortunately, you have arrived at this point through your own efforts. You must surely realize that."

"I need a drink," Colby said.

"Me too," Bryce muttered.

"Would aged bourbon do?" Fischer asked.

Colby and Bryce nodded.

"How about you, Fred and Wes?"

"Coffee would be nice," Fred said.

"For me as well, please," Wes said.

"Coffee sounds fine with me too," Fischer said.

Wes began to stand. "Shall I tell the receptionist?"

"No need," Fischer said. "If I can do an elephant, bourbon and coffee will not be difficult."

"Forgive me." Wes blushed and retook his seat. "I forgot."

Fischer chuckled. "It does take some adjustment. Enjoy your beverages, gentlemen."

CHAPTER 31

That was a welcome interlude," Fischer said. "Before we return to the matters at hand, let me enlighten you about the train tickets. As you are now aware, it's a special train and, therefore, the tickets are unique. There are three kinds. Two are wooden and one is sterling silver. The cypress tickets are for those arriving in Penceville, Fontville, or Roseville, with the town's initial beneath the person's name. The gopherwood tickets are for those on their way to heaven and have L.S. inscribed below the individual's name. Incidentally, gopherwood is what Noah used to construct the ark. Gopherwood signifies a safe passage through turbulent times. The silver tickets with gold engraving are for those who would expect no less than the best, due mostly to their prideful opinion of themselves. Of course, you will recall that in the past, Judas betrayed Jesus, who you have come to know as Jay, for pieces of silver. Its misuse does not impugn silver, however. After all, silver did comprise the ticket that stopped the bullet and saved Jay. Incidentally, the silver tickets are also inscribed with L.S. like the gopherwood tickets."

"When I first saw my ticket," Wes said, "I assumed the *L.S.* meant Lafayette Springs where the hardware convention is held. That was a wrong assumption I now realize."

"That is so," Fischer said. "It is fortuitous that the initials were the same. It would have otherwise raised suspicions on your part. The *L.S.* simply stands for Last Stop, nothing fancy. We do have two separate exits from the station platform for the silver and gopherwood ticket holders. These two types of people have a tendency to clash. Your recent train journey exemplified that, so we separate them while they await their appointment."

"Mr. Fischer, the initials weren't really just fortuitous in my case were they?" Wes asked.

A smile crossed Fischer's face. "You are, of course, correct. My plans and knowledge are extensive and all encompassing. *Omniscient* is a suitable word. No detail is too minute to escape my attention. Had your destination differed from the *L.S.*, you certainly would have questioned it. I know you, too. So, it was indeed more than fortuitous. I do gloss over things now and then, if they are not germane to the more important issues under discussion. You caught me; of course, I knew you would."

Wes blushed. "I didn't mean to. I just didn't want Mr. Colby and Senator Bryce to think it was chance. They should appreciate your capabilities."

"Thank you, Wes. That's a nice compliment," Mr. Fischer said. "Now let us return to you, Mr. Colby. Perhaps you would like to take this opportunity to apologize to Wes for what you did to him and his family."

Colby sneered. "I will not. He blocked my attempts more than once. He was a thorn in my side."

Fischer's eyebrows rose. "A thorn in your side, Mr. Colby? You have been the perpetrator, the aggressor, the schemer, the thorn in the side of hundreds of your fellow human beings. As a banker, they entrusted you with their money, earned through the sweat of their labor. It is a solemn responsibility. Many fine bankers exercise their duties seriously and remember that it is people they serve. You foreclosed on Wes's father when his wife was ill, without an inkling of compassion. You destroyed the reputation of honest bankers so that you could illicitly acquire their banks. You embezzled, falsified records, and stole from widows, no less. You conspired with Senator Bryce to bankrupt businesses. That forced people out of work and brought suffering to countless families. Need I go on, Mr. Colby? I have recited but brief highlights of your career. Shall we pursue vastly greater detail?"

"That's enough. It's business," Colby said. "I'm not the only banker that does it."

"Sadly, I know that," Fischer replied. "Those that have gone before you are waiting for you now, Mr. Colby. You'd best hang onto your wallet. The others I shall deal with when their time comes. It seems not a one of you remembers the Ten Commandments. If you do, you consider them the ten proposals. They are ignored as though an unlimited waiver or exemption has been granted."

"Well, you never helped me any," Colby said. "Where have you been?"

Fischer sighed. "Mr. Colby, you behave like a spoiled child. You had fine parents who took you to church and Sunday school. And your Sunday school teacher, Mrs. Ellis, took a great interest in your progress and encouraged you. Do you remember?"

Colby squirmed in his seat. "I do, now that you mention it."

"You see," Fischer said, "I frequently work through other people. Sometimes, I arrange circumstances to nudge people in the right direction, which is often not so easy. My work cannot overcome the gift of free will I bestowed upon the human race. The widows you stole from sobbed genuine tears in your banking office. Not one tear moved you one bit. If that cannot reach you, then what can? What chance do I have when you ejected me from your life so long ago? I have made more attempts to reach you and turn you from your wicked ways than you would wish to hear about. Not one worked because you had no interest in them. Even on this trip, you were twice rescued and didn't realize it. You assume that nothing has been done for you. The fact is, we attempted everything that could have been tried. You have been totally obtuse to those efforts."

Colby crossed his arms. "Oh, really. Tell me how I was rescued twice during the trip. I don't remember either time. I don't believe it. What was I rescued from?"

Fischer leaned forward. "The first time occurred when you opened the window on the train. Did you feel as though something pulled at you through the window, Mr. Colby? And that your scarf choked you, almost as if in a noose? Did you not wonder how merely opening a window could create such a perilous situation?"

"I was nearly killed," Colby said. "Of course, I remember. It was some defect with your train and that tunnel. It wasn't natural. It shouldn't have happened."

"Congratulations. You just spoke a truth, Mr. Colby," Fischer said. "Indeed, it was not natural. Now let me ask Fred and Wes a question. Did you two notice anything peculiar while you struggled to free Mr. Colby?"

"We certainly did," Wes said. "There were strange black shadows floating around. At one point, they resembled fingers opening the window. It was eerie. I don't know what it was; it seemed to be pulling Mr. Colby and with great power."

Fischer nodded. "Those shadows and that unnatural force were real. The devil was trying to pry you, Mr. Colby, from the train and take you directly to hell. He wanted your soul without delay, and he wished to deprive both you and me of this meeting. My judgment is something you deserve to hear, so you understand it is not whimsical or capricious. It is based on reason and justice. An open window at night poses a danger only to those with silver tickets. For those on their way to purgatory or heaven, there is no risk. The devil holds no sway over them."

"The devil? I don't believe in the devil," Colby said.

"That presents a great advantage for Satan as far as your soul is concerned, Mr. Colby," Fischer said. "It allows him and his cohorts to proceed with their business freely with no defenses on your part. That creates an ideal environment for the devil to accomplish his goals. Devils are fallen angels and quite dangerous, cunning, and highly intelligent. They cannot nullify your free will, but they can certainly influence the decisions you make through distortions, lies, and deception. They have done a number on you, Mr. Colby, I am sad to say."

Colby's eyes narrowed. He glared at Fischer. "You still didn't tell me how you rescued me."

"Permit me to ask Fred and Wes one more question," Fischer said. "Did you observe anything else before you managed to free Mr. Colby from the window?"

"I remember small white flakes of ash that fell onto Mr. Colby's scarf," Wes said. "They drifted away before we freed him. I noticed them because they were so bright."

"Those tiny white ashes were the Holy Spirit coming to your aid, Mr. Colby," Fischer said. "The devils left immediately. You were freed from their grip and their efforts to take you to hell prematurely. Had you not opened the window in the first place, you would have avoided that sordid affair. The improper exercise of free will has consequences, Mr. Colby."

"Well, maybe you did something for me, and maybe you didn't," Colby said. "When else do you claim to have saved me?"

"Perhaps you recall your night in the line shack and the violent storm that battered everything?" Fischer asked.

"It would be difficult to forget," Colby said. "The storm was horrible."

"Indeed it was, and you were terrified too. You instructed Gus to make sure he locked the windows. You remembered what happened on the train. You were fearful because of it. Rightfully so, I might add. Do you recall the door of the line shack, or shall I relate it?"

"How would you know?" Colby asked. "You weren't there."

"My dear Mr. Colby, you forget who I am. Must I perform some tricks, as you say, to remind you?"

Colby took a deep breath and exhaled. "No need. The door beat against the frame because of the wind. Flashes of lightning lit up the gap under the door. Black shadows were there too. Awful shadows. It seemed like something was trying to sneak in. I could feel it. I made Gus block the door and stuff a towel under it. You're not telling me that was the devil too, are you?"

"You are catching on, Mr. Colby," Fischer said. "Actually, many of them. They wanted you, Senator Bryce, and Mack. All of you at once. For them it would have been a major coup. Do you remember what happened next?"

Colby rubbed his forehead. "I remember a piece of wood exploded in the stove. White ash flew everywhere. You mean to tell me—"

"Quite correct, Mr. Colby. That white ash was the Holy Spirit once again. The storm abated shortly thereafter. In that case, we rescued the three of you. Gus, of course, was in no need of saving. They couldn't have touched him."

Colby frowned. "What difference does any of this make if it doesn't change what happens to me?"

Fischer hesitated, a sad look in his eyes. "As I stated earlier, to find yourself in hell thinking it was a fluke, a mistake, or that you were somehow abandoned or misunderstood would be a disservice to you. Now you clearly understand why hell can be your only destination. You pursued it with all the vigor at your disposal. You are a man of great persistence and high intelligence, Mr. Colby. Had you used those traits for noble purposes, your situation now would differ considerably. And for the better, I assure you. At this point, there is nothing more you or I can say or do. My judgment simply recognizes that which you have chosen for yourself. Sadly, there are far too few extenuating circumstances to mitigate the outcome. My mercy is bountiful, but my justice is absolute. It is now time for me to address Senator Bryce. I give you the option of staying or continuing on your way, Mr. Colby. Should you decide to stay, I shall expect no interruption. What is your choice?"

"I prefer to stay," Colby said.

"No interruptions?" Fischer asked.

Colby gazed at the floor. "No."

"Very well," Fischer said. "And now to you Senator Bryce. Let me say outright that I know what you are thinking. Because of your political skills, and I would call them otherwise, you believe you can hoodwink me with honed rhetoric and meaningless diatribes. Should that fail, you are willing to trade information on Mr. Colby for consideration. First, remember who I am. I am God the Father. I know you better than you know yourself. Second, I certainly know all that Mr. Colby has done and you as well. There is nothing you can tell me that I do not already know. Do you understand your predicament, Senator Bryce? Your life in politics is of no assistance to you here. In fact, it has been your downfall and by your own choice. Just as Mr. Colby's choices have been to him."

"This is distinctly unfair," Bryce said. "I suspected as much, and now I know. You have a monopoly, and I have railed against them as a senator."

Fischer erupted with laughter. "Senator Bryce, you indeed have used the rhetoric of monopolies in your campaigns over and over again with much success. In the meantime, you have utilized every possible political shenanigan to centralize your own power, to create a monopoly for yourself. You achieved that, but it is not based on any valid accomplishment or whiff of virtue on your part. As for me, purgatory and heaven are indeed my purview, as is judgment following death. I am God. You would not exist without me. During your lifetime, the gifts of free will and reason provide you wide latitude. Free will means you have the choice no matter what I might prefer. There is no monopoly in that. Once your life is spent, then I am the arbiter. There is no one else. Call it a monopoly if it makes you feel better. In any case, the last day comes for each person. There are few who are unaware that they shall answer to me. Many choose to ignore their inevitable judgment. Often for their entire lives. When the consequences finally become apparent, as they do for you now, protestation and indignation are common. You and Mr. Colby have displayed both. You ignore what you have known for a lifetime and then blame me for your ignorance. It is akin to blaming me for free will when you make a bad choice. So please, Senator Bryce, use your intelligence honestly. Political maneuvering does not work here."

"Politics is a special vocation," Bryce sputtered. "Politicians are *special*. Our duties require us to do things the way we do. We're different from other people. Most of the politicians are like me. That's where I learned how to do it, from other politicians."

Fischer grimaced. "Politicians certainly consider themselves unique. As an elite group, they expect special perks and privileges. Also, exemption from many of the laws they impose on others. Do you suppose I should grant them waivers from the divine laws, Senator Bryce? I must say, far too many politicians have become a most contemptible lot, no matter what the century or place. You find every conceivable way to connect with those of your ilk, so you may enrich yourselves and accrue great power. You are easily corruptible; you pass your corruption on to any and all who will take their fill of it. You campaign with platitudes of virtue and the noble deeds you will accomplish and then promptly forget your pledges until it is time to campaign again. In your audacity, you profess your many years of sacrifice as a public servant. Those words should be struck from the language. Too many politicians are a public leech, drawing excessive salary and lavish benefits while doing nothing that serves the public. You mock the word *sacrifice*, the practice of which would be as foreign to you as that of honesty. So, is it your belief, Senator Bryce, that special dispensations should be made for politicians? Perhaps I should lower the standards for them because they are so very eminent? In other words, politicians deserve a preferential or special treatment by virtue of who they are?"

Bryce smiled and his eyes brightened. "I think that's an excellent idea, Mr. Fischer. Politicians certainly deserve such consideration, and I applaud your understanding. They simply cannot be expected to behave like others. I was afraid you weren't seeing that, but you were obviously thinking it through as you spoke. Yes, I think you have drawn the proper conclusion. I commend you for it."

Fischer chuckled. "I am most grateful for your blessing, Senator Bryce. However, those were absurd rhetorical questions. As representatives of the people and though their public pronouncements, politicians should exemplify virtues and truth as a beacon to the general population. Legislation and rulings, which can have profound effects on an entire population or enterprises, require substantial thought, attention, and diligent consideration of the consequences in all respects. Because the politicians exert influence upon entire constituencies, one could argue politicians deserve more stringent standards. They possess the capacity to adversely affect many others and, therefore, bear a greater responsibility. I am glad you made your point, Senator Bryce. However, the countervailing argument seems to carry greater merit."

Senator Bryce groaned. He wagged his finger at Fischer. "I think you underestimate the hard work we do and the long hours we put in."

Fischer's eyes narrowed. "I am well aware that there are highly principled politicians who devote themselves to their elected task and conscientiously fulfill their duties with honesty and integrity. They are, unfortunately, too few in number. More often than not, their efforts are overrun by the mediocrity and shady machinations of the others. Hard work and long hours are too often a byproduct of backroom deals, election rigging, political calculation, and shakedowns of businesses through threats of government intrusion or outright intimidation. Then, of course, there is the time spent in collecting bribes, the cover-up of corruption, and other malfeasance. In addition, don't forget the efforts required to destroy one's political opponents through innuendo, deception, lies, fabrications, and blackmail, if needed. On occasion, it never hurts to arrange a photo opportunity on the church steps to remind the electorate of your sterling qualities. That takes time too. Does any of this sound familiar, Senator Bryce? Is this the kind of hard work and long hours you were speaking of?"

Bryce stiffened and crossed his arms. "Those kinds of actions would be reprehensible. I would not be associated with them."

"Oh, really? Perhaps you would explain the bribe you paid to a municipal worker in Mr. Quinton's hometown to eliminate the public parking adjacent to his hardware store. Let's see, I also seem to recall a threat against my train. What was it?" Fischer rubbed his forehead and glanced down. "Ah, yes. You planned for a government agency to shut down my train for safety violations. Do you remember these two instances, Senator Bryce? Shall I go on? There are hundreds more. We could spend hours discussing them."

Bryce shifted in the chair. He swallowed hard. "Others did it too. It was accepted practice."

"Acceptable to those who suffered from your misdeeds, Senator Bryce?" Fischer asked. "You cared only for yourself. Earlier you were willing to rat out Mr. Colby if it would help you."

"I didn't say that," Bryce stammered. "You said I was thinking it. I never thought it, Lamar. Honest. He's lying again."

Fischer shook his head. "What a shame, Senator Bryce. Mr. Colby is the closest thing you've ever had to a friend. When trouble comes, friendship means nothing to you. Do you realize how vile you have become? Sadly, both you and Mr. Colby have been incorrigible for a very long while. I wish it had not come to this, but you both made your choices. You brought this judgment upon yourselves."

Bryce and Colby slumped in their chairs and stared at the floor. Neither could think of a word to say.

"Before you leave," Fischer said, "there's an additional matter. It's out of the ordinary, but I could not resist the request considering who made it."

CHAPTER 32

The office door opened. Serafina's voice floated across the room. "Your guest is here, Mr. Fischer."

"Thank you, Serafina. Please send her in."

Wes, Fred, and Fischer stood as Mabel Hawthorne walked toward a chair next to the desk. She carried a folded newspaper in one hand. Colby and Bryce remained seated and glared.

Fischer shot Colby and Bryce a stern look. "You two don't stand for a lady? Where are your manners?"

Mabel sat and smoothed her dress.

Colby sneered. "What's she doing here?"

Grant Fischer patted Mabel's arm; she trembled. "Mabel, no need to be nervous. Those two can do nothing to you. Thank you for your courage and your kindness."

Fischer stared at Colby and Bryce. "Mrs. Hawthorne is here at her own request to address you on a specific matter. That will take but seconds. Before she does, there is an opportunity to cover other issues that all of you will find compelling."

"What is this?" Bryce demanded. "We don't have to—"

"Silence," Fischer said. "Let's begin here. Mr. Colby, you stole half of Mrs. Hawthorne's savings, and you, Senator Bryce, short-circuited any investigation by the Bank Regulatory Board. Your criminal complicity is crass and cowardly. Would you have done this if she were your mother? Will either of you take this last opportunity to apologize to Mrs. Hawthorne? This is not her request but mine."

Colby and Bryce stared stony faced at the distant wall in silence.

"I thought as much." Fischer turned toward Mabel. "Tell them what they really stole, Mabel. I don't think they have any idea."

Mabel clutched the newspaper with both hands, took a deep breath, and looked directly at the two thieves. "What you stole, Mr. Colby and Senator Bryce, was our savings. Those savings came from my husband's forty years of labor. He worked long hours and many double shifts and overtime. There were times he was away from the family for months at a stretch. You didn't ask; you just did it. Had you ever asked for help, my husband would have given whatever he could. He was a generous man and would not ignore a person or family in need. You stole part of his life. But it's more than that. You also stole from the sacrifices both he and I made for our family and for our later years. The times we didn't eat out, so we could save a bit. The movies we didn't go to, so we could save a bit. The shortened vacations, so we could save a bit. You stole part of our lives. After the theft, I had to sell the house and most of our belongings. So you stole memories as well. I suppose I will never understand how you could do those things. It makes me very sad."

A long silence filled the room. Fischer gazed at Colby and Bryce. "Any apologies?"

IT WAS MORE than he could bear. The chair tumbled as Wes vaulted from his seat and shot toward Bryce and Colby with clenched fists. Bryce and Colby cowered in their chairs and leaned away. Raised arms covered faces frozen in fear.

Wes glanced at the desk. "Mr. Fischer, I've had enough of these ill-mannered ne'er-do-wells. If they can't treat a lady with respect, they need an etiquette lesson, army style. If you and Mabel leave for a few minutes, I'll take care of the instruction. Fred can go too. I can do this myself."

Fischer stroked his beard as he stared at Colby and Bryce. "Interesting idea, Wes. Perhaps—"

"You can't allow this," Colby screamed. "It's not fair; it's not right."

Fischer chuckled. "Funny coming from you. Not fair. Not right. When did you become an expert in those subjects? Let's see . . . fair? It would be one against two. Perhaps that's not fair. What about right? Come to think of it, you two deserve a good whipping. Can't argue with that." Fischer rubbed his brow and glanced at Wes. "You're sure you wouldn't need Fred's assistance?"

Bryce whimpered, "You can't do this."

Mabel tugged at Fischer's sleeve as she shook her head from side to side. "Please, no more violence, Mr. Fischer."

Fischer turned his head toward her. He winked with his left eye, which was hidden from the others.

Refocused on the pair, Fischer said, "Mr. Colby and Senator Bryce, a thorough thrashing might prove salutary. There is no doubt that Mr. Quinton would provide a masterful pounding. His anger at you is justified. Does righteous indignation come to mind?"

Colby looked ashen as though the fear of God had overcome him. Actually, it was the fear of what God might permit Wes to do. Colby stuttered, "We're sorry. We're sorry. I apologize, Mrs. Hawthorne."

"Me too," Bryce added.

"What wimps." Wes shook his head in disgust. "You apologize under pressure. Otherwise, you're real tough guys. Tough on women too."

Wes stepped back and righted his chair. His stare drilled through Colby and Bryce for a half minute before he sat. "I'm sorry, Mr. Fischer. Those two can say and do whatever they want to me. But when it comes to other innocent people, like Mabel, I don't deal with that very well. She's my godmother, too."

Fischer nodded at Wes. "Perfectly understandable and, yes, there is a duty to protect and assist the innocent. That's what you did on the train journey. Those two deserve a healthy beating, but it's far too late for that."

"Too late? Why?" Wes asked.

"The time for it would have been many decades ago when the lesson might have transformed a life not yet fully entrenched in malevolent ways," Fischer said. "Take, for example, a school bully who preys on the scrawny classmate and knocks him to the ground. It's an unequal match. The bully is the true coward. What's grand is when that scraggy victim jumps back to their feet and decks their tormentor with one punch. That has instantly reformed many a bully and to his benefit for a lifetime. For Mr. Colby and Senator Bryce, such a lesson would've had to occur long before now."

Wes looked down and shook his head. "Rats. I'm sorry for what I just did. Justice seems to ride a slow horse at times."

"Don't forget," Fischer said, "that justice comes in many forms. It can take place even when you're not aware of it. Sometimes you even find it in black and white."

Wes shrugged. "Did I miss something?"

"IF YOU WOULD, please hand me the newspaper, Mabel," Fischer said. "That's what I was referring to, Wes. The black and white."

Mabel unfolded the paper as she passed it to Fischer.

Fischer laid the newspaper on the desk. "I usually don't do this, but there's a good reason for the exception." He scanned the front page. "Interesting. Today's paper, the *Tribune*, from the state capitol. Here's the headline: 'Task Force Exposes Vast Banking and Government Corruption.' The line below it reads: 'Late Senator Bryce and Banking Magnate Colby at Center of Probe.'"

"What?" Colby shouted. "That's a lie. More tricks."

Fischer raised the paper so Colby and Bryce could see the front page. Stock photos of them stared back. "I'll read several paragraphs of the article so you can judge if anything rings true."

> A special task force investigating banking and state government corruption expects to issue indictments soon, according to informed sources. The governor secretly convened the task force two years ago, due to the relentless efforts of attorney Sam Knight.
>
> Sam Knight represents Mrs. Mabel Hawthorne and another widow, both allegedly defrauded by banking magnate Lamar Colby. Knight also alleges that complicit state banking regulators failed to investigate the cases because of corruption linked to Senator Bryce.
>
> Senator Bryce and Lamar Colby died in an auto accident earlier this week as did two of Colby's close associates. Although the investigation initially centered on Bryce and Colby, sources say the probe will also snare other lawmakers, government agencies, Colby's banking empire, and other financial institutions. Sources suggest the deaths of Bryce and Colby will not adversely affect the probe or its outcome. The task force has already assembled extensive evidence.

> Attorney Sam Knight has been a member of the task force since its inception. Today, he expressed confidence that there will be restitution for the many victims. He is certain that scores of convictions and resignations will result.
>
> Late this afternoon, the governor announced that Sam Knight has been appointed to fill the remaining four years of Senator Bryce's term. By senate rules, Senator Knight will retain all seniority previously held by Bryce.

Fischer looked up from the paper. "That's the meat of it. You'll each find a copy of the paper in your luggage. There are plenty of other related articles including a nice one on Sam Knight."

Colby and Bryce slumped in their chairs. They resembled recipients of a good beating, absent the bruises and black eyes. Thin smiles decorated Wes's and Fred's faces.

"Bless Sam," Mabel said. "He never gave up."

"No, he didn't," Fischer replied. "Sam's work for you and other defrauded clients was pro bono. He wanted only justice and restitution; he achieved both. For your information, Mabel, your family will receive full restitution, plus interest and damages. All of your grandchildren will be able to attend college because of it."

"I'm so grateful." A tear rolled down Mabel's cheek.

"You should also know," Fischer said, "that Sam, despite his lack of political ambition, will later be conscripted into running for governor and win handily. By the end of his term, corruption in the state will be found nowhere except in the dictionary. He will refuse to run for a second term. He will feel his work is done, and he will return to his law practice."

FISCHER TURNED TOWARD Mabel. "I must apologize to you, Mabel. You returned to address Mr. Colby and Senator Bryce briefly on a particular matter, and we've been sidetracked ever since. The floor is yours."

Mabel straightened the crease in her dress and swallowed. Her gaze turned to Bryce and Colby. Her soft green eyes made it impossible for theirs to turn away. She could see they expected the worst and rightfully so. What she had to say would not be what they anticipated. Not at all. Perhaps it would help them in some small way. She had already done it, years ago. They just didn't know it.

Irritation grew on Bryce's face. "Can we be done with this?"

"Sorry," Mabel said. "Senator Bryce and Mr. Colby, you have not been kind to me. I want you to know that I forgive you both. I actually did so years ago. That does not mean I forget. Those memories need no mothballs to preserve them. But I have forgiven you."

Bryce and Colby stared at her with open mouths.

"I'm ready to go, Mr. Fischer," Mabel said.

Fischer escorted her to the door at the back of the office.

WITH HIS HEAD bowed, Fischer returned to the chair behind his desk. He laced his fingers together. His face lifted toward the men. A touch of sadness grazed his eyes as they met those of Colby and Bryce. "It gives me no pleasure, but it's now time for both of you to go."

A portion of the wall at the far side of the room slid open. Dim lighting revealed a vestibule with two bronze doors, each accompanied by an attendant. Colby picked up his travel bag, inched toward the doors, and grabbed his suitcase with his free hand. Bryce, a step behind, angrily jerked his luggage from the floor. The attendants opened the doors. A dark corridor, faintly illuminated by red lights, sloped downward. Sporadic flickers of orange, yellow, and red mingled with beckoning black shadows in the distance. Faint moans rumbled from the bowels of darkness. Colby and Bryce trudged through the doors and crept forward. Bryce looked back, glared at Fischer, and spat on the floor. A faint stench of sulfur momentarily lingered. The attendants closed the bronze doors. The sliding wall returned to its original position.

CHAPTER 33

Fischer stared down at his hands and sighed. "It's always poignant when souls leave this office in the manner Mr. Colby and Senator Bryce just did. The best I can do, once they've reached this point, is to make them aware that my justice is unimpeachable. They need to know that my efforts to reach them during their lives continued until exhausted by their deaths. Even then, most remain defiant, argumentative, accusatory, and in denial. I hoped that your presence might facilitate a degree of comprehension on their part. Unfortunately, it did not. It did, however, make it more difficult for them to deny their offenses, at least insofar as they pertained to you. So, thank you, Fred and Wes, for your help. It certainly was not my intention for the train journey to be an unpleasant experience. You deserved the opposite. That is how it shall be for you from now on. Good people bring me boundless joy. It is like the friendship shared by the two of you. I know you are both gratified by it."

"It's special beyond words," Wes said. "I can't imagine the trip without Fred."

Fred patted Wes on the back. "The same for me. Without Wes, it would have been like an empty book."

"Wes, there are a few things I would like to discuss with you, to set the record straight, if you wouldn't mind?" Fischer said.

Wes's brow furrowed. "I was afraid of this. I'm sorry, Mr. Fischer. I know I've messed up at times." Wes swallowed and looked down while he fumbled with his watch. His eyes widened. "Does Fred, does Fred—"

Fred and Fischer stared at him.

"What's wrong?" Fred asked. "You all right?"

"It's nothing, just my watch," Wes said. "Caught me off guard. It's not important."

"It's not trivial either," Fischer said. "You have a remarkable eye for detail and a memory to accompany it. Tell us about your watch, and I'll explain what happened."

Wes's shrugged. "It's pretty straightforward. After I woke on the train, I saw my watch wasn't working. The crystal was cracked too. The time was 10:07. I remember because I fiddled with it for a while. It still didn't work. Out of habit, I'd look at it now and then. Of course, the 10:07 didn't change. After a day, I stopped looking. I don't know how I broke it. But just now I looked and—"

"It shows 12:55 precisely," Fischer said.

Wes lifted his arm and showed the watch. "That's right. It's not working now, but it must have for a while. How did you know that time?"

Fischer chuckled. "It involves celestial physics, which you will have to take on faith. Your watch broke as it struck a shelf the night you died. That's why you don't remember breaking it. That's the 10:07 time. When you died, your soul entered eternity in which there is no time. Broken or not, your watch would not have advanced since time had ended for you. The question becomes this: Why did your watch advance exactly two hours and forty-eight minutes to 12:55?"

Wes rubbed his forehead and gazed at the watch. "I think I may know. I was trying to estimate how long I was off the train in Penceville: time at the station, walking, the stores, the café, lunch with Gus, time with my dad, time with Jay and the children. I'm forgetting something."

"The buckboard ride," Fred said.

"That's right," Wes said. "All together, that's probably close to three hours. And I think I saw a watch repair shop in Penceville. I did; I remember the shop now. Why would that be there? Wait a minute. My dad's shop had a clock. It was on the wall near the checkout. So there is time in Penceville. That must be it. Penceville is part of purgatory where there is time. While I was off the train, I was back in time, so my watch moved forward. Is that it? That's hard to wrap your mind around."

Fischer grinned. "Splendid. That's precisely what happened. Had you looked, your watch was working in Penceville. There is time throughout purgatory because each person has their particular time to complete. Therefore, there must be time there. In eternity there is not, although some jokingly call it *all the time in the world*, even though that's not technically correct. It is difficult to grasp. Even Einstein struggled with it."

"That makes me feel better," Wes said. "Sorry I interrupted you before. You were saying something about setting the record straight. I was worried that maybe I received the wrong ticket."

"Heavens no," Fischer said. "I wanted to talk to you about your brother."

Wes's brow furrowed. "Tommy? Is he all right?"

"He is fine. You will see him in heaven."

"Thank God. I mean—"

Fischer chuckled. "You're welcome."

Wes rolled his eyes and shook his head with an embarrassing smile.

"What I wanted to discuss is the blame you have put on yourself for his death," Fischer said. "You have carried that guilt ever since that awful day during the war. You could not have reacted any quicker. No one could have. He wasn't even supposed to be in that sector. In war, as you are well aware, mistakes happen. Things often go badly. You did all you could have. There is no blame on you, Wes, none whatsoever. I'm sorry this has needlessly burdened you for so long."

Wes buried his face in his hands and sobbed. Fred put an arm around him and pushed a handkerchief into his palm. Wes dabbed his eyes and straightened in the chair.

"Thank you, Mr. Fischer," Wes said. "I always thought I'd failed Tommy. I guess I didn't realize how much it has affected me all these years."

"You've had nightmares from it," Fischer said. "That's what first aroused you on the train. You won't have them anymore. And because there was no blame, there was also no need for redemption on your part. Your mind told you there was, but there wasn't."

"I'm not sure what you mean, Mr. Fischer," Wes said.

"Let me approach it this way. What did Timmy mean to you on the trip?"

"I like Timmy," Wes said. "Why, he's like a little brother. I had to look after him and protect—"

"Do you understand now, Wes?" Fischer asked. "You didn't have to protect Timmy for redemption because of what happened to your brother. You needed no redemption for that. You would have protected Timmy anyhow because of who you are."

Wes slowly shook his head. "My gosh, I hadn't realized that. We don't always understand things very well, do we? I mean, people."

"No. It's complicated sometimes," Fischer said. "You see, I know you better than you know yourself. Now, if you feel up to it, there's another topic I'd like to address."

Wes nodded. "I'm ready."

"Very well," Fischer said. "It's the matter of justice. I know that wrongdoing and a frequent lack of justice have been distressing to your sense of propriety. Alas, in the world of man, justice is too often lacking, inadequate, or, at times, overzealous. It is a source of frustration and exasperation to those who cherish it. Even the highest courts can ignore the wisdom of the ages and lofty principles and arrive at atrocious decisions through foolishness, agendas, and illogic. When a child can easily see what is right and jurisprudence rules otherwise, then where is justice? Flawed rulings often result in dastardly consequences similar to those that result from the actions of unscrupulous politicians. Those effects can be extensive and reverberate throughout an entire population. The administration of justice is truly a solemn matter requiring extraordinary diligence.

"And there are also the injustices of everyday life in every imaginable aspect. Those can become overwhelmingly wearisome. You and your family, Wes, have had their share. So did Mabel and others cheated by Mr. Colby. The justice does not always come in your lifetime. But it does come. Your father knew that. It often brought him a sense of peace at which I know you marveled. I am the ultimate source of justice, taking into account even the minutest of factors and blending in whatever mercy is due. The imperfect and often absent justice in the world was an affront to you, Wes, because you knew it should be better. I concur with your thoughts. Perfect justice comes only from me.

"Death is when my justice is administered for the life one lived on earth. Death is also the gateway to eternity. Life is fleeting and short. Eternity is forever. People would do better if they heeded that. Your dad understood my justice better than most. I think you now do as well."

"I do," Wes said. "I wish I had grasped it as well as my father did. He had more patience; I should've done better."

"Well, that's covered," Fischer said. "If I can answer any questions, I would be pleased to do so."

"Wes asked me something this morning that I couldn't answer," Fred said. "He wanted to know what I will do in retirement. Of course, he didn't know what *retirement* meant when he asked. What will we be doing, Mr. Fischer?"

"It's an excellent question," Fischer said. "In the world, there is much that is splendid and many admirable and enjoyable leisurely pursuits. You will find heaven beyond your fondest dreams. I will give no specifics. It's preferable that it be a complete and delightful surprise. You will be there shortly. You will not be disappointed. Perhaps, I should add, you will not face any issues similar to those you recently confronted on the train."

"That's an improvement already," Fred said.

"And how about you, Wes?" Fischer asked. "You look pensive."

"I was wondering about the shooting," Wes said. "What if the silver ticket wasn't in Jay's pocket when Mr. Colby fired the gun? Would Jay have died? Or what if the bullet hit me? Would I have died again? And if we hadn't reached you in time, would you have died? It's confusing. I have no idea."

"That's quite a question," Fischer said. "It's hypothetical because the alternatives did not occur. Nevertheless, neither I, nor Jay, nor the Holy Spirit, for that matter, can die in the sense you are thinking because we are God. We are, however, extinct to people who choose to ignore us through the improper exercise of their free will. In their minds, we are dead, so to speak. That does not mean we don't try to reach them in many ways unique to their situation and character. As long as there's life, we try. We are successful in many instances but not always. As for you, you would not have died again on the train. Any other questions?"

Wes's brow furrowed as he rubbed his chin. "I'm realizing some things that hadn't occurred to me before. It's all so incredible. I'm second-guessing myself."

"Go ahead and ask," Fischer said.

"When I woke on the train, my feet bothered me," Wes said. "Jay brought a foot soak and dried my feet afterward. It reminds me of the Bible when Jesus washed his disciples' feet. It was an act of humility and service. Jesus set the example. Of course, I'm no disciple like them."

"Jesus has not changed. What Jay did for you was Jesus being himself," Fischer said. "As for you, Wes, you very much followed Jesus in the manner in which you lived your life. That makes you a disciple. It's not the times, it's the way of life."

"I hadn't thought of it like that before," Wes said.

"Most don't but it's quite true," Fischer said. "Disciples are needed in all eras."

"There's also something that Fred must have already known but couldn't tell me," Wes said. "I knew there was something special about them when I first saw them. It's still astonishing, but everything is now. Mr. and Mrs. Holyfield are Mary and Joseph. I know Mrs. Holyfield is Jay's mother because she told me. It all fits."

"You are quite correct," Fischer said. "Mary and Joseph are a help and blessing to me and to all. They care for the children and babies that are passengers on the train. They love them and watch over them as family."

Wes frowned and looked down at his hands. "The children and babies have all died?"

"I'm afraid so," Fischer said. "It's heartbreaking that their lives have been so brief. Some died from accidents and others from illness. Many of the small babies were miscarried. Some were taken before they were born because they were unwanted. It's terribly tragic. It brings a great darkness to society when the innocent and defenseless become expendable. Next, it will be the elderly, the disabled, and those with mental illness. Eventually that society shall be torn apart by its disregard for life."

"And Timmy and Blackie have died too?" Wes asked.

Fischer nodded. "Yes, a lightning strike. It was instantaneous. Timmy and I had a nice chat earlier. He's a delightful boy, and I know both you and Fred are quite fond of him. He showed me the chess set and toy dog."

"We'll watch over him," Wes said.

"Thank you," Fischer said. "He will like that. He cares deeply about both of you. You've also made new friends of Nick and

Daniel, who admire you. They died in battle. They were both decorated war heroes like you, Wes."

"I don't know why it is, but the best often seem to die at a young age," Wes said.

"I take very good care of them," Fischer said. "The world could use more like them."

"Will I see my father again soon?" Wes asked.

"It won't be long at all," Fischer said. "In heaven there is no time; it's eternal. When your father arrives, it will be as though he was always there. It's difficult to explain and comprehend. You will be pleased to know your mother is in heaven, so you will see her along with your brother. There are also many ancestors you have never met before. It will keep you busy."

"If you don't mind, Mr. Fischer, there are a few questions that may be a little silly," Wes said.

"Please ask," Fischer replied.

"I was thinking about the bird's-eye maple wainscoting in the passenger car," Wes said. "With Mr. Colby's second shot, the bullet hit right in a bird's-eye. It took a while to find it. The strange thing was, there were holes in other bird's-eyes too. Has that happened before? Shots where the bullet hit the bird's-eye? The odds wouldn't favor it, but I can't make sense of it otherwise."

"It's a question no one has asked before," Fischer said. "Yes, each hole was from a bullet. It has not happened frequently, but the train is quite old. It's a simple matter to deflect a bullet to a bird's-eye. That is for me, Jay, or the Holy Spirit. It eliminates the need for repairs. We aren't bound by probability and have a little fun now and then. It's remarkable that you noticed it."

"The only other question has to do with my hardware store," Wes said. "My will leaves it and the lumberyard to my store manager, who's been a good friend for a long time."

"He's a fine man and grateful for what you did," Fischer said.

"What I want to ask . . . this really is silly," Wes said. "In Penceville, I bought a dowel jig that I especially wanted for the store. I planned on ordering more at the convention but—"

"Not to worry," Fischer said. "A salesman stopped by the store yesterday. Your friend bought all he had and ordered more. He has an eye for detail like you. Does that answer your question? It's not silly at all."

Wes smiled. "Good."

"Would you like me to fix the cracked crystal on your watch before you go?" Fischer asked. "Up to you."

"Well, if you have time." Wes blushed. "I'm sorry, Mr. Fischer. I keep forgetting."

Fischer laughed. "Yes, it does take time doesn't it? It's fixed."

Wes raised his arm and glanced at the watch. "Like new."

"If you have no more questions," Fischer said, "the door at the back of the room opens to a hallway that leads to an exit. You'll return to the location where the young man first came for you. You may take the path to heaven whenever you wish. The pathway begins at the back of the area. It's only a short walk to a wooden gate where your luggage awaits you. If you want to eat or have a drink before you go, feel free to do so. There's no rush. The tavern has excellent ale, by the way."

Wes rose. "Thank you, Mr. Fischer. An ale sounds good. We'll drink to you."

Grant Fischer grinned. "Off with you, boys."

CHAPTER 34

Fred and Wes exited the building into gleaming sunlight.

"There you are," Timmy said. "Blackie and I have been waiting for you."

"Were glad you did," Wes said. "Mr. Ables and I are having some ale before we go. Want to come with us?"

"If Blackie can come. What's ale?"

"It's a type of beer," Fred said. "And Blackie can come."

A bright and cheery atmosphere filled the tavern. Timmy picked a booth by a bay window. Blackie jumped onto the seat and gazed at Fred and Wes while they slid into the booth. Wes felt his pocket and pulled out a biscuit for Blackie. The dog curled in the seat nibbling away at the goody.

"Would you like a chocolate shake, Timmy?" Wes asked as the waitress approached.

Timmy grinned. "That's my favorite."

Two ales and a shake with a straw soon arrived. Wes looked at Timmy and smiled. "You've already been to the big office, Timmy?"

"Sure have," Timmy said. "Mr. Fischer and the others talked with me."

"What others?" Wes asked.

"They're on the 'oddographs' I got," Timmy said.

A puzzled look crossed Wes's face.

"Can you show us?" Fred asked.

Timmy removed a bundle of three-by-five cards from his shirt pocket. "It's in here somewhere. Here it is." He laid a card on the table. Timmy beamed. "See." There were three signatures: Father, Son, and Holy Spirit.

Fred grinned. "*Autographs* is what you mean, Timmy. Give me a card, and I'll print it for you."

"I still have a lot to learn," Timmy said. "I hope I don't run out of cards."

Wes took a handful of cards from his shirt pocket and passed them to Timmy. "We all have a lot to learn."

Timmy added the blank cards to his stack and wrapped them with a rubber band. "Thanks, Mr. Quinton. I want to be just like you."

Fred rubbed his jaw as he eyed Wes. "You look different. Can't put my finger on it, but there's no doubt about it."

Wes chuckled. "Do I have ale foam on my nose?"

"No. I'm serious," Fred said. "You're sitting straighter. Your shoulders are back, your head is higher. Eyes are different too. Brighter. Not as sad."

"That's nuts," Wes said.

Fred tapped Timmy's arm. "Take a good look at Mr. Quinton. Tell us if anything looks different."

Timmy glanced at Wes. "He's different."

"You sure?" Fred asked. "You didn't look long."

"He looks like Nick and Daniel except no uniform," Timmy said.

Wes squinted at Timmy. "What do you mean?"

"You look like you're at attention, except you're sitting." Timmy said. "Nick and Daniel look like that when they're sitting."

Wes shook his head. "Well, I'll be."

"Do you feel different?" Fred asked. "There must be an explanation."

"I don't know." Wes gazed out the bay window. A sparrow flew skyward from a branch and out of sight.

Wes closed his eyes and rubbed his forehead. "It's my brother. The war. I didn't save him; always questioned myself. Should've reacted sooner. Should've been faster, a hundred what-ifs. The doubts became guilt, an albatross, a weight you can't measure in pounds. You wonder if you still have the honor and duty of a soldier, seemed to tarnish even that. Mr. Fischer took away those doubts, the guilt, and that horrible burden. I do feel different now. I think that's why."

"Oh, Wes," Fred said, "your honor and duty were never tarnished."

Wes's eyes became moist. "I know that now. I can finally hold up my head again."

Fred patted Wes's arm and nodded. "That's the difference. Timmy saw it too."

Wes took a sip of ale and stared out the window. "Fred, I owe you an apology. I put you on the spot at times. Asked things you couldn't talk about. I'm sorry. Seems silly now, but I thought I was on my way to Lafayette Springs."

"That's probably the hardest thing about being the conductor—not letting something slip," Fred said. "Thank goodness for the *L.S.* on your ticket."

Wes's eyes brightened. "The ticket. I almost forgot; I bought you a retirement gift. I'm embarrassed to say, I nearly left it on the train." Wes removed a package from his pocket and handed it to Fred.

Fred removed the ribbon and paper. "My goodness." He placed the statuette of a conductor on the table. The raised hand held a beige ticket.

"Holy cows! Where did you find that?" Timmy asked. "It looks just like Mr. Ables."

"It's from an antique shop in Penceville," Wes said. "I painted the ticket so it looks like gopherwood."

Fred smiled. "It's a wonderful gift. Really thoughtful. Thank you, Wes."

"You know, Fred," Wes said, "I'll forever think differently when I hear a train whistle."

Fred stared at the ticket in the statue's hand. "It's been that way for me ever since I became conductor. Isn't it odd? You work on the ticket your whole life, and most people never think about it."

"Even more remarkable, you can almost choose the one you want," Wes said.

Fred wrapped the figurine in a handkerchief and slipped it into his pocket. "Shall we go?"

Timmy slurped what remained of his milk shake. "I'm ready. Blackie is too."

Outside the tavern, sparrows chirping in the trees greeted them.

"Do you know the way, Timmy?" Wes asked.

Timmy pointed. "That way. Hold my hand. I'll show you." Timmy took Wes's hand with one of his and Fred's with his other. "Let's go, Blackie."

With Blackie in front, they followed the path toward the wooden gate.

CHAPTER 35

Crinkled brown leaves, with dapples of red, yellow, and orange, dropped from elm and maple trees populating the cemetery. A groundskeeper in green overalls raked the fallen foliage into piles. Wes Quinton sat hunched on a concrete bench, his head lowered, and his hands clasped over the curved end of a worn cane. A tremor of his right hand ceased when he grasped it with his left. Age spots dotted the wrinkled skin on the back of his hands. Eighty-three years old, Wes thought. Never expected to live so long.

The Indian summer day warmed Wes's flannel jacket. He drew its sleeve back. The cracked crystal of his watch stared back at him. How or when it had broken he couldn't recall. The watch, otherwise, kept perfect time. He glanced at the stooped figure trudging from one nearby gravestone to the next. Wes and the man had talked for hours. Actually, mostly Wes recounting his dream. The other man placed a bright bouquet in front of each gravestone. Wes read the names chiseled into the marble headstones: Mabel Hawthorne and her husband, side-by-side; Wes's parents, also, side-by-side.

Chin to chest in silent prayer, the man lingered for a moment and then returned to the bench. "Want to stand for a minute, Wes? You've been sitting since we arrived."

Glancing up, Wes nodded. The man grasped Wes's arm as he struggled to an upright position. Wes leaned on his cane and shuffled his feet on the grass. The two slowly circled the bench. Wes nodded once more, and they both sat.

"That's better," Wes said. "We've been sitting too long, Tommy. My fault."

"You never told me about your dream before, Wes. Why not? Gosh, I am your brother."

Wes shrugged and stared at the ground. "Don't know. We never talked about the war much, either. The dream happened during the coma from the mortar blast. The vision seemed real, but it wasn't. My feet weren't cured like in the dream. They were severely wounded. I thought you were dead from the mortar round. Later, in a letter from home, I learned you survived. The dream was wrong there too. I couldn't tell anyone about the visions after a head injury. They would think I was crazy."

Tommy rubbed his chin. "Probably so. Wouldn't look good in a medical record. But your dream was wrong in another way. You weren't too late when the mortar hit. You did save me. You always knew that, though."

Wes turned toward his brother. "That's not right. I jumped out of my foxhole. I intended to shove you into yours. I didn't make it in time."

"You did, though," Tommy said. "An injured soldier from my unit saw what happened. He told me at the evacuation hospital. I didn't remember because I had a concussion. The shrapnel from the mortar would have hit me square in the chest. Would've killed me on the spot. When you pushed me, I twisted while I fell. The shrapnel hit the side of my chest. It collapsed one lung and sliced blood vessels on that side of my chest. I survived because of emergency surgery at the field hospital. You did save me, Wes. I wouldn't be here now except for you. I thought you always knew that."

Wes's face was blank. He stared at Tommy. "That can't be. I know I was too late."

Tommy shook his head. "No. Your push did it. You don't remember because you were knocked out too."

Wes sat motionless and swallowed hard. Tears filled his eyes. "I didn't know. All these years and I didn't know."

Tommy handed Wes a handkerchief and wrapped an arm around his brother's shoulders. "I'm glad you know now. Thanks, brother."

Wes sniffled and dabbed his eyes with the handkerchief. "I guess that's what older brothers are for."

"I'm glad I didn't die like in your nightmare," Tommy said. "It's strange, but other parts of your dream seemed to come true, partially anyway. Like the hardware store. After the war, we talked about starting a business. You insisted on a hardware store. We didn't know much about hardware. You chose that corner store for sale in town. You also said we should buy the lot and warehouse next to it for a lumberyard if it ever became available. That's what we did, Wes. Like in your vision. Remember?"

Wes nodded. "I thought hardware and lumber made sense for our town."

"Now I understand why we carried a selection of chess sets in the store too," Tommy said. "I always wondered why."

Wes chuckled. "Many of our customers did too. We sold plenty of them over the years."

Tommy's eyes narrowed. "We traveled by train to hardware conventions for years. You always fidgeted on those trips. You glanced at everyone who entered the passenger car. You were expecting someone from your dream to show up?"

Wes looked down. "It's silly, I know. You can see why I kept the story to myself."

"Then there's the bank," Tommy said. "That didn't happen like your dream."

"Not exactly," Wes said.

"Your friend from the army did open a bank, but it was in our town," Tommy said. "You talked him into it. You told him the town was growing and could use a second bank. Many townspeople opened accounts there. I don't remember any Colby at the other bank."

"No Colby," Wes said. "But remember the city banker who ran that bank for a year? One of Sam Knight's clients found irregularities in his business account. Sam quietly involved the bank examiners. That banker went to jail for embezzling. He thought chiseling small town folks would be easy. Turned out, that wasn't true."

"I'd forgotten about that," Tommy said. "That was thirty years ago. Sam became a lawyer at your suggestion, didn't he, Wes?"

Wes nodded. "He didn't know what to do after the war. I thought he would make a good detective or a lawyer. He had that kind of mind. He hadn't considered either of those occupations. He decided on law school."

"I'm glad no one lost their homes or their accounts," Tommy said. "I wonder if things would have been different without your friend's bank." Tommy rubbed his forehead. "Maybe your vision was an omen, Wes. Maybe a guide too. Is that possible?"

Wes shook his head. "No, Tommy. Too much doesn't fit. Fred seemed real in my dream, but I don't know anyone like him. But I do think about train whistles differently because of Fred. And then there's talking with God. Don't ever tell anyone I did that, even if in a dream."

Tommy glanced at his brother. "The way you told the story, it sounded like God. What he would say; how he would speak. The church reverend talks like that. You don't talk that way, Wes. How would you remember it so well more than fifty years later?"

Wes shrugged. "I can't explain it. My feet weren't healed though. Don't forget that. In the dream, Jay cured my feet."

Tommy rubbed his chin. "You mentioned once what an army nurse told you about your feet at the evacuation hospital. Do you remember what she said?"

"She said it was a miracle I didn't lose both feet," Wes said. "Infection was taking hold. The surgeons scheduled amputations for the next day. The next day, my feet turned the corner."

"Maybe your dream was about keeping your feet, Wes. Not about a cure. Did you ever think of that?" Tommy asked.

Wes looked down, his forehead furrowed. "Never considered that. The nurse did call it a miracle. The hospital beds were full of amputees. It still seems like a stretch, Tommy. It was only a dream."

Tommy sighed and leaned forward, placing his elbows on his knees. He rested his chin in his cupped hands. His head tilted toward Wes. "You're probably right, Wes. Timmy was important in the story, but there was no Timmy either."

Wes stared at his younger brother. A thin smile appeared on Wes's face.

Tommy's eyes squinted. "What, Wes? Why are you staring at me like that?"

"You remind me of Timmy," Wes said. "The way you're looking at me with your head angled."

"I thought in your dream, Timmy reminded you of me?" Tommy said.

"He did." Wes slowly rubbed his brow. "Maybe . . ." Wes tapped on his cane and gazed at the barren trees. "Maybe . . ."

"Come on, Wes. Maybe what?"

"Maybe you *are* Timmy," Wes said.

"How could that be?" Tommy asked. "I died in your story."

"You died in the nightmare at the beginning of my dream," Wes said. "Later in his office, Mr. Fischer told me I had done everything possible to save you. In the dream, Timmy was in great danger when Mack grabbed him, but we were able to save Timmy. And yes, Timmy did remind me of you. You were Timmy. Timmy was saved. That has to be it."

Tommy sat upright and stared ahead, momentarily silent. "I'll be darned. That makes sense. Maybe the whole dream makes sense, Wes. And maybe you really did talk to God?"

"You would think that strange and me nuts," Wes said.

Tommy smiled. "Probably; no, definitely." He glanced at the sun and shivered. "What time is it, Wes? We ought to be heading home."

Wes pulled back his jacket sleeve and showed Tommy the time on his watch.

"It is late. Time to go, Wes."

"We better not forget him." Wes raised his head and scanned the cemetery grounds. "Where is he?"

"Probably chasing squirrels," Tommy said.

"Why don't you call him, Tommy?"

Tommy glanced at his brother. "Are you kidding? That's your job from now on."

Wes chuckled. He reached into his pocket and withdrew a bone-shaped treat. He held it up. "Blackie. Want a biscuit? Come here, boy."

A black Pomeranian pup scampered across the grass toward them. He jumped onto the bench and munched on the treat.

"Wes." The voice sounded from behind the bench. Blackie hadn't barked. Wes knew that voice.

Wes and Tommy turned as the man came around the bench. He wore green overalls and held a rake. In his early thirties, he had shoulder length chestnut hair and sparkling blue eyes.

Wes's eyes widened. His mouth dropped as he stared at the man. "It can't be . . . Jay?"

Jay smiled. “Who else?” He shook Wes’s hand and introduced himself to Tommy who gazed in disbelief.

“I told you I would see you again soon,” Jay said. “Mr. Fischer asked me to repair your watch crystal. It’s fixed. I’ll stop by again sometime.”

Wes pulled back his jacket sleeve. He and Tommy glanced at the watch. The crystal was like new. The brothers looked up. The rake leaned against a tree. Jay was gone.

THE END

ABOUT THE AUTHOR

Bruce Berger, the son of a naval officer, grew up in thirteen different locales and attended ten different schools by the time he finished high school. He graduated from Hampden-Sydney College. An M.D. degree followed from the Medical College of Virginia. He completed an internal medicine internship. During his service in the U.S. Navy, he travelled to ten European countries. Thereafter, he specialized in radiology and entered private practice. In the 1990s, he retired from medicine to devote more time to his family. He lives in Florida, where he has volunteered many hours to charitable activities.

AUTHOR'S STATEMENT

Purposefully, I have tried to make this a relatively "clean" novel without gratuitous violence, language, or other situations.

I have not asked anyone to write an inflated review of this novel. If you read the book, I would appreciate your honest review on the internet. You can do so using a pen name. Reviewed books are more likely to be considered by other potential readers.

Thank you for your purchase and taking the time to read this novel. I hope you found it worthwhile and memorable.

Printed by CreateSpace, An Amazon.com Company
Available from Amazon.com and other retail outlets
Available on Kindle and other devices

Made in the USA
Columbia, SC
17 August 2017